A Thorn in the Garden

THE TAKEN SERIES
BOOK FOUR

E. C. RODERICK

Also by E. C. Roderick

For all inquiries about this book, contact:
E. C. Roderick
1217 Wilshire Blvd.
P. O. Box 3282
Santa Monica, CA. 90403

Cover Design: Mary Ann Smith

Editor: Candy Leonard

Library of Congress Control Number: 2025911102

ISBN (Ebook): 978-1-7374357-9-2

ISBN (Paperback): 979-8-9923020-0-4

ISBN (Hardback): 979-8-9923020-1-1

Publisher: Sandy Pier Press
Los Angeles, California

If all else perished, and he remained, I should still continue to be; and if all else remained, and he were annihilated, the universe would turn to a mighty stranger.

—Emily Brontë

A Thorn in the Garden

PART ONE
The Return

One

1

768, August.

MY EYES FLUNG open as I gasped for breath, drawing in as much air to fill my lungs. The air replenished me, and it was fresh, clean, and fragrant with the scent of pungent woodland. Nature bloomed and surrounded me. Sunlight fell intermittently between the heavy boughs above, blanketing my face in warmth as they swayed with rustling leaves from the dancing breeze moving the humid atmosphere over the earth. An innate feeling came over me that space and time had breached and sealed. A sharp sense of panic and terror electrified my blood as my consciousness coalesced. Once again, the world had suddenly changed and what I had left was no more.

I felt Leif's chest rising and falling beneath me while lying on top of him as he lay over damp vegetation, realizing something had happened. Lifting my gaze to see his face, our eyes met as he looked at me through the slits of his eyes, and my fear began waning. The solid grip he held around me slightly loosened, and he, too, seemed more at ease now.

"Are ye alrecht, *ceisdein*?" he inquired carefully in a low, calm voice.

"Yes, I think so," I replied mindfully also as I newly felt the extreme aches in my body.

"Guid," he groaned, surely feeling the same way. "It appears we have been transported by the manner in which I feel. I reckon our experimentation with yer new instrument a success."

"Yes, it would seem so," I agreed.

"This bodes weel fur our future endeavors across time."

"It is optimistic. Now we can monitor the phone's usage for every opportunity we leap to gauge when it'll wear out to prevent us from being stuck without any way to return."

"Aye. We shall carefully record its usage tae impede the predicament," he agreed. Then, he drew in a deep breath and said, "Yet, fur the present, let us untwine ourselves." He promptly loosened the binding rope from our position on the ground and awkwardly began unraveling the cord, withdrawing it from us.

"Did you leave your horse here?" I asked, remembering Blaze and hoping that he was nearby.

"He instead remains at the fort," Leif answered. "Once we have arrived at it, we shall acquire my horse and be fully awaur of the current state of affairs."

"I don't remember exactly, but how long of a hike will it take us to arrive there?"

"It lies not far from haur. 'Tis not too burdensome a trek."

"All right," I accepted.

Once the rope had been loosened and nearly removed from us, he mindfully shifted me off to his side and leaned upward to sit. He then proceeded to unravel the rope completely, wrapping it into a tight bundle and shoving it into his traveling parcel as I pushed myself upward to sit also. As he was organizing and fixing his parcel, closed, I took a minute to regain my orientation. When he soon finished and was satisfied with it, he carefully got to his feet and stood tall before me, ready to leave the area. Proffering a hand, I slipped my palm into his, and he assisted me from sitting to standing, sturdy.

"We must proceed tae Fort Hoosic before nichtfall," he said, glancing up at the sky and gauging the position of the sun. "Micht ye be fit presently tae trek?"

"Except for a bit of a headache, I'm okay. I think." I lightly rubbed my brow.

"A pity yer head ails, I weel ken," he sympathized, placing a gentle palm over my shoulder and caressing it. "Hold fast. 'Twill pass, however." I nodded, agreeing, knowing it would. "Alrecht, let us go." His hand slid from my shoulder, and he turned, starting to pace slightly ahead of me in the direction we must go.

Turning away from Crazy Eye, we began in the opposite direction, hiking between the primitive woods. Moving amid massive trees whose limbs reached the sky like skyscrapers along city streets. The humid air felt extremely warm as we trekked, particularly while dressed in many layers of garments to which I was no longer accustomed. But as we made our way, I admired the earth glowing from the bright yellow sunlight falling between the trees upon our proceeding feet while the rays radiated down on us and illuminated patches of surrounding vegetation. The summer season was evident, and I thought how odd it was that the world could so abruptly transition from one weather period to the next and appear incredibly transformed from the dense, spindly woods and snowy winter season we had immediately left.

With no horse to benefit our journey, I had forgotten how arduous hiking on foot through this wooded mountainous region could be. I wondered about the actual length of our trek, having no idea if we'd arrive at the fort in merely minutes or if we were facing hours while we had now settled into the rhythm of our hike. However, approximately an hour from where we experienced our temporal leap, we entered onto a small but cleared, desolate dirt path and hiked southeast to some relief from the more arduous ground covered by thick vegetation.

I kept staring at the massive trees surrounding us. Their aged impressiveness struck me like the last time I was here, and the abundant sound of unfettered wildlife encompassing us also impressed me. While I enjoyed the singing birds among the forest and other small, harmless fauna and flora carpeting the woodland floor, I also hoped there would be no surprise from a hungry, ferocious animal to interrupt our safe journey.

It had been many years since I'd seen this country, and the memory of it suddenly came rushing back like a tidal wave, overwhelming my mind and heart. The instant memory of being here was vivid. My initial impressions and all the following things that had happened to me remained as if I had never left.

"Are ye alrecht, *ceisdein*?" Leif asked, noticing me as we hiked the path.

"I'm just remembering everything—that's all. It's all so clear," I answered.

"Och," he realized. "'Twas many years ago."

"Yes. But I remember it as if it had just happened."

"The memories bode precisely within my mind as weel. I clearly recall all of our days together. I have endured the haunting of our rift and persevered with hope fur our reunion fur numerous years," he said. I glanced at him as he was retrieving his timepiece from his waistcoat pocket. As he held it, I immediately recognized it. It was the one I'd given him as a gift for his birthday when we were first married. "And now, my prayers are answered," he continued as he returned his eyes to mine with perceivable deep gratitude that was particular to our reunion and for the time we now shared.

"Mine too." I smiled diffidently at him as I reciprocated the truth in his gaze.

"A blessing without reservation or question."

"Yes." I nodded gently in agreement, then paused thoughtfully.

He glanced down at his timepiece again and promptly closed its face as we continued walking. "What did you tell everyone when you had returned without me after I'd disappeared that spring long ago?" I resumed asking him, curiously wondering while observing him tucking his timepiece back into his pocket. He turned his eyes toward me again and met my gaze the moment his timepiece was concealed.

"'Twas a most injurious experience when ye vanished from me," he remembered solemnly. "I wisnea certain how I micht explain it entirely tae anyone. I was greatly grieved tae have lost ye. 'Twas akin tae when Abenaki had stolen ye from me, originally. The feeling eviscerated my being. Yet 'twas worse—inexplicably so —fur this occurrence left me at a fundamental loss. I had nae notion whatsoever how I micht retrieve ye. My impetus was tae seek immediate assistance from others tae aid in my search of ye. Yet, it swiftly came tae mind that the notion was futile."

"Why?" I asked curiously.

"I wouldnae have been assisted by anyone if I had disclosed the truth. The truth would have marked me a lunatic or a sorcerer who had disposed of his wife. I would have been cast a leper and expelled, at best, should I instead not have been condemned tae death."

"I see..." I realized horribly. "So, what did you say, then, as a result?" I wondered still.

"I reckoned tae relay a partial truth micht serve best than saying naught at all in order tae prevent suspicion of me. I had abandoned the Hoosic in tormented spirits on the fateful day of my loss. All perceived the grief I had borne upon my arrival in Boston. So, I explained tae all who had inquired that ye had been stolen from me once more," he expounded, looking grimly at me.

"Who did you say stole me?" I responded, returning his unsmiling gaze.

"I wouldnae say."

"You didn't even blame a fabricated kidnapper?"

"Such a falsehood would have garnered a posse tae seek ye. As ye would have never been discovered and returned tae me, aspersions waur certainly tae take form, and suspicion would have been cast upon me, inevitably."

"Oh."

"Instead, 'twas sensible fur people tae construe from the partial truth which I had told without any further enhancement."

"I understand," I replied, nodding a little. "So, what's the general belief about my disappearance that people believe?"

"Many believe Indians abducted ye from me again," he informed me.

"Oh."

"I let the tale lie. It places their inquiries tae rest."

I nodded a little in response, clearly remembering my experience with the Abenaki during the massacre at Fort William Henry and all the accompanying terror as I was taken to their territory.

I let my eyes fall away from his poignant gaze when I heard him unintentionally kick a pebble in the dirt trail while we walked. I glanced at it, watching it as it bounced off to the side into the vegetation. I felt his eyes lingering on me, still. So, I returned to looking at him, feeling the familiar devastation he had experienced when we lost each other to time's unfair whim and hardship. I reached for his hand and slipped my fingers among his, lacing them together. His hand contracted around mine, securing them, and his eyes turned from me as he resumed looking ahead. Silence ensued between us, and my thoughts remained unspoken as I knew he was thinking also.

We continued hiking over the trail for a while without speaking, letting our concentration fall to our walking path before us. Although our silence was comfortable, my pondering returned to fixing on the many years I had been absent from him while he lived in this century. He said it had been ten years since he'd last seen me. The four years since I had missed him, according to my own era, left me devastated as I lived empty days without him also. I imagined how much more amplified the heartbreak must have been for him as he lived tormented days that had multiplied beyond my own, leaving him utterly broken. I was fortunate and blessed to have living memories of him wrapped in the form of our children to keep, hold, and love. However, the trauma for him, I was sure, was nearly unbearable as he was relegated to intangible memories of us in his mind, along with the visions of paintings he had commissioned of me that hung in *Taigh Grás's* halls, and the imagining of my death along with our unborn offspring haunting him.

Aware of the weight he felt in his being, I sensed the feeling of our thoughts, both unmistakably running parallel as we continued hiking the trail. While my mind wandered, I found myself thinking of all that he was missing, in addition to his extended family, whom I had grown to know and love so well while living here with him years ago.

"Leif?" I started, breaking the quiet spell between us as we moved over the inclining path.

"Aye?" he responded simply as he concentrated, guiding me carefully along with him.

"What do you think people will say when they suddenly see me again?" I wondered.

"Certainly, they will be full of wonder. They will be beside themselves with happiness tae see that I have found ye, at last," he said, glancing at me and steadying his gaze to mine. "Ye have been sorely missed by all, *ceisdein*." The expression in his eyes and the tone in his voice were wholehearted, grave, and true.

"I've missed everyone very much, too. I'll be so happy to see them again," I said, reciprocating his feelings. He mindfully clasped my elbow and gave me a soft, heartening look, then proceeded to return his attention to assisting me up the steep incline we were now climbing in companionable silence.

Two

Fort Hoosic was finally seen through the trees in the clearing. Now, being late in the day, Leif checked his timepiece and informed me that it was half past four o'clock and that we had reached our destination in time before the sun went down. Here, his horse, Blaze, was stabled, and this is where we were also to lodge the night. Additionally, provisions from here were going to be granted to replenish us for continuing our journey the next day as we made our way toward meeting Beth and her family, far away in Concord.

The small fort was a mere blockhouse with one minuscule barrack and stockade outfitted with a skeletal militia regiment. When we neared the fort, men were staring and gawping at us as their eyes fixed on me. Given the peculiar looks on their faces, questions, and intrigue, they were astonished. Feeling self-conscious as I glanced around at them while entering behind the stockade with Leif, I had forgotten how much I'd felt like a misfit in general by being here. Particularly in the presence of men. Men here had no reservations about ogling women as they pleased or openly commenting about women's appearances and their wishes for them to suit themselves, regardless of whether the woman referred to was in their presence. The idea of subtly for the sake of indiscretion alone was certainly a foreign concept to these men, underscoring my insecurity while Leif and I moved toward the stockade.

Despite being appropriately dressed and escorted by Leif through the grounds, I was especially aware that I was the only woman on the property, which highlighted my discomfiture over-all. Careful not to return the men's curious stares to avoid being bold or rude, I was conscious to remain modest with my gaze and ignore their looks as Leif steered me past the stockade and started us through the open quad into the fort.

The moment we continued moving behind the stockade into the courtyard, the captain of this outpost was seen rushing out from the only barrack toward us. Promptly arriving, he respect-fully saluted Leif by clicking his heels together and bowing, obvi-ously recognizing him. When the captain straightened from his bow, Leif returned a polite verbal acknowledgment. After briefly but politely addressing each other, the captain turned an inquisi-tive eye toward me and oddly stared for a second before returning his attention to Leif.

"Might this be your long-lost wife, Your Grace?" the captain asked in his New England accent, seeming patently hopeful.

"She is, indeed, Captain Nichols," Leif said, appearing inde-scribably relieved, determined by the clear, joyous look on his face.

"What wonder! Thanks be to God. 'Tis a blessing," Captain Nichols expressed gladly while looking astonished through his gaping grin and wide eyes, genuinely impressed.

"Quite. Praise God. He has bestowed His blessing upon us, indeed," Leif agreed undoubtedly.

"Quite, indeed." Captain Nichols nodded accordingly. "Pray, might I have the honor?"

"Certainly. I present tae ye, Her Grace, Duchess of Monteith," Leif replied, politely introducing me to the captain.

"A certain pleasure to make your acquaintance, Your Grace,"

Captain Nichols courteously greeted, dipping his head accordingly toward me.

"Thank you, Captain Nichols. It is very nice to meet you as well," I replied politely.

"The pleasure is mine, indeed. We have long prayed for this day. I cannot say how devoted His Grace has been in your retrieval, for he has been as predictable as the spring season in his venture to have you returned to where you belong. I am certain you are most pleased to be restored."

"Yes, it's wonderful. I'm extremely grateful. Thank you, Captain Nichols."

"Indeed. Indeed." The grin on his face lingered as he transiently scanned our unblemished appearances, then faded slightly. His brows also faintly drew together, giving him a wondering look. "It appears you are untarnished by the elements," he noted freely, returning to looking at Leif with a weird and remarkable expression.

"Aye, 'tis a further blessing we are fortunate tae have remained unscathed. I was prepared tae bring my wife new clothing in my search fur her," Leif replied easily, appearing unfazed by the captain's blatant curiosity.

"Wise, indeed," Captain Nichols said, agreeing.

"Aye."

"Of all this time, how might you have discovered your wife at last, Your Grace?"

"She was discovered amongst the Iroquois at a trading post."

"A friendly nation," Captain Nichols acknowledged, despite the sudden scandalous and unfortunate expression on his face.

"They are our allies," Leif said.

"Of course."

"I merely traded fur her and 'twas done. Now, she is within my possession once more at last."

"Quite a wonder! You are further blessed, indeed, Your Grace. 'Tis miraculous," Captain Nichols responded, maintaining the remarkable look on his face, letting his amazement be known. But he shortly composed himself while gazing at Leif's deadpan face. "Pray, do come indoors and have some nourishment. I am certain Your Grace must be famished presently and weary from your travels, nonetheless."

"Thank ye, Captain Nichols," Leif replied appreciatively. The captain acknowledged Leif with a final bow, then promptly turned from us when he proceeded to lead us through the courtyard toward the barracks from where he had come.

As we entered the barracks, Captain Nichols invited us to sit in chairs at a stretched pine table in the middle of the room. Finding places at the table, and while we were seating ourselves, a Huron woman, whom I immediately learned had been captured as a slave, entered from another door within the room. She promptly served us plates of salted venison, boiled cabbage, and carrots with hard cider. My natural inclination was to smile and thank her for the food when she served me. But I abruptly abstained from doing it as I realized my response to her would be misconstrued by the other officers at the table. I was aware of being keenly studied by their observant eyes as they drank and proceeded to eat their food. As a result, I didn't want to bring any unusual attention to myself like I'd unwittingly done before in my previous visit to this era.

Reticent to engage these strange men, I instead sat quietly, simply eating my food. Being carefully observant also, I listened to the conversation Captain Nichols was having with Leif concerning the latest occurrences between the Crown and Massachusetts Bay Colony.

Later, after completing our meal and when the discussion between Leif and Captain Nichols had ended, Leif and I were kindly shown by the captain himself into his cramped quarters to rest for the night. Though it was protocol, he graciously relinquished his bunk to us on the pretense of having the need to attend to other matters waiting inside his adjoining office, and that he would occupy that room for the night, instead.

Once we had settled ourselves inside the captain's quarters for the night, I was grateful that we were going to sleep in the security of the fort with a roof over our heads tonight instead of being forced to camp outdoors in the forest, as I nestled with Leif over the hay mattress. I was happy to be here with Leif while reflecting before finally closing my eyes, when suddenly homesickness began emerging earlier than anticipated, awakening a pang in my heart. The thought of our children and my family swept into my mind and overshadowed the thought of every modern-day convenience that had existed, that was no more now. As my mind centered on our children before going to sleep, the ache in my chest was present and was sure to expand the longer I remained away from them. So, I wasn't sure how I was going to cope with this.

I released a little sigh, trying to quell myself, and shifted in Leif's arms as I sensed him drifting toward sleep. Despite being thoroughly depleted from our hike to arrive here and from the effects of quantum leaping, I struggled to relax and drift off to sleep. Guilt over my decision to be here with Leif compounded my emotions, and I wished to hug and kiss our kids once more before finally submitting to unconsciousness.

"Try tae rest, *mo leannan*," Leif said softly in a mollifying tone against my ear as he kissed it. "We have a long journey set upon us fur the morrow."

"I'm sorry for keeping you awake," I apologized.

"Nae matter. Sleep tight." He pressed his lips over my crown, and I decided to close my eyes despite my wakeful mind. But as I forced myself to settle, my body ironically began relaxing, and I found my thoughts quieting. Soon, I drifted and peacefully fell to sleep.

THE NEXT MORNING, Leif awakened me to the dawning sun. As I groggily removed myself from bed, I noticed that he had already dressed himself and was ready to leave the fort. Still half asleep, though, as I moved to dress myself, I was having difficulty and found myself growing frustrated with my garments while attempting to lace my pair of bodies around my torso. I was surely out of practice with this manner of dressing and wished to simply have a bra to put on without petticoats and laces instead.

Leif suddenly appeared, standing closely before me, and gently gathered the lace from my fingers. Letting him take the string from me, he mindfully proceeded to entwine the front holes of my pair of bodies with it for me. Tightening the garment snugly around my torso as he laced it, my breasts were now securely supported, and I was glad to receive his help.

"Thank you," I said, observing his careful fingers working the lace through the upper holes now.

"Yoo're welcome, *ceisdein*," he said softly as he was paying close attention to what he was doing. The warmth from his steady breathing breezed over my brow as I sensed the close proximity of his lips near my crown. When his fingers arrived at the top holes, he worked the lacing through them and tied them securely. "Waur micht yer stomacher be?"

"It's on the bed," I answered, pointing to it beside us. He quickly lunged for it and carefully slid it behind the front laces he had just tied over my shift against my breasts.

"Thaur we are," he said in a soothing voice, observing his work with satisfaction.

"Thank you," I responded again, grateful to him.

"Aye," he replied simply and snatched up my short-gown from the same location on the bed, holding it open for me. "Permit me." I smiled at him, perceiving the tenderhearted look in his gaze, and his lips gently curved upward. Stepping toward him a little, I turned and slipped my arms through the sleeves, and he proceeded to pin it closed down the front for me. Within a minute, I was nearly completely attired after the final pin went into the fabric, concealing my torso. As I gathered my muslin apron, he withdrew it from me and tied it perfectly around my waist, finalizing my appearance.

His careful thumb and forefinger clasped my chin, and he tilted my head back, forcing my gaze to meet his. Fusing his eyes to mine, he merely stared at me, soft and warm, and my cheeks began to burn. I thought he was going to say something or give me a little kiss, but he didn't. Instead, he held my gaze for a second in silence. As I returned to looking at him, I perceived his admiration for me in his eyes. His thumb brushed my bottom lip, faintly parting it, and then his fingers slipped from my face, leaving me slightly lost.

"We must depart," he said alternatively. I nodded, aware of our readiness now. He lightly gripped my elbow, prepared to guide me out the door, and we left the room.

When we entered the courtyard, the dawning light had transformed into new lemon-yellow and cadmium-orange hues across the awakening sky, as the large, warm-glowing sun climbed above the eastern horizon. Continuing through the quad together, Blaze was detected a distance ahead, already saddled and prepared for journeying, waiting by the stockade entrance with a soldier tending to him and Captain Nichols beside him also. As we arrived at his tall ebony stallion, Leif seized my waist and easily hoisted me into the saddle when the captain proceeded to greet us.

"Good morn, Your Grace," Captain Nichols cordially initiated, looking at Leif.

"Guid morn tae ye as weel, captain," Leif politely replied.

"I pray your accommodations were suitable, Your Grace?"

"They waur fair, captain. I thank ye."

"Quite good, Your Grace. Have you acquired your necessary provisions?"

"Aye."

"Very well. Then, Godspeed, Your Grace."

"Thank ye, kindly, captain."

"As you will be missed in these parts, forthcoming, we are

grateful that you will remain soundly with Her Grace. 'Tis been an honor to serve Your Grace whilst within our company."

"Yer assistance tae me, Captain Nichols, will forever be remembered."

"I wish you well, Your Grace."

"Ye as weel, captain."

"God bless you."

"May He bless ye also."

"Farewell, Your Grace."

"Farewell, captain," Leif concluded, then proceeded to secure his pistols inside his holsters at his hips. After he swiftly finished, he adroitly tossed himself high into the saddle snug behind me and wrapped an arm around my waist, making sure to hold me in place.

Clicking the inside of his cheek, he started Blaze through the stockade out of the fort, beginning us on our journey again. As we came across the clearing, we returned to the lone path heading due east.

Three

F rom Fort Hoosic, we soon passed Fort Massachusetts when the road grew lonely away from soldiers and with just the two of us traveling on the Mohawk Trail through the forest. We followed the trail for hours, with rest stops taken along the way to relieve ourselves and snack by bubbling streams. By dusk, we entered the small settlement of Shelburne Falls, where we lodged at a homestead for the night. It took us two more days from there before reaching Leominster, when I realized we were completely bypassing Northampton, where Beth's sister, Suzanna, resided with her family and where Beth's and Leif's other proper-ties remained, along with his cousins.'

"We're not going to visit Northampton?" I curiously asked Leif.

"Nae. We are tae arrive at Leominster, instead," he disclosed simply behind my head as we rode along on his horse.

"Why are we missing it?"

"I huvnae any business tae which I must pertain in the area."

"You don't?"

"I rent our property in Northampton tae tenants, presently."

"You do?"

"Aye."

"Oh."

"Since I have already collected their dues early this spring before arriving at Fort Hoosic in search of ye, thaur isnae any need fur my sooner return."

"I see," I understood. "So, we're headed straight toward Boston, then?"

"We shan't arrive thaur punctually."

"Why not?"

"I have acquired anither property that I wish fur ye tae see before our arrival at *Taigh Gràs*."

"You have more land?" I expressed surprise.

"Aye. I reckon that ye will be fond of it as it lies by the sea. 'Tis named *Sàmhchair*."

"*Sàmhchair*," I echoed. "What does it mean?"

"It means tranquility."

"That's a pretty name," I admired as his lips lightly brushed my ear, and the warmth from his breath caressed my skin as he spoke.

"It pleases me that ye fancy its name. I hope that yoo'll find the property equally suitable."

"I'm sure I will. How long ago did you acquire it?"

"Before we waur first wed. When Fin had taken his leave from us fur Boston whilst we remained in Northampton at *Taigh Bheinn*, I had given him money tae purchase the land fur me," Leif explained.

"You did?" I responded, greatly surprised as I wasn't aware of this.

"Aye. When we had traveled tae Concord fur our wedding day, I had given orders fur construction upon a new hoose upon the new land."

"Really?"

"Aye."

"I had no idea."

"I meant fur yer ignorance of it."

"Why?"

"I had intended it as a surprise, fur 'tis my wedding gift tae ye. This different location was meant fur our retreat from Boston... 'Twas completed the spring of yer disappearance..." His voice became soft as it trailed into silence. He leaned his warm cheek against the side of my head and rested it. The short stubble on his jaw gently scraped my cheek, and the sensation was familiar and comforting. I inhaled a little, leaning my back into his chest as he was holding me while on his horse. "My affection fur ye is boundless as the sea," he returned, gently speaking into my ear.

"Mine is too," I whispered and moved my hand over his as he held the reins with his other hand and caressed my fingers over his knuckles. He switched the reins into his other hand and took my palm into his, enfolding it as he wrapped his arm around my waist again. His fingers contracted over mine, securing them, and I felt the highlighted bond between us.

"Where is Tranquility located?" I wondered.

"She lies in Nahant just beyond Lynn," he said.

"Oh. How long will it be before we arrive there?"

"Within two more days. We shall reside thaur fur the duration of whit remains of this season before our retirement in Boston."

"Oh. I'm sure that will be nice."

"Aye, I imagine it as weel."

"But, when will we see Amity in that case?"

"She will be collected from Beth at the commencement of October before we shall depart fur Boston."

"So, we'll wait a while before seeing everyone?"

"Aye."

"I'm anxious to see all of them. I'll be happy when the time comes."

"I greatly anticipate our visiting them as weel. With certainty, they will immediately rejoice upon laying eyes upon ye again," he said.

"It's been so long."

"Indeed. Beth and her husband, Patrick, are currently blessed with three bairns if I huvnea already informed ye."

"Three?" I responded, significantly surprised.

"I gather that I huvnae told ye already by yer response."

"No."

"Forgive me."

"Of course, it's okay. There were so many other things we talked about, as you had informed me when you found me again." Aware of the three girls Beth previously had, along with her niece, I couldn't imagine how much fuller her hands must be with a number of extra children.

"I reckon thaur waur many topics tae discuss, which preoccupied our attention."

"Yes, certainly."

"Weel, now, tae have ye fully informed, Beth has laddies in addition tae the lasses with which she has already been blessed."

"My goodness. Sons?"

"Aye."

"Her hands are full. I can surely imagine," I joked a little. Leif chuckled, knowing the mischief all too well.

"She and Patrick will soon have anither bairn," he informed me.

"Another?"

"Aye."

"How amazing." This was all I could say since I was in sheer astonishment. "Is she happy?"

"She must, of coorse."

"Yes," I imagined that she was happy after all that she'd experienced in suffering Finley's loss. "I've prayed for her happiness."

"I, too."

"I keep thinking about her girls also. How old did you tell me they are now?" I wondered again.

"Mairie is eighteen years of age, Doireann is seventeen years,

Alice is thirteen, and Amity is twenty-one at present," he reminded me.

"I can't believe it," I gasped, exceptionally surprised by the large amount of time that had passed between us all. "It seems like yesterday when I last saw them."

"I reckon it must."

"I'll hardly recognize them anymore when we see each other."

"They are certainly tae recognize ye, fur ye huvnae been changed the merest wee bit," he assured. "The laddies will be pleased tae meet their aunt as weel."

"What are their names? And, how old are they?" I asked interestedly.

"Timothy is nine years of age, Earnest is seven, and Henry is five."

"A nice little brood," I acknowledged.

"They are a hearty lot indeed," Leif agreed.

"Does Beth's sister still live in Northampton?"

"Aye, she does. She has anither laddie and a lassie, presently, as weel."

"She does?"

"Aye. Her William is ten years of age, and Liza is six."

"That's so nice. It sounds like she's doing well also."

"She and her family have been quite weel, indeed. All have been blessed."

"Yes, I believe so. What about George and Henry? How old are they now?"

"They are strapping lads now, nearly as old as Beth's eldest lasses."

"Really?"

"Quite."

"It's all so hard to believe how much everyone's grown."

"Certainly, a difference, I ken. Time is a mysterious element."

"Yes, it really is." I fell quiet as I was left suspended in thought, finding it difficult to believe that the children I had known only four years ago were now young adults. The timeline that I found myself in now was mind-boggling.

I sensed Leif laying a kiss on the side of my head behind my ear, and he became silent, too. The silence that descended on us was gentle and companionable while the sound of the horse's hooves clopped over the dirt in the trail as the animal rocked us along the way. Leaning my head against Leif's shoulder now as he secured me with an arm around my waist, I closed my eyes, thinking about the differences in our eras and how much time we'd lost with each other before letting the horse's relaxing sway drift me into a nap.

Four

~∞~

Two days later, just past sunset, we arrived in the village of Lynn by the seaside. The air smelled fresh and pungently salty. A breeze lightly stirred from the nearby ocean, but the atmosphere remained warm and uncomfortably humid this evening. The horse's hooves clopped over cobblestone streets as we passed collections of lantern-lit windows from surrounding dwellings. In a matter of minutes, as we proceeded through town, the navy blue Atlantic Ocean fully came into view. Sparkling beneath the moonlight as the moon hovered over the water, the moon appeared as an enormous blood-orange orb suspended in the dimmed ultramarine sky.

Ocean waves audibly crashed over rocks and sand against the sides of the causeway when we crossed the peninsula into Nahant, known as the island. After entering the island, we followed a single path, veering left until it forked, heading us right onto a narrower trail. Continuing along the path, I wondered how much farther we had to go; traveling on horseback for days now was taking its weary toll on me, and I dreamed of having the comfort of a reclining passenger car seat in which to ride for the time being since I was ready to dismount only to rest. Instead, I had leaned my head against Leif's shoulder miles back and sank into his solid chest in order to relax for the rest of the journey toward our final destination. Now, I found that I could barely keep my eyes open as my head began bobbing against him, and sleep was all I craved.

As we continued curving along the road, we soon cleared the last group of trees, and a field glowed beneath the moon. Emerging in the clearing and also illuminating in the moonlight was a large, dark, three-story, four-gable house resting on a sea-blown bluff. Not too far from the house, a barn and a coach house were detected, and a paddock remained beside them. As I noticed we were advancing toward these extra structures, it seemed this was where Leif was heading us first.

When we arrived at the paddock, I raised my head off his shoulder and straightened my posture as he finally halted Blaze. Promptly dismounting Blaze, Leif reached around my waist and easily pulled me off his horse, mindfully placing me onto my feet over the grass. When I came to the ground, my legs felt like gelatin, and my posterior was too sore. To lie on a cushy mattress was what I desired most, and I couldn't wait to sink my head against a nice, soft pillow. As Leif's attention turned to Blaze, I patiently stood near the gate he had swiftly opened and watched as he led his horse into the enclosure. After he removed the saddle and unbridled him, Blaze now freely relaxed and lay on the grass inside the fencing.

Securing the gate again, Leif gathered the saddle and reins into his arms and strode toward the barn with me walking beside him. Pushing the large barn door open, he entered inside, and I followed him into the pitch darkness. He abruptly stopped near the entrance, causing me to shortly bump into him as he proceeded to rummage by the dark wall. Curiously wondering what he was doing as I stood close, he promptly returned forth into the moonlight, entering at the opening, holding something in his hand. He knelt on the ground, and I observed him starting a flame from the tinderbox he had retrieved from inside. Taking a moment to start a flame, when the match was lit, he straightened to his feet and lit a hanging lantern on the front wall beside the barn's opening with it. Extinguishing the match, he snatched the flaming lantern's handle, unhooking it from the wall, and turned toward me with it swaying in his clutch.

"Hold it fur me, *ceisdein*," he requested when he faced me. I gathered the lantern from him and observed him return to the tinderbox left on the ground. He quickly organized its contents, then shut it closed and collected it into his hand. After returning the box where he had found it, he turned toward me, and I suddenly gasped when I was unexpectedly scooped up high off my feet into his powerful arms, completely caught off guard.

"What are you doing?" I inhaled with a little nervous giggle.

"Carrying my bride into her new abode, of coorse," he said obviously.

"Oh." Another giggle eluded me, and I suddenly felt strangely shy. He grinned, and I caught the pearly gleam of his teeth in the pouring moonlight, inspiring my own smile. He started pacing with me in his arms from the barn's opening, forgetting to shut the door behind him, and trekked us across the grass clearing toward the house.

As we advanced over the illuminated field, the salty breeze from the ocean wafted around us, and the night sky was brilliant with inundating, brightly shining stars. Except for the nearby sound of the breaking ocean and the breeze rustling the tall grass around us as it also caressed us, the atmosphere was melodic and soothing.

Within five minutes, Leif was climbing granite steps to the front door of the house. Now standing beneath the portico, he tried the door, and it immediately opened. Still holding me, he moved indoors into the large foyer and easily shut the door at his back with the heel of his foot.

"Welcome tae *Sàmhchair*, *mo leannan*," he said quietly into my ear. I turned my gaze toward his in the shadows to thank him.

But before I could utter a word, his lips warmly came over mine in a tender kiss. "I hope it pleases ye," he muttered against my mouth.

"I'm sure it will. You're so sweet. Thank you," I whispered between his kisses.

Withdrawing his lips from mine, and while I still held the lit lantern, he mindfully continued through the dim foyer into the corridor until he rounded a staircase to his right and conscientiously climbed the steep steps as I propped the flickering lantern in my grip before us to guide his path. When we arrived on the second-story landing, he turned left, strode through a different hallway, and entered the first room on the right. Lowering me now, he eased me back down to my feet and took the glowing lantern from me. I observed him proceeding across the room as the wood planks creaked beneath the heels of his boots and placing the lantern over a large, white, alabaster mantelpiece above the fireplace. As the lantern was set over the mantelpiece, the flame in it settled, and the room was subtly illuminated in orange and yellow hues. Shadows were cast and bounced over the walls and furniture, animating them among the darkness.

"It seems very nice in here," I remarked pleasantly as I glanced around our new surroundings, taking stock of the elegant décor in the bedroom. He smiled in response, observing me.

I noted the many tall, narrow windows that would let in an abundance of sunlight during the day. Snowflake white wainscoting bordered the yellow ochre, distempered painted walls, which I was sure were going to make the room appear cheerful as daylight filled it. A large crimson Oriental area rug covered a portion of the wide-planked oak hardwood floors, enhancing the room's warm scheme. A Chippendale writing desk and chair, along with a pair of Queen Anne armoires, a dresser, a dressing table, and a gilded free-standing looking glass, added to the inviting décor. And lastly, but certainly not least, was the master mahogany four-poster canopy bed at the back of the room, luring me to instantly fling myself over it and sink my head into the plush-down pillows.

"The bedchamber pleases ye, then?" Leif inquired after a moment of watching me acquaint myself as I carefully moved around the area.

"Yes, very much," I replied gladly, returning my gaze toward his.

"I'm quite pleased that it does," he said, smiling at me. I began toward the bed to sit, but before I had reached it, he caught my hand in his as he stood near me in the middle of the room, apprehending my steps instead. "Permit me."

"Yes, of course. Thank you," I realized suddenly as he indicated his wish to undress me. Giving me a little wink, a smile swept my lips before he started.

Remaining still and quiet before him, I watched his fingers gently come beneath my chin and mindfully begin removing my fichu from around my neck. When it was withdrawn, he let the delicate muslin material slip from his fingers to the foot bench at the end of the bed. Then, his fingers moved to the front of my short-gown, and he carefully proceeded to unpin it. The air was silent between us, except for the faint sound of our breathing as we stood closely facing each other while he mindfully worked the pins loose from the cotton fabric, and I patiently observed him.

After a moment, my short-gown was fully unpinned, and he removed it from my shoulders. When the garment came off my arms, his hand lightly tossed it onto the foot bench with the first garment. Then, his fingers returned to me and began untying my petticoats. Once completely untied, they slipped from my waist to the floor, and he moved to unlace my pair of bodies from the front of my torso.

While watching him disrobing me, I sensed his intentions as I anticipated our time in bed tonight. When my pair of bodies was being loosened from around my torso, freeing my breasts, I was aware of his warm breathing escaping him, caressing my brow as he worked the lace away from its lower holes. Soon, the lace had come completely undone, and he pulled the undergarment away from my torso, dropping it onto the rest of the accumulated pile of clothing on the foot bench. Simply attired now in my pair of stockings and shift, I stepped away from my petticoats puddled at my feet, and he bent to scoop them up, lightly tossing them finally with the other loose garments on the bench.

Taking the initiative in kicking my slippers off with my toes, I leaned to untie my garters and removed my stockings. As I was withdrawing them from my calves, Leif thoughtfully gathered them from me and added them to the bench. With bare shins and a shift, I was ready for bed at last. So, I started from him again, intending to comfortably slip myself into bed, when he caught my wrist in his clasping hand, preventing me. Our eyes returned to each other's, and I sensed him reaching for the hem of my shift. Gathering the hem, he raised my final garment over my head, completely removing it from my body.

"Remain as ye are," he wished in a soft voice. I gave him a little smile and stood before him entirely bare. His eyes slowly rolled over my nakedness, and I felt the heat from his stare burning my skin. An inspired grin eased over his face, slowly curling his lips, and the amorous look in his eyes was doubtlessly perceived.

With his gaze adherent to mine, my coursing blood began heating me, and the strange warmth in my stomach began kindling as the urge to be with him distinctly emerged between my thighs. Without a word, emoting from his adherent eyes, he commanded my attention as I watched him begin to undress himself directly before me.

In silence, I patiently observed him remove his coats from his shoulders as he watched me look at him. I knew not to falter from my natural instincts of modesty and glance away from him as I perceived a brazen craving in his gaze. But the subtle nervous smile curving my lips betrayed my diffidence, and his lips indolently tilted into a licentious smirk, conveying his awareness of me.

Deliberately undressing, he had finally removed his breeches and now appeared in his billowing flounce linen shirt. He then pulled the shirt over his head and easily tossed it with the rest of the clothing pile, revealing his nakedness with unfettered pride. Hard and erect, fully ready to proceed to conclude the evening, he reached for me and scooped me off my feet high into his robust arms, moving us toward the bed where he placed me, at last.

Then, his lips came over mine, and he began kissing me. Returning his kisses, the heat in my blood began to rise. My lips parted for him, and he thrust his tongue deep into my mouth, kissing me with ardor. His tongue moved zealously within my mouth, and I thought I might faint from his final momentum before going to sleep tonight. But not ignoring my own hunger for him, I lightly scoured his back with my raking nails, wanting desperately to be with him.

As we kissed each other, I knew he needed me, all of me, too—underscoring my own need for him also. He pushed a solid knee between my legs and spread my thighs apart, and I sensed his formidable shaft brushing between my cleft, seeking my entrance. Then, in one vigorous thrust, he surged into me, filling me to the end, and he moaned as he joined us together. My breath was stolen from me at the sudden, powerful sensation of him plunging into me. Taking him in, I adjusted my hips more comfortably, wrapping my legs snugly around his hips, completely receiving him to the hilt, welcoming him.

He drove himself with escalating force. My body opened and closed as he boldly moved between my thighs, and he began swallowing me whole in an ocean of advancing euphoria. My body, inviting him on each thrust, begging him to return as my walls became slick, pulled me closer toward the height before the fall.

I began tightening around him. My flesh, gripping him, beckoned him to remain—to savor him for as long as we existed before our dissolve. The sensation of our union compelled me to ascend higher, where I felt the reward advancing closer. I was imminently going to be hurled from this distance and crash into a swirling abyss of ecstasy. So, I held onto him as he vigorously drew us closer to this summit.

Helplessly, he thrust deeper and with more vigor, penetrating me to a new end when I believed all had already been discovered. But before he had reached the barrier of this unfamiliar depth, I was brought to the crest right before the fall when he surged in one last uncontrollable, insatiable thrust, and I tumbled off the ledge.

I began shuddering in his arms. My chasm thundered as it violently pulsated around him. The sensation of my depths gripping and squeezing him, begging to keep him, sent shockwaves throughout my nerves as they were electrified and launched me into pure ecstasy.

"Leif!" I cried out, soaring on a plane of joyous delirium. He released a guttural roar into the curve of my neck, and his breath burned my skin. I was scarcely aware of him expelling himself, throbbing between my thighs, as his essence poured into me.

He suddenly collapsed, nearly suffocating me while fully embracing me in his arms, satisfied. My legs slid from around his hips as I held him also. His seed escaped me while we embraced in silence for an undetermined moment, listening to each other's breathing finally settle. And I could hear our hearts pounding in synchronicity until their rates slowed, returning to normal pulses.

Lessening my grip over his shoulders, I gently stroked his back while remaining affixed, still resting, unspoken. He grew flaccid in my arms, and my flesh began closing, forcing him out. Leif shifted and rolled onto his back, and I felt empty inside once more. Wrapping an arm around me, he drew me against his chest, holding me securely.

Stillness came over us now as silence did, too, and we simply rested together, consumed in bliss as sleep finally took us away.

Five

The brilliant sunbeams entering the windows of our new bedroom as dawn broke the next morning awakened me. I glanced over my shoulder among the pillows and noticed Leif's bedside was empty. He was also nowhere present in the room as I glanced around after yawning and rubbing the sleep from my eyes. I assumed he must have risen before daybreak as he so often did to begin his morning.

Feeling rested, I decided not to lounge in bed this morning and removed myself from the quilt covering me. The mattress was raised high off the floor, and I carefully climbed out of bed, down the large step until shortly planting my feet onto the rug. As I stood for a second, scanning the room and absorbing my surroundings once more, the bright sunlight illuminated the charming décor, enhancing its cheerful impression. But I immediately noticed the already warm air and realized the morning heat was only a sample of what was surely to be another sweltering and humid day as it grew later.

Barefoot, I started crossing the floor and discovered the privy closet at the back of the room. Entering it, I curiously glanced around and was suddenly pleased to see how relatively spacious it was by colonial standards. There was even a dry sink made of oak with a washbasin, a full pitcher of fresh water, a small bar of soap, and a cotton towel next to it. Additionally, I discovered an unused pair of wooden boar bristle toothbrushes and a small jar of tooth powder, which was made from ground pumice stone, charcoal, oyster shells, and salt. I remembered then that I needed to concoct a paste made of baking soda and crushed mint leaves for our oral hygiene instead of using this corrosive toothpowder. Opposite the sink was the chamber pot in a corner, on which I instantly sat and gladly relieved myself.

When I had finished, I approached the sink, poured water from the ewer into the basin, took the bar of soap, and proceeded to wash my hands and freshen the rest of my body for the morning, without using the copper tub, which needed to be filled by hand. Afterward, I returned inside the bedroom and proceeded to don a fresh dressing gown that I had found hanging in one of the armoires, along with several other unworn gowns meant for me. While dressing myself, I noticed that the fabric of this gown appeared newly fashioned, but the scent of the ocean had subtly settled into the fibers as my petticoats brushed against my nose when I brought them over my head to position them at my waist. It suddenly occurred to me that this wardrobe had been prepared and waiting for me to wear for many years while I was absent.

Once I had finished fully dressing and was satisfied with my appearance, I came out of the bedroom into the hallway facing the banister. I glanced from one end of the corridor to the other when I noticed bright sunlight shining through an open door to a room at one of the ends. Drawn toward the glowing daylight lighting a portion of the hallway, I naturally began pacing in that direction. When I arrived at the end and crossed the threshold, I entered into a spacious room, which by all accounts was a nicely arranged library with rich, well-fabricated Chippendale furniture and other lovely décor. Another crimson Oriental area rug was laid over the wide floor planks, embellishing the Prussian blue wainscoting and snowflake white painted walls that were embellished with land-scape and seascape paintings.

"Och, guid morn tae ye, *mo ghaol*," Leif greeted warmly, suddenly noticing me entering the room. He was seated behind his desk, preoccupied with a letter he was in the midst of composing, as he promptly tapped the nib of his quill on the parchment and inserted the quill in the holder on the inkstand.

"Good morning," I said pleasantly, pacing toward him as he was now giving me his undivided attention. When I arrived, standing close to him, I leaned and pecked my lips over his, happily greeting him.

"Yoo're quite dear," he responded affectionately as I withdrew my lips and straightened myself again. I smiled at him, and he reached for my hand, taking it into his. "Tell me, how ye micht have slept?" he asked, grinning benignly at me. His other hand slipped around my waist, and he easily drew me over his lap to sit.

"I slept really well, thank you. How about you?" I replied, gazing closely into his dark blue eyes, glimmering like gems as the morning sunlight caught their crystal-like luminescence from the bold rays entering the window beside his desk and chair.

"I slept as the dead," he said, winking at me. I giggled, and his lips discernibly curved into a knowing smile that spread warmly across his face, bolstering the playboy look in his eyes.

"Then, you're certainly well rested," I teased.

"Inarguably," he chuckled lightly.

"Good. How long have you been awake?" I wondered simply.

"Och, I have been roused since five o'clock this morn."

"Why so early?" I looked at him, somewhat surprised at the unusual time.

"I have a few matters tae which I must attend and reckoned my start tae see them completed early in order that I may spend the rest of my time with ye later."

"Oh. What are you focusing on?"

"Och, I merely toil upon matters that ye are certain tae find dull."

"I see."

"However, now that ye have come, shall I acquaint ye with the hoose before we take our breakfast?"

"But I interrupted you while you were still working. Wouldn't you like to finish with what you were in the middle of doing first?"

"I fear not."

"Why not?"

"Ye tempt me. I am not willing tae proceed with matters whilst I presently prefer tae weel acquaint ye with yer new hoose, instead."

"Are you sure?"

"Quite."

"Well, if that's what you wish."

"Indeed."

"All right."

"Very weel. Once we have had our meal afterward, I shall return haur tae resume my duty."

"Okay," I agreed. Still holding my hand, he brought it to his lips and pressed a gentle kiss on my knuckles.

"I pray this hoose micht please ye," he continued when he drew my hand from his supple lips.

"I'm certain it will."

"Yet, I must make ye awaur that we huvnae any servants tae aid us whilst residing haur in the interim fur the remaining season. They wait at *Taigh Gràs* as this visit fur us is impromptu," he apologized.

"That's okay. Please don't be concerned. We'll be just fine on our own."

"Shall we?"

"Of course we will. Remember how much I enjoy it when we're all alone with each other without any help, anyway?"

"I do recall ye having mentioned a bit of the sort once before."

"Our first Christmas together is when I told you that."

"Ye dismissed the servants without my permission."

"Only because I wanted to be alone with you," I said, obviously. He smiled at me, and I saw that he was amused.

"Tell me again why ye must be secluded with me, " he asked specifically, keeping his smiling, mining eyes fastened to mine.

"But you already know why," I replied softly, suddenly undermined by bashfulness. His grin slanted, and the corner of his mouth lifted higher. He simultaneously arched an eyebrow, prodding me, and gave a taunting, devilish look that was knowing.

"Not precisely. Now tell me," he elucidated, keeping the roguish look on his face. I felt my cheeks abruptly warm, and the heat in them began to burn. The goading smirk on his face deepened, creasing his masculine cheeks until his lustrous incisors were exposed. I knew he perceived the blushing hue on my face, making me further flush as I was unable to avoid answering him.

"Being alone together..." I started, faltering in my response as I paused and wondered how to express myself without sounding brash.

"Aye?" he prompted.

"I was just going to say that we don't have to worry about the attention of others when we're alone," I suggested.

"Ye mean whilst we fornicate?" he replied candidly. My eyes suddenly widened. "Ye may speak plainly, Your Grace, fur not a soul can hear ye but I."

I suddenly arched an eyebrow at him, too, with a coy, little smile out of surprise and embarrassment. I didn't know why I was reacting to him this way.

"Fine," I forced myself to say as I agreed.

"Fine?"

"Yes."

"Aye? In whit regard?"

"I'm agreeing with you."

"Are ye?"

"Yes."

"How precisely do ye agree?"

"Precisely that I like it because no one can hear us fucking," I blurted, surprising myself for boldly stating it. His eyes abruptly widened with his brow lifting high, and a brisk chuckle escaped him. "Well, you can't get angry at me for saying it because you wanted me to tell you."

"I bear the responsibility of coorse," he said, chuckling some more.

"You're so noble," I teased.

"But ye amuse me," he responded, now smiling clearly at me after laughing.

"I'm glad that you find me entertaining," I giggled.

"Ye quite delight me, indeed. I am stirred already before the day has merely begun."

"That's not my fault."

"How is it possible when ostensibly it is yer doing?"

"I don't understand how it can be because I'm actually rather innocent, to be honest," I replied sincerely, giving him a quizzical look.

"Mmm," he considered. "Mayhap, ye are that."

"I am—comparatively."

"Yet, 'tis not an excuse, however."

"Why not?"

"Ye lure me. Despite yer innocence, 'tis yer doing."

"How?"

"By yer beauty and yer heart," he said.

"That's really nice of you to say. I'll admit."

"I'm quite sincere."

"It seems that you are, which is why I think you're so sweet," I replied, perceiving the truth in his playful expression.

"Also, by yer cunt," he remarked bluntly.

"Leif!" I suddenly gasped as I chastised him. I gaped and unbelievably shook my head at him. He chuckled again, clearly entertained.

"Why, I enjoy yer cunt tremendously. It satisfies me greatly. It is supreme."

"You're absolutely unthinkable," I scolded again.

"Yoo're glorious." He smiled shamelessly at me. Despite him, my own lips helplessly betrayed me as they curled into a guilty little smile. The crowfeet at the corners of his smiling eyes were enhanced, and the warm, rakish look on his face was distinctly visible as we gazed at each other for a lapse.

"Well, if we're speaking plainly, Your Grace—" I resumed, except I paused for a second as I reconsidered being too bold with him, careful not to encourage him at the moment.

"Aye?" he urged, looking expectantly at me.

"I was simply going to say, rather honestly, the same thing about you," I replied.

"In whit regard, precisely? Again, dinnae be coy with me, Your Grace."

"If that's what you really wish."

"Indeed, it is."

"All right, then. I meant to say that your big, powerful cock sends me beyond the stars. Is that better for you to know?"

"Och!" His brow shot upward, and his eyes widened as he abruptly laughed. "Ye have taken me. Yet, I am not at all a wee bit guilty fur it. I merely remain intrigued about whit I have caused."

"Only you would know, Your Grace," I giggled.

"Indeed," he agreed, nodding and grinning simultaneously. "My, how far we have come from the days of Northampton."

"Yes, we have, Leif," I replied quietly as my modesty returned.

"Ye scarcely stood tae gaze at me when I caught yer eyes with mine. And when I smiled at ye, ye turned from me. Why had ye?"

"You made me feel shy and nervous. That's why."

"Had I?"

"Yes."

"Why do ye reckon?"

"Because I liked you—and I was attracted."

"Waur ye?"

"Couldn't you tell?"

"Ye waur bashful of me," he acknowledged.

"Yes, I was. And, you know that I was."

The corner of his mouth tilted, and the smirk was telling. "Micht ye be so, still?" he asked mildly, looking genuinely at me now. I nodded a little, noticing the soft grin curving his lips. "Why micht ye be? Ye ken me weel, presently."

I shrugged a bit again, not able to articulate the exact answer, and hesitated. But he gave me a little encouraging look.

"I don't know, honestly..." I started as I thought about it. "Maybe it's because you might frighten me a little. When we're together—the way you touch me—it's intense... and I want to do everything to please you because I love you. It makes me feel wonderful to be with you. I'd do anything for you."

"As I shall fur ye." The smile on Leif's face remained tender, and the look in his eyes deepened with further affection. I sensed his fingers wrapping around the back of my head and seeping into my loose ringlets. He compelled me toward him as he drew my lips toward his and pressed his mouth over mine. He began kissing me with gentleness and warmth, conveying his deep and abiding love. As our kisses escalated, his breathing became unsteady, and so did mine. I parted my mouth, allowing his tongue to slide inside and dance with mine. His lips emitted the heat rising within me as we carried ourselves to another place. Suddenly, he pulled away, breaking our kisses, and leaned his brow against mine, panting.

"Ken that I shall forever loove ye, Sylvie, more than ye will ever loove me in return," he expressed unevenly as his steamy breath caressed my lips. Grasping my waist with both hands, he urged me off his lap to my feet again and straightened himself from his chair. I stepped away a little, giving him some clearance as he stood before me now. He reached for my hand, took it into his, and pressed a meaningful kiss on the inside of my wrist. "I shall acquaint ye with *Sàmhchair* at present, lest I bed ye instead."

"That's something to consider," I accepted demurely.

"Come," he said, leading me out of his library while keeping my hand in his.

Six

Returning with him through the corridor, he proceeded to introduce me to the rooms surrounding the master bedroom on the second floor. When we crossed the hallway on the other side of the staircase, we entered one of the final rooms on this level. As I stood in this particular room with him, I noticed this one was slightly smaller than the two previous ones, and compared to our room, it was even smaller. But with a full four-poster bed closely facing us, including the beautiful Chippendale oak armoire, matching dresser, and nightstand furnishing the room, it was appealing. And, with the same Prussian blue painted wainscoting, light yellow ochre distempered painted walls, and large windows letting in abundant sunlight, the atmosphere was bright and cheery.

After acquainting me with this bedroom, Leif guided me toward an adjacent doorway, and we stepped past the open door into the final bedroom. This room mirrored the one before it, and I thought this current one was another lovely room also. When I had finished absorbing this bedroom, he guided me back through the hallway somewhat farther in the opposite direction until we soon came to a narrow flight of stairs.

Climbing up the winding stairwell, we arrived at the third level and proceeded through a short hallway. Two other rooms were located here, and we faced one of the two doors leading into the separate rooms. Leif reached for the door handle closest to us and led me inside this new bedroom, which had vaulted ceilings and was furnished like the previous vacant bedrooms seen on the second floor.

After he showed me this bedroom, I followed him into the last bedroom inside the house, which was positioned across the hallway from us. Although it resembled the previous room with its vaulted ceilings, this one had two alcoves instead, one of which had a window seat. Also, unlike the last room, this one faced eastward and received the morning sun as its brilliant beams entered the windows, illuminating the space with cheer.

"This is a large house," I commented while pleasantly examining the current room in which we stood.

"Suitable fur the family I longed fur us tae have," he responded with a gentle grin. I smiled, and he reached for my hand again, ready to lead me out of the room.

Leaving it, we returned downstairs from the third and second floors. He toured me through the drawing, sitting, and dining rooms, all of which had large, slender windows and beautifully crafted flooring painted in geometric black-and-white checkerboard designs. From the sitting room and kitchen windows, I loved that I could see the beautiful, expansive, unobstructed navy blue Atlantic Ocean, with the beach below the slope from where we were perched.

Finally, there was a second privy closet hidden in the corridor, replicating the one upstairs in our master bedroom, but this one lacked the copper bathtub; I concluded my tour through the entire house. As we returned to the kitchen, I thought that I would very much like it here. The house was warm and picturesque with a lot of charm.

"How micht ye fancy it?" Leif asked as he observed me gazing out the kitchen windows at the animated ocean glinting beneath the morning sunshine.

"I love it," I said, turning my gaze toward him. He grinned, and I smiled also.

"I shall present the remaining property once we have had our breakfast before I return tae business."

"Okay."

When I glanced away from him and looked around the kitchen again, I noticed the cupboards were empty. I suddenly wondered what we were to eat this morning and returned to looking at him, intending to inquire.

"Thaur is dried cod and fresh eggs tae eat," he said, noticing the question on my face before I had the opportunity to ask.

"Oh." I nodded, realizing.

"Later, I shall drive us into the village tae acquire bread and ingredients fur yer cooking."

"That would be nice."

"Yet, fur the present, ye may find the cod in the pantry." He moved across the kitchen toward a door and pulled it open, revealing the nearly empty food storage room with only a few bags of flour and oats, along with the dried fish. "We shall have it stocked once we return from town." I nodded again in response, and he winked at me with a subtle grin. "Presently, permit me tae collect eggs fur ye from the coop."

"But where do we get fresh water?" I asked, suddenly realizing there wasn't any of it around.

"Of coorse. Come with me." He began leading me from the kitchen through the connecting mud room until we came outside by the back door and showed me a large freshwater trough where rainwater collected. He also pointed to the small well only steps away, past the gable just beyond the nearest corner of the house.

After he showed me where to get fresh drinking water, we returned inside the house. I watched him promptly snatch up a basket from the counter by the large dry sink and return through the mudroom on his way outdoors again. While he left to collect us eggs, I began familiarizing myself with the kitchen more intimately.

Once I had familiarized myself, it wasn't too long afterward before he came back with plenty of eggs in the basket for me to use. Instead of returning to his library to quickly finish his correspondence, as I believed he would, he stayed in the kitchen with me, slicing the salted cod into small portions after skinning the excess skin and cutting the tail away. Collecting a bowl from the cupboard, I began cracking eggs into it as I watched him grab a bowl for himself to place the fish into. He reached for the pitcher and poured fresh cold water into the bowl with the cod, soaking it to leach the excess salt from it.

While it was soaking, he moved to the stove and hunched over the large basket beside it. Gathering some kindling from the basket along with some wood, he opened the oven door to the cast-iron stove and began arranging them inside. As I started scrambling eggs at the counter, I glanced over my shoulder at him when he reached an arm over the nearby counter and snagged the tinderbox off of it. Opening the box, he retrieved its components and placed them on the floor before setting the beeswax candle upright in its tin holder. Snatching up a piece of flint in one hand and the flint striker in the other, he proceeded, striking it several times downward in the direction of the box with char-cloth in it.

Then, seizing one of the many brimstone matches, he dipped it into the box, and it flamed at the tip. Promptly covering the smoldering char-cloth with a tin plate that fit perfectly inside, he took the flame and lit the candle. As it now burned, he retrieved the jute match resting by his foot and lit it with the candle's flame. With this new match steadily burning, he stuck it into the oven and proceeded to light the tinder with it. Quickly catching fire, the tinder around the wood began burning, igniting the small logs on fire in the oven, and the stove started heating.

Afterward, Leif promptly drew up the narrow copper tube

over the flaming match, immediately extinguishing it, and proceeded to return the box's contents inside. After everything had been collected inside the box, he closed it and placed it back beside the stove on the counter as he stood, now checking the burner plates.

Soon satisfied that the stove was nearly ready for cooking, he turned from it and approached me at the counter, where I was removing the remaining skin from the softened fish.

"I shall go tae the cellar and retrieve a bit of lard and wine," he said.

"All right," I replied simply, nodding a bit. He turned from me and left the kitchen, and I started deboning the cod.

When Leif returned, I had just finished deboning, and all the ingredients were prepared for use. He took the cast-iron skillet off the counter in the corner near the stove and placed it on one of the burners, warming the pan. Within a minute, the pan was hot, and I cut a bit of lard to place in it. The skillet immediately started sizzling, and I gathered the fish into it.

The cod quickly cooked along with the scrambled eggs, and as I was preparing our plates for eating, Leif placed silverware for us to use on the table instead of the simple flatware I'd found in the hutch before pouring us glasses of Madeira. With small wine glasses now filled, he proceeded to seat himself at the head of the stretched maple table as I placed a full plate of prepared food before him. Seating myself close beside him, we began eating, enjoying our morning meal together, staying comfortable in the kitchen, instead of in the formal dining room.

Seven

After breakfast, Leif brought me outdoors and toured me around the anchorage for a while. It was an expansive property as I gazed around the landscape once we had climbed down a rocky trail on the bluff onto the beach from where the house overlooked the ocean. Strolling now over sand, I observed small nearby waves calmly crashing onto shore while admiring our new location as we leisurely paced along.

The animated water, sparkling beneath the shining sun, was a mixture of cobalt and ultramarine blue. It was pristine and clear, with flecks of turquoise as it rolled over the golden sand. As I took in my surroundings, it seemed we were the only ones inhabiting the peninsula. The air was hot and uncomfortably muggy, but the sky was a crystal-clear cobalt blue without a cloud to be seen.

We came to a cove surrounded by large rocks, but the shaded sand was smooth as my bare feet pressed into it. When I glanced over my shoulder past the surrounding rocks, our burnt sienna house with lampblack shutters could easily be seen up on the bluff, with beachgrass around it. It sat near the rocky slope, not too far from where we were walking.

"Do we have any neighbors?" I asked curiously, gazing around our secluded location and enjoying the view from the cove.

"A Master Welles and his family reside on the west end of the peninsula. He is a tenant of ours," Leif answered, turning his gaze toward me.

"Are they the only ones?" I inquired with surprise.

"Aye. This is all our land," he informed me, pointing around our location as far as the eye could see as the peninsula curved away from us from the cove.

"My goodness!" I was thoroughly amazed. A grin eased over his face in response, but it was suddenly tempered. He appeared meditative instead as he looked at me, making me wonder about the change in his expression. "What is wrong?"

"Naught." He lightly shrugged.

"But you're no longer smiling."

"I'm merely recalling my moments haur."

"Oh. Did something bad happen here?"

"Not at all."

"Then what are you remembering?"

"I frequently visited this place."

"You did?"

"Tae gaze upon the sea in my melancholy," he disclosed, seeming glum as I suddenly realized him referring to his time spent alone during our separation. "'Tis tranquil haur..."

"Yeah, it is tranquil here," I agreed softly, observing that his expression had become nearly unreadable now. He shifted his gaze from me toward the ocean ahead and silently gazed at it for a moment, simply watching the water flow and ebb over the sand. The sound of the waves caught my attention, and I also turned my gaze out to sea, listening and watching in silence.

"As time passed to nae avail, thaur waur many a day I believed that I micht never lay eyes upon ye again, Sylvie," he resumed in a temperate voice, breaking the lull between us and revealing his deepest fear that had been hidden until now, and that was the raw truth. "'Tis strange, fur although such a thought had entered my mind, I equally believed 'twas not tae come tae pass. A flame within my breast granting me faith never snuffed, yet merely grew when in doubt and forced my belief that I shall hold ye once more.

"I visited this place tae bathe in the sea, aplenty. When I had come tae do so, my spirit lightened with the restoration of hope—that I would find ye one day. So... I never relinquished faith. Nor, ever relented my search of ye. Yet, distantly, I kent that if it never meant tae pass during my living days that we should reunite before perishing, I would meet my end knowing my effort wisnae in vain as my loove fur ye remained boundless and true within the pit of my being. The pulse of my heart that ye are." He shifted his solemn gaze toward me again, and I glanced up at him, meeting his eyes. A knot formed in my throat, and a sudden tear slipped down my cheek. He mindfully raised a palm to my face, and I sensed his thumb gently stroking the droplet away. "Not anither tear, *mo ghaol*," he semi-whispered. "We have shed enough already." I swallowed down the knot in my throat while gazing into his tender eyes, realizing again my acute elation that we were blessed to exist together again. An affectionate smile gently eased his lips, returning contentment in his expression while gazing quietly into my eyes for a moment. "Join me, tae bathe."

"I would like that," I whispered from the hoarseness in my voice.

"Grand," he replied, still grinning softly.

Attired leisurely in a simple linen shirt and breeches and without any stockings and boots, he stood beside me barefoot in the sand, proceeding to remove his shirt from himself. As he undressed, I glanced down at myself, merely dressed in a shift and an underpetticoat for the sweltering heat, and began untying my skirt. When it was briefly untied, I let it slip from my waist, and it puddled at my feet. Then, stepping from the pool of fabric at my toes, I withdrew my shift as he was now bare-chested and taking his breeches off his legs.

Soon disrobed as we stood before each other in the cove, he suddenly darted from me, and I watched him jogging ahead toward the shoreline. Smiling while observing him, I found myself giggling as he whimsically splashed into the water up to his waist. Then, he abruptly dove beneath the surface and emerged with his hair soaking wet. Inspired, I swiftly trotted after him, ready to splash into the water and join him, anticipating the enjoyment of his company. But as soon as my toes reached the shoreline, the sparkling turquoise surf splashed frigidly over my calves, instantly chilling my warm skin and stealing my breath, causing me to automatically screech.

Unlike the mild Pacific Ocean, I was used to, this water was simply cold to start, and it stifled my breathing. Immediately balking, I backed away from the rushing waves, suddenly hearing Leif's audible laughter. Glancing up from my wet feet while moving from the water, I noticed him promptly approaching me from the ocean while heartily chuckling.

Being not too far, he swiftly emerged from the surf and scooped me up into his arms when he arrived. Instantly carrying me back into the water with him, I helplessly squirmed in his binding clutch, expecting the frigid water to wash over my skin again as I breathlessly giggled, and he laughed. But my giggling immediately curtailed the second the cold water hit my flesh. I gasped, hyperventilating, as he was submerging us. When it came around his chest, my body was completely immersed as he continued holding me, and it seemed I couldn't adjust to the water's temperature soon enough.

"How far will you take us offshore?" I inquired unevenly, among stifling giggles, while shuddering in his arms from the frigid temperature enveloping me. The inspired look on his face while he continued moving us into deeper water told me he intended us to go far, since he didn't answer.

When I felt him beginning to float, I glanced back at the shoreline and saw that he had certainly swum us far from it. He buoyed me over himself, and our naked bodies brushed against each other, with his hand lightly gripping my waist now. Now attuned to the water, I comfortably exhaled as my breathing became regular and smiled at him. We ceased swimming farther at this point and began calmly floating beside each other instead. Floating on my back close to him, I sensed his palm brushing over my thigh and buttocks until it settled comfortably onto my waist again. I placed a hand loosely around his as it lightly rested on my waist, also anchoring myself close to him.

"How micht the seawater presently suit ye?" he asked while grinning enjoyably at me.

"Much better," I replied, gladly smiling back at him.

"Splendid." The large smile on his face creased his cheeks, and his eyes glimmered from the bright sun. They seemed as pristine and animated as this ocean enveloping us, I noted. "I meant tae bring ye tae this place at the cove upon our honeymoon during the spring after we first wed."

"Really?"

"Aye."

"It feels like this is our honeymoon right now," I said actually. I shifted my arm and raised my fingertips toward his face, tenderly stroking his square jaw while cupping it.

"It quite does," he agreed. "'Twill be our honeymoon experience among our eventual visit tae Hawaii."

"Yes, I suppose it will—and I'm loving it so far," I responded, sensing his palm lightly stroking my tailbone and buttocks some more.

"Is it so?"

"Yes, absolutely so," I upheld. He grinned again, and I perceived his enjoyment of me. As I floated over him while buoyed on his back, his firm penis kept brushing my thigh as I held his intense gaze and thought in all aspects how perfectly beautiful of a man he was.

"I think of the nicht we spent within yer bathing pool," he said as his grin turned languid along with the dreaminess in his eyes.

"You do think of it?"

"Aye."

"What exactly do you think about as you remember it?"

"I think of yer luring me into the water as ye swam and yer seduction of me."

"You think I seduced you?" I giggled suddenly, giving him an absurd look.

"Ye did entirely that," he said undoubtedly, smirking at me now.

"I did no such thing," I protested, giggling again.

"Ye most certainly had."

"I'm really blameless despite everything. You know?"

"I do indeed ken. Blameless ye are not. Despite all," he laughed outright.

"Of course I am. Why would you think otherwise?"

"I believe otherwise as I have never knoon a lass in all my years who is as unbound as ye have proven yerself tae be with me."

"I doubt that," I said with some irony, teasing him. His brow lifted, and his eyes widened in surprise. "You're guilty of sexual indulgences with your past liaisons. Given what I'm continuing to learn about you, your exploits were past any decadence that I could ever imagine. I'm sure. So, that makes you the wild one between us—if anything."

"Ye accuse me of hedonism?" he responded, feigning shock.

"You bet I am. You even admitted it to me."

"Ye micht have a notion."

"I certainly do."

"I am not ashamed of it, however."

"I know you're not—which makes me nervous."

"Pray, tell why?"

"Because I think you have no guardrails."

"Guardrails?"

"Yes. Boundaries, I mean."

"Yet, I have."

"Like what?"

"Shall I grant ye an example?"

"Yes, of course."

"It is quite certain that I have never taken a lass against her will. Nor, have I introduced her tae pleasures she wisnae willing tae experience."

"You know what?" I narrowed my eyes on him.

"Aye?" he replied, grinning like a guilty rake.

"Even though you're honorable not to have ever violated a woman, you're still a cunning seducer. A complete one. You made those women fall in love with you, so you'd get them to do anything you wanted them to do for you."

"Preposterous!" he chortled.

"It's true," I maintained, amused by his unexpected reaction as I giggled.

"How micht it be?"

"I'm your last specimen," I replied obviously, teasing him.

"That ye are, indeed."

"See?"

"Mayhap," he hinted.

"Sure, you do. You're just being facetious."

"Ye reckon that I am jesting?"

"You are, absolutely."

"Mmm." He seemed to consider as he pursed his lips.

"What?" I urged, curious about the thought in his mind.

"As ye have accused me of being a lecher, of which I assure ye that I am above such character, will ye do naught tae serve me, after all?" He winked at me, and I laughed.

"You already know that answer from me," I replied confidently.

"Yoo're dear. I'm raither charmed."

"I know you are because you've corrupted me."

"Not entirely."

"You're working on it, though."

"Impertinent lass."

"So, what if I am?"

"Yoo're challenging me."

"You're perceptive."

"Ye may regret it."

"Are you going to punish me?"

"Fur being pert."

"I'm not so sure I'll regret it," I giggled, teasing him. He chuckled, obviously amused.

"Ye have much tae learn from me, *mo leannan*," he said, smiling at me with appeal in his eyes.

"I'm seeing that."

"Ye enjoy my instruction."

"I'll admit that might be true. But I want to know something specific from you now that I'm thinking about it since we're touching the subject."

"Aye?"

"Did you ever make one of your courtesans dance naked in front of you before?"

"I cannae say that I have," he said honestly as I noticed the hue in his cheeks flushing either from the sun or something else. I narrowed my eyes on him again.

"I don't believe you," I said, lightly shaking my head.

"Whyever not? I dinnae lie tae ye in the merest," he responded, chuckling.

"Then why are you laughing? I'll tell you why. It's because you're completely guilty, of course."

"I cannae be guilty as I huvnae any shame. Recall? Now, permit me tae get a word in edgewise."

"Fine. Go ahead. I'm listening."

"I shall inform ye, however, that aye—"

"Yes, what?" I interrupted.

"I have indeed witnessed courtesans dancing nude before me."

"I knew it!"

"'Twas of their own volition, however," he said, trying to sound innocent.

"You're not fooling anyone, mister!" I scolded playfully.

"Master! Ye leave me slain, fur I am most affronted." He unexpectedly pinched my buttock cheek, and I yelped. He laughed, and I started giggling, completely amused.

"So, they would just dance for you on their own accord?" I questioned, giving him a skeptical look as I smirked at him now.

"Aye," he replied in a reassuring tone.

"You obviously found them entertaining when they'd do that for you," I chastised playfully.

"Of coorse."

"Of course," I echoed ironically.

"How else micht I find them?"

"Right. You're innocent. I forgot," I mocked.

"I am, however."

"Hardly."

"I am sincere."

"So, those women spontaneously danced for you?"

"It pleased them immensely tae do so."

"Interesting."

"They waur inspired tae entertain."

"What do you mean?"

"They entertained those at bacchanalias."

"Bacchanalias?" I suddenly gave him a shocked look.

"Aye."

"You're familiar with those?"

"I do admit."

"You're beyond hope," I said, shaking my head in disbelief.

"Am I?" he laughed, amused.

"Absolutely. You have no authority to be appalled by people dressed in swimsuits at the beach."

"A notion weel regarded as Rome prevails."

"How many have you attended?"

"A fair number whilst in Europe."

"You're scandalous!" I accused. Leif laughed heartily, clearly entertained by me as I gazed unbelievably at him. "My goodness! The nerve. You have a lot of surprises up your sleeve. I mean, how on earth can you possibly say that I'm the one who seduced you when you're clearly already familiar with questionable revelries and women doing that for you in the first place?"

"Yet, I shall inform ye of how ye are the superior nymph," he justified.

"I'm listening," I replied in amusement.

"Understand that not a single one of those lasses had ever presented themselves in such a manner in which ye had whilst dancing before me that particular nicht at *Serendipity*."

"Is that so?"

"Quite. They could have never invented such a presentation as the dream of it would have been incapable of entering their minds. Yer secret manner of dance isnae courtly but entirely salacious in nature. Deeply ribald. Bawdy tae the extreme."

"Salacious? Ribald? Bawdy?" I laughed incredulously.

"Aye." He gave me an unequivocal look combined with enthrall.

"Holy cow! I can't believe you just called me dirty."

"Utterly indecent," he chuckled.

"No one's ever said that about me before. But then again, you're the only one I've ever done that for," I disclosed, attracted to his enlivened expression. Settling himself from laughter, his grin remained wide, and the gleam of his teeth enhanced the charm on his face. "I felt really foolish dancing in front of you like that, you know."

"Ye deserved it. Entirely warranted. Even better fur I enjoyed it —significantly," he said bluntly with an unsympathetic look.

"Yoo're a seductress of the likes nae soul has ever seen. One of the highest order. A siren."

"I don't know if you're flattering me or insulting me. It's absolutely hard to tell." I shook my head unbelievably at him again.

"'Tis flattery that I am bestowing upon ye."

"Well, thanks," I responded ironically, and he laughed again.

"But once more, I am most sincere." He gave me a true look now, and I felt my smile weaken a little as I felt suddenly shy.

"There's a lot of power in your flattery of me," I said sheepishly.

"I am weel awaur of it." His tone turned mild, like the look on his face now that his smile lessened. But he winked at me and returned to smiling fully, causing me to smile, too.

"I think you should be concerned," I warned, teasing him some more.

"How micht ye reckon?"

"You've enabled me to have power over you."

"Ye have always had it, however."

"But now I can use it."

"Are ye not awaur that ye have been using it already? Which inspires my proceeding question tae pose. How micht ye use yer power upon me willingly?"

"Hmm. I haven't really thought about it, actually. I'm not sure... Maybe, one day, I might have you serve me wine and cheese all day while I simply lie around in bed."

"Nude?"

"What do you think?"

"Done. Whit else?"

"Maybe I'll have you cook an extravagant meal for me also."

"I implore ye. My culinary art skills are raither lacking," he said genuinely with a pitiful smile. But then he arched a brow as he suddenly smirked instead. "Yet, punishing me fur my lack of skill may be pleasing. How micht ye do such a thing tae me?"

"You are definitely hopeless," I giggled, lightly shaking my head at him. He gave me a goading smirk. "Fine. In that case, I will, in fact, perfectly punish you if you ever cook for me anything I don't like."

"Perfectly?"

"Yes."

"In whit manner"

"It's a secret."

"Not permitted."

"Really?"

"Aye. Therefore, divulge yer punishment."

"I haven't thought of one yet, actually."

"Have ye not?" He gave me a doubtful look. I smiled at him, unable to hide my guilt. "So, ye taunt me."

"Only because you're awful."

"How awful?"

"Incredibly."

"Ye flatter me."

"You're so wicked," I giggled. He laughed, and his face flushed, clearly diverted.

"Inform me of whit ye will have done tae me should I disappoint yer expectation of me."

"I'm not going to tell you."

"Yoo're naughty."

"Naughty?"

"Aye."

"For not telling you?"

"Yer secret is indecent, certainly. Otherwise, ye will divulge."

"What a supposition. But you'd already know about indecency. I don't think I can shock you even if I told you. So, why bother in that case?"

"Shall I punish ye fur yer cheek? Yoo're certain tae be stunned by me on the account."

"Okay, then. Since you're so eager to know how horribly you'd be treated by me if you ever failed to cook something pleasant for me, know that you will be forced to pleasure me until you physically couldn't do it any longer. You'll beg me for a break, and I won't give it. Simple as that," I finally informed him, confessing and looking smugly at him. He suddenly erupted into laughter, and his hand slipped from my waist, releasing me from his hold. Now, treading water in front of each other, we laughed together.

"What's so funny?" I asked curiously while laughing.

"Death by pleasuring ye wulnea be the slightest torture," he said, chuckling.

"You're making fun of me," I realized.

"Yoo're innocence utterly delights me."

"Now you're saying that I'm innocent? After you just said I was salacious and bawdy?"

"Yoo're all of it," he replied, settling from laughing now.

"How in the world can I be all of those things when they contradict?"

"Yoo're innocent due tae the fact ye dinnae ken the power ye truly wield."

"I'm not a silly teenage girl," I mocked, also calming from giggling and looking at him with a little smirk.

"I micht say that ye are more akin tae Baubo raither than an adolescent lass."

"Baubo?"

"Aye, the Greek goddess of mirth. Are ye not awaur of her?" He looked at me, somewhat surprised, as his brow faintly drew together.

"No. I'm not," I admitted, shaking my head a little.

"Weel, I shall enlighten ye."

"Please do."

"Being a goddess, Baubo was fully awaur of her wielding power."

"What did she look like?"

"Bonnie, of coorse. Yet, she wisnae chaste. She was an elder goddess."

"She was?"

"Aye. 'Tis said she was mirthful, bawdy, and sensual."

"Oh."

"She restored Demeter from melancholy efter her daughter Persephone had been stolen by Hades of the underworld as he took her tae his realm."

"Really?"

"Aye."

"But I don't think I come close to sharing any of her characteristics."

"The difference betwixt ye and Baubo is the innocence ye hold fur yerself, whilst she had naught of the sort and was aware of it," Leif explained.

"Hmm. Interesting... Well, then, who would you be akin to if that's the case for me?" I replied.

"Some have likened me tae Dionysus on more than one occasion during my youth," he mentioned matter-of-factly.

"Bacchus?" I responded, nearly laughing outright as I smiled widely at him.

"Ye awaur of this god, apparently."

"I'm not all that ignorant of ancient Greek and Roman mythology, you know?" I said, admiring the grin gracing Leif's face. "Funny, though, that you would be likened to that god. Wine and pleasure were what he was all about. I can absolutely see how that is fitting for you to be likened to him even now."

"Yoo're the wine upon which I drink and which stupefies me," he flattered, smiling at me, too. I giggled, suddenly feeling bashful, as he concentrated his gaze on me, seizing my eyes with deep enthrallment. He reached an arm forward, and I sensed his palm beginning to take my waist, ready to draw me close to his body again.

"Not if you can catch me first," I laughed and playfully slipped from his grip as I started swimming away from him.

"Let me not catch ye weel and guid, *àilie dhubh*," he joked audibly from behind me and proceeded swimming after me. Swiftly arriving close, he was now swimming alongside me while I was making my way back to shore. "Why must ye elude me?" he asked laughingly.

"Because you're Dionysus and Eros combined!" I squealed between giggles, and Leif continued laughing.

"Ye will drown me!" he gasped.

"Not my fault when you are both."

"A mighty combination ye declare."

"It explains a lot."

"Elucidate."

"I can't. It's embarrassing, and it will only expand your ego even further."

"Thaur is nae reason fur ye tae be chagrinned when I'm weel awaur of yer witty tongue. As fur my *ego* as it waur—I assume ye are referring tae my sense of self-import?"

"That's exactly what I mean."

"Yet, I am of import."

"Conceited, just like the gods," I joked.

"Yoo're meaning my virility," he understood quickly.

"What else would I mean?"

"Ye continue tae flatter me."

"Oh my gosh! You're a monster!" I laughed again, realizing I had accidentally just inflated his self-opinion to the maximum.

"Yoo're a nymph, lest we forget, who enjoys the attribute of my cock," he teased.

"Leif!"

"Aye?"

"Stop embarrassing me!"

"I shall not. Ye must hear me."

"No!"

He continued laughing, and so did I, as I tried pulling away from him while we swam, but I couldn't. Instead, he followed alongside me, and I anxiously strove to remain out of his reach. So, when we came to shore, I arrived splashing out of the surf, returning over the sand as I darted from him. Still, he was too close to withstand while he was immediately at my back, jogging behind my heels, chasing me. There was no escaping him, though I ran with all my might over the hot sand, determined to get to the house.

Giggling breathlessly while now galloping toward the slope, I heard him chuckling close behind me, exciting my anxiousness to elude his capture. When we soon reached the bottom of the hill, I lost my breath as I began vigorously climbing the gradient toward the house amid the tall beachgrass. As I made my way, I had become nervously aware that he nearly snagged my waist in his pursuit to capture me, as I was certainly aware of his intentions to take me to bed.

The moment we reached the crest, I dashed ahead of him through the beachgrass, feeling it whipping me like silk against my naked skin before finally arriving at the back of the house. Throwing the door open, I rushed inside into the mudroom and entered the kitchen without a minute to spare when he snatched my waist with an arm, whirling me around to face him.

"Yoo'll never escape from me, nae matter how michty ye try," he said, panting and smiling as I gazed into his excited eyes.

"You keep proving that to me," I laughed, gasping for air also. He pulled me against his body, and I sensed his hard penis poking my flat stomach. Suddenly, hauling me from beneath my arms, he raised me off my feet and held me against his chest, forcing me to gaze eye level with him. I naturally wrapped my arms around his neck and encircled his hips with my legs, anchoring myself to him. Our bodies pressed snugly together, and I felt our hearts pounding synchronously within our chests while our irregular breathing began settling.

"Yoo're a flighty wee hummingbird which I have captured," he panted lightly.

"I thought you said I was a nymph," I uttered breathlessly,

feeling his large palms gripping my buttocks as he stabilized me in his arms.

"Tae be certain, ye are all that spellbind," he replied.

I smiled at him and tightened my arms around his neck. As I gazed into his sparkling ultramarine eyes, they were amorous, and I perceived the depth of his attraction to me. He leaned his mouth toward mine, and I pressed my lips onto his, parting my lips slightly. His tongue instantly slid inside, and I began kissing him with the heat of my own desire, longing for him to fill me. Anxious moans and panting passed between us while we kissed as he urged us down on the kitchen floor.

PART TWO
A Little Honeymoon

Eight

We arrived in the nearby village of Lynn as planned to purchase some fresh loaves of bread from the baker, along with other ingredients such as flour and butter. We also purchased coffee beans from the coffeehouse and tea from the teahouse, along with various hobnobs and necessities from the mercantile. As we continued gathering stock, our stay on the peninsula was proving to be very enjoyable.

Because this was my first visit to town, I was particularly enjoying myself while discovering this new place as we strolled over cobblestone walkways after parking our horse and buggy at one of the posts lining the street. The sun shone brightly, and ivory-white clouds drifted by in the cobalt sky as a breeze from the ocean whipped the humid air around us.

We entered a selection of shops that caught our attention. While we were inside one shop and as Leif was making some purchases for me, I couldn't help noticing how everything seemed so expensively priced compared to the time before, when I was last in this colony—despite Leif having informed me months ago regarding this economy when he was with me in my era.

"Prices for things have really increased," I commented as we were leaving the general shop after purchasing some seasonings that included salt, pepper, sugar, ginger, and cloves, along with some candles and tins.

"'Tis due tae tariffs the Crown has levied upon goods imported into the colonies," Leif replied as we began strolling over the walkway again.

"I remember you telling me earlier about the current cost of goods, but why the exorbitance of it, though?" I asked curiously, feeling unfortunately naive about what exactly was occurring with England now.

"The Crown reckons English subjects shan't bear alone the burden from the war tae replenish the treasury when they already pay increased tariffs as it is," he answered.

"But, couldn't the government distribute the impact of the cost more evenly across the board so that it doesn't target certain areas more significantly than others in the empire?" I wondered.

"These colonies are the wealthiest in the empire. Therefore, the Crown deducts the cost from us. Whit is more, the Crown decrees that English subjects had borne substantial costs fur the war with France whilst maintaining lax tax policies fur the colonies it had defended. Thus, a proclamation has been made that we in these colonies shall reconcile the difference by paying the balance in taxes that is timely due. England carries great debt from the war, mind ye. Her coffers are far depleted, leaving her in peril upon the condition she disnae recover the loss."

"I see…" I responded thoughtfully. "I remember that you saying there've been riots in Boston because of the economic strain, but that they've since settled. Right?"

"Aye. The mobs have quelled tae an extent."

"You mean they haven't fully?"

"The strain presently results from the many troops stationed in the city tae enforce the Townsend Act as the military snuffs smuggling into the colony."

"Aren't more people inspired to riot because the military is there doing that, though?"

"They have done fine tae control the streets. Any man partaking in such an event or having organized it will be arrested, imprisoned, and hanged. Any allegation of a man's participation in such matters will lead tae his death without question also."

"Oh."

"Absolutism has rooted itself within Boston as Tyranny is weel seen."

"I'm surprised, then, that anyone would have the initiative to protest. I mean, aren't people afraid of even thinking of doing it?"

"'Tis the Crown's directive, of coorse. Many do fear the Crown's punishment. Yet, thaur are those who defy the Crown nonetheless."

"They're surely brave for doing it," I acknowledged, realizing the fear the Crown impressed upon the people to control them, as I understood that mentioning one's political leanings could get one killed. It was certainly a frightful time now. Leif didn't respond to my remark. He glanced at me instead as we continued walking with packages in his arms.

"I have recently received word regarding Master Hancock," he alluded, catching my attention further. Leif shifted his gaze ahead to mind his steps on the uneven walkway.

"What have you heard?" I looked at him for a second longer before returning to looking ahead.

"The navy has seized his *Liberty*."

"*Liberty?* You mean that would be one of his ships?"

"Aye."

"Really? What for?" I glanced at him again with surprise.

"Tidesmen have accused him of smuggling."

"Really?"

"Aye."

"Does he smuggle?"

"Aye. Boston is weel awaur of him, and Hancock disnae distress."

"He doesn't at all?"

"Nae."

"Why?"

"The risk of being accused didnae outweigh the measure of his smuggling success."

"Until now, apparently."

"'Twould seem."

"I didn't know he would be in that sort of business," I said, still in surprise.

"He is shrewd," Leif commented.

"Does he have to pay a fine for being accused?"

"He will be charged tae pay coin in addition tae further consequences."

"You mean he's been arrested also?"

"He has been charged with the crime."

"He's in jail now?" I gave Leif a shocked look.

"He has been arrested. Yet, tae his fortune, he remains free from imprisonment till his trial. However, fortune is telling when he risks being condemned tae hang fur treason should magistrates decide tae finally punish him. A chilling example they micht make of him."

"Oh, my goodness," I uttered under my breath, stunned over this news.

"Hancock is a Whig and a financier of clandestine affairs of which Sir Francis Bernard, our governor, is far awaur."

"Really?"

"Sir Bernard detests Hancock and has set his sights upon him."

"Oh no."

"Indeed, it disnae bode weel fur Hancock."

"It wouldn't seem so at all," I agreed worriedly. But I knew that Mr. Hancock survived his trial, as history had shown that his name was written on the Declaration of Independence by himself and was displayed in my era. What I didn't know were the intimate details of his life, involving the sacrifices he must have made to survive the Crown's oppression, which led through the American Revolution. So, I was concerned about his general well-being as I considered the threat he was now facing from the English government.

"Hancock has many men who are fond of him, however. Those who admire him partook in mobbing the streets once the navy seized his vessel."

"Seriously?"

"Truly."

"He is one of many pied pipers who rule men's sentiments against the Crown, as he commiserates with disposed merchants who favor him." I nodded a little in acknowledgment. "His flamboyance and audacity have acquired the governor's attention. The governor is awaur that Hancock makes him appear like a fool tae the king, involving the lack of explanation tae his opulence."

"So, they can't explain why he's so much richer than he should be?"

"Quite. Hancock slights Sir Bernard without compunction. Therefore, Bernard despises him," Leif said.

"I see." I became quiet as we continued walking, thinking for a moment. Leif also became silent as he minded the path we were on toward our buggy. "If taxes on imported commodities are causing prices on things to climb, what will everybody do if it all becomes unaffordable? Couldn't the colony tax itself to lessen the burden from the Crown?" I asked, returning to our conversation.

"'Twould be treason should the colony implement such a measure."

"Would it?"

"Certainly. Tae do so, the colony would be declaring independence from the king. The colony would never survive the king's wrath and panishment as a result of such a declaration and consequence. Aside from it all, Bernard is a Loyalist tae his being. Therefore, he would never betray the Sovereign."

"Oh," I realized.

"But what is anyone to do when things become unaffordable?"

"Due tae hidden machinations at play, will they persevere? I reckon so. Therefore, the price upon guids will remain attainable."

"What schemes are you referring to?"

"The nefarious art of smuggling."

"Is it substantially prevalent to affect the market?"

"Considerably. The navy is at its wits' end striving tae curb it."

"So, plenty are escaping repercussions from the Crown, then."

"Those who dinnae escape capture are imprisoned tae waste away, if not fortunate tae hang."

"So, you've told me," I understood frightfully, swallowing the dryness down my throat. "How are the Hutchinsons? Do you still see them?" I inquired, changing the subject as I suddenly remembered them from Boston.

"I do not encounter them as I once had before," Leif said indifferently.

"Really? Why not?" I asked curiously, noticing his demeanor change.

"They are of wee interest tae me. Master Hutchinson is presently Lieutenant Governor."

"He is?"

"Aye."

"Oh. Well, why don't you care for him anymore?"

"Since his reversal of opinion on his opposition tae the Townshend Acts, he works in favor of Parliament against Whigs as he now loathes the subjects of Boston."

"Why doesn't he like the people of Boston anymore?"

"It originates from when he was closely murdered by them."

"What? Why on earth?" I gave Leif a stunned look, realizing the outlandish thought.

"Men rebelled against him fur his support and instillation of the Stamp Act in the city. He escaped being burnt alive when his hoose was torched after ransacking by the mob."

"My goodness! That really happened to him?" I shook my head in appalling disbelief.

"Aye."

"When did all of this happen?"

"Four years ago, it occurred."

"That's incredible. Don't you believe it's a bit extreme to want to kill someone over differences in political beliefs?"

"Politics inherently determines men's lives," Leif said. I didn't immediately respond as I thought about what he just said.

"So, you don't like Mister Hutchenson because of his political change that's affecting people negatively."

"Tae acknowledge it simply."

"I know you said that for the colony to tax itself would be treason, but it seems like a viable solution to everyone's woes—including the Crown's—if the king would simply agree to let it happen. Then, maybe the motivation for rebellion might be dispelled. It could possibly help carve out a more peaceful path between here and England."

"A novel notion tae consider. Yet, England will never regard such a proposal."

"I know England would never peacefully allow for a separation. But what about compromising? It could very well wind up saving lives."

"Plenty of men who disagree with Parliament complain that tariffs ought not be collected from them unless they have a seat in Parliament," Leif continued, informing me.

"That seems fair, though," I replied sincerely.

"Conceptually. The truth of the matter is that the nobility and landed gentry wulnae agree to permitting the lowborn tae acquire more power than they already have, which is none."

"Why not? I don't understand."

"The reason being it may very weel tip the balance of power

71

from the king and cause strife within all the empire, which may result in more than fur whit many have gambled, presently."

"Oh," I replied simply. I suddenly realized again how very different this political world was from my own, and it reminded me of its uncertainty, making me question if we'd ultimately be safe here as we spend our lives. "So, Mister Hutchinson isn't well loved anymore," I remarked as I resumed thinking of him and his wife, whom I had really liked.

"He is weel loved amongst Tories as Bernard. Yet, undoubtedly, due tae his near mortal experience at the hands of the mob, subjects of Boston, in general, have lost an ally as he forfeits his admiration fur them."

"I see. What a shame, really. I just remember how nice everything was between us with Mister and Missus Hutchinson many years ago. I keep thinking of the time when they came to our Christmas party and how we had enjoyed ourselves with each other."

"The ball was long ago, indeed. Much has changed since that period."

"How sad," I replied regrettably as I thought about them. "He gave Oakley to us to purchase. Remember?"

"Clearly."

"I wonder how she is. Is she still alive?" I asked, remembering the horse that Leif had given me.

"She is quite alive and fit."

"I'm so glad to hear that. I'd like to ride her again. I hope she'll remember me."

"She is certain to recall ye." He glanced at me and smiled. I smiled at him also as I fondly remembered my horse and the wonderful moment when he had surprised me when he presented her to me. It was a very dear day we had shared together, and I deeply cherished the memory of it as warmth kindled inside me while thinking of it.

Leif shifted all the packages he was carrying into one arm and gently wrapped his freed fingers around my elbow. The warm-hearted feeling between us was apparent, and the feeling enveloped me with sheer happiness as I forgot the serious conversation we had just had. He guided us through the light pedestrian crowd until we soon arrived at our buggy. After placing the packages inside, he seized my waist, lifting me slightly as I placed my foot on the footstep and assisted me onto the seat. Swiftly unhitching Blaze and grabbing the reins, he took his place beside me in the buggy and drove us out of Lynn, returning us over the peninsula into Nahant for *Sàmhchair*.

Nine

M uch of our time here was spent in leisure. Days of swimming in the ocean, walks, or picnics on the beach, and moments in bed together blissfully consumed us. On occasion, Leif would slip into his library to correspond and tend to business affairs while I preoccupied myself with preparing meals in the kitchen for us to enjoy.

This morning was quite pleasant, with intermittent bright sunlight peering through drifting white cumulus clouds. However, the air was muggy after the heavy rain from the night, which was sure to amplify the heat as the day wore on. As often as I tried ignoring the weight of the heat every day, I longed for air-conditioned rooms to escape the swelter. Still, as I opened the windows and shutters this morning, a noticeable onshore breeze entered the kitchen and tempered the atmosphere to my comfort and satisfaction.

After breakfast, Leif returned to his library to complete his remaining business for the morning. While he worked, I decided to take a blanket and a book with me down to the beach and relax on the sand. When I laid my blanket out on the warm sand near the shoreline, I sprawled myself over my stomach on it and began enjoying myself while reading the book I'd snagged from his library.

The ocean waves were lightly crashing over the sand, and their sound was hypnotic, further relaxing me. Titanium-white clouds suspended in the cerulean sky continued drifting overhead as the hot sun beamed between them down over me. Adjusting my hat from the bright sun to see the print on the pages better, my eyes were growing heavy, and the feeling of drowsiness was overcoming me as I tried to concentrate on continuing to read. But I finally decided to close my eyes only for a minute before returning indoors.

But, when my groggy eyes opened again, it registered that I must have dozed for more than my intended minute as I drowsily realized the sensation of a large hand gently stealing over my waist and backside with light caresses. As my gaze sluggishly began focusing from under the brim of my straw hat, Leif's smiling eyes became distinct as they closely hovered over mine. I became aware that he had eased himself down beside me over the blanket, and I smiled at him.

"Shall we forever remain in a state of undress?" he inquired in a low, tender voice as I was conscious of his palm slowly stroking beneath my shift, the only article of clothing I was wearing today. His hand gently meandered over my thigh and buttocks, further garnering my attention to him.

"I think it suits us nicely," I replied as my sleepy eyes held his. His shirt was untucked and the collar open, revealing the light blonde hair on his chest. He proceeded to lie comfortably beside me after sitting.

"Do ye not care fur yer repute, Your Grace?" he asked while pushing the hem of my shift above my waist, exposing my entire backside.

"I don't think it's at all threatened. Who would ever find us here in this isolated corner of the world?" I replied dreamily, noticing the large smile on his face creasing his ruddy cheeks. His ultramarine eyes glimmered like the ocean and were full of amour and affection while I stared at them.

"A vessel, mayhap, micht discover us," he said. His golden hair had grown long, well past his shoulders, and was untied, hanging free in the breeze. Portions of it obscured his face as it wafted, and tendrils carried over his eyelashes. He raked a hand through his wayward strands, replacing all of them behind his shoulders, clearing his face. "Whit micht ye say if a vessel mayhap appears upon us, presently?"

"A ship? You think one could see us?" I asked skeptically while smiling at him.

"One very weel micht. They do sail these waters."

"Do they really?"

"Aye."

"But, the chances of one coming by seem very slim. So, I'm not worried."

"'Twould be wise if ye waur tae consider tae have a bit of caution."

"Why?"

"One micht appear."

"Hmm," I regarded, shifting my gaze from him and glancing toward the vast encompassing ocean meeting the horizon, only seeing waves as they broke on the shore. "But I don't see a single ship, and I've never seen one since we've been here. So, I think we're safe from being discovered."

"Yoo're disclaiming my warning, then?" I noticed the smirk tilting his lips now, and he suddenly looked fiendish.

"Yes."

"Yer poise will be yer undoing."

"Really?" I giggled.

"Certainly."

"Why are you warning me?" I smiled at him, having an inkling about him. He rolled me onto my back and positioned himself, hovering directly over me, grinning amorously into my eyes.

"Ye will very weel ken the reason why," he half-whispered, delivering a single tender kiss on my lips. I giggled again, and he proceeded to bestow plenty of soft, little kisses over my lips. My mind began to float, leaving my surroundings behind.

Consumed by his delicate, small kisses, I was hardly aware of him lifting my hem higher, passing my bare stomach, until my nipple was revealed. When his palm found my stiffened nipple, his fingers began gently fondling it, and a faint little moan eluded my lips.

While he continued kissing me, I returned all of his sweet affection, wanting more as the warmth of his massaging fingers over my breast diluted my mind, and the delirious feeling of euphoria emerged, heating my blood. The sensation of his stroking fingers roving past my breast now, drifting downward over my stomach with more warming caresses, continued beyond my navel and meandered lower until they arrived at my pubis and finally slipped between the cleft between my thighs.

His endeavoring fingers began to open me, spreading me apart, and my depths liquified as I helplessly lost myself in his touch. Then, a long, thick finger slid beyond my entrance, deliberately surging into me, and my breath unevenly drew into my lungs. He slowly proceeded to pump it inside me, and a light little moan eluded my lips. With each ebb and flow, I felt the heat escalating throughout my body as searing blood coursed my veins, and the embedded warmth between my thighs migrated within my abdomen, giving rise to a deep-seated aching for him to bury himself completely within me.

"Why do ye smile, *àille dhubh*?" he inquired in raspy tones against my lips as he was kissing me.

"Am I smiling?" I moaned, unaware.

"Ye are. Why?"

"You already know why," I breathed, realizing now that my lips were, in fact, upturned. He pressed a kiss over my mouth again and deepened it as the pad of his thumb began stroking my clitoris in conjunction with his inserted finger, deliberately thrusting inside me. I sensed his lips also curving into a grin over my mouth. My lips parted to catch a breath, and his tongue surged into my mouth, completely stealing my wind. The light, gentle kisses he had bestowed on me turned into craving. He began devouring me as his scorching lips swept over mine and powerfully latched with a forceful tongue. Gently seeping my fingers into his silken crown, I received his kisses with the yearning of my own intensifying heat. Anxiously dancing my tongue against his, the sublimity he was creating between my thighs concentrated the growing ache for my ecstatic release.

Withdrawing his lips, his fingers slipped from me also, and a whine of dissatisfaction escaped me. He suddenly shifted and adjusted himself stably over me with elbows propped beside my head. Then, his lips resumed kissing as they began trailing intently over my cheek and down along my neck. When I sensed his lips slowly moving lower toward a breast and latched onto a nipple, suckling, my breath caught as he drew it deeply into his mouth. Sucking and rolling, he fervently kneaded it with his tongue. Purposefully, he manipulated my swelling nipple, tenderizing it until it ached and giving rise to higher pleasure.

Finally releasing it, glistening from his mouth, and paining me a little, I caught a glimpse of the satisfied grin curving his lips and knew he would continue to satiate and please. He promptly returned his lips to my heated skin, and they wandered across my stomach, burning me and sending my blood searing throughout my body, quickly turning my liquified depths molten.

As his lips arrived at my pubis, I felt him parting my legs as he propped my knees and fitted his mouth comfortably between my thighs. Glimpsing at his crown dipping below, I was particularly aware of his fingers separating my cleft. He pulled me far apart and gazed for a moment. Closing my eyes, I returned, lying motionless on my back, anticipating his fingers. Wanting him to do whatever was at his will, I wriggled my hips a little, spreading my thighs wide, inviting him to take and use me in any manner.

Then, welcoming fingers proceeded, stretching me far apart, and the fire of his breath consumed my clitoris and entrance. His breath steamed my flesh, and I thought I might die from the burning aching rooted in my belly. Sensing the searing tip of his tongue beginning to gently stroke my clitoris, my senses spun. But the world seemed to be still when I opened my eyes and saw the quiet sky.

His tongue pursued going around it again, causing the same dizzying effect as I helplessly returned to closing my eyes. As it moved around once more, his tongue pressed against my hole and pushed inside. Gravelly groans from his throat escaped him as he thrust it in and out of me, sucking simultaneously. Incited moans also eluded my lips as escalating delirium began overwhelming me. When his tongue completely retracted from my entrance and stroked upward, his mouth returned to my clitoris and paid it acute attention.

I gasped at the wild sensation he forced upon me that focused my consciousness precisely on the heart between my thighs. Deliberately dragging his tongue around it, then over it, he began to gently suck. Then, suddenly releasing my clitoris, his tongue drew around it again, repeating the motion, and sucked. Gasping at the intensely pleasurable sensation, I was hostage to his driving spell.

As he focused there between my cleft, my clitoris began swelling with tenderness, and it ailed between pain and pleasure. Feeling raw with every nerve in it alive, I whined as I buried my fingers into his silky crown, pressing his face snugly between my thighs, only to have him fulfill the need to have him inside me.

Suddenly, my clitoris began throbbing, pulsing with the beat of my heart. He stopped sucking and pressed his tongue onto it, gently but firmly, and concentrated on my tiny organ. I disintegrated. My nerves throughout my abdomen electrified, sending shockwaves past my hips and thighs, right down to my toes, cramping them. Launched into euphoria, I rapidly soared into a realm of pristine rhapsody. I felt as if I was on fire as my little organ wildly spasmed, and the electrical shocks enveloping my body annihilated me.

An audible cry escaped me in the middle of climaxing, and before I completely tumbled from ecstasy, I hazily sensed him shifting forward above me when his hand moved between us and fumbled with his breeches. Before I realized it, the keen sensation of his formidable shaft abruptly surged into me before my pulsing abated, reversing the end of my collapse. Filling me to the hilt, he panted and groaned as he intently began thrusting, opening my eyes again to gaze into his.

Assuming his rhythm, he moved amorously within my depths, compelling me to join him as he journeyed toward the summit. No words passed between us, but panting and moans as our lips brushed against each other and adhered between tender and melding kisses. Syncing us with every thrust, my thighs fit his hips and naturally rocked, welcoming the penetration to the end of my depths.

Diving deeper, he kissed my cervix and rolled my uterus with vivacity, grunting and panting while achieving our dissolution in the sweltering atmosphere surrounding us. Each surge forced my breath from my lungs as rapturous moans passed my lips, and the beaming sun above seemed to boil us without mercy. Droplets of preparation had formed on his brow and began streaming over his face, dripping over my lips. My tongue involuntarily emerged and licked the salty droplets away.

The enamored look in his deep blue eyes brimmed with delirium, echoing the sublime sensation he created far within me. The inferno was around us and within us, and I believed I was melting away and thought I would die. Unrestrained gasps and groans emitted from us, and I was aware of myself tightening around him as he vigorously continued in and out of me. He hardened further as if he'd turned into stone. The drilling became distinct and complete, as the details of his engorged organ were precisely felt inside me, causing me to fully ache to receive all of him to my core.

The cusp was nearing as he drew me with him to our end with each measure. Then, the crest arrived, and we hurtled together from the summit into rapturous oblivion, where we soared.

My body began shuddering beneath him, and he roared a feral roar originating from his gut. Crying out as my depths clamped down on him, I stiffened in his embrace as he seized and exploded into me. My nerves electrified as my depths wildly grabbed his shaft, hitting me with intense waves of euphoria. As the convulsions within me obliterated my senses, I was scarcely aware of Leif as he violently throbbed between my legs and expelled himself inside my chasm, completely overrun by his overflowing release.

While pulses abated, I glided downward in a haze back to emerging reality, landing softly on a plane of bliss. An extra roar emitted from Leif before collapsing over me, and he heaved over my breast. I felt his chest rapidly expanding and contracting over mine while my own quick breath was settling. I reached my arms around his back and held him, feeling his ragged breathing warmly caressing my cheek and neck as his face rested against mine.

When we calmed, ocean waves were heard again crashing over the sand, and the world around us returned, with the brightly shining sun radiating down on us, accompanied by a light, humid breeze. He stirred a little from my embrace and raised his gaze toward mine. His lips sluggishly curled into a spellbound grin, and the affection in his eyes was apparent. I smiled dreamily at him as I looked up into his gaze, feeling utterly fulfilled. He leaned, pressing soft, tender kisses over my lips, and the light flavor of salt was on them. I kissed him in kind, loving him equally.

Everything seemed like a dream. But it was all real.

As our kisses stilled between us, he carefully reared upward, and I sensed him pulling out of me, leaving me void while his essence emptied from me and flowed between my thighs. He lethargically rolled onto his back beside me and scooped an arm beneath me, lifting me over him to rest on his chest, facing him. Cradling his palms over my cheeks, he forced my gaze to his and momentarily stared into my eyes without a word. Perfect satisfaction and contentment were pronounced in his eyes. I smiled, and he smiled, too.

He drew my lips over his and bestowed more little kisses that were sweet and benign. As they lightly trailed from my lips toward my cheek, my starry-eyed gaze turned toward the glinting, animated ocean. While glancing at the shoreline, enjoying his gentle kisses now, a mass of titanium white sails bobbing over the water unexpectedly appeared, and I was suddenly amazed as I reconsidered Leif's earlier warning about these shores. As I stared at it in surprise, the ship seemed to be quickly approaching the shoreline, heading directly in our direction.

"Leif?" I uttered softly in uncertainty, attempting to distract him from his granting kisses.

"Aye?" he muttered against my cheek, preoccupied with his lips over my cheek and neck.

"There's a ship over there," I notified.

"Whaur?" he replied inattentively.

"Over there." I pointed out to sea for him to notice. But he remained inattentive and preoccupied with me. "Look," I insisted while continuing to point at it as the euphoric haze of recent love-making dispelled from my senses. Still disregarding, I shifted in his arms as he held me in order to sit beside him instead. He promptly fastened his arms around me, preventing my intention, and playfully smirked. "Won't you look to see what I'm trying to show you? It seems to be sailing right toward us."

The smirk on his lips disappeared. His brow suddenly raised, and his eyes widened with abrupt realization. Immediately relinquishing his embrace, his arms slipped away from around my waist, and he eased me off his chest, placing me beside him. As he swiftly proceeded to get to his feet, he grabbed his spyglass, which was left close to his opposite side. Standing tall in front of me now,

I started to my feet as well and stood beside him, curiously looking at the approaching vessel while he pulled the segments to his spyglass open. Holding the instrument to his eye, he peered through it at the advancing ship.

While the large schooner was clearly coming into view, it soon arrived extremely close to shore when it appeared to drift not as quickly as the sails were drawing downward, and it began anchoring before us. Noticing it was heavily armed with many cannons peering from the portholes and lacking the Union flag, a wave of alarm seeped through the marrow of my bones.

"Are they pirates?" I asked dryly, suddenly realizing our vulnerability.

"'Tis my *Freiheit*," Leif calmly answered, recognizing it and seeming unfazed. Instantly withdrawing the spyglass from his eye, he shut it closed and turned his gaze toward me. "Promptly attire yerself, *ceisdein*. We have company."

"Who are they?" I asked curiously, confused.

"'Tis Captain Sinclair and his crew who have arrived," he said.

"Oh," I replied unknowingly.

"Make haste, loove. He and his men will shortly come tae shore," he responded before I could inquire any further. So, I swiftly leaned to collect my book and blanket off the sand as he caught the men on deck of the schooner waving at him from afar. As Leif waved back at them, I made no delay to meet his request to avoid being seen in my sheer shift by any of these new, strange men, and started away from him. "I shall soon be indoors with the captain," Leif informed me from behind before I'd gone too far.

"Okay," I replied, glancing back at him and nodding a little. Then, turning from him, I hurried across the sand toward the slope near the house.

Ten

I rushed upstairs to our bedroom and went to the privy closet to cleanse myself from salt, sand, and the aftermath of our lovemaking. All the while I washed from the washbasin, I wondered who Captain Sinclair was and the reason for his unexpected arrival. But by his response, Leif didn't appear at all surprised by the visit of this man and crew, which made me consider that he was likely expecting him. I was surprised that he hadn't mentioned anything about it to me.

When I had finished, I collected fresh clothing from the armoire and dresser drawers and proceeded to dress myself. First, pulling a pair of clocked stockings over my legs, I tied them with silk ribbon garters, then slipped my toes into a nice, simple pair of slippers. Afterward, patiently donning fresh peach linen petticoats and a peony chintz short-gown, I finally moved toward the dressing table and sat before the looking glass, ready to fix my hair. Not having assistance or the time to coif my ringlets, I made due by skillfully fishtail braiding my hair into a long plait down my back, leaving wispy ringlet tendrils on the sides, framing my face. Finally, I pinned a petite lace pinner on top of my head, then left the bedroom for downstairs, acceptably attired.

As I descended the staircase to the first floor, I heard a couple of male voices emanating from the dining room. Leif's voice being among them, I paced toward the sound of the conversation, curious to know about our visitor. Once entering the dining room from the hallway, a slightly tall man with raw umber hair, appearing in his forties, dressed in white breeches, a matching waistcoat, and a navy blue coat, stood near Leif before me as I approached the threshold. The men ceased speaking with each other and turned their attentive gazes toward me the moment I appeared, pacing deeper into the room.

"Captain Sinclair, I present tae ye my dear wife, Her Grace, Duchess of Monteith," Leif introduced politely as I arrived to stand with them by the window closest to the hearth. The captain's light blue eyes briefly widened with understanding as a pleasant smile curved his mouth. His clean-shaven cheeks also abruptly flushed while gazing at me. A little awkward lull ensued as he stared for a prolonged moment with a look resembling embarrassment mixed with charm, and I smiled a little unevenly at him.

As he gazed, I suddenly wondered whether he had seen Leif and me together on the beach as his ship approached the shore. I abruptly glanced away from him toward Leif, meeting his admiring eyes before the heat in my cheeks rose. Captain Sinclair immediately interrupted his stare, suddenly seeming aware of himself. He sharply clicked his heels and bowed to me. When he straightened, he appeared more collected, and he returned to looking at me.

"I am most honored tae make yer acquaintance, Your Grace. 'Tis quite an unexpected surprise. A blessing tae His Grace, indeed. I have heard much about Her Grace as His Grace has done naught, but speak of Her Grace in the highest regard. Her Grace is quite beloved by His Grace, told by his word. 'Tis clearly understood why, as Her Grace's vision of loveliness is striking. It pleases me greatly tae witness both of ye reunited at long last," the captain said pleasantly to us as I noticed how ruddy his complexion had become, which went beyond the sun exposure from sailing the high seas.

"Thank you, Captain Sinclair. It's very nice to meet you also," I replied modestly, smiling unevenly again at the Scotsman. My glance bounced from him toward Leif as I was aware of his observant, steady eyes on me, and I gave him a little smile. Leif reciprocated a confident grin, then returned his attention to the captain.

"Micht His Grace forgive my being bold when I say tae him that Her Grace is markedly stunning," Captain Sinclair further complimented when shifting his eyes toward Leif again.

"Indeed, she is most bonnie, Sinclair," Leif agreed appreciatively, without a doubt. The captain's face flushed some more, and I continued to notice. When I was about to politely begin a little small talk with him to learn something about him, Leif turned his eyes toward me again, catching my glance.

"Will ye be too kind, *mo leannan*, tae replenish our rum?" he requested benignly.

"Yes, of course," I replied easily and immediately started away from them for the sideboard where it was kept, along with bottles of Madeira behind the doors. When I arrived at the cabinet and opened it, I easily spotted the rum. Retrieving it, I returned to them and refilled the glass tumblers they were each holding in their hands.

"Thank ye, Your Grace," Captain Sinclair said gratefully to me as he received his filled glass from my fingers when I returned his tumbler to him.

"Yes, of course," I responded nicely. A small grin lingered on Leif's face when I also gave him his glass filled with the liquor while he kept his eyes on me, watching. I demurely smiled back at him, aware of the captain observing us. Like the captain, Leif brought his glass to his lips and took a light swig from it, but his eyes never left me as he drank, causing my self-consciousness to emerge. He gave me a subtle wink, inspiring a little smile to curl my lips.

"The captain and his crew are on leave haur fur an interim

before returning tae sail," Leif informed me after swallowing his rum and bringing his glass down from his mouth.

"Oh?" I responded interestedly.

"Aye," Leif confirmed.

"This is a surprise. Isn't it?" I replied, looking curiously at him.

"Not in truth, as he visits these shores upon every summer season."

"Really?" I responded.

"Aye," Leif said, and I glanced at the captain again.

"How interesting. You and my husband must be good friends to visit him regularly, Captain Sinclair. So, I'm very happy to welcome you here also," I said kindly. He grinned and lightly dipped his head toward me in acknowledgment.

"I thank ye most kindly, Your Grace," he replied politely. "'Tis my great honor tae receive yer welcome."

"Certainly," I replied favorably. "How long will you stay?"

"'Twill be for a sennight," he answered.

"A week?" I responded.

"Aye."

"I see. And, where will you sail afterward?"

"We sail tae England, Your Grace," he politely informed me.

"That's a long journey, I understand."

"The journeying is quite the same when the sea is one's home."

"Yes, I suppose it is," I considered. "Do you have a family which takes you to England?"

He glanced at Leif and briefly hesitated before clearing his throat and looking at me again.

"'Twill not be kin which brings me tae England, Your Grace, as they remain on highland ground in Scotland," Captain Sinclair said.

"Does that mean you won't have the chance to see them while you're in Scotland?" I asked.

"'Tis unfortunately that it will be the case, indeed," he replied.

"Oh, I'm sorry to hear it. When was the last time you visited your relatives? You must miss each other very much."

"Aye. 'Tis been many a year since having seen one anither. I nae longer count the days as I am wed tae the sea," he said. I nodded without a word in response, suddenly feeling sorry for him as I realized he was a bachelor without any family close at hand as a result of being nomadic on the perilous ocean. He grinned at me again, and I returned a polite smile.

"Well, certainly while you're here visiting, consider this place a refuge when with us," I sympathetically offered him.

"I fear Her Grace is the most genteel of any woman that I have ever met, fur which I am deeply indebted as I thank her," he replied, sounding truly sincere, then lightly bowed toward me.

"You're welcome, Captain Sinclair," I said when he straightened and looked at me again.

"Sinclair presently witnesses but a few of the plenty reasons fur my adoration of my wife and why I hold her most dearly," Leif said to the captain.

"Yoo're weel blessed, Your Grace," Captain Sinclair acknowledged, saying this to Leif.

"That I am, Captain. That I am," Leif agreed with certainty. Both of them took more swigs of rum from their tumblers, and a small lull came between us. "Now, inform me of yer voyage from the West Indies?" Leif resumed, interestedly, changing the subject of discussion once they'd finished drinks.

"'Twas miraculously fair," Captain Sinclair answered.

"Certainly?"

"Quite, in fact."

"How was it possible?"

"Grace from Heaven. Even the fresh gale we had encountered journeying north was met with a bit of rain," he said to Leif.

"Was it all, indeed?" Leif's brow rose in surprise as he also appeared impressed.

"'Twas so," the captain verified. "Unspoiled days and wind carried us weel over the seas."

"The reason being fur yer early arrival," Leif surmised easily.

"Aye. Thus, I didnae dare risk a seaman's curse when bringing the lads tae port into Boston by forbidding their whims tae delay us when taking leave upon the shore," Captain Sinclair explained.

"A wise decision," Leif agreed.

"Aye. The Mount and Alley of Boston would have certainly led tae certain trooble in one respect and permitted likely predicaments with the navy in anither regard."

"Aye," Leif agreed again, nodding accordingly. He suddenly glanced at me and gave a half-smile when a thought seemed to enter his mind. Shifting his eyes back toward Captain Sinclair, he continued saying, "Pray, remain. Make yerself at ease whilst my wife is certain tae please and satisfy by preparing fur us a perfect meal. Her charms in the kitchen will spellbind yer palate as she is most talented in the art of cuisine."

"I am most grateful tae His Grace fur his generous invitation," Captain Sinclair said. Leif turned his gaze toward me again and gave an encouraging look that was gentle and imploring.

"If you'll excuse me, Your Grace?" I said politely to Leif, following his lead. He took my hand, held it in his, and lifted it to his lips, placing a gentle kiss on the back of my knuckles. After kissing my hand, he released my fingers, and I curtsied before him before retreating to leave him alone with the captain in the room.

When I passed through the doorway and returned to the corridor for the kitchen, the conversation between them resumed. Briefly wondering what to cook for dinner while making my way toward the kitchen, the sudden thought of what to prepare came to mind. Without any assistance or time to spare for creating anything elaborate, since I knew we were all shortly growing hungry, I quickly decided to prepare the lobsters that Leif had caught earlier this morning in the traps, which were kept in a large saltwater bucket right outside the mudroom door. Including roasting carrots and potatoes and toasting bread, then layering it with buttered garlic and salt, in addition to sweet plum bars for dessert that I intended to make, I was confident that a flavorful meal would be served to their liking.

❧

NOW THAT TWILIGHT HAD ARRIVED, Leif and Captain Sinclair continued their casual conversation in the dining room long after dinner had been served and enjoyed, much to their delight. While the captain's men settled onshore with fishing and bonfires, the relaxed atmosphere that Leif and I had grown accustomed to was suddenly disrupted by the loud sailors now among us. Aware of our new surroundings, I realized I needed to be conscious of my appearance by abandoning my habitual comfort of dressing in my shift. Additionally, I felt it necessary to generally maintain a low profile whenever I wanted to go out alone onto the beach to relax with a book on the sand, simply to ensure I was properly seen.

But later in the evening, when I came downstairs from the bedroom dressed in my dressing gown, wanting a simple, fresh glass of water before I was completely ready for bed, I was surprised to hear Leif and the captain still discussing, their voices resonating through the hallways from the dining room they hadn't yet left. Expecting that by this time, they would surely be ready to end the evening and retire for sleep. It seemed, however, that they were wide awake in the middle of a serious conversation about business affairs of which I was unaware.

As I passed by the room they were occupying on my way to the kitchen, I glanced through the threshold and saw several open ledgers and large maps spread out across the big dining room table. Leif was leaning over them with a quill in hand and an inkstand beside him, studying the papers while the captain marked one of the maps, holding a chart divider over it.

"Haur lies Hollow Point, which remains clandestine. A fair location tae be used," Captain Sinclair said to Leif.

"Has it been explored?"

"It has, well indeed, Your Grace."

"Is it deep?"

"Considerably. With scant sunlight entering the cave, all that is seen is obscurity. And the slope of the earth, as it bends about the sea, conceals it entirely from afar. It cannae be discovered unless one surveys the land with scrutiny upon foot. Yet this cannae be achieved unless the vessel survives the breaks betwixt the rocks," Captain Sinclair explained.

"Aye. Guid. I shall claim it immediately," Leif replied.

"As I reckoned, fur it lies not far from haur."

"Guid. How has it been ye who discovered it in this case?"

"By happenstance, whilst on the run from the navy," the captain answered.

"Quite fortunate," Leif remarked.

"Indeed—tae say it lightly," Captain Sinclair agreed with discernible relief in his voice.

"Certainly," Leif agreed, also with the same relief. "Weel, then, the remaining stores are tae be held thaur, till brought tae these shores once the stores haur have been emptied."

"Aye. 'Twould be an efficient manner tae move stock from one location tae the next."

"Assuredly. Whit is in cargo, presently?" I heard Leif inquiring as I continued moving through the hallway, passing them inside the room.

"Casks of rum, fine linens, silks, and wool," Captain Sinclair replied.

"Fine. Whit else?" Leif asked, sounding satisfied.

"Glass, sugar, molasses, paper, and tea," Captain Sinclair informed him.

"Alrecht. Lead, copper, and paint are already supplied and await collection," Leif also informed the captain.

"Very weel," Captain Sinclair responded. "Shall we proceed tae take a proper inventory of the guids at present?"

"Aye. Git the lads tae disembark it. I shall take an accounting whilst 'tis being done. Afterward, have them haul the stock away from shore tae store it within the nearby cave with the rest," Leif said.

"I shall promptly order Turner tae git the lads tae work," Captain Sinclair replied, as I assumed he was referring to his first mate.

"Guid," Leif said.

Suddenly, a pair of footsteps echoed across the oak floors from the dining room, traveling down the hallway in the opposite direction as I entered the kitchen. Retrieving a glass from the hutch, I poured fresh water from the ewer on one of the counters into my clean glass. Subsequently, the house fell quiet as I made my way back through the hallway, and I assumed Leif had also left with the captain as I climbed the staircase to the bedroom, finally ready for bed.

As I returned to bed, their conversation replayed in my mind as I now understood that, without a doubt, Leif was smuggling goods into the colony. He had already mentioned potentially doing this to me years ago, during the war, when Lord Loudoun blockaded Boston. He alluded to it again just months ago when he found me in my era and we discussed his business dealings and success, suggesting that he continued his hidden business ventures. Having an idea of what occurred to criminal smugglers, and particularly because of his perilous position with the Crown, I prayed that he would never be exposed for breaking the law. The thought of it not only troubled my wakeful hours in the back of my mind but kept me awake at night many times during a night like this, when he would be joining me later in bed.

Hours past midnight, I awakened to the sound of the door opening and closing in the bedroom when I recognized Leif's silhouette entering. He quietly paced deeper into the room until he came to a stop in the moonbeams pouring through the window and proceeded to undress. When he had soon finished, he sidled into bed close beside me, naked and warm, and slipped an arm around my waist, drawing me snugly against him.

"You're coming to bed so late," I muttered sleepily, lacing my fingers with his.

"I beg yer pardon," he apologized in a low voice and pressed his lips on the back of my head with a kiss. "I reckoned ye waur fast asleep."

"I was until I heard you coming into the room," I yawned.

"Och," he realized regretfully.

"What kept you?"

"Matters of business."

"With the captain?"

"Aye."

"Oh," I understood, yawning again. "Were you able to finish all of it?"

"Nae. 'Twill require the duration of the captain's stay till 'tis weel done."

"So, you'll be preoccupied with it for that long?"

"I fear so."

"I understand your business."

"Shiploads have arrived, and I must regard it."

"I realize. There's no one who would accuse you of this, would they?" I responded worriedly.

"I am covert in my dealings, as are all who deal with me. My register is balanced with the Crown's tariffs, so the extra guids are not suspected." The reassurance in his words and voice put me at ease, and I nodded in acknowledgment. He planted an accompanying kiss at the back of my head, and another yawn overcame me. Ready to fall back to sleep, I peacefully resettled in his arms now and became silent as I instantly began drifting. I sensed him gently laying a final kiss on my neck, and I was carried off to sleep in the comfort of his secure embrace.

Eleven

The next morning, Captain Sinclair and his first mate, Turner, shared in our company for breakfast with us at the dining room table, which had been cleared of ledgers and maps from the night before. The conversation between the men, while genial, was sparse after they agreed on how their day was to be conducted regarding further offloading the ship's cargo. When breakfast was finished, Captain Sinclair and Officer Turner graciously excused themselves from me and promptly left the table with their attention on the business facing them for the day. Leaving Leif behind, he and I remained alone together in companionship and took our time ending our breakfast with cups of tea.

Afterward, I understood Leif's attention to his new business affairs, so we separated as he started his tasks. So, I decided to preoccupy myself with light chores around the house to start my morning. When I had finally finished tidying our bedroom and dusting the dresser, I returned downstairs to the dining room to collect the used dishes from breakfast. Entering the kitchen with the last of the plates in hand, I began washing them in the hot water, filling the pail with a bar of soap and a wash rag.

When the dishes were cleansed and dried, I proceeded to

return them to the hutch. While working to complete the last of this chore, I glanced out of the windows past the beach at the brilliant Prussian blue ocean glittering beneath the sun, admiring the scenery. *Freiheit* was spotted directly ahead in the nearby middle ground from where I stood by the windows, anchored not far from shore. As my gaze lingered on the bobbing ship, sailors were seen on the large masts and on deck going over the rigging while the brilliant ivory-white sails had been lowered from the masts and tied to the booms.

As I gazed out the windows at what the sailors were doing on the ship, I sensed a hand stealing around my waist as lips affectionately pressed against my temple in a tender kiss. I suddenly became aware of Leif's touch, pleasantly surprising me. My eyes turned from the windows toward him and met his gleaming, warm blue eyes.

"You're as stealthy as a ninja by the way you sneak up on me without me noticing," I giggled, feeling his tickling kisses beginning to nibble on my ear.

"Whit micht a ninja be?" he faintly chuckled against my skin.

"A Japanese warrior," I informed him.

"Micht one be as deft?" he asked, kissing my neck now.

"No one is as skilled as you are," I replied, giggling again at his tickling lips.

"That may be due tae the fact that I am matched by the charge of my desire to have ye within my arms at all times."

"Making you a force of nature?"

"Mayhap, indeed," he chuckled.

"Don't be so aware of yourself. You may not be able to stand upright, because your head might be too inflated by your ego for you to see straight," I teased.

"Yoo're warning me of arrogance?" he laughed, entertained.

"A cautionary tale never hurt anybody."

"Wise indeed. Yet, mayhap, ye micht heed my caution as weel, as ye brazenly see fit tae warn yer husband."

"Oh?"

"Aye."

"What warning could you possibly have for me?"

"I shall rain upon my garden tae suit her glory, fur every droplet doth a petal receive births magnificent blooms tae behold which have been conceived."

"Any excuse to get me into bed, Your Grace. Shame on you."

"On the contrary. 'Tis my duty and my liking. Therefore, shame falls moot upon me."

"You sure know how to impress by being blunt and romantic simultaneously."

"Then, you are wooed?"

"Ever since—" I interrupted myself, not wanting to stroke his ego any further and reveal myself to him again.

"Ever since?" he insisted, interestedly.

"You already know."

"Nae. I dinnae ken. Ye huvnae ever told me."

"Haven't I, though?"

"I reckon not."

"Oh. I thought I had. Plenty of times."

"Yet, yoo're mistaken, fur I recollect every word fallen from yer sweet lips tae my eager ears."

"Your eager ears?"

"Forever," he said, causing me to smile. "Now, do as I wish. Tell me regarding yer being wooed by me."

"Well, I was just going to say to you—that ever since you first kissed me was when I realized that I loved you," I admitted after all these years of keeping this little secret.

"Ye mean whence we shared the cave whilst in flight from the French as we fled Fort Carillon?"

"That's exactly the time." I felt him grinning against my cheek as he pressed his lip there.

"Aye," he muttered.

"Did you already know?" I asked, somewhat surprised.

"Ye returned my kiss. Therefore, I kent ye felt fur me."

"Nothing's changed."

"Have we not grown in our loove?"

"Yes, we have."

"Aye. Then, in truth, 'tis not I who is a force of nature, but the loove shared betwixt us which drives the element we own."

"You should be a poet."

"Come tae bed."

"But I thought you had a full day's work ahead of yourself today."

"A respite is in order."

"Already?"

"Aye."

"But the day's still fresh and I doubt you've done everything you've set out for yourself to do so soon."

"Pray, dinnae abandon me."

"I'll never do that. You know it."

"But ye play me fur a fool."

"How?" I giggled, entertained by him.

"Ye resist me, and so I am tortured."

"Tortured?"

"Aye."

"Aren't you being extreme?"

"Never, when I am graced by yer presence at every moment within every hour. Whether within my thoughts or as I behold ye within my sichts, ye take possession of my very being."

"Leif," I sighed, trying to distract us from his luring intentions, knowing full well we'd lose the remaining day to ourselves and that he'd regret being hard-pressed to make up the difference to achieve his obligations for today.

"Whit is it, *mo ghaol*?" he asked distractedly, attentive to the gentle kisses he was laying over my ear and neck.

"You're being very irresponsible right now," I replied.

"Reprimand me as ye micht. 'Twill not alter my mind."

"A stubborn man is definitely a foolish man."

"Yer prose is lacking."

"I'm a pediatrician, not an artist, and certainly not a poet."

"Forgive my criticism. Yoo're extraordinarily weel learned. Of coorse."

"Thank you."

"I am beholden tae yer scholarship."

"It's nice of you to recognize that."

"Whilst it is true, ye remain in need of further mentorship."

"I do?"

"Aye."

"In what way, specifically?"

"In my manner, Your Grace," he said, speaking softly into my ear.

"Is that so?" I felt him nibble on my ear, and I giggled again.

"Certainly."

"Well, may I suggest that your recommendation for my further education be delayed?"

"Denied."

"But, they're sailors everywhere, and Captain Sinclair might come to the house looking for you, if you're not already available to work with him, since he's expecting you. And, since there's no one to receive him when he enters the house, he's obviously at liberty. So, what if he happens to overhear us fooling around, because of that?"

"Dinnae worry. Sinclair wulnae make entry upstairs."

"But if he hears us?"

"Though the door will be shut?"

"It doesn't matter. You're a feral man, Leif."

"Must ye blame me?" He laughed against my cheek as he kissed it now.

"Of course I do."

"Yet, ye inspire my behavior, and therefore I am helpless."

"Don't even think of pointing your finger at me. You are far from helpless," I said, smiling.

"Ye enjoy having me as I take ye," he muttered confidently between another kiss on my cheek.

"But I'll be distracted knowing the captain has the freedom to wander the house, and I'm worried about it."

"Micht it be since we waur seen by him already?"

"Is that for certain?" I gasped, acutely embarrassed, and stiffened in Leif's embracing arms.

"He spied us whilst upon *Freiheit* yesterday."

"Oh no!" I breathed, and my embarrassment solidified.

"Dinnae mind it."

"Of course I mind it."

"'Tis of nae consequence as the man isnae a pietist."

"Well, I'm not an exhibitionist."

"I warned ye of vessels sailing our shores. Pray, think naught of it. Presently, mind and come tae bed." He turned me in his arms, facing him now, and held me snug against his body. He kissed my brow, and I relaxed again in his embrace. His hard shaft, restrained within his breeches, boldly pressed against the fabrics concealing my flat stomach, and I couldn't help smiling at him before consciously giving him a reticent look. "He wulnae mind us, but retreat tae shore and mind his crew instead, should we be heard by him," Leif assured, reading the careful look on my face. "Though he be wed tae the seas, he is dignified."

"Hmm. He does seem it," I considered.

"Then?"

"I have no idea what I'm going to do with you. You're too charming for your own good," I playfully chided, and he arched an eyebrow, smirking too. He was guilty and he knew it. "Fine. Apparently, I'll be wasting my breath dissuading you," I giggled, shaking my head.

"Ahh, yoo're a guid wife. Now come tae bed before I carry ye tae it," he chuckled.

AFTER OUR LOVEMAKING, all I wanted to do was lie in bed for the rest of the day, and I knew that Leif felt the same way. Except he was well aware of the work he needed to achieve before it became too late, and he regretted having to leave me in bed as he remained lounging beside me.

"Micht the hours remain longer? I dinnae care tae abandon ye whilst in bed," he muttered as if he were wistful.

"Well, look where your shenanigans got you? Now you no longer care to be serious about your work."

"I cannae be blamed due tae yer temptation," he teased.

"How unfair of you to blame me," I giggled.

"Ye wield far too much power over one as mere as I."

"Hardly." He suddenly playfully pinched my buttocks, and I yelped, laughing.

"Fur yer cheek, of coorse," he chuckled.

"Then are you going to lounge with me for the rest of the day and forgo your responsibilities? If you do, that's what we call playing hooky where I'm from."

"Playing hooky?"

"Yes. It's mostly what adolescents do to avoid their responsibilities in school."

"Micht that be so?"

"Yes."

"Ye do say that I am incorrigible as a lad, therefore I very much desire to play hooky."

"As you wish," I giggled, amused very much by him.

"Och, ye will lead me tae my ruin," he teased again. "I must tear myself from yer spell lest the day not be gone, *siren*." As I stared into his stellar blue eyes, I could clearly sense their warmth. The brilliant sunlight entering the nearby window made them glimmer like topaz gems. He paused for a second and seemed to rethink himself. He grinned and planted a delicate kiss on the tip of my nose. "Now, then, micht ye fancy a tour about my ship as I meet Sinclair onboard?"

"Oh, that would be a nice surprise." My eyes suddenly widened at the unexpected realization.

"I witnessed ye admiring her from the windows whilst ye waur minding the remaining plates in the kitchen earlier."

"Really?"

"Aye."

"Well, yes, I was admiring your ship. It's very pretty."

"Then, accompany me upon a tour as I introduce ye tae one of several that are mine. Yet, I must have ye awaur that 'tis not customary tae have lasses aboard any vessels."

"It is?"

"Aye."

"Why not?" I gave him a confused look.

"Sailors regard it as bad luck."

"Really?" I replied, surprised.

"Aye."

"Hmm..." I pondered it.

"Nonethelss, I shall have Sinclair warn the lads. He is a man of reason."

"All right," I agreed. "So, you have other ships than the one I also know of that harbors in Boston?" I asked in amazement, unaware that he seemed to have a fleet now.

"Thaur are four of them that I own. *Freiheit, Eagle, Intrepid,* and *Sylvina*," he informed me.

"You named one after me?"

"Why would I not?" He kissed the top of my crown, and I was suddenly very warmed.

"I don't know what to say... I'm extremely touched that you'd think to do that," I whispered.

"Yoo're moved," he perceived easily.

"Deeply so."

"The pulse of my heart, ye out ken how my heart was crippled during yer absence. I commissioned a vessel in yer name as an emblem of my loove fur ye. Ye waur a mere ghost. A memory haunting my every deed. I was cursed. Ye followed my existence though ye waur not haur tae join me. Every hour was strife. Therefore, *Sylvina* was created," he said softly.

"Oh, Leif," I uttered beneath my breath and tightened my embrace around his torso.

"*Sylvina* sails the Caribbean Seas. I expect that she will appear in Boston's harbor at a later season."

"I see. Will I get to see her then?"

"Aye. She is the queen of all my vessels."

"Is she really?"

"She outclasses any other ship within Boston and is the envy of every merchant and seafaring man within the vicinity."

"Oh, my goodness," I responded, further impressed. "And the other ships you have? Where are they?"

"*Eagle* sails tae France whilst *Intrepid* is scheduled to make her return tae England," he said.

"These are ships you've acquired since the war, when I've been gone?" I surmised, impressed.

"Aye." I simply nodded in response, beginning to realize the level of his business success evidenced in his significantly expanded fleet of ships that he had acquired since the French and Indian War. "Forgive me fur interrupting yer chore within the kitchen, yet shall we attire tae have a tour of *Freiheit*?"

"Yes, that would be very nice," I agreed. "I'll finish in the kitchen later while you're working."

"Very weel. Let us rise from bed." His robust arms slipped from around my waist, freeing me to carry out the task of getting dressed.

When we were both properly clothed, he stepped toward me and took my hand into his, then promptly led me out of the bedroom for outdoors, putting us into the brightly shining morning sun. The sunlight beamed warmly down on us, making me instantly hot. But the thick humid air was tempered by a gusty salt-laden breeze tousling my ringlets and skirts, and Leif's unbound hair, mussing it everywhere over his golden head.

The wind blew us around as he led us through beachgrass and down the trail on the slope. The sense of our pleasure as we anticipated spending a portion of this morning together was felt between us, as I was aware of his eagerness to present this particular ship of his to me.

Twelve

There were several jolly-boats beached on the sand, I noticed when we arrived at the shore. A number of sailors were preoccupied with plenty of noticeably large, weighty chests, casks, and barrels distributed across the sand near the beached boats, as they were laboring to move them away from the shore. Apparently, they were relocating them out of sight. Assuming these were the goods I overheard Leif and Captain Sinclair had been referring to last night, I wondered about it.

"Where are they taking it all?" I suddenly inquired, turning my curious attention toward Leif as we neared one of the jolly-boats. He glanced at me and didn't answer right away, making me think he might not have heard me. Except his glance betrayed him.

"They bring it tae the cave," he replied after a second, appearing indifferent, however.

"Oh." I understood, then, that it was important to keep the goods hidden from authorities in any way possible, and the troubling thought of Leif's line of business secretly plagued me again. I hoped he'd never get caught smuggling and suffer the legal consequences. It was a sharp, unsettling feeling. So, I quickly pretended that everything was all right and pushed my worried thoughts away to save my outlook.

But before I could inquire any further about the storage, as I was still tempted to do for security purposes, believing that a warehouse could better serve to hide his secret goods, I realized that would put him at a disadvantage to monitor the security of his products since such a building might only be found in the nearest town of Lynn away from our property here where the cave was located. So, in reality, the cave was an ideal location for his contraband.

Leif seized my waist and swung me into the facing boat. Then, I observed him swiftly toss himself inside after me. As we sat in the boat facing each other, three other sailors hopped inside and joined us.

Like the others in the boat with us, Leif naturally pulled the oars out as he situated himself with them. While handling his grip on one of the oars, he dipped the paddle into the water and proceeded to row. Several sailors immediately took the initiative by pushing us out over the rolling waves, helping us gain momentum. Then, Leif and our accompanying sailors began rowing us more smoothly away from the beach toward *Freiheit*.

We found ourselves far enough from shore now as the men kept rowing. A greater distance between us and the land was created, and I admired the scent of the surrounding saltwater. Bobbing over moderate breaks and the breeze caressing my face with the beaming warm sun shining on us, I was soothed and simply enjoyed us being rowed over the glinting water in tranquility. I caught Leif's glance and realized he'd been staring at me while working his oar. He grinned and winked at me, and I naturally smiled at him, feeling a strange sense of bashfulness seeping into my consciousness and distracting my ease. The grin on his face broadened, and the heat in my cheeks rose. Aware of him noticing me, I nervously glanced away from him at the seagulls flying above our heads, incapable of understanding myself sometimes when in his presence.

Feeling his penetrating eyes concentrating on me, I compulsively glanced toward him and caught the subtle smirk on his face while he maintained his transfixed stare. I gave him a little grin, and he winked at me again. Then, I shifted my gaze toward *Freiheit* at a closing distance that seemed to creep nearer, conscious of myself and fully aware of his focused attention on me as he continued rowing.

Redirecting my own attention to our attraction for each other, I gazed over my shoulder at the seascape and at the beauty of the shoreline as it curved away from us while the men heaved on every stroke. Skillfully, they rowed and paced themselves well. As we traveled the length from the shore, *Freiheit*'s stature incrementally grew from the water into an impressive schooner ahead of us. In time, which proved to be not too long, our boat tapped her hull, and *Freiheit* appeared as a fearsome warship of her time. She reminded me of clipper ships I'd seen in paintings from the past hanging in museums. Her attending crew, immediately aware of us, lowered one of the rope ladders as Leif assisted one of the accompanying sailors in knotting our boat to her.

After securing our jolly boat to the hull, I was instructed by Leif to carefully climb the ladder with his assistance as he followed directly behind me. As I slowly climbed the rungs, mindful of my skirts, I was mentally scolding myself for not wearing trousers instead. I had a pair in the armoire for myself that I'd neglected. Leif had left a pair for me to have, understanding my fondness for them. Ironically, I hadn't thought to wear them until now. I had grown so used to wearing a linen shift, short-gown, with petticoats here currently now that the sailors had arrived, since those garments didn't trap the heat against my skin and instead let me breathe.

As I made my cumbersome way upward with Leif closely behind me, I finally reached the deck with assistance from a couple of crew members who grabbed my wrists and arms and hauled me over the platform. I was promptly guided away from the ledge, and Leif easily appeared beside me as the sailors released me from their help.

Captain Sinclair suddenly appeared among his crew and politely greeted us aboard. The unexpected look on his face suggested that he was particularly surprised to see me accompanying Leif. Captain Sinclair was caught off guard by his curious expression. Feeling as though I might be imposing, I automatically gave Leif an uncertain look as I began wondering.

"My wife is present tae explore *Freiheit*, Sinclair," Leif informed him.

"Och, aye, of coorse. As ye wish," the captain stammered as he realized.

"Prior tae recommencing our affairs," Leif said.

"Certainly," Sinclair agreed, then turned his eyes toward me. "Pray, Your Grace stroll the vessel tae yer liking, as it may please ye."

"Thank you, Captain Sinclair," I replied politely. He lightly bowed his head toward me in response.

"Indeed," he replied nicely when he returned to looking at me before turning his attention toward his men. "Move about lads! She is not a siren! Ye have seen a lass before! Carry on!" Sinclair spoke audibly to his surrounding crew, crowding us as they curiously stared at me. He abruptly waved them off, and they immediately began dispersing to resume their duties. Sinclair then stepped aside from us, permitting Leif leeway to begin guiding me across the deck away from him. Leif took possession of my elbow and started us on a leisurely walk along the length of the deck from the bow.

While admiring the beautifully crafted schooner as he strolled us along past cannons protruding from their ports, I was aware of the rest of the cannons below deck peering from portholes as we arrived by the ship's hull. Noticing them all, I suddenly got to thinking.

"Are all of your ships so heavily armed?" I wondered, turning my gaze up toward him. He turned his eyes toward me and met mine. The expression on his face was nonchalant and relaxed.

"Aye. They are," he said.

"Is it common?"

"Quite."

"Oh," I realized as I glanced upward at the massive masts, and quickly averted my eyes from the glaring sun back to his. "This is a very large ship. Are the others this large?"

"Larger, in fact," he replied.

"Really?"

"Aye."

"You said Sylvina was the grandest one. That one must be massive if that's the case," I speculated, comparatively.

"She rivals the navy's frigate," he said.

"Oh," I responded simply, ignorant of the various ship classes but still impressed. "Because you have a fleet now, I can only believe what you've told me about how well your business ventures are going. You seem extremely successful."

"Whit I imparted was true."

"Yes, I can see that now. Not that I didn't believe you. It was just hard to imagine—that's all," I explained. Leif nodded a tad in acknowledgment. "So, Captain Sinclair sails here every year to deliver merchandise?"

"Aye."

"You said *Slyvina* comes to port in Boston?"

"Aye."

"That being because it's the financial capital of the colony," I assumed.

"Correct."

"But why is that? I mean, wouldn't you use her the same way as you use *Freiheit*?"

"*Sylvina* not only has the ability to contain more loads, but she is also a ruse tae maintain the appearance of business being conducted properly by paying the tariffs on the amount of guids within her hull," Leif explained.

"I see," I replied, nodding thoughtfully. "So, *Freiheit* comes here like your other ships?"

"Aye. The cargo delivered haur is a convenience fur merchants within this vicinity. They collect their guids from these shores since the distance tae transport them from Boston is less than having tae move them out of Boston north tae this region. Furthermore, the cost tae them is less since thaur are nae tariffs and the cargo is unique," he explained.

"Right," I understood, nodding a little. "How do the merchants acquire everything belonging to them from out of the cave?"

"'Tis arranged by me in order that they may collect whit is theirs."

"Do you help them move their goods?"

"They have their own men accompanying them. I merely record their acquisitions as they retrieve them."

"I see."

"So, normally, everything's retrieved from Boston's port," I understood.

"Aye," he said. I nodded again, realizing the effort and distance merchants had to make in order to obtain their merchandise to sell in various localities throughout the colony. A far cry from the network of trains, planes, and trucks that easily hauled goods across the modern U.S., where I was from.

"I remember the blockade Lord Loudoun had installed in the harbor," I recalled.

"He had all of Boston at his mercy."

"Yes, he did," I remembered terribly. "He told me that he caught smugglers and executed them."

"Aye." Leif's face suddenly turned impassive, and his gaze

shifted from mine toward the seagull sitting on the railing near us as we passed it by. It abruptly flew away into the clear blue sky, and he watched it vanish.

"If you hadn't been fortunate enough to accomplish removing him from the continent through your political contacts in London, I'm afraid to think how hard it could actually be for everyone now, in spite of the government's current taxes. Everyone's financial recovery would be that much worse, since it takes time to achieve anything. Who knows what could have happened to us as well? I'm so grateful that you've had the opportunity to become so successful in your business, Leif. It's incredibly reassuring," I said, thinking about our financial security if we were to live here in the future as planned. He shifted his eyes back toward me, and the expression in his eyes was genuine and earnest.

"Ye needn't worry. I have acquired our security entirely fur ye," he responded sincerely without smiling.

"I don't know what to say. Except, that I'm truly humbled and grateful to you," I replied with the same honesty. The corner of his lip subtly curled upward, and the half smile on his face appeared gentle.

"Ye mustn't thank me," he responded.

"Why?"

"My loove fur ye naturally determines my duties without complaint."

"Why do you spoil me so much?"

"Yoo're far from daft. Is it not at all apparent otherwise?" His eyes twinkled in the sunlight, and he was right; I already knew. But I only wanted to hear him say it. The affectionate expression on his face confirmed the fact, and I sensed that he wanted to lay a kiss on me if it weren't for the obstruction from the large brim of my pretty straw hat and the ship's surrounding crew. So, the smile on his face widened, exposing the pearly gleam of his teeth and highlighting his endearment for me.

"So, when will the merchandise in the cave be collected?" I asked, resuming our conversation.

"From now till the end of September before we shall take leave tae Concord," he answered mildly.

"Oh, you mean that'll be when we'll see Beth and her family?" I couldn't help the excitement in my voice as I anticipated the visit.

"Aye. 'Twill be a splendid visit."

"Yes, I'm sure it will be." We were arriving by the center mast, and I heard the flag whipping in the breeze. I glanced up at it, tousling around on the flagpole, and noticed that it was solid white instead of the expected Union flag, and oddly grimaced as I curiously wondered about it. "Why is there a truce flag flying on the ship?"

"Thaur are men amongst the captain's crew who speak Patois, Creole, and French. Thus, 'tis flown," Leif answered as I returned my gaze toward his.

"Why does it matter if anyone speaks those languages?" I looked at him, slightly confused, as we were now approaching the steps to the upper deck, not too far ahead.

"Those men pose as prisoners from the West Indies," he answered inexpressively.

"Prisoners? How come?"

"Ye mean why?"

"Yes."

"'Tis done tae deceive the tidesmen."

"Who are they?"

"Customs officials."

"Oh. Why must they be deceived?" I abruptly gave him an unusual look.

"They are in exchange tae disarm the tidesmen from inspecting our wears and alerting other officials."

"I don't understand. That doesn't sound right, " I commented. I looked at Leif for an answer, but he gave me a deadpan look. That's when I knew that I shouldn't press him further. I returned a glance at the foreign-speaking men and contemplated that they were all Black. A sudden realization came to me that their involvement had to do with the slave trade. I felt more uneasy at this point as it dawned on me how far this network of Leif's smuggling enterprise had really gone.

"Ye mustn't be concerned," he responded, appearing assured.

"Why not?" I asked, looking obviously at him.

"The lads wulnae rot in prison. Sinclair purchases their freedom fur returning them tae his crew."

"Well, I'm glad that they won't suffer in jail. But your enterprise is smuggling," I replied, certainly worried. He held my gaze without responding for a moment, as I tried reading the unemotional look on his face. "Aren't you concerned about any of it?"

"Not in particular," he said candidly.

"Why, though? I hate to think what'll happen to you if you're caught. Is it worth the risk?"

"Aplenty."

"How?"

"Primarily, I am wildly cautious, and I have overcome the difference the king has unjustly taken from me, and far more. My enterprise secures our independence. Fur that, 'tis worth my fight and happiness."

"I certainly see your point. I just worry."

"Try not tae do so," he encouraged.

Still, despite his confidence and what he'd just said, I was fearful of his jeopardy. He continued to look at me without a reply, but I perceived his fixed attention on me as he studied my response to this new information.

"How long have you been smuggling for certain?"

"Since Loudoun's blockade," he informed me.

"That long?" I looked at him in surprise.

"Aye."

"You've either been lucky, or you're extremely skillful at evading the government by having crooks within it helping you."

"A bit, aye," he admitted, unfazed.

"So, the ones in government helping you, do you really trust them? I mean, what if they betray you at one point and reveal what you're doing to other authorities?"

"They wulnae betray me," he responded, appearing confident without fault.

"How do you know that?"

"These men are Whigs in secret and receive a stipend from me fur their trooble."

"Really?"

"Truly."

"Still—I don't know—I feel it's extraordinarily risky given all that you've been up against with the king."

"As I have said, it disnae concern me. My operation is surreptitious. Also, my repute and apparent obedience tae the king remains unquestioned as I continue tae serve him," Leif explained.

"Then, he never relieved you of military duty after all?"

"But he has. My point precisely being that he has granted my liberty from the army as he perceived my honor fit. Therefore, I shall not be questioned, and ye mustn't continue tae worry."

This time, I didn't reply easily, and instead simply gazed at him while considering what he was telling me.

"So, you say that you can actually trust these certain officials not to betray you in any way?" I continued after a second.

"Aye, and the bit of coin they receive from me aids in their ignorance as weel," Leif said indifferently as he gave me a reassuring look. A sigh escaped me as I stared at him, thinking this situation was fearful, and realized that I was resigning to his knowledge of the operation he was leading, as it far exceeded my competence and awareness.

"I told you the last time that you better not get caught. I still mean it," I said, considering him.

"I'm weel awaur of yer sentiments," he replied composedly.

"Just be careful," I warned again.

"Yoo're my most prized possession. Of coorse, I shall take utmost care tae maintain our safety," he vowed. Without responding, I simply continued looking at him, adhering to his word, determined to never break his promise. "All is weel, *mo ghaol*," he reassured again, conveying his oath to me by the steady look in his eyes. I nodded a little, better convinced but still remaining concerned for him.

He shifted his earnest gaze ahead and continued guiding me over the deck as we began climbing flights of stairs at the stern. Arriving on the upper deck, we proceeded to stroll along it, and the seriousness of our conversation evaporated as we resumed our comfortable companionship, which kept my worrying thoughts at bay as they lingered distantly in the back of my mind.

After touring the upper deck, Leif led me down the staircase toward the second deck, where he showed me to a door and reached for its handle. Pushing it, he opened the door and led us inside a large cabin belonging to the captain, I had immediately presumed. As I scanned the spacious area from where we stood near the entrance while Leif closed the door, sealing us inside, the captain's quarters appeared impressive.

The air was stuffy inside, heightened by the outdoor heat and the thick scent of the salty ocean, mixed with the sweet, smoky aroma of cigars, burnt firewood, and male musk. The abundant slanted windows at the back of the cabin admitted plenty of bright daylight. After noticing all the windows and how brightly lit these quarters were, my gaze landed on a large Queen Anne writing desk with a couple of spyglasses, maps, and a compass sprawled over it. An oval ebony dining table, adorned with a large candelabra, was also at the center of the room, before a full-sized four-poster bed positioned at the back, by another row of slanted windows. I also observed the beautifully, intricately carved, rich mahogany wall moldings spanning all of the walls with mounted sconces. Finally, a matching mahogany built-in daybed covered in rich burgundy velvet blankets and matching silk pillows was seen beside me. But when I discovered the hammock hanging in the corner opposite where Leif was standing near me, I glanced at him again and asked curiously, "Have you known Captain Sinclair for a while now?"

"'Tis been twelve years," he replied.

"Since the war with France?" I responded, surprised it had been for this long.

"Aye."

"Then, you know him well?"

"Quite, indeed."

"Oh," I realized, nodding a little. "Has he been working for you since then?"

"Aye. He has been within my employ ever since."

"Then he's trustworthy?"

"His loyalty and honor are untarnished," he answered irrefutably. I nodded again in acknowledgement, relieved to understand this.

"What about people in Lynn? Don't they have a clue about what's happening here?"

"The subjects of Lynn resent the Crown and hold nae favors fur it."

"Really?"

"Aye. Furthermore, the navy hasnae inspected these shores, leading tae the belief that subjects of these parts huvnae informed and they dinnae welcome such officials."

"I see."

"My vessels have landed these shores fur many years without qualm. 'Tis a safe harbor. Pray, be at ease, at last. Will ye not?"

"I'm trying. I can't have you dead, Leif."

"I shall not part from ye by the Crown. I swear it. I shall never let ye ken any such burden. Do ye recall my oath tae ye when we newly wed?"

"You told me that you'd never leave me."

"Aye. I shan't ever abandon ye. Never. We shall forever be," he promised gravely again. I nodded once more in response, holding his adherent, stalwart, transfixed eyes gazing into mine, believing him as I trusted his words and held faith in God that it was true.

I felt his hand slipping around my elbow again and possessing it as he proceeded, leading us toward the door. Grasping the handle, he pulled it open, escorting me out of the captain's quarters and returning us outdoors into the sunlight.

Nothing else was said, laying the issue to rest while we began climbing down the first flight of stairs and arrived again on the first deck. He had me returned to the jolly boat and rowed by sailors to shore without him as he resumed his remaining business with Captain Sinclair.

Thirteen

_T_oward the end of the week, nearing Captain Sinclair's and his crew's final stay, I was distracted from reading while relaxing in the sitting room by a curious sound emitting from the hallway near the staircase. The strange tapping sound against a wall grabbed my attention, so I straightened from the sofa with a book in hand and left the room to find the source of the unusual noise. Rounding the corner from one of the corridors, Leif was discovered carefully pounding on the wall of the staircase with a light hand. As I inquisitively approached him, he seemed to be intently listening for something within the wall as he leaned closely toward it while tapping.

In a second, he stopped thumping his hand against it and placed his fingertips on a seam of one of the moldings, beginning to trace over it. Then, at a certain location, his fingers pressed onto the wall, and suddenly, a panel popped open. He promptly widened it, revealing a concealed door to a hidden closet, to my surprise.

"What are you doing?" I asked curiously, amazed at the unexpected cubicle.

"I am in the course of retrieving Sinclair's payment," he

informed me as he stepped through the passageway and entered the dark closet. Observing him rummaging within the obscured space for a moment, he grunted as he proceeded to push a substantially large oak chest out of the closet and into the hallway opening with considerable effort.

"What's in there?" I asked curiously, watching him struggle as he brought it fully into the aisle of the corridor. He straightened from hunching over the chest and briefly dusted his palms off.

"A holding of five thousand sovereigns," he revealed, taking a breath from his hefty exertion in moving the obviously extremely heavy chest.

"Five thousand?" I echoed, significantly impressed as I looked at him in disbelief.

"Aye. 'Tis entirely whit is owed tae him and his men fur the year's journey," Leif said, turning to close the secret door and hiding the closet again.

"Oh," I realized.

"Sinclair's men will come shortly tae collect it," he informed me.

"How soon?"

"Within the moment. Oblige me, *ceisdein*. Peer through the window tae see whether they are near the back door," he requested.

"Sure," I replied easily and started away from him for the mudroom.

When I entered the mudroom and arrived at the window by the door, the men were clearly seen approaching closely. I promptly opened the door for Captain Sinclair and his several sailors, and they entered the house as they greeted me. Then, following me through the room into the kitchen and into the leading hallways, they arrived at Leif standing behind the chest, ready for them to take it away.

"Five thousand," Leif confirmed to Sinclair.

"Grand," Sinclair replied with a satisfactory nod. He sharply motioned to his men to haul the chest away. They instantly moved to handle it and carried it back through the corridor, vanishing around the corner for outdoors. "We sail on the morrow morn fur England."

"Till next season, then," Leif replied, anticipating his return.

"Aye," Sinclair said. "A pleasure, Your Grace."

"Certainly. Godspeed."

"Thank ye, Your Grace."

"Indeed," Leif replied with an agreeable nod. "God bless ye as weel, Sinclair."

"May He bless ye also, Your Grace."

"I thank ye, certainly," Leif responded. Then, Sinclair turned his eyes toward me and mildly smiled.

"I am most obliged tae Your Grace's kindness. My sincerest pleasure tae have made her acquaintance," he genuinely said to me.

"Thank you, Captain Sinclair. It was very nice meeting you, too. Please be safe on your journey," I replied nicely.

"The Lord Almighty permitting," he said.

"Yes, I pray so," I responded.

"I thank ye," he said graciously.

"You're welcome," I replied, giving him a kind smile. Holding his hat, he bowed before me, and when he straightened, he tucked it beneath his arm.

"By your leave, Your Grace," he concluded courteously as he looked at Leif, ready to leave.

"Guid evening, Captain," Leif permitted politely

"Guid evening, Your Grace," Sinclair said to Leif and respectfully dipped his head toward him. Captain Sinclair then turned from us and proceeded through the hallway in the opposite direction, vanishing from sight as he rounded the corner, heading out of the house for *Freiheit*.

DAYS LATER, since Captain Sinclair and his men had set sail aboard *Freiheit* from our shores for England, a number of different men newly appeared here at *Sàmhchair* as Leif anticipated their arrival. They were merchants from nearby Lynn and from Concord and Boston afar, who had traveled the distance to obtain their ordered merchandise, all to avoid tariffs levied by the Crown. Many of their items included contraband from France, Portugal, Spain, and Italy, of which I had become aware. Wagon-loads of goods overflowed their beds and trailed off our property by trains, making our location appear like a distribution center for the area.

Fortunately, as I had understood it, the locals supported this enterprise, and this location was of no interest to the government. Flying under its radar and with the military focused on Boston and its harbor, the Crown was stretched thin to discover and control what was occurring on the periphery. Therefore, I got a better sense of Leif's confidence in how he was conducting his business. Still, I couldn't help but mind the needle pricking me with concern, though minimal, as I tried pushing it aside. I, nevertheless, was unsettled that if somehow, he was exposed, I knew that I'd be beside myself with terror of the consequences he would suffer in the event. So, I held on to faith as I prayed for his overall safety while he earned his living and we lived our lives.

By late September, the visiting merchants began to dwindle in numbers as they obtained their goods, leaving the cave empty of stockpiles. And, when October arrived, the property was cleared of anyone else, and we returned to our lonesome selves. Soon afterward, we had shuttered the house for the season, and Leif was now loading the last of our belongings onto the back of our horse-drawn chaise as I sat on its cushioned leather bench, waiting for him to join me on the seat and drive us away.

Given that he had made earlier arrangements with Beth to visit her, my eager anticipation to finally see her, along with her family, again, happily excited me. Fortunately, it was only a day's journey from Nahant to Concord, and the sky was clear cobalt-blue with mild sun warming the temperate atmosphere as it brightly shone down on us.

When Leif briefly finished situating our belongings, he easily tossed himself up onto the seat, sitting close beside me, and grabbed Blaze's reins as he was harnessed to the chaise. With a couple of little clicks inside of his cheek, Leif started Blaze on a trot, moving us easily along the way over the narrow road.

As we rode through the grassy field, *Sàmhchair* dwarfed into the background, and soon we entered a wooded path. Sunbeams fell between the fur and pine trees, latticing the vegetated ground in golden hues while the salty ocean breeze stirred their boughs. Soon entering the causeway, Lynn was near, and we were now passing through the town's cobblestone streets. Within minutes, Lynn was falling a distance behind us, and we were riding on a lone path heading south toward Concord, surrounded by dense woodland. It seemed to be a good day for traveling, and I was highly anticipating seeing Beth and her children again with happiness.

Approximately an hour and a half into our journey, the sky ominously clouded over the intensely shining sun, among clear skies from the early morning. Sprinkles started falling from above between the trees, dampening the path and changing the surrounding woodland aroma.

But by the time we had arrived in Concord, heavy rain was pouring on us as twilight was settling into the evening. Now bumping over wet cobblestone streets, Leif finally stopped our chaise before a large three-story brick dwelling with viridian green shutters and four dormers protruding from the roof. The painted white portico with a pair of Doric columns over granite steps added to the house's charm.

Leif dismounted the driver's seat and promptly tied Blaze to the hitching post, then swiftly arrived beside me, reaching for my waist and assisting me out of the chaise onto my feet over the stone walkway when a groom promptly appeared. The groom immediately tended to our horse and chaise while Leif lightly took my arm and began escorting me up the limestone steps leading us toward the front door. As the groom proceeded to take our horse and chaise away, we arrived at the viridian green-painted front door. Leif quickly grasped the large brass knocker and rapped on it a couple of times. Without hesitation, the O'Donoghues' front door opened, and we were promptly welcomed indoors by a stolid, tall, ebony-skinned man with short, kinky gray hair who was clean-shaven and appeared stern and dutiful.

"Your Grace," the man politely greeted Leif in an even voice as he closed the door behind us while we entered the foyer from the inhospitable rain.

"Hullo, Abel," Leif responded cordially while proceeding to remove his drenched hat from his head. "How micht ye fare this rain-filled evening?"

"I am well, I thank you, Your Grace," Abel answered without any hint of emotion on his face. "How might you fare as well, Your Grace?"

"Apart from being caught in this dastardly rain, I am very weel, thank ye, Abel," Leif replied as Abel, who I soon learned was the O'Donoghue's butler, dutifully took our wet outer garments from us.

"I am pleased to learn of it, Your Grace," Abel said in a distinctly smooth, baritone voice.

"I have Her Grace, Duchess of Monteith, accompanying me upon this account," Leif informed Abel. Abel promptly turned his mocha eyes toward me and graciously bowed in acknowledgment.

"Your Grace," Abel greeted politely when he straightened and looked at me.

"Hello, Abel. It's very nice to meet you," I responded cordially.

"I am most obliged, Your Grace," Abel replied evenly, then returned his attention to Leif. "Permit me to escort you into the drawing room."

"Aye, very weel," Leif responded naturally.

"Master O'Donoghue instructs me to inform you of his tardy

return for this evening's dinner as he pertains to his pressing matters in town," Able respectfully told Leif.

"I see," Leif accepted.

"Yet, Mistress O'Donoghue eagerly awaits your arrival," Abel also informed Leif.

"We pleasantly await our reunion with Mistress O'Donoghue as weel," Leif responded. Able faintly dipped his head in acknowledgment, then turned to escort us as he began leading us through the nicely furnished house into the drawing room.

When we entered the drawing room and paced deeper into it, Leif kindly gestured for me to make myself comfortable on the Queen Anne sofa near a series of many paned little windows behind it. As I proceeded to sit among the silk cushions, Abel exited past the threshold, leaving us to ourselves. Leif moved to seat himself in the large matching winged chair, askew from me. Within minutes, several light footsteps were heard advancing through the nearby hallway until the lovely sight of a beautifully gowned Beth entered the room with Amity, Mairie, Doireann, Alice, and her three young boys. The sight of them all astonished me with delight, and I suddenly stood from my seat on the sofa as we immediately recognized each other and rushed to greet each other with joy.

Instantly embracing each other, we uncontrollably began weeping, overjoyed by our reunion and grateful, as she persistently uttered through abundant tears that it was by God's grace that we see each other now, and I lived to be returned to the family. It took us a noticeable moment to settle our emotions and collect ourselves. When we released each other from embracing, we both took a second to clear our appearances and gazed at each other in happy awe. As I looked upon her, her gentle modesty and sincerity were easily remembered, and the lovely remnants of the young woman I knew remained despite her golden hair that had grayed and little crow's feet at the corners of her brilliant light blue, sparkling eyes.

"You appear extraordinarily well, sister," Beth said in her soft-spoken tone as she studied my appearance through tearfully joyous eyes. She dabbed away her slipping tears again as Leif naturally pressed his handkerchief into the palm of my hand. I took the handkerchief and wiped my own emerging tears again, clearing my vision.

"Yes, I'm very well," I admitted, nodding my head in accordance as I dabbed my eyes dry.

"'Tis a marvelous blessing," she replied with obvious gratitude and amazement.

"Yes, it very much is," I agreed, equally as grateful.

"What grace has been bestowed upon us by God that you are safely restored to us, Sylvina."

"There aren't words enough to express how wonderful it is to see you again, Beth, and how thankful I am for it," I replied, trying to stifle my tears and my choking voice.

"We all share your sentiment. It has been too many years hence that have dispelled."

"Yes."

"Yet, you appear not a day aged," she remarked, truly amazed. I smiled nervously at her, not knowing what to say. She returned a genuinely warm smile. "God has been good to you," she concluded. I smiled unevenly again.

"Yes—He has—in many ways—because I'm here again with you," I said. Then, I glanced at the sweet individuals surrounding us as they curiously observed, noticing all of her children. "God has been good to you as well, Beth," I commented sincerely, returning my gaze toward hers as I tried to redirect her attention.

"Aye, as I praise Him." She nodded accordingly when my eyes dropped to her extremely round belly. Her hand slid over her stomach, and the gentle grin curling her lips faded somewhat when her gaze slipped down from mine and glanced at my own flat stomach. She quickly returned her eyes toward mine, catching herself, and the look in them obviously conveyed compassion as they turned full of regret. Sympathy was clearly perceived while gazing back at her, and my heart suddenly dropped. I was remorseful that I couldn't tell her anything about the truth, and the pain she was evidently feeling for me precisely weighed on me. I couldn't help my own smile from vanishing also as we gazed at each other. Perceiving it in her eyes, I knew she believed that I had lost my pregnancy.

"You indeed appear well in spite of it all, Sylvina," she started again after our small lapse. I smiled unevenly at her again, feeling extremely guilty that I couldn't simply tell her the truth about my own happiness with my children. Instead, I meekly looked at her with sadness I couldn't hide. "I pray for you to soon receive a new blessing," she said sympathetically in a heartfelt tone.

"Thank you, Beth. You're so very kind," I replied sincerely. She gave me a gentle smile in response. Then, she turned her gaze toward her surrounding, on-looking children and said politely, "Pray, permit me to introduce you to your nieces once more and to your new nephews."

"Thank you," I replied and followed her attention toward them.

"They have gravely missed you," Beth said. "Pray, children, do not be bashful. Come, meet your lovely aunt."

The children gave reticent but sweet little smiles as they curiously kept their stares on me. I couldn't help smiling so happily at them as I wondered by their questioning gazes if they found me a little unusual. Perhaps, I swiftly realized, it was the fact that we were all new to each other after my many years of absence from their lives. My own surprise, I was sure, got the better of me also as I gazed back at them, clearly surprised by how much the girls had all grown, and my charmed amazement by them and their handsome little brothers. I was clearly impressed.

The girls had practically grown into lovely young women. Eighteen-year-old Mairie certainly resembled her dearly departed father, Finley, with her ruddy complexion and shiny copper hair escaping her fine linen cap. Her sisters, seventeen-year-old Doireann and thirteen-year-old Alice favored their mother, with their alabaster skin and wispy platinum strands peering from their caps.

But when my eyes landed on Amity, I had to take an extra moment to comprehend that she was a beautiful twenty-one-year-old woman now. Closely resembling her aunt with the same complexion and hair and endearing facial features that were sweet and lovely, I observed the mesmerized sparkle in her light blue eyes as she realized my return. Although I detected in her gaze an air of childlike innocence attributed to her deafness, it distantly reminded me of when I knew her as a very young girl. The deep fondness that I held for all of them struck me again—especially when I gazed at Amity.

Beth gestured toward the children, instructing them to step forward and greet me. The girls first stepped toward me and respectfully introduced themselves with individual curtsies and delicate smiles. After she reintroduced the girls, Beth's three young sons approached and courteously introduced themselves with gallant little bows and interested expressions.

As I was getting acquainted with my new nephews, I learned Patrick, age nine, was the eldest, followed by Kenneth, age seven, and Abraham, age five. After our fair introductions, she excused her boys from us as their governess had come to collect them. While they were leaving the room, two pleasant black maids crossed the threshold, entering the room with large trays, each full of tea and enticing edibles. They set the trays over the tea table, and I was happy that we were going to share tea together since I had also grown slightly hungry.

After the maids had perfectly positioned the trays on the table, they promptly began serving us proper portions of tea and bannocks smothered in butter and cranberry preserves as the girls assumed their polite places beside me on the sofa and in extra surrounding chairs, joining us with Beth. Beth began conversing with me, courteously bringing me up to date regarding the latest occurrences throughout the local community.

I learned about her present daily routines, which I found fascinating, involving not only her children but also encompassing the extra particulars regarding her involvement with the almshouse, where many destitute widows and their children, along with orphans, were living. According to Beth, many of them had arrived at this devastating disadvantage due to the war with France and were now suffering. As I listened to her explain their situations and the tales of her personal accounts while assisting them, my compassion and concern for them were strongly felt as I admired her generosity and commitment to her family and to those less fortunate.

While Beth and I were talking, the four girls sat quietly, listening to our conversation and meticulously observing me. The girls seemed entranced as they curiously stared at me with wondering and questioning gazes. My own awareness of them heightened my curiosity about them also. Occasionally, I subtly exchanged glances with them and easily perceived their gladness to see me again, along with the shock in their staring eyes. When I glanced in their direction, a smile came to my lips. They returned demure, little smiles also, and seemed nearly too shy to respond otherwise. But my eyes specifically caught Amity's several times, and I subtly waved my fingers at her with a tender smile. Meekly, she responded in kind, and the bashful smile curving her lips warmed my heart.

As the conversation between Beth and me drifted and waned, I noticed Doireann appearing to wish to join us. I gazed at her and smiled while she sat in the chair beside her mother, across from me.

"So, tell me, how have you girls been doing for so long? I've missed you so much," I prompted kindly, beginning a conversation with them.

"We have been well, Aunt Sylvina, I thank you for inquiring," Doireann replied politely.

"How very nice to hear. I'm so glad," I said, truly. "What has kept you busy during all of this time since I've been away? You've all grown into such lovely ladies. I'm afraid that I've missed so many of your achievements."

"Well, mayhap, I shall like to share news to inform you that Mairie is presently betrothed," Doireann cordially informed me of her older sister in her shy manner.

"Is that right?" I responded, amazedly, turning my surprised attention toward Mairie.

"Aye, it is true, Aunt Sylvina. I am betrothed to Master Hardy's nephew in Lexington, young Master Henry Rhodes," Mairie demurely informed me as she blushed. I swung my gaze toward Beth with an unbelievable look.

"'Tis a good match," Beth responded, approving proudly as she looked at me.

"I can't believe it. Where has the time gone between the time she was the height of my elbow and now?" I replied.

"Time seems to flow as a leaf upon a river. One blinks, and 'tis swept away, no longer found," Beth said wistfully.

"Yes, I suppose you're right," I agreed, nodding a little. I returned my gaze to Mairie, and the flushing hue in her face appeared to deepen as she demurred with a bashful grin.

"Master Rhodes and I shan't wed till I am twenty, however," Mairie said in a modest tone but obviously seeming somewhat disappointed.

"I see. Well, it's perhaps good to wait a little. Don't you think? You know, in order to become established," I replied supportively.

"Aye, mother would agree," Mairie said with a faint sigh.

"Master Rhodes must secure your future endeavor prior to your wedding. You are very well aware of it, my dear Mairie," Beth responded to her daughter.

"You are correct, Mother," Mairie agreed with a slightly faint heart. I discerned her eagerness to marry Mr. Rhodes and fathomed she must certainly be in love with him. I gave her a heartened smile, and she reciprocated a sweet one of her own.

"Aunt Sylvina?" Doireann suddenly began, her voice filled with curiosity, interrupting us.

"Yes?" I replied nicely, shifting my gaze back toward her.

"Pray, tell your experience whilst being captive to Indians?" she asked inquisitively without a modicum of reservation, as the eagerness to know was visible in her wide eyes. I was taken off guard by her question as I unexpectedly looked at her. I cleared my throat a little, realizing I was abruptly put on the spot, and wondered how I was going to approach her burning question.

"Doireann, Aunt Sylvina may not wish to revisit her trials. Pray, be considerate. You must mind yourself, child," Beth chastised as she clearly read the hesitation on my face.

"Yet, we do care to learn of it, Mother," Doireann disregarded, though her tone was respectful and soft.

"Pray, kindly think of your aunt, Doireann," Beth reminded.

"It's all right," I politely interjected instead. "There isn't much to tell, anyway."

A momentary pause in the conversation ensued with a bout of discomfiture encroaching as everyone's gazes were transfixed on me. I felt the topic was unavoidable as all of them stared at me, anticipating some kind of explanation from my own lips.

"Pray, Aunt Sylvina, what experience had you?" Doireann inquired carefully again.

"Well, uhm..." I started conscientiously, suddenly remembering the incident that had happened to me after the fall of Fort William Henry some years ago, when Abenaki warriors had abducted me.

"Aye?" Doireann prompted me.

"It was actually very frightening," I remembered.

"Was it your belief that you will be killed and eaten?" Alice, the youngest sister, innocently wondered, appearing as engrossed as her sisters, to what I was going to say.

"No. Thankfully. I didn't fear being eaten. I simply didn't know what was going to happen to me—and that was frightening enough," I reminisced horribly.

"Yet, you believed that you were to be killed by them, none-theless?" Mairie conjectured with captivation.

"At first, yes, the thought was there," I admitted.

"Is our aunt not a brave woman? The frontier was perilous," Alice remarked, duly impressed with fear.

"The frontier remains so, Alice. But our aunt is truly brave," Doireann said to her younger sister. "Our dearest Aunt Sylvina has survived, and we are all forever grateful and blessed."

"Most indeed," Alice agreed wholeheartedly.

"I wonder, however, for are Indians not known to commit such atrocities? Therefore, how were you spared, aunt?" Doireann questioned inquisitively, looking quite terrified of the idea of their own captivity.

"Would it not be by the grace of God?" Alice replied gratefully, giving Doireann an apparent look.

"Yet, had they not taken you for a slave?" Mairie inquired before Doireann could respond.

"I wasn't aware that I had been enslaved when it happened. My only concern was escaping since I didn't know what was in store for me after experiencing—" I suddenly broke off, apprehending the details I was about to reveal of my experience at Fort William Henry.

"Truly?" Doireann closely interrupted, clearly astonished.

"Yet, they enslave all whom they capture and do not eliminate. To not understand so, it must have been a devastating trial for you, Aunt. Having your adventure would have certainly tested my faith and will to remain alive—out of mere fright if naught at all," Mairie said frightfully.

"Indeed. I have heard many atrocious tales of their ferocity and harm to women in their raids. However, you appear quite well, Aunt. 'Tis miraculous," Doireann replied candidly, implying the sensitive nature of the topic concerning a woman's particular vulnerability in circumstances of hostility. As I gazed at the girls' inquisitive stares and given their looks of concern, I knew they were wondering whether I had been scandalized by bodily harm.

"I'm very grateful I wasn't harmed by them in any way," I said truthfully, putting their uneasy questions to rest and settling their concerns.

"Yet, I remain remorseful, aunt," Doireann continued sympathetically.

"I'm well, though," I reassured carefully.

"Blessed be the case. Regardless, as I cannot restrain from pondering how our poor baby cousin has been lost in your plight and that we are immensely grieved," she replied terribly with noticeable compassion in her delicate voice, supported by the deep sadness in her eyes.

"Alrecht, lasses, that will complete yer inquiries," Leif interceded suddenly, and I glanced at him, noticing his deadpan face.

"Aye, it is quite enough," Beth agreed abruptly also. "Your uncle is correct. Aunt Sylvina need not experience the past any longer. We are immensely grateful to our Lord and Savior that she has been restored within our protection and is in fine health. We are quite blessed and happy. Naught else need be said."

The girls immediately became silent, and the conversation dropped. An uncomfortable lull ensued for a moment. As the conversation obviously stumbled, it didn't naturally resume, and we sat in each other's company, awkwardly having tea in silence. When the girls had finished their tea, Beth excused them from us, and they quietly withdrew from the room, leaving us alone together. At this point, Beth resumed a lighter discussion with Leif and me about our visit to *Sàmhchair*.

Fourteen

L ater, at four o'clock, Beth kindly showed us into the dining room to have dinner, where we met her husband, Patrick, who had shortly returned from town and was waiting for us to join him at the table. Patrick was an older man, appearing in his fifties, whose long, thick hair was white as snow, tied into a loose tail at the nape of his neck by a large black silk ribbon matching his pristinely tailored, crisp, dour suit. Given the spacious scope of the O'Donoghue house, containing a full staff of servants, and his well-groomed appearance, Patrick was undoubtedly a formidable pillar of Concord's financial community.

His light gray eyes were vibrant and friendly as he smiled cordially at me upon our greeting with an unassuming bow. When he straightened, and though he appeared amiable, earnestness and reservation were discernible in the air of his character. I wondered if he was a man of reasonable humor in spite of his strict demeanor. His politely smiling eyes told me he was guarded but contented with mirth, too, in the likely company of male peers.

"A great pleasure to make yer acquaintance, Your Grace," Patrick greeted formally with politeness in a distinct Irish accent.

"Thank you, Mister O'Donoghue. It's very nice to meet you as well," I replied nicely.

"Might I have the liberty to kindly propose, as we are family, that I be addressed simply as Patrick?"

"Yes, of course," I replied, smiling at him.

"I thank ye most kindly," he said, bowing before me again.

"Please regard me as Beth does. As you've said, we're family. There's no need to be formal by not calling me by my first name," I suggested politely. "I'm so happy to meet you and that we're family."

"I, as well," he replied courteously and grinned amicably. "'Tis most gratifying that ye have been reunited with us. You have been missed terribly."

"Thank you. Yes, it is exceptionally nice to be here with everyone again," I agreed.

"I pray your journey to arrive was not much of a hindrance in the rain."

"We managed well, thank you."

"Splendid. It soothes me to learn of it." Patrick then shifted his attention toward Leif. "Seamus. Always fair to see ye once more."

"Ye as weel, Patrick. How micht ye fare?"

"Occupied quite commonly."

"Aye," Leif understood.

"As I am certain ye well agree."

"Indeed."

"Then, pray, let us discard our tribulations fer a wee bit of leisure and dine in the delightful company of our wives. I am certain ye are famished by the hour," Patrick politely offered as he encouraged us to take our places at the dining table.

Leif guided me toward our seats at the stretched mahogany table and seated me near Beth at one end. Then, he found his place near Patrick on the opposite side as the children filled vacant seats around us, making themselves comfortable to eat. As several waiters began serving our plated food, the casual conversation started between Leif and Patrick until we were fully served. Then, the light discussion between them curtailed, and Patrick promptly said the blessing. When he concluded, everyone began eating their meal, and he resumed conversing with Leif. At that time, Beth and I were inspired to discuss between us, while the children sat quietly listening, according to their refined upbringing.

The conversation between Beth and me was light and polite as I caught tidbits of our husbands' discussion about their business dealings, the economy, and politics. When dinner ended, Patrick and Leif lingered in leisure at the table, still discussing current affairs, while I was invited to join Beth and the children in the drawing room for further relaxation. There, the boys played with their wooden toy soldiers on the floor, and the girls performed singing and minuets on the harpsichord. Afterward, they were inspired and impressed me further with recitations of poetry.

During their performances, Amity quietly sat beside me on the sofa and attentively watched her cousins. It seemed she was enjoying them when I glanced at her and saw the gentle smile on her face. For a second, she glimpsed at me, catching my eye, and an affectionate little grin passed between us, amplifying my fondness for her. When the other girls finally concluded their presentations, I applauded them well, and I was thoroughly amazed by their accomplishments. After my applause, I glanced again at Amity with a smile, and she raised her fingers, proceeding to animate them as she remembered the sign language I'd taught her to use years ago. To my absolute delight, she and I began communicating with each other. It seemed she was eager to finally express herself to me, and started asking me as many questions as I had in mind to ask her.

"Where have you gone, aunt?" she inquired immediately.

"I'm sorry to say that I've been unintentionally too far away for so long," I answered as generally as possible.

"I have missed you greatly," she responded.

"I have missed you equally," I communicated. She smiled again, a little nervously this time.

"Yet, to where did your misfortune take you that you could not be recovered?" she asked timidly.

"Forgive me," I said, sadly shaking my head a little with a look of sincerest regret. She didn't respond as I perceived her searching eyes delving for an answer while staring fixedly at me. Then, the registration emerged in them, and I knew she realized that something uncanny was the reason for my long absence in their lives.

"I am sorry," she said, remorseful about everything. I clearly saw her deep regret over our separation and how severely she missed me. I reached a hand over hers while it rested in her lap, and she promptly wrapped her fingers around mine, squeezing them as if to never let them go. I reciprocated the sentiment of our embracing hands, and it seemed we might weep from dismay over lost time and joy at being here with each other again.

"I'm well, though. You mustn't worry," I assured her.

"Praise be to God," she replied as we fought back tears seen in each other's eyes.

"Yes," I agreed. "Your uncle tells me that you're doing well."

"Yes, Aunt," she responded with a slight nod also, as I was hoping to steer the conversation into calmer waters.

"I'm so glad to learn this from you." I smiled, heartened.

"Has Uncle informed you of my ability to scribe, also?" A demure look of pride came over her face with a shy smile.

"I believe that he did," I informed her. She nodded a little again in acknowledgment.

"Shall I demonstrate it to you?"

"Yes, of course. That would be very nice."

"As you wish." The smile on her face grew, and now she appeared filled with eagerness to please. "Permits me to be excused, and I shall fetch my blackboard and chalk."

"All right," I agreed gladly.

Our fingers unclasped each other's and she promptly stood

135

from her seat beside me, then purposefully withdrew from the room. Beth and her girls had been intently observing with interest as they sat quietly around the room. While we patiently waited for Amity's return, we remained in companionable silence as all of our novel insights had been presented and discussed. By this time, as I had glanced at the young boys, they were now resting speechlessly on the floor, no longer interested in entertaining themselves with their toy soldiers. They had become listlessly ready for sleep as their eyes drooped and fought to remain open since the evening had grown late.

Beth rang the servant bell, and immediately, the governess arrived in the room. Without a word, she approached the tired boys and encouraged them to their feet. Gathering them with her, the boys obediently followed her out of the sitting room and disappeared into the corridor the moment Amity returned, joining me on the sofa again. Beth and the girls resumed their attention on Amity and me, anticipating the start of our new conversation. With the chalkboard positioned in her lap and her fingers poised to write with the white chalk, she proceeded to move the slender chalk piece over the board. When she had quickly finished writing, Amity showed me what was written, and my eyes skimmed over her words as I read, "You and Uncle will return with me to *Taigh Gràs*?"

"That's right. We're returning home together," I signed to her as I gently spoke to include our onlookers in the discussion also. She quickly erased what was written and wrote again.

"I am most pleased," she wrote and smiled at me.

"I can't express how very happy I am about it also," I communicated.

"Uncle is joyous once more," she swiftly wrote after erasing her previous words.

"Yes, I'm as happy as he is," I replied.

"For too many years, Uncle experienced melancholy in your absence. He suffered. No other happiness would come to him," she disclosed. "Plainly, at present, I perceive that he is no longer forlorn, as you are here." I smiled unevenly in response, feeling a distinct pang in my heart, realizing the extended grief Leif had intensely experienced, as I had heard this from her and knew the aching all too well. Amity's brow was faintly knitted as I held her searching gaze. She stared at me momentarily, and I perceived the concerning question in her eyes. After a silent lapse, her eyes fell from mine, returned to her chalkboard, and proceeded to write some more. When she had finished, she slightly raised the board toward me to read what she had written. "Pray, where has our baby cousin gone?"

I returned to looking at her, suddenly unable to explain or lie about any of it. I stalled. Simply gazing at her wondering eyes, the deep concern in them was visible, and I hesitated to say anything.

"I cannot say," I found myself silently signing to her in reply after a moment, unintentionally excluding our observers. The wrinkle in her brow deepened as they drew upward, and the awful sadness appeared, her eyes glazing over as tears emerged. Before she could fully react, I reached my arms around her and drew her into a sound embrace, attempting reassurance that I was all right in spite of everything that had happened. Holding her in my arms seemed to suddenly prevent her from weeping, as she brought her arms around me also and secured them. While embracing each other, the sense of her understanding the state of my overall well-being was felt since she relaxed in my arms, causing me to do the same, as some relief came over me.

Aware that Beth and the girls were watching, I couldn't dwell on the realization that they believed I had miscarried our first child. The thought of it closely brought me to tears as the weight of all the lies bore heavily on my heart, and knowing how incapable I was in revealing the truth to them. So, Amity and I simply embraced for an undetermined moment, comforting each other without the spectacle of tears.

"Might all be well?" Beth inquired delicately, breaking the lull.

I moved to release Amity, and her arms slipped from me as I returned my attention to Beth, who was facing me from where she sat. Her look of apparent concern was obvious as she gazed at us.

"Yes, everything is just fine," I assured. I gave her a modest smile in accordance, and she reciprocated a slight but kind one of her own.

"I am much relieved," she said, appearing slightly eased. It seemed she was about to say something else when the clock suddenly chimed ten, drawing our attention to the time and interrupting her. "Dear. How late the hour has become," she commented.

"It seems that it has, Mother," Mairie realized and agreed.

"It has come for us to retire," Beth determined as she politely fought back a yawn. "I shall have my maid, Annabelle, introduce your chamber, Sylvina."

"That's very kind, Beth. Thank you," I accepted.

"Indeed, you are most welcome," she replied. She rang the servant bell again, and within a minute, her maid appeared past the threshold as she advanced into the room. Beth politely instructed Annabelle, and I soon followed her out of the room after Beth and my nieces pleasantly wished me a good night.

I hadn't realized the true exhaustion that I felt until Annabelle was leading me through candlelit corridors and up the staircase, and finally arriving at my bedroom for the evening. With Annabelle's assistance, I was soon disrobed down to my shift and tucked into bed before she moved to hang my clothes in the armoire and stoke the flames in the fireplace since the evening was cool. When she was satisfied by the strength of the fire, she left the room, closing the door behind herself.

Finally, alone now, I automatically exhaled and my eyes immediately closed while I started relaxing beneath the welcoming down blanket and quilts with my head sinking into the downy pillows. The recognizable sound of Leif's and Patrick's muffled voices traveling up the heating ducts into the room from the sitting room below soothed and quickly lulled me to sleep.

But sometime, much later, I was slightly roused from slumber when I sensed Leif sidling into bed close beside me. He wrapped an arm around my waist and drew me against his naked body with my back against his chest.

"What will we ever tell them about our children?" I muttered drowsily with the troubling thought as I laced my fingers with his.

"I shall ponder the explanation as I devise a likely tale in time," he said softly, realizing himself having awakened me. He contracted his fingers around mine and gently pressed his lip on the back of my crown in a tender kiss, reassuring and soothing me. Satisfied by his answer, I didn't reply. Except my fingers tightened around his. His fingers responded and our hands were solidly joined as I peacefully drifted back into a dream, glad he was holding me.

PART THREE

Taigh Gràs

Fifteen

D awn, the next morning, after eating breakfast with Beth's family, Leif and I left the O'Donoghue family in Concord for Boston with Amity in our company. Patrick offered for one of his coachmen to drive us toward our destination using his coach. So, Leif had the smaller chaise towed with the O'Donohues' coach, and we began our journey out of Concord with Leif, Amity, and I bundled warmly inside the coach from the cool October air with his horse, Blaze, hitched to the coach along with the other horses.

The rain had ceased overnight, and the day was left with bright cobalt, sunny skies as white cumulus clouds drifted high overhead in the atmosphere. However, as a result of the rain, the road was left muddied, which slowed our carriage as we traveled through the woods. I gazed out of the window, observing the towering colorful maple trees and viridian evergreens surrounding us while we passed them, and the encompassing sound of abundant sparrows chirping invisibly among their boughs resonated throughout the forest. The songful birds emanating, along with the brightly shining sun and crisp fall air, made the scenery idyllic.

Anticipating our arrival at *Taigh Gràs,* I wondered what

Boston was like now compared to when I last visited. I assumed much had changed. Aside from new political leaders executing the king's law and determining the social climate, I was more looking forward to reuniting with familiar household faces, along with neighbors and friends, than considering any of the surrounding politics.

Hindered by the waterlogged trails, the ride inside the coach was sluggish and topsy-turvy, and the sway contributed to my motion sickness. So, I closed my eyes, willing the nausea to dispel as I leaned my head against Leif's shoulder. He drew an arm around my shoulder and pulled me comfortably against him. As I began relaxing, I found the sickness easing as soon as I fell asleep.

When I opened my eyes, the sun began setting along our journey, and I wondered how soon it would be until we finally arrived in town. It was well after dark when we finally arrived in Boston. Driving over the Neck, passing the gallows, making our way over cobblestones through town now, we passed single dwellings and brownstones with flickering lantern-lit windows along the streets. The red moon hovered brightly and low on the horizon, appearing like a gigantic blood-orange disk as if it were falling toward Earth. It was beautiful and also struck an odd chord of ominousness within me that I couldn't explain, as it was over the town, illuminating the sparkling black Atlantic Ocean beyond. The night air was mild and smelled thick with a combination of salt and chimney smoke, instantly reminding me of the night I had first come here to stay when Leif and I were newlyweds. I deeply inhaled the unique aroma, remembering every detail of it.

The road curved left, and we went around the bend. Following it until it straightened again, it gently curved right, and soon we finally arrived at our property. *Taigh Gràs* could finally be seen advancing through the trees as it glowed beneath the moonlight as we approached. My stomach suddenly somersaulted with excitement; it had been far too long since I was last here, and I wondered what to expect.

As the coach rounded the pebbled driveway, it came to a halt at the front of the house, finally. Promptly, our groom, Samuel, appeared as if he had been waiting for our arrival and hurriedly approached the carriage. He quickly opened the door for us as our driver continued holding the reins to the horses and locked the wheels with the brakes. Leif immediately moved out of his seat and stepped out of the carriage as he kindly greeted Samuel.

"Your Grace," Samuel respectfully greeted Leif as he bowed toward him. When he straightened from bowing, Leif swiftly turned toward the open door, reaching for my hand, and assisted me out of the coach. After being planted on the ground, Leif turned from me and also reached for Amity, assisting her to stand beside me. As she came to arrive at my side, I turned my glance toward Samuel, giving him a polite acknowledging smile, remembering him from when he was a young teenager; to my surprise, the simultaneous moment as our footman, Elijah, also abruptly appeared from the house, approaching us with purpose.

"Elijah," Leif spoke, kindly acknowledging him also, as he arrived and immediately began retrieving our belongings from the coach.

"Your Grace," Elijah replied politely with the same affability and bowed toward him. When he straightened, he promptly resumed removing our luggage from the carriage, and Leif seized my elbow with a gentle hand, beginning to steer me away over the path toward the granite steps of the mansion with Amity closely following.

Walking up the steps, we arrived beneath the large portico supported by whitewashed fluted Ionic columns, and the front door widened as it was pulled fully open for us to enter by Quinn, our butler, and Leif's manservant. Stepping aside from the door, Quinn made way for our entry into the grand foyer I clearly remembered from before.

"Welcome, Your Grace," Quinn politely greeted Leif as we now stood inside the foyer. Before Leif replied, Quinn's eyes instantly shifted toward me, and his eyes widened with a modest grin of surprise as he immediately recognized me.

"Thank ye, Quinn. 'Tis guid tae see ye," Leif responded good-naturedly while stepping us away from the open door, letting in the cool air as luggage was going to be promptly brought inside. Leif moved us deeper into the area away from the draft, where we stopped and stood facing Quinn.

"'Tis indeed pleasant tae see that you have arrived well, Your Grace," Quinn replied.

"Aye," Leif acknowledged, agreeing. "My wife has returned tae *Taigh Gràs*. As ye recall, it is Her Grace who presently appears?"

"Most certainly, Your Grace," Quinn said to him, turning his remembering eyes on me now. He graciously bowed toward me and straightened with a mild smile that was sincere and genial. "Welcome home, Your Grace. 'Tis a true blessing to have you restored to us. You have been missed greatly by all."

"Thank you, Quinn. It's very nice to be here again. I've missed all of you extremely as well," I replied, truly, politely returning his genuine smile. As we stood beneath the flickering candlelit chandelier, I noticed that he had aged by ten years since my absence, and he now appeared to be in his fifties. His hair had grayed, and the lines in his face had deepened, but the calm stoicism and earnest demeanor I remembered about him remained unchanged. The approachable reception, with a willingness to please, was evident in his quietly welcoming eyes.

After his greeting, I silently glanced at my surroundings as Leif gave Quinn further instructions and remembered how I was once immensely happy living here with Leif. Nothing at all about my surroundings had changed, as if they had been encapsulated by the alterations of time. They were completely the same as I had left them. I noticed, however, that no other servants were around us as I admired the many landscape paintings I'd distinctly remembered still hanging on the surrounding walls.

My attention turned from one of the paintings toward Elijah

as he entered the foyer carrying as much luggage as he could manage, and we made eye contact. He diffidently grinned at me, and I smiled in return, perceiving his wonder and heartfelt gladness that I'd returned. Although the look on his face didn't seem surprised that I'd returned, like Quinn, it appeared that they were expecting my appearance. I realized then that Leif had prepared them with the knowledge of my homecoming through correspondence, likely when we were previously staying at *Sàmhchair*.

When Elijah swiftly turned from the baggage he'd placed unobtrusively in the corner by one of the walls, he swiftly returned outdoors to collect more of the remaining luggage as I wondered about the absence of the rest of the household staff. But Quinn shortly stepped aside after Leif completed giving him instructions, and my gaze suddenly recognized Mercy appearing from behind Quinn when he turned toward her where she silently and dutifully stood. He briefly instructed her to come forward to stand directly in our presence before he withdrew from us to execute Leif's wishes.

Mercy stepped forward and curtsied before us, and I couldn't help the automatic smile that came to me as I was tremendously happy to see her again. Remembering our kindred connection and the fondness I held for her immediately compelled me to rush toward her, wrap my arms around her with an embrace before a word was uttered. Forgetting protocol, impulse determined my affection for her, and I naturally hugged her with my heart.

"Mercy... I'm so very happy to see you again," I said gently while embracing her. She didn't respond and remained rigid in my arms as I held her for a moment. When I released her, letting my arms slip away from her, she took a step backward, and I easily noticed the shock on her face. She looked at me, speechless, with wide eyes, and I quickly wondered if I'd done something wrong. Perhaps I was too forward? But we were always companionable with each other in the past, though. So, I was slightly confused. I coincidentally glanced at Leif and realized the innuendo on his nearly impassive face. I had indeed broken the rule of propriety, as I had forgotten. An awkward feeling came over me, accompanied by an uneven little grin, as I returned to looking at Mercy and perceived her uncertainty, also accompanied by a spark of mirth in her eyes.

She mindfully curtsied before me and straightened, standing silently while demurely gazing at me. As we stared at each other for a second, I observed her twenty-seven-year-old appearance, which was different from the seventeen-year-old girl I had known. I opened my mouth, ready to apologize for startling her with the liberty of my emotions, when I felt Leif gently slipping his fingers around my elbow and holding it. My eyes shifted toward him, and the taciturnity in his gaze determined my restraint.

"Her Grace is most pleased to see you, Mercy," Leif politely said to her, pardoning me and explaining my reaction.

"Yes'm, Your Grace," she said modestly to him, understanding, then turned her eyes toward me. "'Tis verily joyous to see you returned, ma'am," she responded sincerely with a gentle smile reflecting the brightness in her eyes. She curtsied again and straightened, looking at me with the same familiar connection we once shared that I recognized.

"Thank you, Mercy. It's so very nice to see you. I hope you've been doing well?" I responded, smiling at her.

"Yes'm, that I have, I thank you," she replied.

"I'm so glad you have," I said, truly.

"I pray that you are well, ma'am," she said genuinely. I thought I detected a hint of concern in her voice when I also discerned it in her eyes as she stared at me.

"Thank you, Mercy. I'm very happy to be here again," I acknowledged truthfully without answering her question, knowing the question and regret regarding seeing the expected child born between me and Leif was absent, and was at the forefront of her mind. Incapable of explaining any of it to her, I gave her a weak smile instead.

"Pray, presently show us tae our chambers, Mercy," Leif kindly instructed her, sparing a cumbersome moment.

"Yes'm, Your Grace," she responded dutifully and started from us out of the foyer, heading toward the grand staircase.

As Leif began guiding me away from the foyer, keeping his fingers gently wrapped around my elbow, we, with Amity among us, proceeded following Mercy through the passage when I unexpectedly heard several unfamiliar male voices subtly resonating a distance from us through the corridor originating in the dining room. It seemed the occupants were freely socializing as laughter from them emanated, and my curiosity was piqued as I was certain it wouldn't have been servants being so lax. Furthermore, as I amazingly glanced around at my unchanged familiar surroundings while pacing for the staircase, the halls were noticeably quiet, otherwise. The many servants I'd remembered from before, roaming the house, performing their duties, were absent. Regarding the late hour, however, I easily presumed that most of the servants had already retired for the night.

Following Mercy up the staircase, we rounded the first landing, passed the grandfather clock, and continued to the second floor. When we reached the top landing and were about to round the banister into the corridor, an unknown twenty-something-year-old man with auburn hair and blue eyes abruptly met us as he was ready to descend the steps in a hurry. Suddenly surprised by our appearance as we bumped into him, he sharply moved backward and stepped aside, permitting us to pass him and continue on our way.

"I beg your pardon, Your Grace. Good evening," the young man said with a humble, conciliatory look as our gazes met. I quickly noted that his accent was clean and proper, and he was from London. I instantly wondered who this stranger could be, as he was evidently familiar with Leif.

"Guid evening, Captain Miller," Leif replied formally,

acknowledging him. "Ye micht take care tae mind yer steps, so not tae stampede the innocent."

"Forgive me, Your Grace. I shall heed your warning," Captain Miller responded to Leif's suggestion, suddenly appearing significantly embarrassed as the hue in his face immediately rose hot pink. He sharply bowed before Leif again with respect. He straightened, visibly chagrinned as his eyes bounced from Leif between me and Amity and landed on me for a second longer before returning to Leif's unemotional gaze. But Captain Miller glanced at me again, and the inquisitive wonder on his face was discernible.

"I present my wife, Her Grace, Duchess of Monteith," Leif said to him, introducing me to the captain as he maintained a deadpan expression. But the young man's eyes suddenly widened at the realization, and the expression on his face turned more humble as the clear embarrassment remained. He briskly clicked his heels and bowed before me this time. When he straightened, it seemed he was at a loss for words as he stared at me for a second.

"I am most rude. I beg for your pardon, Your Grace. 'Tis an utmost pleasure to make your acquaintance," he said reverentially to me after finding his voice.

"This would be Captain Miller of the army," Leif informed me as he politely spoke. Considerably, I was silently struck and unexpectedly surprised to learn that a British soldier was freely roaming the halls of *Taigh Gràs*.

"Hello, Captain Miller," I greeted courteously, despite my surprise.

"Your Grace," he replied graciously.

After the captain's polite acknowledgment, Leif turned his eyes on Mercy as she had stopped short, leading us away from the landing due to our abrupt encounter. Understanding Leif's implicit directive, she recommenced pacing through the corridor, and Leif began steering me and Amity away from the captain as we returned to following her. As we began walking from the captain, I caught a glimpse of Amity as she briefly glanced over her shoulder at him. My gaze further turned over my own shoulder, and I noticed his eyes lingering on Amity as they stared at each other for a moment. Amity suddenly returned her gaze ahead, away from him, as we continued pacing through the hallway, and he dropped his gaze toward the stairs, which he now began descending.

I couldn't help glancing at Amity before returning my attention to where we were heading, and I perceived her cheeks brightly flushing in the candlelight flickering in the sconces along the walls. Witnessing the furtive glance they had just shared and the resulting hue in her cheeks quickly gave me the impression that there was a hidden attraction between them.

Meandering our way through a series of hallways, before approaching our bedroom door, we arrived at Amity's doorway first, where Leif had instructed Mercy to stop us. In his usual kind manner, he further directed her to tend to Amity in my place before dismissing her for the evening after she completed the task. She curtsied in response and opened Amity's bedroom door, guiding her inside. As Amity's door was carefully closing shut with them inside, Leif continued guiding me with him through the rest of the quiet corridor toward our own room.

Soon arriving at our bedroom door, Leif reached for the silver handle and turned it, opening the door for us to enter the room. As I preceded him into the room, I heard the door closing behind me until it clicked shut. I turned, facing him as he stood by the door, realizing we were finally alone once more, and smiled at him as I was glad to bring myself to rest. His lips turned upward, marking the warmth in his sparkling, smiling eyes, and I perceived that he was as pleased to be here, too, finally.

"Permit me once I have removed my coats," he suggested and started from the door, heading toward his armoire. I quietly watched him swiftly remove his greatcoat as he arrived at the large wing chair positioned beside his armoire and stopped short. Carelessly tossing his first coat over the seat cushion of the chair, he promptly removed his second coat from his square shoulders and mindlessly dropped it over the previous coat. Remaining in his waistcoat, fine linen shirt, and breeches, his boots resonated over the wide plank oak floor as his heels clapped against it while striding toward me.

Arriving where I stood, he came close before me and carefully withdrew my cloak before reaching his fingers toward my stomacher, beginning to unpin my gown. He grinned at me before dropping his gaze to mind his fingers while removing the pins, and his warm breath caressed my brow as I observed his mindful concentration while his fingers moved over the silk covering the front of my torso.

"I am joyful that ye are present with me, haur at *Taigh Gràs*," he uttered in a low voice. The tenderness in his tone was apparent, and he raised his gaze from his working hands, meeting my eyes again. Distinct affection and elation were clearly perceived, and I softly smiled at him. Aware of his penetrating eyes, I knew his happiness and his desire to express it as he was compelling my shyness to surface.

"I'm happy we're here together, too," I said softly in a near whisper. He grinned gently, and I could sense his affection as I gazed into his eyes.

"The lecht of my soul and ballad of my heart restores the pulse of my heart as I gaze upon her glory," he said quietly. I smiled at him again as my self-conscious gaze fell toward his fingers that had stilled over my breast. "Micht ye remain bashful of me?"

"I think so," I admitted mutedly,

"Why?"

"I don't know."

"Do ye not?"

"No."

"'Twill always be so?"

"I think it will."

"Then, it will remain a mystery," he fathomed, and I returned my gaze to him despite my shyness. He smiled again, seeming deeply charmed.

"Do you like that I become bashful of you?" I asked.

"Aye."

"Why?"

"It strikes my fancy tae ken that ye perceive my loove and affection fur ye as it is great."

"Oh," I realized.

"Aye," he reinforced tenderly. "Micht ye ever tire of me?"

"Never. You know that." I observed the gentle grin gracing his face and the truth he already knew in the depth of his adoring eyes.

"Hence, telling me, beckons my heart tae forever hold ye as I desire it more every day of my living."

"Really?"

"Now more than ever, since I nae longer remain haunted by yer memory and have discovered ye within my possession once more," he disclosed. "My torment has been dissolved at long last. 'Tis as though I had never knoon misery as my eyes gaze upon ye. Tae touch ye again, soars my spirit toward the reigning heavens. Thaur I dwell when I am with ye."

I smiled softly as I dearly gazed into his eyes feeling a knot forming in my throat, and my vision began blurring as they welled with heart-warmed tears. Incapable of words, I delicately raised my palms over his firm biceps and stroked upward as my arms slipped around his broad shoulders in an embrace. Tightening my arms around him, I buried my face in his neck as I blinked, and silent tears slipped forth, rolling down my cheeks. His arms came around me and solidly drew me against him. Feeling the concreteness of his body glued to mine while he anchored me in his powerful arms, I knew he knew my feelings for him.

"We shall remain as we are till time's end," he half-whispered. I tightened my arms around his neck in response, believing it would be so.

We held each other unspoken for an undetermined moment

until I released my arms around him, and he eased me back down onto my feet. Closely standing before each other, he clasped his thumb and forefinger over my chin and lifted my watery gaze toward his. I sensed his other palm reaching into his waistcoat pocket and withdrawing his handkerchief. He carefully placed it upon my damp cheek and dabbed my tearful eyes clear. When he was satisfied with my appearance, he returned his handkerchief to his pocket without removing his deep, meaningful eyes from mine.

His gaze locked mine to his, and I sensed his palm gently coming over the side of my face as the pad of his thumb tenderly stroked my cheek and lips. I raised my palm to the back of his caressing hand, lacing my fingers with his. His fingers contracted around mine and his hand slipped from my cheek as he brought my knuckles to his soft lips, placing a significant, tender kiss on them. After, he let my fingers slide from his and silently returned to undressing me.

As I quietly watched him disrobing me, the familiar sentiment between us was soothing and calm and rich with unyielding love and companionship. The silence in the room pervaded save for the crackling sound in the burning fireplace as sap from the logs popped in the roaring flames. While standing before each other as his fingers worked my clothes away from me, my mind began wandering and reverted to the encounter we had with Captain Miller and Amity's reaction to him afterward.

"I didn't know that we would be having any guests," I commented modestly as the thought occurred, breaking the silence between us.

"Aye, a number of them are billeting at *Taigh Gràs*," Leif replied, unfazed while concentrating on the unlacing of my stays.

"Oh," I realized, uncertain of the fact.

"A large contingency of soldiers has landed, as the Crown immediately sent them tae instill order within the streets resulting from the abundant rabble-rousing and rioting inspired by the seizure of Hancock's *Liberty* by the navy," he continued. I nodded in response, remembering what he'd told me about what had happened to Mr. Hancock's ship earlier. However, I wasn't aware of the number of people's adverse reactions to it that would warrant a government response with the use of the military. But then I remembered the Second Amendment in the Constitution and the reason it holds a prominent place in the Bill of Rights. "Since Parliament's passage of the Quartering Act, I have also been forced tae billet soldiers haur as all within the city," he said.

"For how long?" I asked curiously, feeling concerned.

"Indefinitely," he responded with a hint of displeasure in his voice. I suddenly felt uncomfortable about the unusual situation of us having to house strange men from the military. Living with them was not only likely to impede our privacy but also our freedom to live without the concern of others infringing on our lives. Then, my experience in Northampton entered my mind, furthering my unease and skepticism.

"Indefinitely…" I echoed pensively under my breath.

"'Tis not a preferred situation as it remains," Leif acknowledged after hearing me.

"What kind of soldiers are they? Are the ones living here enlisted?"

"They are officers who billet at *Taigh Gràs*. Captains and lieutenants," he informed me precisely. I didn't immediately respond as I considered whether knowing their ranks made them any better behaved than their subordinates. But I reasoned that officers must have been cultured and typically refined since they had the means to purchase their commissions, unlike the enlisted who were generally pressed into service and came from harder backgrounds.

"What are they like?" I inquired after a second.

"As in whit manner?"

"Are they respectful of women?"

"They originate from esteemed pedigrees and are genteel toward lasses, if this is whit yoo're inquiring, and remain respectful of men who outrank them," he answered.

"I see," I accepted. "But I wonder if there aren't any barracks for them to live in instead of being here?"

"Those remain insufficient about the city. Furthermore, such provisions are not availed tae ranking officers. Woefully, *mo ghaol*, we must obey the Crown along with every other subject, noble or not, who has quarters tae spare the king's men." My brow knitted at Leif's explanation, discouraged as nothing could be done to change our circumstances. "We shall manage as we micht, of coorse," he suggested realistically, seeming to read my thoughts and putting my mind at ease.

"I suppose we will," I resigned as the words automatically spilled from my mouth.

"Now, ye are freed," he remarked as he finished unlacing my stays and withdrawing the garment from me, leaving me simply in my under petticoats, sheer, fine linen shift, stockings, and shoes.

"Thank you," I said gratefully as I naturally proceeded to kick off my shoes and immediately free my confined toes.

"Aye," he acknowledged with a wink and little smile. I started from him toward the bed, eager to slip myself beneath the down blankets and rest against the inviting pillows. "Shall we not remove yer stockings prior?"

"I'll keep them on since they help keep my feet warm while sleeping," I preferred, aware of him watching me crossing the room and climbing into bed after removing my petticoats.

"As ye wish," he replied simply and began undressing himself now. When he had soon finished, he easily gathered my clothing with his and merely placed it all on the long foot bench at the footboard. Then, rounding the post as he approached his bedside, he turned the covers down while stepping on the lower bed step and eased himself over the mattress, replacing the blankets over himself as he comfortably lay back with his head sinking into the fluffy down pillows.

I turned my gaze toward him, admiring the light hairs on his bare chest. Catching my eyes, a warm grin curled his lips, and he reached an arm around me, drawing me snugly against his spooning naked body. Fitting me comfortably against him, his arm slipped over my waist as his large palm naturally found and cupped my plump breast beneath my shift. I felt his lips press against the back of my crown in a tender kiss, and I entwined my fingers with his as they rested over my breast.

"*Tha gràdh agam ort, àille dhubh,*" he uttered softly.

"I love you too, Leif," I whispered. His fingers tightened with mine as he continued holding my breast.

Subsequent words drifted from us, and we settled in silence in each other's arms, peacefully spooning. The tiredness from our day's journey easily overcame us now, and my eyes helplessly closed as his breathing immediately became regular with sleeping. The feeling of being home again at *Taigh Gràs*, in each other's arms as we had been before, encased me in the comfort of secure bliss as sleep claimed me.

Sixteen

∽

The sensation of tender, titillating kisses trailing over my lips, face, and neck carefully roused me from deep sleep. Opening my drowsy eyes, Leif's amorous, gently smiling gaze was recognized hovering over me. Illuminated as an apparition in the moonlight, still escaping through the opening of the slightly drawn velvet drapes over the windows, exposed portions of his shadowed face. The blue incandescent beams partly bathing him allowed me to catch the heated glint in his eyes, along with the indolent grin curving his lips as he stared dreamily at me when he raised his gaze after bestowing kisses.

I sleepily smiled at him, hearing the low-burning fire still crackling near the hearth. He stirred, shifting his body completely over mine and bringing his elbows beside my head, supporting himself as he caged me beneath him. Sensing the weight of himself resting over me, he held his unwavering gaze to mine without a word as he stared into my eyes. My palms naturally stole around his back, and I lightly raked my nails down the length of his spine to the tailbone, returning to the nape of his neck and over again. As I slowly trailed my raking fingers along his bare back, the heat emitting from his body warmed me as my flesh began to burn. Softly leaning his lips over mine, he began kissing me, and my desire grew as my breath was stolen, fully awakening me.

"Do ye nae longer care tae slumber?" he muttered between his kisses.

"I can't go back to sleep now," I gasped as his tongue dove deeply into my mouth.

"Why?" he heaved over my lips as I received his yearning kiss and began kissing him back in response. "Yoo're stirred." His voice rasped and was husky, and his breathing was uneven when he broke from kissing me. He abruptly kissed me again before I could answer, shoving his tongue deeply into my mouth.

"Yes," I admitted when his tongue withdrew, and air filled my lungs again. His lips smiled over mine, and I knew he was satisfied to know.

My fingers seeped into his long, silky hair, obscuring his face, and drew it behind his shoulders, clearing the way for our continuing kisses. Pressing a knee between my legs, he wedged himself between my thighs, urging them far apart. The sudden sensation of his hard organ pressing firmly against my pubis liquified me, and the strange aching embedded within the depths between my legs ignited.

"Leif," I inhaled sharply the second I caught my breath when he released his lips from mine again.

"Aye," he muttered in a gravelly tone, agreeing, now feeling the hem of my shift hitching up my thighs by his determined hand. The barrier was immediately removed from my hips, and the heat radiating from his naked loins seared the bare flesh on my pubis as his groin pressed against mine. His hand continued raising my shift higher along my body until it was entirely withdrawn, and I was bare to his satisfaction.

Warmed by his naked body, I began feeling as if I were suddenly on fire, and my blood turned molten in my veins while the liquid heat between my thighs emerged, beginning to run from within. His palm passed over the cushion of my breast when his fingers seized my nipple and proceeded to toy with it. Tugging and squeezing, the sensation was rough enough to ripen it to his liking and oddly stimulated me with pleasure through the mild discomfort of a little pain.

Meeting his satisfaction, his mouth dove over my protruding nipple, drawing it far inside, and began rolling it over the coarseness of his tongue, tenderizing it further. Hardening more while he ravenously sucked and suckled, my nipple became nearly too sensitive to bear as it was swelling by the passion of his attention. A little whine eluded my lips as I anxiously raked my fingers through his unbound hair. Ignoring my whimper, his tongue continued delighting over my nipple, working it until it was tender. Finally releasing it, his salivating mouth withdrew, leaving warm dampness behind, and it suddenly chilled in the atmosphere as I glanced at what he had done. Fully erect and swollen as a ripened berry, it angrily throbbed, and the pleasure was strangely great.

A moan escaped me, and his devouring lips took my other nipple. Insatiable groans eluded him as his suckling mouth fervently toyed with and manipulated it like the first, impelling my desire for him to satiate his need for me however he wished while my core burned for him. So, I arched my back, encouraging his torment of me, and he indulged himself with my nipple as he willed, to my delight. Turning it tender as it ached, small anxious whines passed through my lips as my breath was stifled from the pleasure and pain.

Satisfied at last, he freed my second nipple as it achingly throbbed, feeling swollen and tender, and I knew it resembled the previous one: ripe to his content. Before I could catch my breath from the deliriously aching he'd caused me, his lips abruptly smothered mine in a plunging kiss. Dancing his tongue again with mine in a deeply rousing kiss, well mounted over me, I sensed his palm moving lower between us when I recognized him seizing his large, swollen shaft.

Stroking the head of his organ along my cleft, I was spreading open. The head kissed my clitoris, and my nerves electrified, catching my breath in my throat. He began stroking it over my plump flesh, and I sensed it awakening while he was growing slick from my dampness. But his breathing quaked when he began brushing the tip of his shaft with longer strokes from the beginning of my clitoris toward the back of my cleft, locating my entrance, and my breath shortened with yearning anticipation.

Over and over, he rubbed the surface of my inviting flesh, growing slicker, until he suddenly surged into me and entered me. Naturally, wrapping my legs around his hips and securing him, my arms came over his shoulders as my body welcomed him into my depths. He plunged to my end on the first thrust, forcing the wind from my lungs in a gasp. A simultaneous groan eluded him from titillation, and he began moving in deliberate, measured thrusts.

On every ebb, he closely pulled out completely before diving to the hilt in return, filling me wholly and pushing my breath from me as he met my cervix and jarred my uterus. Arousing my core with each penetration, my mind began to float as the sensation of him driving himself into me like an unyielding piston purposefully created a euphoric dream taking me over. Absorbed by delirium expanding over my senses, my eyelids drooped as I could hardly keep them open, and I gazed into his eyes through the slits of mine, catching the spellbound euphoria reflecting in his own dreamy eyes staring back at me.

"*Uh*, Leif," I panted incoherently as my climbing need became begging.

"I hunger fur ye, loove. I am enslaved. I relish it with glory," he uttered with each breath while plunging far between my thighs.

His shoulders grew moist to the touch, and tiny beads of perspiration had formed on his brow. He was an inferno and igniting me on fire with him as I felt the burning heat consuming my flesh while witnessing the escalating rhapsody in our joined gazes. My skin grew moist, too, and the well within me poured as the sounds of his thrusts emanating between my thighs audibly resonated between us. As he worked me, he now glided with remarkable ease, and the air permeated the heavy scent of our love-making as it mixed with the aroma of flames in the fireplace.

"I am drowning within yer soul," he strove, saying in scraping tones as his voice and breath shook.

"I'm coming to yours," I whispered between pants.

"Receive me," he expressed desperately.

"I am."

"Aye."

"Yes."

"Yer flesh cradles me."

"I love the way you feel."

"It adores me."

"Yes."

"I am beholden tae it."

"Take it as you like."

"I'm humbled that ye permit me."

"I love you."

"I loove ye more," he said, speaking softly.

"I want you in me forever."

"I must remain," he panted as his hot breath caressed my lips.

"Yes," I breathed.

"Aye."

"I die when you're not."

"As do I."

"What will we do when we're apart?" I gasped wondrously.

"Remain as we are till time's end, fur we shall never part," he replied euphorically as I saw the intoxication in his eyes.

"I'm glad," I managed to say between breaths.

"I as weel."

"I'll never have to miss you again."

"Never."

"Then, I'm especially happy."

"You will have me forever."

"Good."

"We shall always be."

"Yes, we will," I gasped as he continued thrusting into me, believing this to the pit of my soul.

"Have me, now."

"I will."

"I am arriving."

"So am I."

"Glorious," he heaved.

His lips suddenly melded to mine. Fervently kissing me, the raging fire burning within him while thrusting was known as his scorching tongue lustfully rolled over mine, sucking the life out of my lungs. Losing ourselves to the other as he was delving into my depths and dominating me with zealous kissing, absolute sublimity closely appeared on the horizon.

My uterus churned as my body accommodated his massive shaft, impaling me the moment he gripped my legs and crimped them against me. I immediately cried out while the air was sharply forced from me as he rammed himself into the ends of my depths. The feeling of him ripped through me as if he'd abruptly forged into my womb and kissed the core of my heart. Penetrating me more, he deeply hammered me again, striking the same location, causing me to cry out, and I knew his intent was to merge our souls. Bearing the pain with each audible cry, he was achieving our amalgamation as extreme pleasure gave rise, and my eyes began to tear. So, I submitted entirely, letting him use me as he endeavored, manifesting the existence of our union into unyielding reality.

My organs rolled as he pushed himself into me, and I sensed my stomach rise and fall on each thrust. Grunts escaped his panting lips as anxious moans came from mine. Then, my internal muscles began tensing around him while his shaft continued to move, and the sensation intensified with cogent precision on every measured thrust.

Suddenly, my nerves electrified, and I jolted as fierce shockwaves gripped me. Searing electricity charged every nerve in my body, and I shuddered as my depths rocked with vibrant pulses reverberating my being. As Leif instantly released my crimped legs, they swung around his hips, and I tightened them, securing him in place to savor the embedded feeling, ecstatically shaking my core, he imparted on me.

Soaring through euphoria as I climaxed, I seemed to hover in a realm of absolute bliss as I scarcely heard Leif's roar upon my neck when he erupted into me and joined my flight. As I cried out in rhapsody, his feral growl resonated throughout the room as he froze in my arms, and we were together as he commanded.

Fused together, we seemed to marvelously hover a second more in ecstasy before gliding down on its wings.

After I drifted back down from euphoria, I realized we had landed back into reality together when I felt his ragged breathing warmly caressing my neck as he lay silent and still in my embrace. He nearly let all of his weight smother me as he barely supported himself over his elbows while his chest greatly expanded and contracted upon his quick breathing. He drew in large breaths while settling, and I remained motionless with him, blissfully aware of his presence continuing to exist inside me.

While embracing him, I sensed he wasn't going to disengage from me just yet as he lay lifeless over me. Therefore, I knew his desire to hold himself within my depths for as long as time allowed. So, we stayed joined in peace listlessly.

When he grew flaccid, I began feeling the flow of his heated essence escaping me as my chasm forced him out and finally closed. The warmth of his seed mixing with my dampness drained past my thighs, moistening him also as his groin continued resting on mine. He stirred only slightly as he withdrew his face from the bend of my neck and raised his lips to mine. He began placing small, gentle kisses over them with eulogizing tenderness.

"Pulse of my heart," he muttered over my lips between kisses. I smiled as his lips covered mine, loving that I was the reason for his happiness and how I loved him the same. "So we are," he said softly after a kiss.

"So we are," I whispered, echoing his heart. He raised his gaze, and our eyes met. The adoration in his gaze was blatant and raw while he stared transfixed into my eyes without another word. The silence between us was all there while lying there together, staring affectionately into each other's eyes. I felt the careful pads of his thumbs warmly stroking the sides of my cheeks as he continued quietly gazing at me. There was nothing left to be said as I also perceived deep satisfaction and contentment in his soft eyes.

At last, when he decided, Leif shifted from me onto his side. Slipping an arm beneath me, he pulled me over his chest, laying me stretched on top of him, and flung a blanket around us. I tucked my head comfortably into the curve of his neck as he secured an arm around me, now cocooned together beneath the blanket. Crooking his other arm behind his head against the pillows, he came to rest, and I closed my eyes, feeling the throbbing of his pulse against my lips as my face contentedly hid in the bend of his neck. The beating of his heart synchronized with mine, and our breathing harmonized as we soon returned to sleep.

Seventeen

⸎

Brilliant sunbeams entering the windows passed through the partly drawn drapes the next morning, awakening me as I found myself alone in bed. As the cobwebs from sleep began to disappear, my consciousness grew clear. I indolently glanced around the room from the pillows and blankets warmly tucked around me. Leif was nowhere to be seen, nor was he heard in the privy closet feet away. So, I assumed he'd already risen at dawn as usual and began his day, leaving me to rest at my leisure.

Noticing my shift draped over the footboard, I sat up from the pillows, displacing the blankets as they slipped down my naked breast to my lap. I leaned and crawled toward the foot of the bed, grabbing it. Swiftly throwing it over my head and shoving my arms through the sleeves, modestly covering myself, I then climbed out of bed as my stockinged-covered toes met the cool oak floor from the bed step. A slight chill had settled in the air as the fire had died down in the fireplace, I noticed as I made my way toward the privy closet.

When I came into the closet, I immediately sat on the chamber pot to urinate, relieving the tiny ache in my bladder. After I finished, I moved toward the dry sink and poured fresh, cold water from the ewer into the second washbasin, which had remained unused. I then proceeded to cleanse myself with the leftover bar of soap and fresh washcloth positioned beside my basin.

Afterward, leaving the privy closet and returning to the bedroom, I went toward the bed again, where a gold cord hung beside the headboard by my bedside. Arriving at the headboard, I pulled it, ringing the servant bell. Then, turning away, I moved toward the warm hearth, stood before the low-burning flames, warming my limbs, and waited.

Soon, the door creaked open, and my attention turned toward it as it carefully widened the doorway with Mercy appearing. She mindfully passed through the doorway and entered the room, closing the door behind herself and sealing us in before facing me. I smiled, glad to see her. She modestly smiled, and the kindred look in her eyes was apparent. Politely curtsying, she then straightened and quietly approached my armoire. Pulling the doors to it open when she arrived, she turned her gaze toward me again and mildly asked, "Good morn to you, Your Grace. What gown might you fancy fo today?"

"Good morning, Mercy," I replied, still smiling at her, and strode to where she stood. I peered inside the armoire and scanned the abundant choices of gowns. I wasn't sure which one to choose, actually, as I glanced at them. The selection was overwhelmingly close as they all appeared newly fashioned to the current style. I didn't recognize any of my older ones until she opened the third door to the armoire, revealing them to me, as she clearly seemed to have read the look on my face.

"His Grace maintained yo previous gowns yet had new ones fashioned fo you in the meantime, knowin' yo return one day," she explained.

"That's so nice of him," I realized thoughtfully.

"His Grace had it all prepared fo you, ma'am," she acknowledged, agreeing. I shifted my eyes toward her, and her gaze also turned away from the open armoire as her eyes met mine. "His Grace's faith in the Lord did not fail him. So, we is all blessed with yo presence once more, ma'am."

I stared at her for a second, catching myself from the urge to immediately hug her again. But she smiled. I smiled also, and the sentiment between us was kindred.

"Thank you, Mercy. I feel very blessed to be here and to see you again also," I said truly.

"You been sorely missed by all, ma'am. But the Lord Almighty, He do work wonders. Don't He?"

"Yes. He certainly does."

"So, all of us been rejoicin' in the kitchen this morn once the lot of us caught wind of yo return to *Taigh Gràs*," she disclosed about the servants.

"I'm as happy as you are," I replied, smiling, realizing how much I'd been admired by them when I didn't know until now, and feeling my sentiment toward them was mutual. "I'm sure I'll see everyone soon, and I'll be happy when I do."

"Yes'm," she responded, freely smiling at me now. I turned my eyes toward the many gowns presented in the armoire and skimmed them again for a moment.

"Perhaps you might choose one for me to wear today, Mercy. I'm having trouble deciding on one. If you wouldn't mind?" I suggested as I returned to looking at her.

"As you wish, ma'am. Indeed," she accepted demurely and selected a beautiful yellow-ochre silk gown as she withdrew it from the armoire. As she had gathered it into her arms, she strode toward the foot bench and carefully laid it over the large Prussian-blue, velvet cushion. "Might you care to have a bath drawn fo yoself before attiring, ma'am?" she inquired, remembering my rare habit.

"Oh, that would be so kind of you, Mercy. But no one should go through the trouble of preparing any water since I've already bathed," I suddenly informed her as I appreciated her thoughtfulness. Except, I suddenly remembered how upset she'd become once before when I took the liberty to dress myself when I first ever came to live here. I didn't wish to upset her again as I looked at her now. "Maybe I'll have a bath later this evening. If no one would mind?"

"Indeed, ma'am. Yo wish will be pleased fine," she replied easily, appearing not at all troubled.

"Thank you very much, Mercy," I said genuinely.

"No need for thanks, ma'am," she said politely. She started across the room toward my dresser, collecting petticoats along with the rest of my undergarments, and then proceeded to dress me.

When I was finally appropriately clothed, I sat at my dressing table that I'd remembered using long ago, and Mercy was ready to arrange my hair. Instead of a belabored coiffed updo that was typical in fashion here, Mercy remembered the simple French braid I once taught her how to do and had preferred outside of special occasions, as she neatly formed one perfectly centered over my head, leaving whisps of ringlet tendrils loose to frame my face, then elaborately tucking the finished braid at the nape of my neck creating a bun and secured it with diamond and ruby crystal rosette golden pins around it. Adorning my neck with a simple pearl necklace and earrings, my outfit was complete, and I appeared pleasantly ready to face my day.

Thanking Mercy for her work, I stood from my seat at the dressing table, and we left the bedroom together. Pacing through a series of hallways, we arrived at the grand staircase and proceeded down the steps. I was gladly looking forward to seeing the servants again and anticipated going into the kitchen to greet them when we reached the first floor, but Mercy continued guiding me in the opposite direction toward the dining room instead.

When entering the room, she parted from me and withdrew altogether as Leif's eyes simultaneously adhered to mine while immediately noticing my appearance. He was surrounded by a full table of military men in discussion, waiting to be served their breakfast. His face suddenly brightened from the conversation he was having with one of the men seated closest to him by the head where he sat when he realized me. Promptly straightening from his chair, Leif dropped his conversation and strode toward me. The mild grin curving his lips reflected the warmth in his eyes as I noticed them glinting like deep blue sapphire gems when he came standing before me.

Discussions around the table swiftly curtailed as all eyes turned toward us. The room was now silent as I sensed his fingers gently wrapping around my elbow. As his smile turned from me, he began guiding me toward my empty chair at the foot of the table, opposite where he sat. I self-consciously felt aware that I'd become the center of attention by everyone's obvious stares that had stilled on me while we moved toward the table.

As Leif escorted me deeper into the room toward my chair, the men instantly stood from their seats and remained standing. They quietly observed us as we approached, and he pulled my chair out from the table for me to be seated the moment we arrived. After I was comfortably seated near Amity, he stepped away from me, returning to the head of the table, where he easily sat. The rest of the men then returned to sitting in their chairs when I caught Leif subtly smiling at me while gazing in my direction. I automatically smiled as my lips curled sheepishly, conscious of the men maintaining their eyes on me as they witnessed my reaction to him. His smile broadened, and the subtle grin on his face grew.

Aware of his flirtation, I recognized the boldness in his intentional gaze, and suddenly, I couldn't maintain his eyes anymore as my shyness was suddenly compelled. So, I dropped my gaze from him as I glanced at the edge of the table before me. But my eyes abruptly returned to his, automatically looking at him as if he'd determined me, and I saw that his stare had remained. As his eyes fixed on mine again, the knowing grin remained confident on his lips.

"Men," he began, garnering their attention, "I present my wife, Her Grace, Duchess of Monteith." His proud look was also apparent as he continued gazing at me, causing me to smile modestly at him again as their eyes returned to me.

"A great honor, Your Grace," said the man in a well-spoken London accent. He was sitting closest to Leif, with whom he'd been conversing earlier upon my arrival. When he spoke, he spoke for the other men who were also curiously gazing at me.

"Your Lordship," Leif acknowledged adequately to this man as he looked at Leif again. Leif glanced at him and returned to looking at me, saying, "Permit me tae introduce tae Her Grace, His Lordship, Earl of Brimfield."

The earl turned his eyes toward me again, stood from his chair, and bowed toward me in polite acknowledgment.

"It's nice to meet you, Lord Brimfield," I politely replied to him.

"The pleasure is entirely mine," he said, keeping his steady gray eyes on me. He was recognizably a handsome man, I noted, seeming Leif's age, with rich auburn hair that appeared thick and straight, lightly salted silver, tied back into a queue with a wide black silk ribbon, unblemished skin, and straight nose. Although, his lips were quite thin, making him appear as if he could have the potential to be insensitive. Despite this observation, though, the interested reception in his staring eyes was perceivable, coinciding with the charmed smile on his face, which leaned to his overall appeal.

Shifting my eyes back toward Leif as his gaze steadily remained on me, the admiration in his eyes was clearly visible. He proceeded to introduce the rest of the individual men sitting around the table, consisting of lieutenants and captains. Except that Lord Brimfield carried the highest rank as colonel, I had also learned. After introductions, servants appeared in the room, serving tea with light courses for breakfast. As I made eye contact with the servants serving me, furtive smiles of recognition and appreciation were exchanged between us, and I knew they were finally happy to see me, just as I was to see them.

After one of the serving maids, Mable, poured my tea and placed it before me, a friendly grin modestly passed between us before she withdrew to pour Amity's tea. I reached for my full teacup to sip before eating the boiled egg presented to me. After my sip, I carefully replaced the cup over its saucer, aware of the eyes on me in everyone's silence. As I took my fork to eat my egg, I glanced at Leif with his attention now contentedly eating his meal without speaking, when I realized His Lordship had witnessed my exchange with Mable, as he had been observing me from across the table while being served his food, when our eyes met.

Glancing away from him, I returned to looking at the breakfast I was about to enjoy. A conversation between the men resumed, and I began eating, glad to be sharing this meal with Amity as we sat near each other, exchanging pleasant smiles. As discussions around the table matured during breakfast, Lord Brimfield had Leif's attention while speaking as they ate. It seemed the conversation between them was friendly, as their demeanors and exchanges were familiar, given the ease with which they discussed, bantered, and laughed. But as the meal progressed, while I quietly ate like Amity, listening inattentively to various discussions, I intermittently sensed a pair of eyes observing me.

Expecting to meet Leif's gaze, Lord Brimfield met my eyes instead as I unexpectedly caught his surreptitious glance in my direction. I realized then that he had been stealing glances at me throughout the meal. Returning my attention to the diminishing food on my plate, I began to feel slightly uncomfortable as I wondered about the reason for his continuous stare. I wondered whether he had detected something about me that seemed strange or wrong, which reawakened my former insecurities about being a misfit here. But when I glanced up from my plate again and noticed the young mid to late twenty-something-year-old, sandy blonde-haired, blue-eyed Captain Berkley sitting at the middle of the table, turning an inquisitive eye on me after glancing at Lord Brimfield, I knew he was aware of His Lordship's glimpses also.

"Might I mention, quite delicately, to Her Grace, as we are speaking of savages, presently, that I pray her experience whilst within their captivity was of a mild sort," Captain Berkley said to me in a considerate manner, as I noticed his London accent also. Leif suddenly quieted from speaking further to Lord Brimfield and shot a glare toward Captain Berkley. My glance bounced between Leif and the captain as I quickly understood the topic was not only delicate but taboo to address. The comfortable look on Leif's face abruptly disintegrated as he now sternly looked at the captain without any hint of amusement. But the captain glanced at Leif and realized his faux pas, then looked at me again. The look on the captain's face, however, didn't seem at all alarmed by his mistake. Instead, he merely gazed at me unfazed, waiting for my reply as the conversation around the table died down with everyone focused on Leif and me.

"Thank you, Captain Berkley, for your thoughtful sentiment," I said politely, concealing my nervousness as Leif's emitting tension of disapproval was clearly sensed around the table and marked.

"I also pray that she is well," Captain Berkley continued as he maintained his eyes on me in spite of Leif's feelings.

"I'm well, Captain Berkley. Thank you," I replied demurely, realizing this particular man to be considerably bold in his assertions as he lightly trod the narrow path toward disregarding Leif, on the verge of insulting him.

"That will be all toward Her Grace, Captain Berkley," Leif interposed sharply, stoutly staring him down. Seeming stymied, the captain returned obedient eyes toward Leif.

"Indeed, Your Grace. Pray, accept my apology as I meant no harm," Captain Berkley responded with a nod, deferring to Leif as he also sounded subdued in his response.

"Should Captain Berkley be interested in deliberating such affairs, micht he be so inclined tae inquire of my experience amongst the Indians, as I retain tales aplenty tae wet his inquisitive-ness?" Leif questioned instead, dismissing the captain's apology. I got the distinct impression just then that Leif didn't regard Captain Berkley too highly—if Leif instead didn't like him at all. Captain Berkley didn't readily respond, appearing suddenly uncomfortable as he was directly placed on the spot. A nervous grin faintly crossed his face. "I am willing tae entertain, Captain. Inquire as ye please." The tone in Leif's voice was provoking, matching the annoyance and goading in his unwavering eyes while looking at him. Captain Berkley lightly cleared his throat and faintly furrowed his brow, appearing a little thrown off-kilter.

"Er, I presume it may please me to know of their savagery as one has been led to believe of their unholy capability of it," Captain Berkley stated, recovering from uncertainty.

"I see." Leif smirked at him, appearing ironic.

"Yes," Captain Berkley responded simply.

"Have ye ever witnessed a man being eviscerated?" Leif asked plainly.

"I have—for treason, Your Grace," Captain Berkley answered.

"Would such an act be holy?" Leif asked. The captain paused momentarily as his brow furrowed, appearing suddenly upended in thought by Leif's quick logic.

"Yet, what is it that you mean, Your Grace?" Captain Berkley asked curiously, remaining respectful in his tone.

"Merely answer the question, Captain, as I repeated it directly. Is the act of evisceration a holy one?" Leif replied instead.

"As the Crown mandates it, it is considered acceptable," the captain answered.

"Aye." Leif nodded. "Then, would not the Indians' mandate tae tear a living man's heart out from his breast and devour it before himself tae see as he perishes be equally found acceptable tae them? Fur the act in truth is not any more holy than being torn from limb tae limb with one's innards cut from one's belly and strewn whilst one still breaths, that is mandated by the Crown."

Captain Berkley suddenly paused again while looking at Leif, as he appeared not to know quite how to respond.

"Micht thaur be anither inquiry of me, captain?" Leif prodded with a deadpan expression, breaking the captain's spell.

"Is this what you have witnessed yourself from them, Your Grace?" Captain Berkley resumed further asking, sounding revolted, unmasking his shock.

"Aye," Leif replied flatly.

"'Twould be unholy of the highest order to exercise cannibalism, that cannot be likened to what the Crown mandates," Captain Berkley denigrated disgustedly, unquestionably appalled.

"Their committing cannibalism is irrelevant tae the wider point, as ye have missed it entirely," Leif said.

"Then, I beg His Grace to clarify his gist to me," Captain Berkley responded.

"The gist is that the dismemberment of men, be whoever commits it, is savagery at its core and is unholy in the eyes of our Lord as it defiles His image created unto us. Suffice it tae say, Europe's ways are none the better by its own brutality, comparatively, despite the presumed esteem of its sensibilities and sophistication. Therefore, the superior perception from Europe is flawed, as barbarity exists across nations, consequently befitting us all," Leif elaborated.

Captain Berkley suddenly became quiet again and stared at Leif, seeming stumped for another reply.

"I might say to His Grace, as I still contend, that our ways remain better than others removed from England," Captain Berkley said thoughtfully.

"In whit manner, precisely?" Leif challenged.

"Consuming a man is not civilized, purely. Nor is it Christian. Therefore, it is unholy and is demeaning to humanity," Captain Berkley said further, hanging on to his aversion and appall.

"The example of torture is indisputably uncivilized, thereby being Godless by nature. Thus, deeming it cruel and unusual to humanity completely," Leif responded sharply.

"But I beg to say that it is necessary," Captain Berkley differed.

"Fur whit reason?" Leif countered directly.

"For the sake of order," the captain said.

"Order?"

"Correct."

"Tae submit the will of men above others," Leif replied, understanding the captain's meaning.

"To other men who can better determine their benefit," Captain Berkley supported.

"As the ones who acquire absolutism over the meek invariably persecute them fur their benefit. This is the order ye mean?"

"Yet, what else would I mean? As it would, chaos amongst men would reign otherwise. There is a reason why the structure of our society is balanced betwixt men whose stations are above others so that those who are lesser will go without want."

"Why should they not want?"

"They are incapable."

"Of whit are they not capable?"

"Providing for themselves."

"Grant a man an education, and he is freed from bondage. Micht that not apply tae ye, captain, as ye address me?"

"But you have permitted my speaking to you, Your Grace. For which, I am grateful."

"As I am more awaur than ye," Leif said, cornering the captain in his argument.

"Yes, Your Grace," Captain Berkley said, appearing reluctant to admit this to Leif as his lips became invisible when he pinched them.

"All men want, Captain. As much as yerself, should we confront sincerity?" Leif said, speaking the truth.

"I beg, Your Grace when I might say that, I would not believe myself to be so presumptuous."

"But yer presumption remains."

"I am most genuine, however, Your Grace."

"Of coorse, ye are. Yer arrogance is upon complete display, nonetheless." Leif smirked at him, and Captain Berkley obviously appeared chagrinned. "I dinnae fault yer displaying it, as yoo're being honest in doing so." Leif paused, and so did Captain Berkley as he watched Leif bring his teacup to his lips and sip, then return his cup to rest perfectly over the saucer. "Are ye a God-fearing man, Captain Berkley?" Leif resumed asking, continuing his steady eyes on the young man.

"I am, of course, Your Grace," he answered unquestionably.

"I see."

"Why might Your Grace inquire?"

"Have ye ever harmed a man at all, be it just or not?" Leif pursued inquiring instead of answering him.

"I have been spared from killing a man, yet I have punished one. If this is what you are inquiring, Your Grace?" Captain Berkley informed him.

"Aye." Leif nodded. "Yoo're fortunate tae this point."

"Yes," the captain agreed.

"Whit incorporated yer punishment?"

"Imprisonment. Starvation. Flogging—the like," Captain Berkley mentioned indifferently, shrugging a little.

"How severe was yer punishment?" Leif asked, appearing genuine about the question. Captain Berkley shifted uneasily in his chair, attempting to straighten his posture more upright.

"I saw a man's ribs once," he confessed hesitantly.

"From starvation?"

"No, Your Grace."

"I see."

"Yes, Your Grace," Captain Berkley disclosed. I got the distinct impression that details of this conversation would have been divulged if Amity and I weren't at the table. Instead, Leif didn't press, and Captain Berkley didn't reveal further.

"The man didnae perish?" Leif's brow subtly lifted, hinting at his surprise.

"The man was willful," Captain Berkley replied with a look of disdain on his face, remembering the event.

"Mayhap, 'twas God's will in spite of the man's own which spared his certain death, condemning yer lack of mercy," Leif said, looking critically at the captain.

Captain Berkley suddenly became quiet again and stared at Leif, speechless. A lull of heavy silence descended between them, which seemed only amplified by the silence of the other men seated around the table. To say the air felt uncomfortable was an understatement, as Leif intensely looked at the captain for a lingering moment. That silence only broke when the captain turned his gaze away from Leif and shifted it down toward the little remaining food on his plate before himself.

Leif gripped his teacup again and quietly sipped from it, staring at the captain until he was satisfied with the sip of tea taken. The other men continued quietly finishing their food as well, and the impression I received of Captain Berkley just then was that he was, in fact, a brutal man—despite his well-groomed etiquette.

I brought my teacup to my lips and sipped also, wondering if anyone else was going to speak to dispel the discomfiture when I noticed Captain Miller, sitting directly across from Amity and on my opposite side, furtively glancing at her as she was contentedly finishing the last of her cranberry glazed crumpet. He was fairly handsome, also. Blue-eyed and young with chestnut hair, he seemed to share Captain Berkley's age, and I wondered if that wasn't all he shared with Captain Berkley as I considered whether he was as cruel a man as he was.

When Captain Miller caught me observing his glances toward Amity, he suddenly flushed with noticeable embarrassment. He abruptly turned his eyes away from me toward Lieutenant Johnson, sitting beside Amity, instead of maintaining his gaze on her. Lieutenant Johnson looked up from finishing the last remnants of food on his plate, meeting Captain Miller's eyes. Captain Miller sharply turned his eyes from him as they nervously bounced toward mine again. A small, reticent smile swept his face, and I reciprocated a modest little smile of my own.

"I, er, I have read Master Samuel Adams' and Master James Otis' Circular Letter," he began saying awkwardly in the same London accent. This interrupted the strained silence in the room, began a new conversation, and suddenly acquired everyone's attention.

"Have you, now?" Lord Brimfield suddenly inquired, lifting his brow and appearing interested.

"I have, Your Lordship," Captain Miller confirmed in a calm tone as they looked at each other.

"Well, now. Might that not be intriguing?" Lord Brimfield replied.

"What is your opinion of it, Miller?" Captain Berkley asked decisively, sounding mocking as he turned an annoyed look to Captain Miller. No doubt he was chaffed from the conversation he'd just had with Leif.

"Er, well, it appears to be in reaction to the Townshend Acts," Captain Miller responded, still appearing awkward as he didn't quite answer Berkley's question directly.

"Of course, it is in reaction to the acts," Captain Berkley scoffed at Miller. "Yet, you did not say what you believe of their letter. So, we remain curious as to how you regard it. Do you not have an opinion?"

"I cannot say that I have an opinion. No," Captain Miller answered him.

"You leave me perplexed, for every man has an opinion," Berkley said ironically.

"Then, I regret disappointing you," Miller replied.

"You merely care not to express it, for I am certain that you are

a keen man with many opinions," Berkley countered with dissatisfaction.

"My opinions do not matter," Miller said confidently. Berkley
suddenly paused and narrowed his eyes on him, catching Miller's
pointed remark.

"In which case, merely explain to us the letter, Captain
Miller," Lord Brimfield requested.

"As you wish, Your Lordship," Miller politely replied to Lord
Brimfield with a single accompanying nod. "The letter expresses
subjects' sentiments resenting the Crown's latest measures pressed
upon them. Their belief is that the Crown's laws are illegal, as this
colony is not represented in Parliament. Furthermore, they pose
that instead, the colony should tax itself as subjects here are represented in their own assembly."

"The Devil!" Berkley sneered with a curse under his breath,
faintly shaking his head. Lord Brimfield turned a curious eye on
Berkley.

"Evidently, Captain Berkley has an opinion. Would you not
care to share it, captain, as it may be considered?" Lord Brimfield
asked him directly.

"Very well, I shall oblige, Your Lordship. Firstly, I consider it
insufferable that these particular subjects would insult the Crown
through their impudence after all it has provided for them since
their inception. The latest example provided their protection from
our enemy, France. This, England had done for them, has bank-
rupted the empire without so much as a nod of gratitude on their
behalf by supplementing a portion of the cost. Instead, the thanks
we receive for our efforts in their best regard is their treason exhibited in this dastardly circular making its rounds about the city,
expressing their desire to be represented in Parliament with the
intent to leverage themselves with equal power. Have they no
notion what this will do to the empire? Disorder will take shape
and dissolve the empire entirely!" Captain Berkley expressed
animatedly.

"But, the governor, Sir Bernard, has dissolved the Assembly as a consequence of this letter, which has effectively inhibited their ability to govern themselves at all, restoring the Crown's authority over them as they now have been silenced," Miller rebutted, introducing a new fact.

"Yes, and whilst we are here in support of the Crown, its initiatives will be properly realized," Berkley responded sharply. "Sir Bernard will not reinstate the Assembly. You may place your bet upon it."

"Not to account for the stifled ire that is certain to exist as a result of their inability to express their grievances, our mission may prove more difficult than first perceived," Miller recognized astutely.

"Precisely why the Crown sends more of our men," Berkley said, obviously, giving Miller an absurd look.

"The rats will scurry," Lieutenant Brand remarked nearly under his breath, perceivably confident.

"With certainty," Berkley agreed, supporting Lieutenant Brand's sentiment. "We are feared for a reason, and we shall remain so till they understand their place within the empire."

"Stimulating perspectives, officers. I am continually pleased by the hearty debates brought amongst you. Pray, proceed as I am ready to listen more," Lord Brimfield said interestedly, reinserting himself into the conversation. He proceeded to introduce another question to them concerning Parliament's affairs after Captain Berkley's snide remark under his breath regarding Captain Millar's leniency.

I shifted my eyes toward Leif, beginning to tune out of the continuing conversation, and noticed he appeared to have already done the same, indifferent to what was being said since he had taken his broadsheet and buried his head in it, quietly reading. Apparently absorbed in his reading, I decided to excuse myself from the table, taking Amity with me. Though she patiently sat primly at the table throughout the discussions, I felt she was as ready as I to leave the table when I found myself disinterested in listening to any more current political affairs because it had begun to unsettle me.

Pushing aside my encroaching thoughts of what I knew was to come between England and her colonies, I was relieved to escape the dining room with Amity as we passed the threshold and entered the hallway.

Eighteen

After I had escaped the continuing discussion at the breakfast table with Amity and proceeded through the corridor together, Amity expressed her interest in spending time in the kitchen with the cook and the other maids. This reminded me of when she used to do this fondly as a little girl. Now, while she was going to stay in their company, she intended to occupy herself with needlepoint. Thinking that I'd like to take the same opportunity and accompany her to finally visit the maids also, I suddenly felt a hand carefully slipping around my upper arm, arresting my steps as I was lightly pulled aside. Amity simultaneously ceased her pacing, too, when we both swung our gazes around ourselves and recognized Leif's appearance, catching me off guard. With a relaxed expression now on his face, I wondered about the reason for his sudden presence when I unexpectedly looked at him as Amity contentedly decided to resume without me through the hallway, heading for the kitchen.

"I observed ye take yer leave from the dining chamber," he said as Amity's footsteps were heard diminishing from us through the passageway.

"Was I rude to leave the table too soon?" I asked worriedly, suddenly realizing that I might have been while looking apologetically at him.

"Nae matter. Ye may take yer liberty as ye will tae do as ye please," he excused easily without looking at all disturbed.

"Then, is everything all right?" I wondered, feeling my brow knitting with concern, considering something else might have troubled him instead.

"Bring yourself at ease, fur I merely wish tae inquire whether ye have a care tae flee with me, presently?" The look on his face was immediately inviting, contradicting his previously irritated mood while dining at the table. I was quickly relieved as I noticed the mild grin subtly curving his lips and the warm glimmer in his eyes.

"Escape?" I asked, a little confused.

"Aye," he replied, giving a little nod, clearly anticipating with the lift of his brow and broadening grin.

"Where?" I inquired again, smiling quizzically now, curious to know what he had in mind.

"Outdoors fur a wee bit before I must mind my duties for the remaining day," he said.

"Oh," I realized, suddenly very interested. "Will we go for a walk or something?"

"Or something as in a jaunt, if ye fancy it instead," he suggested.

"Really?" I responded, filling up with happy excitement as I perceived the same emotion in his sparkling, deep blue eyes.

"Indeed."

"You mean I'll get to ride Oakley?"

"As ye wish." He winked at me, causing me to giggle when I suddenly threw my arms around his neck and lightly pecked his lips. "Yer favored breeks await ye," he said, obviously smiling and flushing, after I kissed him. I smiled widely as I leaned slightly away from him and gazed closely back into his eyes, feeling his strong arms hold me as I was lifted off my feet.

"I'll change into them right away," I said as we closely looked at each other's smiling eyes.

"I shall have the horses promptly readied and bide fur ye at the stable."

"Okay," I whispered excitedly.

"Tarry not."

"I'll be lightning speed."

"Grand." The smile on his face further widened, exposing the pearly gleam of his teeth as he nearly appeared to chuckle at my enthusiastic expression. Instead, he eased me back down to the floor onto my feet, and my arms slipped from holding him as he released me, also. "Run along lest I bed ye instead," he joked. I giggled, slightly shaking my head at him before turning away and quickly began moving through the corridor, now leaving him behind.

Sensing his eyes lingering on me as I continued farther through the hallway, I spontaneously swung a final glance over my shoulder and caught his eyes. He smiled and winked at me again, causing me to giggle more. Then, I turned and started pacing in the opposite direction. Shifting my gaze ahead of myself once more, my heart cartwheeled with excitement as I continued on my way. But remembering that I needed Mercy's help with my clothes as I changed into more comfortable attire for riding, my hunch was that I'd find her in the kitchen with the other maids, as they were likely preparing their own meal to eat later after they'd finished serving us. So, I proceeded toward the kitchen, happily anticipating my morning.

When I rounded the corner into the corridor that isolated the kitchen, cheerful voices emanated through the hallway, and I recognized their lighthearted bantering and gossiping. Continuing toward the entrance, it occurred to me that their jovial exchange centered on Leif and me being the topic of discussion, as their joy was buoyantly expressed, and I slowed my pace.

"I could not be more happy for His Grace after all them years," I heard one of the maids saying as I slowed my pacing.

"He cannot hide the pleasure upon his face," another one said, sounding suggestive, and giggles between them flittered around the room.

"Can never blame him for it, however," said someone else. I further slowed my pacing toward the kitchen after hearing them, decidedly bringing myself to a stop. I suddenly felt that I didn't want to intrude on their conversation. I considered for a second turning back, but I hesitated since I needed to acquire Mercy's help, presuming she occupied the room with them.

"Now then, you lasses, mind your tongues. We can plainly perceive his joy. No need for words about it, however. He has a right to his happiness after all them years, indeed—wretched and forlorn as he was," said an older maid's voice, pausing the other voices coming from the kitchen.

"Yet, have you not noticed how splendid Her Grace appears?" one of the maids resumed with blatant amazement in her voice.

"Indeed! I merely served her breakfast, and when my eyes lay upon her face, 'twas if the hand of time had never spoilt it." A different maid joined the conversation that I'd recognized was certain to be Mable, remembering she was the one who'd served me at the table.

Unexpectedly jolted by some fear, I realized my unchanged appearance could easily draw their suspicion of me, and suddenly, I worried about their gossiping. I didn't want them to suspect anything about me that wasn't true, which could lead to Leif's and my further strife and ultimate demise. Being considered as someone to have been touched by witchcraft, or worse—as being outright labeled a witch—terrified me. So, I remained frozen in my steps, wondering what to do: to bravely make my appearance to them with my usual confidence and kindness or not and retreat from them altogether instead.

But I'm going to have to face them sooner or later. It's impossible.

How can I ever explain away the way I look? Maybe I could simply say that I've been blessed to have the appearance of youth run in my family and hope that might suffice. People here aren't so ignorant that they aren't familiar with family traits, so I hope that I can rely on this realization when it involves my appearance.

"Imagine that?" someone remarked, equally astonished.

"Truly? For I have not yet seen Her Grace," a different maid responded curiously, impressed.

"Most certainly. She remains as beautiful and lovely as the day she first arrived. She pleasantly smiled at me upon my serving her breakfast," Mable said, thoroughly mesmerized.

"Did she do that?" someone asked, sounding stunned.

"She did, indeed," Mable confirmed. "Her manner, as pleasant as it were, remains unspoilt."

"Stunning she ain't changed, then."

"True that."

"Seemin' as she ain't changed as you say, how is it she survived them frightful Indians after all and not come out of sorts from bein' rescued from 'em by His Grace?"

"By the grace of the Lord, for which I's thankful fo it, indeed," Mercy was recognized saying in a soft-spoken tone while I was noticing that she hadn't added the fact of my hugging her last night when meeting her again.

"Indeed, Mercy. By the Lord God's grace," said the older woman among them.

"Yet, you reckon she been harmed by them Indians, nonetheless—'spite her unspoilt appearance?"

"Should she have been harmed, what might it matter? His Grace's love for her is unchanged. It has remained apparent in his melancholy all the years of her absence whilst he searched her return," the older woman responded, that I was beginning to recognize as our cook, Remember. "Never would he abandon her in his devotion. Harmed or not."

"Yet, she ain't got their infant no longer, so I'm told," a maid continued.

"No doubt the fear of lookin' at them Indians put into her soul caused her loss if she wasn't downright violated by 'em that caused it instead," another woman speculated plainly.

"A sore tragedy, indeed," lamented another, sounding deeply genuine.

"How might she ever recover with His Grace? A tragedy indeed for them both."

"We all remain sad for their great misfortune, indeed," Remember said sympathetically as her voice became soft. "To see them whole again with their babe would be a complete blessing. Nonetheless, we have her restoration with His Grace to be a great blessing unto itself."

"True that, Remember. True that," Mable recognized humbly with noticeable gratitude in her tone.

"Being the God-fearing man that he is, let us pray that the Lord Almighty continues to look upon him with favor by providing him another blessing that will bring them both joy," Remember continued.

"I shall pray for it, too, Remember."

"I also. A babe of theirs in this house would be most fitting."

"Aye, we all shall pray for it, indeed."

Overhearing their heartfelt discussion somewhat settled my fear by restoring my confidence in the genuine relationships I'd once had with each of them, and I hoped that was enough to stifle any potentially suspicious explanations of how young I still appeared in the eyes of time. Still, I also knew that there wasn't anything I could do to curb their curiosity about me, but I prayed rumors wouldn't take shape to get the better of us and destroy Leif and me in the process.

In addition, while I felt some degree of guilt about keeping the truth hidden from them, I wasn't even close to the brink of simply disclosing anything to explain myself and the situation. I realized that to enhance the chance of safeguarding myself with them. So, I resumed my pace toward the kitchen and slowly approached, mindful of them as they continued to speak. When I crossed the threshold, I demurely entered the kitchen and politely appeared with the added intent to acquire Mercy's assistance.

Immediately, everyone's eyes turned in my direction, aware that someone was entering. Noticing them also as I caught a glimpse of Amity peacefully embroidering while seated on a stretched bench belonging to the servants' dining table, my eyes landed on them as I stood by the threshold, happy to see their familiar faces.

Unexpected gazes of shock and happiness reflected in their wide eyes, and gaping smiles adhered to me as the gossip between them abruptly stopped. Appearing stricken from a single word, Remember suddenly approached, ceased before me, and curtsied, followed by the other maids surrounding me with curtsies also when other male household servants entered through the opposite door. Several of the male servants were holding full trays of used dishes and set them over the counters while noticing me, too, to their unanticipated surprise.

"Your Grace!" Remember expressed happily, fully smiling at me when she straightened from curtsying.

"Hello, Remember," I said, feeling the same happiness as I stared at her kind, maternal face, which appeared matronly now compared to the last time I'd seen her. The genuine reception in her eyes immediately put my insecurities at ease.

"'Tis a splendor to see you again, ma'am," she sputtered blithely as the male servants had crowded around also. My impulse was to embrace her, but I quickly remembered Mercy and refrained from breaking protocol since I didn't want to be forward as I thought of their comfort.

"It's wonderful seeing you again, too, Remember. Seeing everyone again is extremely nice," I replied, equally glad while glancing at everyone's staring faces. Not knowing exactly what to say, we simply looked at each other at a loss, pleasantly smiling, as the kitchen became quiet.

"You remain lovely, ma'am," Prudence remarked shyly with a kind smile.

"Indeed, you do, ma'am," Mable agreed in the same manner.

"Thank you. I tend to favor my mother's traits, and I continue to be very blessed because I see all of you again," I responded awkwardly, hoping they'd accept the reason for my unchanged appearance.

"'Tis a glorious blessing which God has bestowed upon us that you have been restored to us, indeed, ma'am," Remember agreed.

"God is very good, for certain. I'll always praise his goodness," I replied, agreeing with her.

"'Tis a miracle," Remember said.

"It is a miracle," I agreed, and we smiled at each other.

"I pray that you are well, ma'am," Elijah said sincerely from behind everyone else, where he stood with the other male servants, breaking the little lull.

"Thank you, Elijah. You're very kind. I am doing well," I replied as my eyes discovered him.

"How fortunate, ma'am. 'Tis a pleasure to know," he said, and I gave him a kind smile.

"I hope you've been well also?" I asked him.

"Aye, ma'am, I am well. I thank ya most kindly for askin'," he said with kind eyes.

"I'm so glad," I said, smiling at him. Shifting my eyes between everyone's awed gazes, I continued inquiring sincerely, "I hope all of you have been doing well, also?"

"Aye, ma'am. We all remain in good health, as you are most kind for wonderin'," Remember said graciously, speaking for the group. I smiled in response before I could say how happy I was to know this when she proceeded, "You have been sorely missed, ma'am. 'Tis a true blessing to experience your presence once more at *Taigh Gràs*. We are overjoyed, indeed."

"Thank you, Remember. I've greatly missed all of you, and my feelings for everyone are mutual," I replied.

"We recall your kindness, ma'am. Our fondness for ya shall always remain," she said. Then, she looked at me with more consideration as another thought seemed to suddenly enter her mind. "Pray, how may we serve ya, Your Grace?"

"Oh," I realized. "I wish to see Mercy, thank you."

"Indeed, ma'am. She is here, ma'am," Remember replied respectfully, informing me. She immediately turned her gaze toward the crowding maids and gave an indicating nod toward them in order to let Mercy pass between them. Everyone stepped aside for her to come through, and she approached me. Before leaving with her, though, I told everyone to have a pleasant morning. They curtsied and bowed. Then, Mercy proceeded with me out of the kitchen, and we headed for my room, where she assisted in undressing me from my gown into my riding habit, which included a more comfortable pair of trousers especially fashioned for me to suit the occasion.

Nineteen

After I had finished appropriately dressing for a morning of riding, I left the house and meandered my way past the gardens and orchards until I moved through one of the fields where the stable was located. When I arrived, Leif was waiting for me with our horses prepared, as one of our stablehand, Ethan, was ready to assist. Ethan had just walked Oakley out of the stable while leading her by the reins and stood her next to Blaze as Leif was holding him by his reins. The horses whinnied when I came near, and both Leif and Ethan suddenly noticed me approaching them.

A grin swept Leif's lips, immediately brightening his face with a twinkle in his eyes as I came to stand close beside him.

"Good morn to you, Your Grace," Ethan said with a kind smile as he bowed.

"Good morning, Ethan. It's very nice to see you," I responded.

"You as well, Your Grace," he replied respectfully after straightening. Leif promptly gave his horse's reins to him to hold, then stepped toward me, lightly clasping my elbow and guiding me toward the side of my beloved horse, Oakley.

"Up ye go, *ceisdein*," Leif said, speaking in a low, gentle voice above my head before lunging to support my foot as I pulled myself up on my horse and sat astride. I slipped my boot into the stirrup and made myself comfortable in the saddle high on her back. As I straddled Oakley, I was happy to be with her again as fond memories of riding her returned. When I was settled comfortably over her back to Leif's satisfaction, he turned for his own horse and adroitly mounted Blaze in one swift move.

Ethan gave Blaze's reins to Leif, then passed Oakley's reins to me, and I took them from his hand. As Leif naturally positioned his reins comfortably in his hand, he turned his gently smiling eyes toward me.

"Shall we?" he asked.

"Definitely," I replied, smiling, excited to share a morning with him like this, anticipating our fun.

"Then, let us proceed." He gave a little wink, turned his gaze from me, and looked ahead, urging his horse forward. I began pacing Oakley comfortably alongside Blaze. Leif and I started our horses on a walk into the nearest field, leaving Ethan behind as he returned to his chores.

As we continued onward, the stable soon fell from view along with the well-hidden mansion behind the trees. We entered the second field, which was removed from where our cows and sheep grazed and where wildflowers grew in the early spring and fall, before it was tilled for planting hay and later harvested. After passing over the next field where corn and wheat grew, we came upon a thick band of massive pine and blue spruce trees, shading us from the temperate sun, which was brilliantly shining. The air was fresh and crisp as the boughs rustled above our heads, reminding me of the time Leif and I had ridden our horses here.

I smiled and started Oakley on a light canter, incidentally leaving Leif slightly behind. He swiftly caught Blaze up to me, and we cantered our way out of the cluster of trees into the final field where our pond was discovered and currently swarming with ducks, geese, and swans swimming in the sparkling water. Passing the pond, I saw the road ahead separating our property from the Common and incited Oakley into a light gallop, with Leif immediately matching my fast pace beside me.

The cool October air briskly broke across my face, chilling my cheeks, as the joy of having fun inspired laughter from me. I glimpsed at Leif when he glanced at me and caught the bright ruddiness in his face glowing with sheer delight, while he smiled and chuckled too. Returning our gazes ahead, he followed me deep into the Common until I began slowing Oakley into a walk again, and he equally strode Blaze close beside me.

"Yoo're delighting," Leif remarked, enthusiastically grinning at me while taking note of the gleeful expression on my face.

"I am," I replied without a doubt.

"'Twas my hope fur ye this morn."

"You're so sweet. Thank you."

"My great pleasure, of coorse," he said. "If I had it upon my whim, I would spend my every wakeful moment within yer presence whilst the sun shines. Yet as the moon appears, I ken that I shall keep ye within my arms whilst I dream."

I felt my cheeks warming and gave him a little smile in response, suddenly incapable of knowing what to say as diffidence swept through me. I abruptly broke, discerning the obvious captivation in his steady gaze when I turned my eyes down toward the reins I was holding. He unexpectedly shifted in his saddle and my eyes immediately returned to him, observing as he deftly eased himself off Blaze down onto his feet. Wondering what he was doing as he shortly stepped toward Oakley, he reached his hands upward as I sensed him seizing my waist and began pulling off my horse toward him.

"What are you doing?" I asked curiously as my hands naturally came over his shoulders to steady myself as he drew me forth.

"Let us stroll, presently," he said, bringing me to stand on the ground before him.

"Okay," I agreed, wishing we could walk now, too. Grabbing

both reins to our horses, he started leading us on a leisurely pace over the short grass that had begun turning hues of yellow ochre by the fall season, with our horses trailing behind us. A flock of sheep was grazing a distance away from us when I turned my glance and noticed beyond them a dense cluster of numerous white canvas-pitched tents before the gallows raised on the hill. I wondered about the massive collection of tents as we entered a band of towering evergreens, now moving in the opposite direction.

"Soldiers camp haur as barracks and billeting quarters are at a scarcity about the city," Leif explained when I asked him about it.

"Oh," I realized abstractedly. "How much more military will come here?"

"As much as warranted," he answered. I turned a worried look up at him, and he met my gaze. The look on his face conveyed a combination of encouragement and assuredness with persuasive consideration. "Peer through the wood thaur." He suddenly pointed through the trees ahead of us in the direction where we were walking. I turned my gaze away from him toward where he was indicating and unexpectedly realized where we were. I instantly recognized the pond in front of us. "Do ye recall it?"

"Of course I do," I replied, smiling as I returned to looking at him. I realized he'd successfully dispelled my concern and that I was assuaged by delight. His eyes twinkled, and his lips turned upward, enhancing the glad expression on his face, warming me. I glanced away from him, turning my gaze back toward the pond. I fondly remembered that this was the pond on which we used to ice skate during my first winter here when we were newly wed.

"I missed this place," I couldn't help saying in spite of my previous worry a second ago. I observed the beautiful trees surrounding us and the water facing us, glimmering flecks of gold beneath the shining sun. I sensed him turning his gaze toward me, and I shifted my eyes from the pond, and our eyes met. I realized he was smiling at me as a result of what I said. I slipped my hand into his. He gently clasped it and proceeded, leading us through the trees as we continued strolling near the pond's shore.

Soon, a number of men, recognized as camping soldiers, were coming into view between the trees, bathing in the water, and Leif proceeded, guiding us the other way in a different direction away from them, until we emerged from the trees, cleared the pond, and entered the field again. After arriving on the field, Leif abruptly turned toward *Taigh Gràs*, and as we'd just seen the soldiers bathing, my mind began to wander.

"Leif?" I started, turning my gaze toward him as we were still holding hands along our stroll.

"Aye?" His calm, warm eyes shifted, meeting mine.

"I never asked you, and I'm so sorry, but your cousins just occurred to me now. How are they? Have they been doing well, like I truly hope?" I asked, sincerely wanting to know after so long and suddenly feeling how much I'd missed them. After remembering all that they'd done for us in assisting Leif in finding me when I'd been kidnapped by Abenaki warriors in the aftermath of Fort William Henry's fall, and taken to the Vermont wilderness. The thought of it all hit hard.

"Aye, weel. They do indeed remain comfortably in Northampton, and all are wed with bairns of their own, aplenty," Leif informed me, appearing glad that I'd asked.

"Really?"

"Aye."

"Oh, that's so nice to hear."

"My recent correspondences from Liam and Fearghus disclose the blessings of the births of their newest bairns."

"Really?"

"Aye."

"How extremely nice. It's hard for me to believe that they've been married and settled."

"Quite understood. Their wives have given them new wee

laddies. Liam's newest was welcomed late August and Fearghus' was welcomed as recently as upon the onset of this October."

"This month? Really? I had no idea."

"Aye. I received this news merely this morn."

"My goodness, what a surprise!"

"Quite."

"I'm so happy for him and his wife—and for Liam and his wife, too."

"I as weel."

"What are their wives' names?"

"Liam's is named Grace, and Fearghus' is named Jane."

"They must be happy."

"Aye, quite."

"I'm glad. How many children do they all have?"

"Do ye mean the lot of our cousins?"

"Well, I meant Liam and Fearghus. But, yes, I'm curious to know about everyone."

"Och, weel. Liam has five lassies and three laddies, whilst Fearghus has five laddies and three lassies."

"The opposite?" I responded with a smile, surprised.

"Aye." Leif returned my smile, along with the obvious look of astonishment. He then proceeded to inform me about the rest of our cousins. Regarding them, their families, and their well-being, involving their daily lives, beginning with Angus, Cole, Roy, Lachlan, and concluding with Bearnard, it was extremely nice to be updated on the latest news. I was truly happy to learn that everyone was generally in good health, leading peaceful and fulfilling lives on their farmlands in Northampton.

"Do you think we'll see them any time soon?" I asked wistfully.

"If it waur not fur the soldiers we billet, the lot of them would visit us this Christmas observance," he answered. I nodded in response and smiled at him a little, glancing away from him as I focused my eyes ahead of us while we continued strolling. My mind suddenly gravitated toward Finley, and the regrettable feeling of his loss dampened my mood. Feeling the depth of how much I missed him amplified my empathy and knowledge of how much more Leif was sure to be missing his brother, despite the erosion of time.

"I miss Finley," I uttered softly, acknowledging sadness for Leif especially.

"Ye mourn him," Leif remarked in an equally subdued voice. I returned my eyes upward toward him. The look on his face was one of sentimentality.

"Yes. I do. Very much," I replied.

"He adored ye like a bairn, though ye tried him so, like a disobedient wee folk." The corner of Leif's lips slightly tilted upward into a gentle smirk, and his eyes grinned at the thought.

"Is that so?" I couldn't help my little smile curling my lips, mirroring his, and I nearly wanted to giggle. "I don't think I was that much trouble for him, was I?"

"Ye waur quite, indeed," he differed with a little playful wink.

"I find that hard to believe."

"Certainly, ye do."

"I think you're exaggerating."

"Indeed not."

"Well, even if you believe that you're not, could you actually blame me for it?"

"I dinnae blame ye at all. Although, Fin presented me with fair warning aplenty should I take a fairy maiden fur a wife."

"He did?"

"Aye."

"Then, tell me what did he say to you in his warning?"

"He told me 'twould be I raither than ye who would transpire being one's captive, as I let yer charm enchant me from whit I kent, thereby stealing my sound faculties and rendering me naught but a fool."

"He said that to you?" A giggle eluded me as I was slightly stunned and humored by the memory of Finley's blunt past observations, and Leif chuckled.

"Most indeed."

"What else did he say to you?"

"Though he perceived my betterment because of my loove fur ye, he feared either ye would eventually steal yerself away from me tae return from whence ye came, or I should become lost in my search tae have ye returned tae me, never myself tae be seen again also."

"Are you serious?" I felt my eyes widen with shock.

"Of coorse. Why mightn't I be?"

"I mean... that's a little bit eerie—considering what we've been through. It sounds a little too insightful. Did he tell you that he had a premonition or something?"

"Nae." Leif shook his head. "He was one tae merely regard whatever was presented tae him and drew forth an opinion."

"But that's extraordinary that he could make such a close supposition."

"Micht ye recall his tale about Laird MacLeod's fairy maiden?"

"Yes, I do remember that story—very well, actually."

"Aye. Weel, Beth also informed ye that Fin never lied thereafter he disclosed his tale tae ye and their lasses regarding His Lordship. Micht ye recall that also?"

"Yes, I remember."

"The MacLeods cherish and keep this ancient fairy maiden's cape till this very day as 'tis the flag which continues tae protect the MacLeod clan," he said. "Thaur are many a mystery which remain unknown and unseen, *àille dhubh*."

I nodded a little in response, becoming quiet. He was right about that, and there was nothing I could say. He raised my gloved hand to his lips and planted a kiss on the back of it, then withdrew it with a wink. I smiled at him and squeezed my hand in his. Tightening his hold around my hand, his lips curved, and a deepening grin spread across his face, heartening the warmth in his expression.

Twenty

After arriving back home and returning our horses to the stable, Ethan took care of them, paying attention to each one as he began unsaddling them. We started on our return to the house as we continued toward the orchards, strolling through them. As we made our way among the trees, he reached an arm up high and snagged a couple of low-hanging, ripened apples. Giving one to me, he kept the other for himself. He promptly bit into it, immediately enjoying its flavor. I glanced at him and took my first bite, recognizing the uniquely delicious sweet-tart taste of our type that he'd bred, and it reminded me of a mix between a Granny Smith and Red Delicious apples. Instantly enjoying mine, too, as I chewed and swallowed, I hadn't realized how much I'd worked up an appetite while savoring my scrumptious treat.

But Leif had swiftly completed his in only several bites before I had completed half of mine, when I noticed him tossing the core aside between the trees while we continued pacing through the orchard. He quickly grabbed another from the next low limb of another tree and began devouring it just as quickly; I understood his hunger, smiling. Little, enjoyable grins passed between us as we ate our apples without a word in companionable silence.

I finished and tossed the core to the ground. Leif snagged a third one and handed it to me. We leisurely walked among the apple and pear trees, where we also delighted ourselves in eating ripe, sweet, juicy pears. Then, reaching the edge of the last orchard, we entered a small clearing, and the gazebo, surrounded by the gardens, was visible at a moderate distance ahead, with the back of the house emerging into view.

Entering the gardens now and feeling somewhat satiated, Leif showed me the new vegetable additions to this extensive garden, consisting of onions, leeks, beets, and parsnips. But it wasn't until he also reacquainted me with our floral garden that he introduced me to the labyrinth of dormant lilac hedges and tall, massive bushes of hydrangeas that would bloom into purple and white hues in the spring before arriving at the center. Pausing as I gazed around our location within the garden, its beauty suddenly struck me, my eyes landing on the more abundant dormant azaleas and clematis flowers. I was stunned by the plethora of blooming red, pink, white, and precious, rare yellow roses that surrounded us as I barely noted the large brass sundial in the center from where we stood.

"This is spectacular! I don't remember us having so many roses," I commented, duly impressed, as I gazed at the plentiful shrubs.

"I had the garden expanded with yer favorite flower having the belief of yer return one day," Leif said.

"You did?" I turned my gaze toward him, and our eyes met.

"Aye." The loving sentiment was clear on his face, and I smiled. "Does it please ye?"

"Of course. I don't know what to say," I replied, significantly touched by all that he'd done for me. I turned my gaze back toward the roses and noticed how the yellow ones brilliantly stood out in the illuminating sunlight. "The yellow ones are so beautiful," I remarked.

"They are precious. An utter rarity. I once kent of their existence whilst visiting Versailles. My vessels sail tae France commonly, and I acquired the name of a rose breeder in Lyon, Monsieur Leroy. He procured fur me perfect specimens. They remain a symbol of the scarcity of yer own glory, which I treasure, along with the hope of laying eyes upon ye once more as the loove I bear fur ye burns as an eternal flame within my breast." His lips softly curled, and the affection in his sparkling ultramarine eyes conveyed the billowing warmth he felt. The ruddiness in his cheeks was apparent and mirrored my own, which had begun burning. I smiled at him, feeling my blood heating me, and my legs suddenly felt strangely like gelatin.

I broke from his fixed gaze, unable to help my sudden reaction to him and the shyness he was capable of compelling from me. Slipping my hand into his, he clasped it firmly, and I guided us away farther along the path from where we were standing, heading us toward the gazebo where we might sit for a moment to rest before returning indoors.

"Do you have a lot of work to do this morning?" I asked while we strolled over the narrow garden path.

"Aye," he replied simply.

"Oh."

"Why do ye inquire?"

"I only wanted us to sit inside the gazebo for a little while, just to spend a bit of extra time together before going on your way for the day."

"'Twould be fair. Yet, thaur is more that I must present tae ye before I mind my duties."

"Really?"

"Indeed."

"What else could it be?" My curiosity was piqued.

"Merely, come," he urged, taking the lead.

We passed the gazebo and entered a small clearing near the back of the house, where it was now clearly visible. As I approached, I saw a couple of male figures through the sunroom windows, looking in our direction from a distance. The nearer we came, the clearer the men came into view. Standing beside each other, they seemed to be gazing directly at us, studying us as we continued to advance. My curiosity was piqued as their vision locked onto us, never wavering, and I wondered what Lord Brimfield and Captain Berkeley found interesting, which kept their attention on us. I glanced at Leif and discovered that he'd noticed them also, as he'd adhered his eyes to them without faltering. Shifting my eyes from him back toward the sunroom windows, my gaze curiously steadied on the pair of men, too.

"Why are they staring at us?" I oddly asked Leif.

"Likely, they remain curious regarding yer new appearance. I also presume His Lordship awaits my accompanying him tae Fort Hill," he said.

"Oh," I realized. "But must they stare? It makes me feel weird like something's wrong with me."

"Ye mustn't mind any notion of the sort." Leif turned his eyes toward me, and I met his reassuring gaze. "Yer beauty has immediately captivated their attention, quite plainly. And, the charm ye possess merely serves tae lure them with further intrigue. 'Tis one matter tae behold yer likeness within a painting, but quite anither matter beheld within the flesh." I smiled at his compliment, and he gave me a little grin before returning his gaze to the staring men in the windows. A slight lull came between us as I began recalling the conversation held earlier at the breakfast table this morning.

"The conversation this morning at breakfast was a little interesting," I commented as I thought of it. Leif didn't respond. "Were you bothered by it?"

"That 'twould rumple yer spirit, aye," he said, keeping his eyes locked onto them, still staring at us. "I am certain that it did not meet yer favor."

"No, it didn't," I acknowledged.

"'Tis inappropriate, and nae one's affair tae pry," he responded frankly.

"You don't like Captain Berkley, do you?" I surmised by the tone in his voice, and reflecting on their discussion this morning.

"He disnae favor receiving orders from those he perceives as being beneath him, although they may outrank him. He is rash and executes himself accordingly. I reckon him egregious in his conduct. Nae, I dinnae fancy him in the least."

"Oh," I understood. "But you seem to be friends with His Lordship."

"I dinnae mind him. We have been weel acquainted fur many years since before the war ended and the time I had lost ye."

"For that long?"

"Aye."

"I see. Did you both fight in the same battle or something like that?"

"Upon several accounts, aye."

"So, both of you have a camaraderie with each other."

"Aye," he replied simply without elaborating more as we had now arrived, stepping over the slate pathway leading toward the matching wide steps of the sunroom's French doors.

As we advanced toward the doors, Captain Berkley stepped toward them and reached for the handle, pulling one of them open for us to enter.

"Thank you, Captain Berkley," I said politely as we came through the doorway into the room, sensing Leif's disinclination to acknowledge the captain.

"Indeed, Your Grace," Captain Berkley replied to me in a respectful tone, stepping aside for us to continue entering the room and closing the door after us. Turning from the door, he slightly dipped his head toward us, and I gave him a demure, little smile, attempting to ameliorate the burgeoning tension sensed between Leif and him.

"I pray Your Grace has spent an enjoyable morn?" Lord Brimfield inquired cordially as his interested gaze bounced between Leif and me before settling on me.

"Yes, thank you, Lord Brimfield. It was very nice," I answered modestly.

"Aye," Leif replied stoutly, attaining His Lordship's attention as his eyes abruptly shifted from me toward him.

"Splendid," he said to Leif.

"Should ye care fur my accompaniment, Brimfield, ye must postpone a moment longer as I am not yet ready tae part from my wife," Leif said.

"Indeed?" Lord Brimfield replied, raising his brow in surprise.

"Aye. Permit my not delaying ye further—must ye promptly take yer leave fur the fort," Leif suggested.

"'Tis no trouble at all. Pray, proceed as you must," Lord Brimfield insisted. They both exchanged acknowledgments with a slight nod, and then Leif returned his attention toward me as he lightly clasped my elbow and continued guiding me out of the room into the hallway.

He led me through the back section of the house, primarily used by the servants. Guiding me through a series of passageways, I wondered about his eagerness to show me what he had next in store, since it was uncommon for him to use this route. Passing several servants along the way as they stopped their steps with curtsies and bows, little friendly smiles were exchanged between me and them as I recognized them, further welcoming me.

As we rounded the corner into the farthest hallway, I realized that we had come near the scullery with the kitchen situated beyond it and opposite from where we were now standing. But Leif positioned us before a door next to the scullery and withdrew a key from his waistcoat pocket. I watched him slip the key into the hole of the iron padlock, turn it, and the lock released. He withdrew it from the door's bolt and pushed the door open as he stepped over the threshold into the room.

As I followed him inside through the doorway, I recognized this new room to be one of our several storage rooms. We walked toward the center of it and stood. There were a couple of large windows letting in brightly shining midday sunlight as the room faced East. While I scoped the area from where we were standing, I realized it had been purely tidied, swept, and cleaned, with barren empty shelves and a single, extensively long table, nearly stretching from one corner of the room to the next, positioned in front of the windows.

"This is a nice room," I commented, turning my eyes toward him after glancing around and meeting his gaze as he was already staring at me.

"Micht ye fancy it?" he asked. I gave him a questioning look, accompanied by an uncertain smile, as I was slightly confused.

"Yes. But what's it for?" I replied innocently, curiously looking at him.

"'Tis fur ye, of coorse," he answered as I noticed the kind, little smile curving his lips.

"For me?"

"Aye."

"I don't understand. What would I use it for?"

"I reckoned that ye micht fancy transforming it into a laboratory of sorts—fur brewing yer elixirs."

"Seriously?" My eyes suddenly became round with utter surprise.

"Quite. The lot of us have generously benefited from yer kind knowledge and care," he said genuinely. "Furthermore, yoo're in need of a proper chamber tae see tae it and the kitchen isnae suitable fur ye tae do as ye please."

A sudden knot began forming in my throat, and I fell abruptly on the verge of tears as my vision began blurring.

"Thank you for keeping me in your heart," I whispered, hearing my voice tremble. I realized all that he'd ever done for me, including this new gift. Fighting back tears, I naturally reached my arms around his neck, pulling myself against his chest as I embraced him.

"I have been preparing fur ye," he said softly against my cheek as he tightened his arms around my torso, holding me firmly against him as my feet lifted from the floor. "I aim fur yer happiness haur with me from the start."

"I'll always be happy no matter where we are, Leif. As long as I'm with you," I whispered, choking down the knot in my throat.

"Not a day has passed without yer possession of my thoughts. Now that I am blessed once more tae have yer existence, I discover that I cannae steady myself tae rest despite it."

"Why?"

"My elation compels me tae seek yer presence whilst I breathe, fur I often think yoo're but a dream."

"Except, are you a dream?"

"I am not."

"Me neither."

"So, I celebrate yer existence."

"I've forgotten how much you spoil me."

"Tae the pit as 'tis my absolute pleasure." Lessening his embrace a little, he eased me down from his chest, returning me to my feet on the floor, and pressed a tender kiss over my brow. "Now," he started again, taking my hand into his and placing the key into my palm. "We shall fill yer domain with the required necessities. Yet, I regret that we mayn't proceed till the morrow as I shall have the liberty tae escort ye about the marketplace tae attain yer guids, fur I have a meeting with General Gage which brings me tae Fort Hill this day."

"You do?"

"Aye. I beg yer forgiveness."

"You don't have to apologize. It's okay."

"Quite generous of ye tae say. I do regret my time away from ye fur the day, nonetheless."

"I'll miss you too," I replied, feeling the same. "So, you're seeing General Gage?"

"Aye."

"But I thought you hadn't anything to do with the army anymore."

"He and I meet upon occasion, however."

"Oh. I didn't realize. So, it's more out of pleasure than business?"

"Customarily," he said.

"Oh."

"Thus, I must part from ye as I presently take my leave. His Lordship awaits me also as he joins me."

"Okay." I nodded a little. "Well, I wish you a nice meeting, then." Leif gave me a gentle, appreciative smile and lightly tapped the end of my nose with affection.

"Remain out of mischief whilst in my absence." A warning brow arched over his eye, and I giggled.

"What mischief could I possibly cause?" I teased, smiling at him.

"Aplenty," he mocked, smirking in return. "Now, will ye not be a guid lass?"

"As you wish, Your Grace," I replied, still smiling at him. He narrowed an eye on me, and my smile widened. Gently tapping the end of my nose once more, he winked at me with an incorrigible little smirk, causing me to giggle again.

"Mind yerself weel," he warned playfully, then turned away as he began withdrawing from the room without me. I watched as his tall, strapping figure strode toward the doorway and crossed the threshold, vanishing around the corner into the next hallway. Left alone in the room now, I began taking stock of my new office and was excited to furnish it and fill it with inventory. There was even an empty ledger near a readied inkstand, I noticed, placed in the middle of the table. So, I moved toward it. Opening the ledger, I took the quill on the inkstand between my fingers, dipped it into the ink jar, and proceeded to make my first entry by making a list of everything I now needed.

Twenty-One

Early the next morning, I happily anticipated going to the marketplace with Leif to acquire the new belongings I needed from the list I'd made the previous day. Once breakfast had been served and eaten in the company of the boarding soldiers without the company of Lord Brimfield this time, Leif and I had withdrawn from the dining room to prepare ourselves for our following errand into the center of town. He and I separated as I was making myself ready to leave, and he went to his library to attend to his business while waiting for me.

After putting on my outerwear and bonnet, Mercy gave me a small, delicate silk, pearl-beaded drawstring purse that Leif had acquired for me from one of his shipments from France. The accessory was a novelty and was becoming one of the latest fashion trends for some women to have. While it was unquestionably beautiful, it didn't seem to be quite functional in holding the hearty weight of collections of silver or gold pieces, as evidenced by my pocket. Still, I was delighted to have it, because it was a gift from him. So, I slipped the pretty silk loop around my wrist, and I was finished and ready to go.

After thanking Mercy for her help, I left the bedroom and

made my way through the hallways toward the back of the house for the third floor, seeking Leif in his library to inform him that I was now prepared to leave. Arriving at the staircase and climbing the steps, I proceeded through the next hallway, passing several rooms along the way, leading toward his library. When I approached the closed door to his study, I placed my fingers on the silver door handle, opened the door, and stepped through the doorway into the room.

Discovering him seated at his desk by one of the windows, his eyes immediately bounced upward from the correspondence, occupying his attention with me as he noticed me entering and closing the door behind me. His face suddenly warmed with an inviting smile as our gazes met. Returning his smile, he abruptly shoved the quill he was using into the holder on the inkstand, returned it, and stood from his chair. Pacing toward me as I met him halfway into the room, he greeted me with a small, gentle kiss on my brow.

"Hi," I greeted him, smiling after his kiss. I'm finally ready to leave whenever you are. Sorry that I kept you waiting."

"Splendid. Not at all fur an apology. I was granted an opportunity tae mind my matters," he replied.

"Oh, good. But you're sure that I haven't interrupted you? You seemed a little busy being in the middle of writing," I considered.

"I have merely finished upon yer entry. Yer timing is impeccable," he assured.

"Great," I said. He stepped away from me, returning to his desk, and glanced at the gold clock ticking over it.

"'Tis high time fur a respite," he determined after glimpsing at the clock. "However, I have a matter of import which must be regarded upon our errand tae the market prior tae our arrival."

"Okay," I accepted impartially, observing him folding the parchment on which he'd written and beginning to melt sealing wax over a burning candle on his desk. "So, where must we go first before the market?" I wondered.

"I shall explain along the way," he replied as he poured the liquid wax over the flap and snatched his stamp, pressing it into the carmine wax, sealing the letter. The wax promptly cooled, and he took the letter off his desk, then tucked it into his waistcoat pocket. "Now, then," he started again, seeming satisfied, and walked toward me. "I have informed Amity's new maid tae prepare her fur joining us."

"You have?" I realized, glad to have Amity's company with us.

"Aye. So long as thaur have been soldiers about the hoose, I have never left her within their company without my being present. She has always joined me wherever I have ventured," he said.

"I see," I understood, knowing his protectiveness over her. And, sure he was well aware of how she's blossomed into a beautiful young lady and the attraction of at least one of these soldiers had for her, I understood his distrust regarding any man being alone around her.

"I reckon that she must be awaiting us presently," he suspected as he strode past me for the garment pegs beside the door where his greatcoat and hat were hanging. I watched him grab his coat and shove his arms through the sleeves. He quickly snatched his hat off the peg and held it between his fingers as I stepped toward him to open the door. Reaching for the door handle before I arrived, he swung the door open for me, and I stepped out of the room into the hallway, with him following and closing the door behind us.

When we arrived on the second-floor landing before the grand staircase, Amity was seen patiently waiting at the foot of the stairs, standing with her maid, Winnet, who held her needlepoint basket clutched in her hands. Noticing us descending the staircase, Winnet curtsied when we arrived, standing before them, and withdrew when I realized Leif had dismissed her from Amity until we returned. Covered in our outerwear, we were ready to leave for the center of town and followed Leif as he proceeded to lead us toward the foyer, where Quinn was found waiting at the front door.

Quinn promptly opened the door for us, and we came outdoors, stepping down the stone steps. Once we had made ourselves comfortable in our waiting carriage, our driver was ready to drive us away from home. Samuel started the horses, which jolted us into motion. We started on the curving dirt driveway flanked by blue spruces until we met the cobbled road leading into the heart of the city.

Now riding over cobblestones with Beacon Hill sighted at a distance and the Common visible directly beside us, the vast flock of pitched, white canvas army tents reflecting the bright sunlight drew my attention while glancing out of the window and discerning several shirtless soldiers tied to posts with their backs exposed to the vicious whips they were receiving unsettled me. Although I had assumed the reason for this brutal punishment these men were receiving was likely due to their infractions, as Leif had explained to me the reasons for them receiving these disciplinary actions earlier, I clearly remembered what had happened to the soldiers in Northampton involving me a long time ago and the feeling for its justification coming over me despite the inhumanity of it. Still, to witness such harsh punishment was disturbing to me.

So, I averted my eyes from the soldiers being flogged and looked at Leif, seated across from me, and Amity, who were also gazing out of the window. The look on his face was one of concentration as he stared at the Common passing by, making him appear absorbed in thought, and I wondered about the reason for his unexpected serious mood.

"So, where are we headed first before the marketplace?" I decided to ask, hoping to distract his earnest vein of thought. He abruptly turned his eyes away from the window and looked at me.

"I have a matter which I must take tae Sir Putnam," he answered without smiling.

"Sir Putnam?"

"Aye."

"Who is he?"

"He is my solicitor."

"Oh. Why do you need to see him?" I asked innocently. I was not only a little curious, but suddenly hit by concern, determined by the look on his face.

"My liberty remains at stake," he disclosed plainly without any emotion in his voice.

"What do you mean?" I looked at him in alarm, as I was also surprised by the calmness in his demeanor, which contradicted the gravity of his words.

"His Majesty has reinstated my service into his army," Leif disclosed.

"Are you serious?" I replied, shocked.

"Utmost earnest that I am."

"I don't understand. How? Or, better yet, why—after all that you've already done?"

"Apparently, I am invaluable tae His Majesty," he said; the mocking note in his voice was bluntly noticed.

"It's beginning to seem that way."

"He will use me tae the end of his pleasure as I serve my penance tae him, lest I forfeit his generosity granting me the retention of my peerage and whit remains of my property."

"He'll never free you," I realized, disturbed by this understanding.

"He may simply execute me instead," Leif replied, forcing this reality on me. "Therefore, I remain humbled and grateful that I am spared tae spend my continuously living days within yer presence."

I couldn't dispute this realization. The gratitude he felt matched my own, since all I wanted for us was to stay living our lives together in happiness and peace. The thought of us living in my era quickly entered my mind as I regarded the refuge it could provide us. But I glimpsed at Amity as she peacefully sat beside me, looking out the window as we traveled. *Couldn't we take her with us to live in my era also, and abandon this place for good for the sake of our lives?* However, explaining the truth to her could realistically prove too difficult: she would likely become extremely distraught and panic at the idea alone. Plus, how could I ever convince her to willingly leave her Aunt Beth, a beloved mother to her, including her adoring cousins, behind, never to see them again? It was impractical. Her happiness in life and all that she had ever known was here.

I shall flounder before I fail. I remembered Leif once telling me that he would face his own self-destruction when he experienced living life with me in my era, after he arrived there.

"So..." I resumed, returning my eyes to his. "You're back in uniform," I acknowledged regretfully, extremely worried now that there was no choice but to accept this fact as long as we lived here.

"As colonel."

"He raised your rank?" I asked, somewhat surprised.

"A further demonstration of His Majesty's kindness."

"When were you made aware of your new situation?" I asked unbelievably.

"Yestermorn. I had been summoned tae Fort Hill tae meet with General Gage. 'Twas thereupon when the general had informed me of my new orders upon delivering tae me a letter from the Crown."

"I see," I replied in a small voice, realizing the sudden new dangerous hurdle we were facing. "You could be sent far away..." I remarked under my breath, acknowledging this fact too. "Will you be sent away?" I asked Leif directly.

"I shall remain within this vicinity with my attention upon Castle Island," he informed me.

"But that's an island. Does that mean you'll be staying there instead of at *Taigh Gràs*?" I asked worriedly, despite its relatively close location.

"General Gage hudnae stipulated that I shall. Presumably, I shall ferry thaur unless he orders me otherwise," he said. I nodded in response, contemplating that I should be grateful that he wasn't being sent away any farther than to the local island, and would be commuting as he stayed home with me. But that situation could swiftly change, and I was further worried that the king had Leif trapped within his will with no end in sight, jeopardizing Leif's safety and the stability of our future here together.

"I want us to be safe here, Leif. But what is happening with the king is making me question all of it," I confessed worriedly.

"So long as I appease His Majesty's wishes without qualms whilst I maintain imperturbable and steadfast demonstration of my loyalty tae him, as done continuously within the past, then he is inclined tae consider my petition and grant the favor fur which I seek," he explained encouragingly.

"What favor do you want from him?"

"I desire a written decree from His Majesty that I shall be granted the protection of my peerage and be proclaimed free of further debt as I return my loyal service tae him in blood upon his wish, fur so long that I live."

"What? You're going to sign your life to him?"

"He already has my life by his whim. Recall that he may take it upon his wish."

"Then, what's the point?"

"The gist being that he isnae a heartless king and that he may grant his mercy upon me micht I petition him. Should he favor me by bestowing his mercy presented within a proclamation, then I shall be left tae carry on peaceably, believing that my family's welfare will remain secure."

"But you said the king could simply renege on any decision or agreement he makes with anybody. So, who's to say that he won't do the same with you again—even after making it into a proclamation?"

"Granted. However, a proclamation from His Majesty isnae a regular contract. Raither, 'tis one which is his written order, recorded. Whilst he may indeed rescind such a decree, should he do so, he will be perceived as fickle, and he is loathed tae have himself perceived as having any such trait. Instead, he determines himself tae be perceived as stalwart in all his decisions declared. Having himself portray any inkling of weakness is tae his detriment. Therefore, as it pertains tae His Majesty's proclamations, he remains bound tae his word," Leif explained with certainty. He seemed fundamentally convinced as I stared at his earnest face and discerned the knowledge in his eyes.

"I see," I said simply, considering what he was saying.

"Hence, I shall petition His Majesty fur mercy."

"Do you really think Sir Putnam can help you achieve this from the king?"

"Aside from Sir Putnam's acute competency rivaling any barrister within London, he originates from London himself and has bent the king's ear upon several occasions tae his successful acquisitions through petitions that the king has granted," Leif said, keeping his eyes locked to mine. I nodded in acknowledgment.

"Does that mean he'll visit the king on your behalf to present your petition?"

"Aye. He will present himself tae His Majesty tae make my appeal."

"Sir Putnam must be very good at what he does and well trusted by you in order for him to appear before the king without you accompanying him," I considered.

"The Putnams have served my MacLeod kin weel fur many years, as weel as myself. Sir Putnam's father had petitioned the king tae return me tae London from Guinea upon requesting the sparing of my life by exiling me tae this colony with my duchy intact, as I served the king in his army during the war. Once his father perished, the younger assumed his father's position with high esteem as his father, and continues tae serve me weel," Leif explained.

"I see... Well, I'm a little less worried knowing that you've got someone trustworthy for handling your legal issues," I recognized. "Still, I really worry about you being in the military. Especially, knowing—"

"Pray, dinnea dwell upon it so. Hold fast onto faith, fur He will see us through come whit may—as He has done already."

I nodded a little again, admiring Leif's strength and determination he found in God, and I hoped to find the same strength he had in his faith, and hold onto it, just as he did while believing in what he said. But my fear about everything lurked, making it difficult for me to fully trust in my own faith that we would remain blessed and continue living our lives together in safety, peace, and happiness.

"Once we have also completed the marketplace, micht ye care tae visit *Sylvina*? She is presently docked at the wharf," he suggested with a subtle, encouraging grin.

"Yes, I believe so. That would be very nice," I said, distracted by the new thought.

"As ye wish." The look on his face seemed satisfied, and so the prior issue was laid to rest.

Hearing the horse's hooves clacking over cobblestones, our conversation drifted, and my attention returned to looking out the window. I continued thinking about our vulnerability to the king and how fearful it was to have one man powerful enough who could determine our fate, while we were now riding north on Tremont Street, passing King's Chapel. Then, the carriage turned right onto Queen Street until we arrived at the corner intersection of Cornhill and King Street, where clusters of brownstones were collected and many pedestrians walked the streets.

When the carriage halted before a brownstone on King Street, Leif reached out the door window, turned the handle from the outside, and opened the door before Samuel had the opportunity to dismount the carriage driver's seat to assist us. As Leif promptly stepped out onto the walkway, Samuel swiftly arrived to hold the door open, and he proffered a hand for me to take. Slipping my palm into his, Leif carefully drew me forth from the carriage, helping me step onto the walkway. Then, he leaned inside the carriage again for Amity. After assisting her out of the carriage,

Leif proceeded, guiding us through passing pedestrians across the walkway toward the brownstone facing us.

After climbing up a flight of granite steps, he reached for one of the door's handles and opened the door, leading us inside the building. Entering indoors, we arrived standing inside a small foyer where an oak bench was positioned against a wall by a window facing the busy street. As Leif was closing the door, we were immediately met by a stout man appearing in his early thirties, striding through the narrow corridor on approaching us.

"Your Grace. A pleasure to see you, indeed," greeted the man in a genial manner, speaking to Leif when he stood before us. The man stiffly bowed and abruptly straightened, looking receptive and serious.

"Master Peal. I pray ye fare weel?" Leif replied politely, instantly recognizing this man.

"Aye, Your Grace. I thank ye. Might you fare well also, Your Grace?" Mr. Peal replied cordially.

"Indeed. Thank ye."

"Splendid."

"Pray meet my wife, Her Grace, Duchess of Monteith," Leif said, kindly introducing me.

"I am most honored to make your acquaintance, Your Grace," Mr. Peal graciously said to me and stiffly bowed again.

"This is Master Peal, apprentice tae Sir Putnam," Leif informed me. Mr. Peal's light blue eyes seemed sincere and kind, though distinctly scholarly as he earnestly looked at me.

"It's nice to make your acquaintance also, Mister Peal," I said politely. He faintly grinned, but his ruddy cheeks flushed, and he seemed suddenly embarrassed. Quickly shifting his eyes from me, he returned his direct attention toward Leif and steadily looked at him.

"Our niece, Miss Amity," Leif continued to introduce as she stood beside him on his opposite side from where I stood.

"Indeed. Also, a pleasure, of course," Mr. Peal acknowledged, seeming already acquainted with her, turning his polite gaze toward Amity. She gave a timid smile, and he respectfully bowed once more.

"Sir Putnam presently expects and awaits Your Grace inside of his office. Pray, permit me to show Your Grace to him," Mr. Peal resumed after straightening.

"Aye, thank ye," Leif said, but turned toward me before following Mr. Peal. "Pray, seat yourselves upon the bench, *ceisdein*, whilst I meet the solicitor."

"Yes, of course," I agreed. Then, turning from me, he began with Mr. Peal pacing away from us through the corridor, leaving Amity and me alone together as she and I moved to sit comfortably on the bench.

PART FOUR

Splinters in The Bone

Twenty-Two

While Amity passed the time contentedly needlepointing the project stored in her basket, I quietly sat beside her on the bench, observing passersby through the windows near me, as well as other pedestrians entering and exiting buildings across the street, all while carriages rolled over the cobblestones. My mind wandered as I considered the actual enjoyment of living here, which was truly serene and peaceful.

The much slower pace of life was noteworthy. It could not only be perceived as idyllic to some in my era, but the juxtaposition of where I came, clearly presented life's common ideals, which were predominantly embraced by the culture here, made my living experience surprisingly content. That's not to say that there weren't outliers, though; I wasn't naive to know that life wasn't perfect no matter where one lived, but this place seemed perfect in many ways despite being aware of the lack of medical advancements not yet made, and the pending disturbance with England lying ahead. But for the time being, at least, it appeared that society here was keeping a peaceful existence, with people living their lives accordingly while generally coexisting with the military presence, despite it.

Still, even though my own world wasn't perfect and had its threats, at least it was stable, and I had the ability to determine my own life without the concern for punishment and death from the government for assuming the right to strive and achieve a comfortable life. Ironically and unexpectedly, I realized the security and extreme comfort offered by living in the future, and what I was sacrificing to root ourselves here strangely didn't disturb me as deeply as it probably should have. Being together with Leif was all I cared about. It didn't matter where we lived. As long as we were together, our happiness existed. And, striving through life, we both knew, was simpler now than it would be for us living in the future. We buttressed each other, and suddenly I realized that I now sensed the same trust he had in God: that we were going to live and be all right, no matter what adversity we might face—as long as we held faith.

I abruptly heard an invisible door at a distance in the hallway opening and closing shut when Leif finally came around the corner deep within the passageway, being escorted by Mr. Peal again. Assuming Leif's meeting with Sir Putnam had concluded, as they approached, I notified Amity, and she proceeded to tuck her embroidery project back into her basket. When they shortly arrived before us, Amity and I stood from our comfortable seats on the bench, acknowledging their presence.

Mr. Peal respectfully greeted me once more before Leif kindly assumed our leave, and Mr. Peal politely escorted us toward the door. Reaching for the door's handle, Mr. Peal opened the door for us, and Amity and I followed Leif out of the brownstone down the steps as he cleared our way to pass between strolling pedestrians along the brick walkway.

"Shall we proceed tae the marketplace, presently?" Leif asked me as we arrived at our waiting carriage.

"Yes, of course. That will be nice," I anticipated gladly as Samuel promptly arrived at the door and pulled it open for us.

"Very weel," Leif responded, beginning to assist me into the carriage. As I took my seat on the bench, he helped Amity inside, and she followed, returning to sit across from me. Then, he effortlessly slid inward over the bench after her and sat beside me. After we'd been situated, Samuel shut the door and resumed his driver's seat, starting the horses again through the streets.

"How was your meeting?" I asked Leif, looking at him with interest.

"It proceeded accordingly. Sir Putnam will promptly sail tae London tae request an audience with His Majesty," he said, informing me.

"Oh," I understood. "I'm glad it went well. When do you think you'll know the result of his meeting with the king?"

"Should all be weel, I shall receive word betwixt three tae six months, subsequently, if not a month sooner, upon Sir Putnam's return."

"Really?"

"Aye."

"That's not as long as I'd imagined. Still, it's enough time to be preoccupied and nervous about it."

"Thaur isnae any use tae dwell upon it, lest we waste our pleasant days tae distress in the duration. I raither we simply heed our blessings fur the time being, instead," he said realistically, seeming composed in spite of the potentially negative outcome. I nodded in consideration and fell quiet since there was nothing else I could say, praying for the best.

We rode a few blocks north on Cornhill until it merged into Union Street just before Faneuil Hall and the nearby marketplace. Now arriving at the marketplace, my worrying thoughts faded away as I became distracted by the bustling crowd moving in and out of shops and between the many vendors lining the street. My mind shifted to a more pleasant state as I relaxed, knowing we would spend the rest of our time leisurely enjoying each other's company while shopping and later visiting his ship, *Sylvina*, at the harbor.

While strolling, shoppers moved past us, and I noticed countless soldiers patrolling as they marched through the streets. But the air between them and pedestrians didn't seem openly charged with hostility, though I was certain sentiments on either side percolated beneath the facade of calmness. I suppose the resentment from residents here hadn't yet breached the surface with an overflow of violence, despite the few episodes of protests that had appeared, because the pervading sentiment was for a peaceful environment to remain. Still, for now, those who had differences with the Crown seemed to keep their ideas undisclosed as they accepted the current state of affairs regarding the government and its presence of soldiers.

Not wanting to spoil my enjoyment, I pushed the subject of politics out of my mind, swiftly returning my attention to the pleasantness I was experiencing this moment. We entered a milliner's shop and I was glad that we had. I admired several winter bonnets on display and various gown fabrics, and Leif purchased the bonnets for me. He also ordered new gowns for me and Amity from the Mantua maker to refresh our winter wardrobes with the latest styles from London. Afterward, we paid a visit to the cobbler, where Leif acquired new pairs of silk brocade slippers for Amity and me, as well as a new pair of boots and buckled shoes for himself.

Then, we arrived inside the spice shop, where Leif purchased a treat of cocoa beans so that I could make hot chocolate in the coming cooler days, which I was eagerly anticipating. When we finally entered the apothecary, we obtained the medicines, compounds, empty glass vials, and containers needed to begin supplying my office for the health of our family and household, and this completed our shopping at last.

Lastly, before our outing was done, we made a final stop at

Leif's wharf to visit his ship, *Sylvina*. I met Captain Barnes, as he approached us on the dock, who sailed this particular ship for Leif. The captain and Leif showed us *Slyvina's* exterior as they struck up a cordial conversation instead of bringing Amity and me aboard, as it was uncommon and scandalous to have women on a ship. Leif was right; it was a far more impressive ship than *Freiheit* and appeared to have a superior command of the great seas, and was also well outfitted with cannons protruding from the ports and portholes along the hull. Well crafted, it was an elegant vessel, and understanding that he had named the greatest one of his fleets after me touched me immensely.

On the way home, later that evening, we stopped at the Lion's Den Tavern to fill our hungry appetites we'd earned. A hearty meal of lobster, clam chowder, and buttered bread was served with cups of tea for Amity and me, and cider for Leif, accompanied by almond cake for dessert. Satiated from our meal, we left the tavern for home and brought ourselves to rest.

Twenty-Three

E arly this morning, Leif left in uniform for Fort Hill to report to General Gage for duty at Castle William before he and I had the opportunity to dine for breakfast together. Recognizing my day would be spent without him, I decided to use this time, with Mercy's careful assistance, to organize the many medical supplies. I placed these items onto shelves within my new medicine room and logged all of the materials.

After spending the morning arranging my lab to my satisfaction, I suggested that Mercy take a break for a little while so that she could attend to her own needs. We left the room together and parted ways as I proceeded, locking the door behind us. I slid the key into the folds of my skirts and put it inside my pocket, then went in search of Amity to join her and finally relax.

I found her in the sitting room with her maid, Winnet, sitting together on the sofa by one of the windows. Amity appeared comfortably absorbed in her needlepoint, like Winnet, who was as attentive to her stocking darning. As I strode deeper into the room, I also realized, unexpectedly, that Captain Berkley and Captain Miller were in their company, sitting across from them in separate wing chairs facing them. While Captain Miller appeared to be concentrating on reading a broadsheet he was holding, Captain Berkley stared at Amity while he was indulging in tea and buttered crumpets with strawberry preserves.

To say that I was a little surprised to see the officers here was understated. They immediately noticed my arrival in the room and stood from their chairs, acknowledging me. Presuming they'd be in the field at this hour like the others, I instinctively knew that Leif wouldn't be happy knowing that Amity was sharing in the company of soldiers—despite having her maid with her—if he or I weren't present especially since he'd told me as much the other day about his skepticism about Amity and the presence of soldiers living with us.

"Good afternoon, Your Grace," Captain Miller began politely with an accompanying bow.

"Good afternoon, Your Grace," Captain Berkley also politely followed suit.

"Good afternoon, captains," I replied courteously, hiding the question of their presence.

Winnet abruptly turned a worried look toward me, and I was aware then that she realized her mistake the second I met her eyes. The color in her ruddy cheeks blanched, and her brow knitted. Granted, she was new to the household and was relatively close to Amity's age, being nearly four years her senior. Despite their closeness in age, she was assigned to aid Amity in all her needs, which included companionship. She should have known better when it came to males, particularly the older and more experienced soldiers. While I perceived twenty-three-year-old Winnet as being a nice companion for Amity, I thought she might be considerably young for the challenge of this position as it related to using life's maturely acquired valued wisdom to help guide her decision-making carefully involving Amity.

Still, in spite of my consideration, the fact couldn't be

neglected that she had significant experience suiting this particular role, as she had familiarity with this kind of responsibility in the past within a different household. Nor was her age a factor in this era, as she was considered a spinster who had prior experience as a governess and a lady's maid. So, I was somewhat surprised that she hadn't persuaded Amity out of the company of these men, while I was sure Leif would have previously instructed her to do so according to his expectations.

Amity looked up from embroidering and smiled, noticing me now in the room. She appeared glad to see me when Winnet immediately stood from sitting beside her on the sofa. Dropping her darning aside, Winnet hurried toward me. As the captains watched her approach, Winnet's look was clearly distraught.

"Pray, Your Grace," Winnet began consciously under her breath the second she arrived, standing directly before me with imploring eyes. "I beg Your Grace for a word," she continued, speaking softly.

Obviously aware of the captains observing, and now with Amity's curious attention added, I simply said, "All right," agreeing, sensing Winnet's eagerness to speak privately. Bobbing a brief curtsy, Winnet started out of the room ahead of me as I caught Amity's gaze before leaving with her maid. I signaled to her my momentary excuse from her presence before my brief return to join her company. She nodded, and I turned for the doorway, following Winnet as she continued out of the room. As we crossed the threshold and rounded the corner, she suddenly ceased pacing, stopping short as she turned and faced me.

"Begging your pardon, Your Grace. Pray, forgive my haste. I beseech you," she pleaded in a soft-spoken voice while genuinely looking at me. Before I could inquire what was apparently troubling her, she continued saying, "I also desperately implore Your Grace to have mercy upon me for permitting Miss Amity to repose in the company of soldiers. His Grace's orders were adamant that their company must be avoided unless His or Her Grace was present. Whilst I had believed it to be a simple order, I am discovering it to be most difficult. There are many soldiers about to elude as they are at every which turn, freely roaming the premises without consideration for privacy, even when the door to the sitting room had been closed to inhibit disturbance."

"Really?" I responded strangely, suddenly struck by surprise.

"Aye, indeed, ma'am," she replied anxiously.

"Who opened the door?" I inquired spontaneously.

"'Twas Captain Berkley who had, ma'am, as he first entered the chamber. Captain Miller later discovered that Captain Berkley had taken a chair within our presence and proceeded to join him as well," she answered.

"I see," I realized, slightly unsettled by Captain Berkley's initial rudeness for disturbing their privacy.

"Therefore, may I plead to Your Grace that you might take pity upon my soul as it is perceivably impossible to evade any billeting soldier here whilst I mean for Miss Amity to possess her solitude in peace by adhering to His Grace's orders. It appears the only haven for Miss Amity is within the surrounding walls of her own chamber. However, she is reluctant to keep there, of course. Alas, I fear His Grace's dismissal of me should he learn that I have failed him miserably," she explained worriedly.

"Thank you for letting me know about the circumstances, Winnet," I replied appreciatively, giving her a considerate look.

"Truly, indeed, Your Grace is most welcome," she said. "Whatever shall I do," she muttered while nervously wringing her hands.

"It's all right. Please don't worry. Everything will be all right. I'm sure you'll not be dismissed," I assured sympathetically while trying to calm her with my tone. "Mercy has been given a break for a moment. Why don't you join her for a little while? It could help ease your worry if you do. I think she's probably in the kitchen enjoying something to eat right about now. You should have something to eat too if you haven't already. And, while you're doing that, I'll be with Amity until you're needed."

"Aye, ma'am. You are indeed most kind. I thank you most truly, ma'am," she replied unevenly, though appearing to become slightly relieved. The wrinkle in her brow also lessened, and she curtsied. "Thank you again, ma'am."

"You're welcome, Winnet," I said, relieved that she seemed to feel better as she took my suggestion and promptly started walking away from me for her break with Mercy in the kitchen.

When I returned to the sitting room, wary that Captain Berkley had been disregarding the commonplace implication of closed doors and had intruded on Amity and her maid's privacy, the captains exchanged tacit looks. Captain Miller appeared disapproving of his companion as Captain Berkley conveyed flippancy toward him with a faint, deriding smirk. Simultaneously standing from their comfortable seats in the chairs again, they nevertheless gave polite but shallow bows in my acknowledgment as I proceeded deeper into the room and placed myself next to Amity after retrieving a book that I'd hidden beneath the cushion to read later.

As I'd made myself comfortable sitting beside Amity on the sofa while she continued concentrating on embroidering, I returned to the page in the book from where I'd been reading and glanced up from the pages before beginning, and caught both men staring at me. While Captain Miller had an apologetic look on his face, Captain Berkley, on the other hand, not only appeared apathetic but entitled in his air by the manner in which he was looking at me. We held each other's gazes for a lapsing second before Captain Berkley proceeded to say, "Pray, might I beg the inquiry to Her Grace if there might be any concern that we captains may have caused without our knowing? For it is our deepest wish that we have not caused the merest distress, as it would never be our intention to affront in the scarcest case."

I suddenly felt a little blank as my attention focused on

Captain Berkley. His boldness in indicating his lack of genuine courtesy was unexpected, and I was stumped for a second.

"I haven't thought of any concerns, Captain Berkley. However, is there something that concerns you that I should be aware of?" I replied, quickly recovering.

"Merely that your servant appeared disquieted, and I should hope that neither I nor Captain Miller have caused dismay to your household," he said as I certainly discerned the smugness in his voice reflect the expression on his face.

"That's very considerate of you, Captain Berkley, but I can assure you there's nothing the matter. Still, thank you for your extended kindness," I responded cordially, lying.

"Most indeed, Your Grace. It pleases me to know that no slight was caused," he remarked. I gave him a small, tepid smile in response before glancing at Captain Miller, who was appearing respectfully observant of my reaction to his companion.

"Please, captains, return to your interests before I joined while I keep my niece company," I suggested.

"We thank you, Your Grace," Captain Miller responded instead of Captain Berkley, seeming more genuine in tone and demeanor than the other. He then returned to reading the broadsheet he was holding while Captain Berkley kept his eyes lingering on me for a moment longer.

Breaking his stare, I turned my eyes down to the open book in my lap and started reading. Except, I hadn't been granted the opportunity even to complete the first sentence when Captain Berkley's voice interrupted the pending silence as he audibly cleared his throat. My eyes immediately returned to him, as did his companion's, forcing me to wonder about the reason for his disruption.

"Are you all right, Captain Berkley?" I asked, a bit concerned.

"Pray, forgive me, Your Grace. Merely a spot more tea will ease my throat's discomfort. It will be shortly soothed," he replied. He steadily drew the teacup he was holding to his mouth and sipped while maintaining his gaze on mine. I gave a little nod in response and was transiently curious about the compulsion for his staring. I knew it was intentional, but was ignorant of his reason for doing it. Aware of his direct attention, I couldn't help feeling a little uncomfortable. Still, I disregarded my edging unease when adjusting the book resting in my lap while bringing it into my hand to return to reading. But he continued saying, "Might I beseech Your Grace's indulgence?"

"For what, Captain Berkley?" I replied nicely, nevertheless curious about his question as I was interrupted once more. Captain Miller lifted his gaze from his broadsheet, abruptly returning it flat over his lap, being also interrupted, and shot an agitated glare toward Captain Berkley. He fixed his eyes on him, which seemed to be a warning in addition.

"I implore, Your Grace, for a discussion," he stated, disregarding Captain Miller's apparent look of dissatisfaction toward him.

"Oh," I suddenly realized, holding innate reservations to engage him, highlighted by Captain Miller's reaction, which only further impressed my skeptical feeling, particularly about him coming over me. "Well, I suppose that might be all right. What do you care to discuss, Captain?" Being considerate in my tone, I also hinted at my caution while maintaining my gaze on his conceited, surveying stare. Certain that I could not be rude, I was half-tempted to be less mindful, although I had to be conscious of myself.

"I generously thank Your Grace for obliging and indulging me in gratifying my request to hold my discussion," he responded, sounding slightly over solicitous and altruistic and giving me the impression that he could certainly be patronizing if I wasn't mistaken about his air; I noted.

"Of course, Captain Berkley," I acknowledged courteously with a slight nod again, studying his alert eyes fixed on mine. He gave a faint nod of his own, acknowledging the permission I'd just given him to proceed.

"Might I kindly first pose a question to begin our discussion, Your Grace?" he began, lifting his brow that remarkably changed the expression on his face to innocent interest.

"Go right ahead, Captain Berkley," I agreed modestly.

"I merely wish to inquire about your origin within the colony?" he asked innocuously.

"Oh," I replied unexpectedly, realizing the question was inquisitive.

"Yes, I simply inquire over my ignorance of the dialect which exists in this region of the colonies, for I have not yet encountered one who shares your diction inhabiting this particular vicinity," he explained.

"I see," I said, suddenly becoming precisely guarded.

"Yes. Therefore, I remain most intrigued as if I may be permitted to be rather bold by confessing to say the manner of your voice is flattering," he complimented.

"Thank you, captain," I said politely, remaining reserved.

"Indeed, you are welcome, Your Grace." The tone in his voice was also polite, but my instinct detected his probing, hidden in the refinement of his tact, and I suddenly realized the greater scope of his capability to easily extract information from the unsuspecting, in addition to his admission to the callous physical cruelty he could inflict on another man. Imagining him as an institutional inter-rogator was abruptly easy, as I believed he'd be quite skilled at it. "Pray, proceed to enlighten me of your origin. I shall be indebted to you for dissolving my ignorance by assisting my better understanding of subjects born in these English colonies," he continued, asking me.

"Well," I started thoughtfully, carefully considering what I was going to permit telling him anything about myself when choosing to say, "I suppose that I will confirm the fact of your suspicion that I'm not native to this city of Boston."

"Yes. Most share the same dialect within Boston and are clearly assumed native, forcing those who are not to protrude—causing wonder, of course."

"Of course." I gave him a shallow smile. He reciprocated a grin that made him appear more genuine. "Then, in that case, I'll admit that I'm originally from a place in the colonies that is too obscure to garner anyone's slightest interest."

"Indeed?"

"Yes."

"Yet, would not any city within New England be of import? I should consider all regions within the empire of significance as the Crown deems," he said, then suddenly thought for a second, catching himself from continuing as he remained holding his exploring eyes to mine. "However, I might perceive your modesty. Forgive me."

"There isn't anything to forgive, Captain."

"You are quite generous. I thank you, Your Grace," he said. I gently nodded in acknowledgment. "As you kindly permit my endeavoring to inquire, nonetheless, I am most curious to understand your family's interest in having uprooted from England to reside in America. Might I ask?"

"I see."

"Yes, I am continuously quite fascinated by the reason why anyone would have done so. England is a fine country. Therefore, I remain curious about why it would be abandoned. Particularly, by one's choosing." The last proton of his statement, I discerned, was precise. Though delivered politely, he was implying, and I understood his innuendo as the platform from which he would be ready to pass a veiled insult to anyone who rooted their lives here. His vain, imperial, classist outlook regarding Americans was certainly evident through his skillfully courteous demeanor.

"Well, Captain Berkley, I'll have you know that my family were natural risk-takers for the betterment of their autonomy from others and found their fortune through industry. Since this kind of opportunity is very well provided for here in the colonies than it is in the Motherland, my family found their success and their reward in it," I answered concisely.

"Then, you are a commoner, Your Grace, if I am not mistaken?" he fathomed.

"Would it be a negative attribute in your opinion, Captain Berkley, if I were classified as such?" I replied directly.

"Err, why—uh-em, quite not. Not at all, Your Grace, would it be any consideration of mine to regard your pedigree menially, might this be your case?"

Menially, I immediately understood his underlying insult and gave him a nice smile, contradicting the shallow look in my eyes as I returned his stare. An uneven grin crossed his face, and I perceived his sudden discomfort as I confidently glared steadily at him.

"Then, you have a noble heart, Captain Berkley," I said, returning the offense. His blue eyes suddenly widened as he understood my equally hidden meaning. Briefly shifting a glimpse toward Captain Miller, I caught the smirk on his face while he was giving him a sidelong glance in response to my reply. It seemed Captain Miller might have appreciated my reply, I assumed, when returning my full attention to Captain Berkley, who still had been looking at me a bit caught off guard.

"Mayhap it may please Your Grace to know that I am compassionate to the lowborn, for I, myself, have an aunt who is removed from the aristocracy by birth as a member of the gentry before wedding into our family."

"Is that so?"

"Indeed, it is quite true, Your Grace. Therefore, I respectfully propose that 'tis possible that Your Grace and I may discover that we may typically agree."

"Interesting."

"Is it not?" A light grin passed over his lips while the look in his eyes remained pointed with discernment despite his concession to admit the position of his own social class belonging to him.

"Which begs me to ask, Your Grace, from which part of England does your family originate? For it simply fascinates me to know that the fault of my curiosity will not subside. Therefore, I do beg your pardon."

"Excusing your curious question about my heritage, Captain Berkley, I believe that I'm more interested in yours," I responded, redirecting the conversation's trend.

"Indeed?" His brows lifted, making him appear surprised—and flattered by the more sincere accompanying grin.

"Of course." I smiled, reciprocating the appearance of his sincerity.

"I'm most humbled that Your Grace would care to inquire of me."

"Then, please tell me. Would your family be from London, Captain?" I asked, easily recognizing the source of his accent.

"Indeed, I am from London, Your Grace," he disclosed, seeming distinctly proud of the fact.

"How nice," I acknowledged nonchalantly while being polite. "Where specifically in London did you reside with your family?"

"You are knowledgeable in the parts of London?" he asked, sounding somewhat surprised. I automatically felt my lips faintly turn upward at one corner, suddenly feeling a little insecure about my accurate understanding of this city. I'd only been there once, long ago, when I was in college, touring it with Dakota for spring break. So, not only had my memory of it faded a little from the time I went, but knowledge of it as it exists in this present century was essentially lacking.

"I'm aware of several parts of the city to know enough, Captain Berkley. So, please continue to inform my interest in your upbringing," I ventured, saying.

"Certainly. I originate from Mayfair with my family, of course," he said with a distinct air of haughtiness. "The Berkleys resided originally in Whitehall for centuries before their relocation to Mayfair upon acquiring more expansive property suitable to their taste."

"I see." I acknowledged with a little nod.

"Yes, plenty belonging to the aristocracy transported themselves from Whitehall to Mayfair, better suiting themselves, of which you may already be aware, of course," he presumed. I slightly nodded again in response, keeping up my appearance in knowing this common fact. *Whitehall*, I did recognize: the very heart of aristocratic power, wealth, and social elitism—and the epicenter of British politics. So, my growing dislike for his unabashed sense of entitlement and derision for those living in this land, which cast them as lesser than he, formed my negative opinion of him at this moment, divorced from Leif's own reasons for disliking him. "Guaranteed a most prime experience living in either Whitehall or Mayfair rather than Captain Miller's own enduring, I assure you," he concluded.

"Why is that?" I asked, somewhat confused by the unexpected belittlement of his companion, who I'd believed was a friend.

"'Tis certain Captain Miller may better explain, Your Grace," he answered flippantly. As Captain Berkley said this, he directed our attention toward his companion sitting beside him.

"I am also London bred, but from Covent Garden, Your Grace," Captain Miller divulged politely in a more modest tone. The self-effacing note in his voice reflected the look on his face and struck a different chord with me as I discerned the earnestness in his eyes.

"I see," I responded courteously, also nodding in acknowledgment.

"Indeed, not much aristocracy or gentry remain in this locality but for Miller's family," Captain Berkley mocked. I turned my gaze to Captain Berkley with an unresponsive look, though I was silently questioning the reason for his jeer. "Middlings have overrun the vicinity, dragging in the paupers. Not the paragon design for the high born at all," he stated.

"My family maintains a nice property in Covent Garden, Your Grace. We are not disturbed by our surroundings," Captain Miller upheld deferentially, contradicting Berkley's conceit.

"I'm glad for you, Captain Miller. It's nice to know that your family is happy where they live," I said pleasantly to him.

"Thank you, Your Grace. They are," Captain Miller responded genuinely. I gave him a slight nod of acknowledgment.

"Will you tell me anything about them?" I asked, more interested in learning about him.

"I shall, of course, oblige, Your Grace," he agreed politely. It was then, during this conversation with Captain Miller, that I learned that he had descended from the aristocracy also, while his family now belonged to the landed gentry. As he divulged this information to me, I also noted the reserved and humble demeanor he displayed. A stark contrast to Captain Berkley's bombast, and it favored my better opinion of Captain Miller.

Captain Miller continued to reveal his family's connections in government, paralleling Captain Berkley's family's political influence, while both captains' wealth had purchased their commissions in the army. Without encouraging a political discussion between us, I logically assumed them both to be Tories, skirting the heavy topic altogether to my comfort.

"It seems you're close to your family, Captain Miller," I assessed nicely.

"I am quite fond of my family, yes," he answered pleasantly.

"That's very nice. Do you correspond with them?" I asked.

"Frequently, I do so with my younger brother, Richard, who guards our younger sister, Jane. It is merely the three of us left after my parents' departure."

"Oh, my condolences to you for your parents' passing."

"Thank you most kindly for your commiserations, Your Grace."

"Of course," I replied sincerely. "Do you mind my asking the time of their passing away?"

"Not at all. 'Twas a year ago from grippe which had struck them ill," he informed me.

"Oh, I am so sorry," I replied sympathetically.

"It was indeed a trying event. Yet, 'tis most fortunate my siblings and I remain well."

"Yes, it's very fortunate," I agreed, certainly. "Have you been assigned to Boston for long?"

"Closely a year, presently," Captain Berkley answered for him, interrupting and inserting himself into the conversation again.

"I see." I returned my attention to Captain Berkley, regarding him, and continued to ask generally, "How do you like Boston?"

"'Tis manageable, respectfully considering. Though one cannot help but notice the copious piety prevailing amongst the residing subjects pacing the walkways," Captain Berkley responded.

"I see." A bit chafed by his disposition, I couldn't help saying, "Well, considering that people overall are judgmental essentially, they are bound to form opinions of others whether conscious of it or not. Since we all come from various life experiences, constructing our outlooks, despite how similar our origins may be, we all carry specific biases relating to ourselves and others. Construing objective opinions about things, people, or their situations is contingent upon our own biases. Really, the standard of opinions accepted in society can be respectfully questioned due to discrepancies among individual perceptions resulting from personal background experiences. In short, opinions are not facts. They are just opinions. Everybody has them."

"Judge not, lest ye be judged," Captain Miller supported.

"Very true, Captain Miller," I agreed. "Opinions are trivial. They don't mean anything. What matters are people's actions."

"Those would be facts," Captain Miller commented.

"Exactly." It seemed Captain Miller and I might share a bit of the same philosophy, I thought, as I gave him a small smile, and he reciprocated a faint grin of his own. "So, it's possible to consider that widely accepted opinions of others could actually be harmful to society at large when those opinions are the catalyst for actions taken against those perceived unfavorably because they are cast as less desirable when they may be innocent of causing any detriment to anyone at all."

"His Grace must enjoy his wife's intellect," Captain Berkley stated, appearing somewhat rigid in his chair as his face flushed. I sensed that he had been insulted. If he received the impression that I wasn't charmed or impressed by him, then I thought it was good, and I didn't care if he'd felt placed by me.

"As I appreciate the value of my husband's own intelligence, he also values my unique perspective on his logic, Captain Berkley. It's kind of you to have recognized this characteristic," I replied to him.

"'Tis intriguing to understand that you are well learned, Your Grace. I care not to cause any discord with your clear ability to reason as I am certain I shall be enlightened by you as well while proceeding our respectable engagement," he said, lobbing another masked discredit adhering to my inference, as the apologetic look in his eyes was contradicted by the faint smirk on his face.

"You're generous to claim an open mind, Captain Berkley. Admittedly, it'll be interesting to know how receptive you are to novel ideas stemming from my perspective, as I may occasionally express them. I'm always interested in a good-natured, little debate sometimes that might inform me of you as well," I replied, cordially returning the challenge.

"I shall be much obliged, Your Grace." He gave a confident little smirk.

"Good," I said, equally understanding as I reciprocated a certain pleasant little smile of my own.

"I thank you for already granting me a bit of awareness into your reason according to Boston's manner of perception, which differs from those in London."

"You're very welcome. The more we are open to sharing our

differences, the likelihood of creating mutual understandings as misinterpretations invariably dispel, allowing us to find the commonality existing between us, which bridges us together instead of the held preconceived ideas that will divide us—I believe."

"An intriguing notion, indeed," he admitted. "Being my first experience in Boston, I am, however, becoming more acquainted with its customs."

"I'm glad you are, Captain Berkley."

"Yes, I have taken an interest in the popular diversion of visiting taverns, as there are no theaters that exist to my preference and liking to attend."

"I see." Revealing this information, I knew he was not only bold but also purposeful and explicit. This was a clear indication of his tendency to be tactless and disrespectful, especially if he weren't blatantly fishing for my acceptance of laissez-faire behavior or outright scandal, since theaters at this time were known for their ill repute. I nearly reacted with clear surprise when I felt my brow begin to rise involuntarily, but caught myself instead as I consciously forced myself to gaze unaffectedly at him.

But Captain Miller did react as he suddenly stiffened more acutely in his chair and gaped at Captain Berkley. Evidently, Captain Miller would have never said what his companion just did by the stunned look he was giving him.

"Pray, Your Grace, I beg your pardon for Captain Berkley's impression that he has given you. It is apparent that he lacks delicacy and refinement in spite of his superior breeding," Captain Miller interjected swiftly, abruptly swinging his gaze toward me and steadily holding my eyes. It was discernible that Captain Miller was not only sharply embarrassed but truly apologetic by the sincerity in his regretful expression for his friend's rudeness.

"It's nice of you to apologize, Captain Miller. Thank you," I accepted.

"Most gracious of you to accept, Your Grace," Captain Miller responded appreciatively. His gaze then bounced from mine down toward the book I was still holding in my hand and returned to me again. "I see that you favor reading. Might I inquire about the title of the book you read?" He pursued unevenly, quickly trying to change the subject and circumvent the cumbersome air that had swiftly descended among us.

"Yes, Captain Miller. I'm entertaining myself with reading Ovid," I said.

"Oh?"

"Yes."

"Which of his poems do you enjoy?"

"I'm enjoying *Metamorphoses*."

"I am fond of Perseus myself."

"Is that so?"

"Indeed. I find his character rich in nature."

"I think I agree."

"I quite admire Sophocles, if I dare say also," Captain Berkley said, wedging himself into the conversation again.

"I see," I replied inertly as Captain Miller and I were called to his attention.

"Quite true. I am most fond of his *Trachinian Women*," Captain Berkley said, resuming as if he'd done nothing wrong.

"That's a tragedy," I recognized.

"Indeed, it is," he said with a single nod.

"What about the story do you like?" I asked Captain Berkley, trying to maintain the façade that I wasn't close to being annoyed by him, as I encouraged the general conversation.

"The precept of how quite easily women are simply tricked into betrayal to harm the men who love them, quite plainly," Captain Berkley answered.

"In truth, you are not sincere, Berkley," his companion replied, clearly doubting.

"I quite am, however."

"Should this be the case, you have missed the gist of the tale entirely," Captain Miller asserted.

"I disagree that I have not."

"I assure you that you have as I contradict your poor interpretation that is not commonly understood or accepted."

"It is understood, however, and therefore accepted amongst those who have once listened to my explanation and reason for it, Miller."

"Be that you explain it or not, your incorrect position of comprehending the play in your manner is obscure as it is rare and most believably has been considered your mistake by those who would apparently know better, therefore placating your ignorance from their solicitude lest you not succumb to their offense by your expanded sense of self-import. I must say the number of those who have taken pity upon you is remarkable."

"Insufferable," Captain Berkley scorned under his breath, scowling also with a glare toward his presumed friend.

"You only had to pay your tutor's attention and listen to him whilst being taught. Not at all a difficult feat for many of us at the time."

"Thus, you will impress, Her Grace, certainly. Proceed to enlighten me, after all, Miller." The tone in Captain Berkley's voice flowed with condescension while narrowing his eyes on his companion with visible irritation.

"Your humility is regarded, Berkley, as you generously offer for me to instruct you in this matter," Captain Miller ricocheted, glancing at Berkley with a slight smirk. Given their responses to each other, I wasn't exactly sure if they were truly friends. Or, if they were, whether this was their normal treatment of each other as they displayed their rivalry. So, I was certainly a little confused by these two men while gazing at them. "Apparently, the lesson that has evaded you, Berkley, is the driven depths of love to which perils it may lead through sacrifice in one's demise found in Deianira by no fault of her own but for the love she had for her husband, Heracles, who failed to return her affection. 'Twas his lack of devotion to his wife by his lust for Lole, which inversely caused his cessation. Poetically justified by the gods, as they had wielded their fate.

"Therefore, Berkley, I will simplify it further in terms which you may understand, is that the arching lesson pertains to the innocence of women subjected to the harmful whims of men."

When Captain Miller finished explaining, a pause in the conversation ensued, and Captain Berkley's eyes narrowed on him as he glared unfavorably with evident disdain. I don't think he appreciated Captain Miller's rebuttal or the challenge he was giving him.

"It would seem this fiber of the tale considerably runs parallel to your mode of thinking, Miller. Typically, idiosyncratic of you, of course. Therefore, I am hardly plagued by you in the merest. Yet, why must you esteem contemporaries like Price and Voltaire?"

"I am not of the antiquated mind and much prefer being enlightened over reason than relegated to stupidity."

"Yet, you are an intellectual fop."

"Your belief, of course." Captain Miller subtly smirked at him, and suddenly, Captain Berkley became silent again, tightening his mouth with narrowed eyes. Then, Captain Miller returned his attention to me with a more pleasant look of politeness and regard. "Forgive my distraction, Your Grace. Might I, however, request our continuation of the topic we were discussing?"

"Yes, of course, Captain Miller," I replied, somewhat surprised by their differences.

"I thank you most kindly, Your Grace," he responded sincerely. "I had merely attempted to inform you that I do favor Perseus's adventures as well as you, with Andromeda being a favorite."

"Really?" I responded interestedly.

"Indeed," Captain Miller said, reflecting his genuine expression.

"That's actually my favorite story also," I admitted.

"Certainly?"

"Yes. He's very heroic."

"Quite throughout, indeed."

"Permit my submission of the tale with him and Medusa striking my fancy's chord," Captain Berkley interposed again, still appearing rather comfortable enough to continue engaging.

"Why is that, Captain Berkley?" I asked, inadvertently curious.

"I also quite admire Perseus's bravery, exhibited in the slaughter of Medusa, as she was evil. An attribute of hers which holds no discrepancy, as a matter of fact," he answered confidently.

"Except, was she actually evil?" I countered, curious to know the reason for his one-dimensional characterization of her.

"Her loathing consumed her entirely, dictating her actions toward men, for every man who ever laid eyes upon her was turned to stone as she revealed herself to them from a beauty to the gorgon that she was."

"But there's more to it. Don't you think?"

"I fear not, indeed."

"Really?"

"I believe so, Your Grace."

"Mayhap, Her Grace will be so generous to apprize us of her viewpoint," Captain Miller encouraged kindly, implying.

"Thank you, Captain Miller. I would only like to say that according to the whole story, an interpretation of it can be that Medusa is a misunderstood character," I said, raising an idea.

"Would you say?" Captain Berkley questioned.

"Yes, I would."

"How might Your Grace infer it upon Medusa's nature?"

"Well, if you would consider that it was told in the story that not only was she once an immensely beautiful woman at one point, who had been a dedicated priestess to Athena, but she had also declined every male's advance toward her because of her loyal service to the goddess. Wouldn't that indicate the real underlying value of her integrity?"

Captain Berkley didn't immediately respond as he appeared

reluctant to grant this consideration. So, I proceeded to say, "I mean, if you wish to draw a more relatable parallel, it could be respectfully similar to a modern nun who is also physically beautiful by the natural constitution of her existence and is strictly devoted to her service to God. In that vein, considering this contemporary period, wouldn't a woman like that be revered and held in the highest regard?"

"It would seem that she would?" he confessed with a trace of skepticism in his voice.

"Seem? You suggest doubt by using the operative word, Captain Berkley. Is it because she would be beautiful and can't be a nun simultaneously, so you question her purity?" I asked directly.

"'Tis not my meaning, Your Grace," he replied, somewhat ruffled.

"Then, what did you mean?"

"I am still listening to Your Grace's argument in championing Medusa, merely."

"I see. Well, I will defend Medusa because she is commonly misunderstood as she is viewed through a pervasive patriarchal lens, which often skews objectivity relating to the female sex. So, thank you for patronizing me with your attention to my perspective as I continue telling you what it is," I responded civilly while innocuously sparring the word *patronizing* into use, pointing to my awareness of him, which could be used and determined as an insult.

"As it pleases, Your Grace, pray do proceed as I am indeed stirred with interest," he said civilly without indicating he'd clued into the subtlety of my backhanded insult.

"So, as you might remember in the story, it was Poseidon who raped Medusa as she was serving Athena. Athena was angry, of course, as a result, but her anger was misdirected since Medusa received her wrath when Athena turned Medusa into a gorgon because of her own jealousy over Medusa's rivaling beauty. By Athena's punishing of Medusa, she effectively blamed the victim instead of laying the blame where it rightly belonged, onto Poseidon. So, Medusa is justified by her wrath against all men as she was unduly wronged. She's a tragedy and deserves sympathy, not to be judged harshly," I concluded.

Captain Berkley fell silent again, looking a little flummoxed at me. But I noticed the ruddiness in his face drain, and he looked pale. It seemed he might have suddenly become embarrassed or offended. I couldn't discern which. So, I stared at him also until he was ready to speak.

"Yet, she was slain nonetheless for the monster she had become," he replied after a moment. The bitter coolness in his voice was restrained but noticeable.

"Her vengeance was warranted. She wasn't evil in the beginning. To be fair, evil can be rooted in us also if we experience any harm to ourselves or threat to our security as we decide to seek retribution, becoming obsessed with it instead after being denied justice for the crime committed against us—which, for the individual who committed the crime was evil for doing it, to begin with. However, then again, everyone has a backstory for what they have done and may seek to be excused for it, only to be given pity. The point being, is that if victims of wrongs were properly served justice by the punishment of those who have harmed, then probably the urge for revenge would be reduced, and perhaps end the cycle of crime altogether," I explained.

"I see," he replied.

"Yes. That would be my understanding."

"Quite a novelty."

"The halting of crime would be a novelty for certain," I replied.

"I meant Your Grace's perception. I thank you, for I have been fairly enlightened by it, of course."

"Thank you for the conversation, Captain Berkley."

"By all means, Your Grace. Indeed." This time, the tone in his voice came through sincerely, and the expression on his face altered toward satisfaction as the snideness vanished. By his reaction, a slight sense of easement came over me as I believed a regard of honest respect had been garnered from him.

As silence emerged among us, it seemed our conversation, in general, had ended. It was also apparent that Amity had finished her time embroidering and started tucking her project into the basket at her feet. After finishing, she drew it by its handle and stood from sitting on the sofa, giving me a prepared look to leave the room with her. So, I also stood from my seat, ready to leave, and as we were about to withdraw, both men came to their feet.

"Good day, Your Grace. 'Twas a pleasurable discourse, for which I thank your generosity," Captain Miller regarded politely.

"You're welcome, Captain Miller. I enjoyed it as well," I replied.

"I also would agree that 'twas intuitive, indeed, Your Grace," Captain Berkley added, sounding equally cordial as well.

"I definitely agree, Captain Berkley," I said.

"Good day, Your Grace," Captain Berkley responded.

"Good day to you, officers." They acknowledged with a bow in unison, and Amity slipped her arm around mine, linking us, as we both agreed to leave the room.

Moving past the doorway to the sitting room, we vanished into the corridor and began our way toward the staircase. When we entered a different corridor along the way, Prudence was noticed leaning with her back against the wall, holding freshly folded linens, while Lieutenant Jones leaned his lips close to hers. It was obvious that the pair were kissing, if not flirting with each other, first. Coquettishly batting her eyes at him while diffidently replying to a personal question he'd asked her, he grinned sexually at her, and she giggled sheepishly. Assuming they were safely tucked out of sight in the depths of the wall's recess in the corner nook, well hidden, they were suddenly startled from their clandestine engagement as we unexpectedly appeared.

Lieutenant Jones abruptly removed himself from Prudence,

stepping away into the center of the hallway before us. He stumbled off guard, and the hue in his face flushed bright red.

"Your Grace!" he blurted, surprised. Immediately bowing and straightening, he looked at me with embarrassment as he tried to assume his respectful regard for my presence.

"Lieutenant Jones," I acknowledged curiously, sounding modest nevertheless. Before having the ability to turn my questioning eyes toward Prudence, she averted her gaze from me. She bobbed a sharp curtsy before swiftly rushing away from the scene, taking flight through the passageway in the opposite direction.

"Begging your forgiveness, Your Grace," Lieutenant Jones started unevenly. Returning my attention from noticing Prudence's hasty disappearance to looking at him, I was certainly wondering about the inappropriateness of what was going on with him and our maid.

"Lieutenant Jones, I don't believe it's proper for you to be interested in any of our staff. You're at an advantage, as you know. We're very protective of members who work for us and don't wish for any one of them to become hurt. I hope you'll understand," I said, calibrating my voice as politely as I could, concerned for Prudence's well-being.

"I do, Your Grace. My truest apologies," he responded deferentially, despite the apparent embarrassment displayed on his reddened face.

"In that case, are you returning to the Common to finish for the day?" I inquired innocuously.

"Quite right that I am, as I have completed my respite, and therefore must report for patrol," he said with a bit of unease remaining detectable in his voice.

"I see. Well then, I won't keep you any later from your reporting for duty," I said.

"Much obliged to you, Your Grace. I shall promptly take leave. Good day to you, of course, Your Grace."

"To you also, Lieutenant Jones."

He quickly started from me and withdrew through the corridor. I lingered my eyes on him a little as I watched him hurriedly diminishing in the hallway until he rounded the corner and disappeared. I wasn't exceptionally comfortable with what I was encountering today with these additional men occupying our house as I returned with Amity and continued our way toward the staircase. But I felt sure to mention this discomfort to Leif when there was a chance for us to be alone together, and I wasn't going to let it escape me.

Twenty-Four

L ater the same evening, when Leif finally came home and we were settling into bed after dinner, I made him aware of the encounter Amity and I had in the hallway as we'd witnessed Lieutenant Jones's sexual advance toward Prudence. As expected, Leif was not even close to being pleased about knowing this had happened to Prudence and was certain to address this issue with the lieutenant. But when I further disclosed to him the interruption initiated by Captain Berkley, followed by Captain Miller's accompaniment while Amity and Winnet were first occupying the sitting room alone, together with the door closed, the indignation expressed on Leif's face was blatant as his brow shot upward. His eyes widened with his lips pinched into a line. The muscles in his jaw also throbbed. He was gritting his teeth while measuring his temper, glaring sharply at me.

"Our niece and her maid waur intruded upon in their privacy despite being shuttered?" Leif questioned collectedly, calibrating his tone as he digested this information.

"Yes. They were," I answered carefully, attempting to mitigate his reaction from becoming more tense. He didn't respond, except that he continued clinching his jaw. "Winnet was very upset about

253

it while trying her best to follow your wishes. But she's undermined when she can't even have Amity safely alone to themselves
without men who are here simply ignoring the simple protocol
behind the meaning of closed doors to a room. Winnet is very
scared that you'll dismiss her because of this when she means to
carry out her responsibility."

"I shan't do anything of the sort. She need not be troobled.
Have a word with her. Will ye not?" Leif insisted.

"I've already tried calming her. But I'll definitely speak with
her again tomorrow to reassure her of her continuing position, so
she feels secure and won't worry anymore," I replied, agreeing.

"Guid. I shall mind these impudent officers as I swiftly aim
them accordingly. 'Twill be done promptly upon dawn of the
morrow."

"Okay."

"Henceforth, keep me abreast should any one of them sway tae
cause any more offense. I shall ken of their disobedience immediately and hold them keenly accountable tae me. Understood?"

"I will. Of course."

"Very weel. 'Tis imperative in order that I may act tae safeguard the welfare of my family and remaining property, particularly regarding the soldiers billeting within our nearest vicinity. 'Tis
the nature of such men as a whole tae trifle with lasses, innocent or
not, tae satiate their needful desires as they quickly discard them by
holding nae meaning," he added, reminding me.

"I'm aware," I replied.

"Aye," he acknowledged with a single accompanying nod. He
paused a second before further inquiring, "Is thaur more else of
any significance which occurred today during my absence of which
I must be made awaur?"

"No. That's all." I lightly shook my head. But, Leif perceived
me and I knew that he was aware of more I had to say. "Except..."

"Except, whit?"

"I had a conversation with some of the soldiers."

"Indeed?" Suddenly, Leif's face turned even more dour.

"Yes."

"With whom?"

"Captain Berkley and Captain Miller."

"I see. Whit did it regard?" he asked as the dour look on his face hardened.

"The conversation revolved around Greek mythology. Specifically about Medusa, Athena, and Poseidon," I answered, staring back at Leif's expression. "But there was more to the conversation."

"Was thaur?"

"Yes. Captain Berkley was being nosey."

"Nosey?" He asked as his brow slightly furrowed.

"I mean that he was asking me all sorts of inquisitive questions about where I was from and was prying."

"I see." Determining the look in Leif's eyes, I knew that he wasn't pleased. "That soldier in particular," he grumbled under his breath.

"What is it about him?"

"Pomposity," he said. "Ye wulnae fear the haven of *Taigh Gràs*, fur I pledge it so." He whipped the blankets over us, covering us well as I watched him from where I was lying on the pillows, tucking us securely beneath them. Briefly satisfied by blanketing us, he rested himself against the pillows also, facing me. As I gazed into his eyes staring back at me, I knew with certainty by the promise he just made that he was steadfastly determined to ensure and maintain the reality of our security and safety here given the razor look in his eyes that echoed the tone of his unadulterated, steely voice. "Rest assured," he said, moderating his tone slightly as he gazed into my eyes.

"All right," I said, aware that he perceived the concerning questions silently running in my mind. But the softer tone in his voice mirroring the look in his eyes now, mollified and steadied me as I felt myself relaxing. I was now comforted. He reached a gentle palm over my cheek and tenderly caressed it when I felt the pad of his thumb lightly sweep my lips. I softly kissed his thumb as it stilled over my mouth and his lips faintly broke into a subtle grin, bringing affection to his eyes.

"Sleep weel, *àille dhubh*," he uttered under his breath, urging me to finally close my eyes. So, I did as he drew me against himself and soundly fitted me with his body. Spooning with him at my back, his arm came around me, fixing me with him, and I drifted to sleep the moment I felt his lips softly pressing upon the back of my crown.

SINCE THE OCCURRENCE with the soldiers involving Lieutenant Jones and Captains Miller and Berkley, it seemed an undebatable understanding among them all had been established and well understood for them not to engage any of us women of the household, particularly with respect to anyone's privacy when doors to rooms were closed, whether rooms were vacant or not. Whatever it was that Leif had said to them, it worked. From then on, soldiers precisely avoided us with the exception of respectfully acknowledging us with polite greetings upon encounters in the hallways or when we dined. This also included strolling the property outdoors, where they remained obligingly considerate as they kept their distances.

Now that it's been a month since this new etiquette had been established, I resumed feeling comfortably at home here again at *Taigh Gràs*. Having the range to be in command of our household and being able to do as I pleased without the hindrance from boarding soldiers, I no longer felt stifled.

Today, Amity, Mercy, Winnet, and I seized this beautiful, mild fall morning to spend in the garden. Many of the maples, birches, and dogwoods had begun bursting deep alizarin crimsons, and cadmium reds and yellows throughout the scene, whichever way the eye turned. A rainbow palette of intense colors exploded as their leaves rustled in the stirring breeze from the shore, highlighted by surrounding viridian evergreens. At the same time, we strolled through the grounds to arrive at the garden.

Amplifying the garden, abundant, fully bloomed thick bushes of towering lavender hydrangeas, densely lower lying rich-purple aster and cornflower shrubs, complementing brilliant yellow sneezeweed and black-eyed Susans that intensified the striking beauty of it all. But the massive amounts of large and small blooming roses, which matured in hues of red, yellow, white, and pink, glorified the panorama. And, the pleasant perfume emitted from all the blooms was intoxicating. It was utterly astounding, amassing the full sense of what Eden must have been like.

Much of our morning was spent here enjoying each other's company. Amity and Winnet sat on one of the nearby marble benches as Amity had begun reading a favorite book of hers and Winnet continued darning stockings. Mercy happily assisted me in pruning roses and collecting an assortment of other blooms to fill our large baskets.

While she and I were contentedly snipping flowers and placing them into our baskets, a thorn from a rose pricked my forefinger, causing me to wince. The sting was sharp and quick, and a droplet of ruby red blood suddenly emerged at the tip of my finger. Shoving my other hand into my pocket, I quickly drew forth my handkerchief and pressed it onto my little wound as I applied pressure to stem the bleeding while Mercy carefully observed me. Assuring her that I was all right, she continued snipping flowers, mindful of her own hands. When the blood on my finger soon ceased flowing, I tucked my handkerchief back into my pocket, thinking nothing of my injury, and returned to clipping more roses to fill in the basket.

As I resumed collecting more flowers, I was inspired to start a conversation with Mercy. I remembered Jerome from the time she had spoken of him to me a long time ago. I was curious to learn more about her and him, and I wondered if she would share anything with me.

"Does Jerome still work for the Crawfords?" I asked her thoughtfully. Mercy slid a little shy glance without a smile when briefly looking away from the flower she'd just nipped from its branch.

"Yes'm. He do," she replied confidentially, placing the white rose among the purple hydrangeas in her basket.

"I see. So, tell me a little about him, since it's been so long. Do you two still communicate?" I wondered.

"Upon a time when we is at church. We do that, ma'am," she said softly, so that I almost couldn't hear. I realized again, that she remained timid to speak about him, or at least to inform me.

"How nice," I acknowledged gently, appreciating her subtlety. I was also glad to know that they still seemed to have their friendship.

"Yes'm," she agreed.

"He's older than you, isn't he?"

"Yes'm. He be."

"By how much? I think I forgot."

"Some bit over fo years, to have you recall, ma'am."

"So, he's thirty-one, then?"

"I reckon it true."

"Oh. Did he marry?"

"No, ma'am. He ain't done that."

"He hasn't?"

"No, ma'am."

"I wonder why not?"

"He ain't been permitted to do so," she said simply, and I realized it was because he was owned without any rights of his own.

"He's creole from the West Indies, isn't he? If I'm remembering correctly from what you've told me already?"

"From Martinique, more truthfully."

"Oh. I hadn't known from where specifically. That would

surely be the reason for why he'd know how to speak French, of course."

"Yes'm."

"So, he wouldn't be indentured. Would he?"

"He ain't no indentured, ma'am."

"I had a feeling."

"But them Crawfords is good to him."

"They are?"

"They ain't never beat 'em."

"I see." I nodded slightly, acknowledging, feeling my brow knit by the abusive concept and reality of being beaten, as I considered what she'd just told me. The fact that he hadn't been beaten by them could be viewed as a demonstration of their compassion and mercy by eighteenth-century mores. The Crawfords must have had some standards of moral ways to treat human beings, I grant. "I'm extremely glad to know that he's never been beaten by them," I said, understanding his fortune.

"Not once, ma'am, did he be whupped whilst bein' owned by them Crawfords, as plenty others been who is owned by different massahs not like Massah Crawford hisself. Jerome says Massah Crawford say words for correction instead of takin' up the switch. So, none of they slaves has experience bein' beat," she explained. "Accordin' to Jerome, Massah Crawford don't agree wif whuppin', so he don't do it to none of 'em that he own hisself," she explained further.

"I'm very glad for Jerome and for the others among him, if this is true," I recognized.

"It all be verily true," Mercy assured. "Accordin' more to Jerome, Massah Crawford be mild spoken. I reckon much as His Grace be wif us."

"I see," I recognized again. "Except, he isn't allowed to get married. Did Jerome ever tell you the reason why Mister Crawford is not allowing him this?"

Mercy paused for a moment, delaying her answer as she

continued arranging the blooms she'd just snipped into the basket at her feet. She hesitated, and I wondered why. Perceiving her reluctance, I thought maybe to change the subject, believing it was preferred by her. But before I could refer to a different topic of conversation regarding the beautiful flowers we were collecting, she continued saying, "It ain't got nofin' to do wif Massah Crawford granting Jerome permission to wed."

"It doesn't?" I responded, somewhat surprised.

"Yes'm. Massah Crawford permit Jerome his wish."

"He has?"

"Yes'm. He done so."

"Then, why hasn't Jerome married if he wants to?"

"'Tis due to His Grace."

"His Grace?" I felt my brow suddenly rise high as I looked at Mercy in surprise and confusion, wondering how Leif figured into entangling himself in Jerome's romantic interests.

"Yes'm." Mercy nodded faintly, keeping her eyes on the next bloom she meant to crop. "Massah Crawford abides His Grace."

"I don't understand. How is His Grace any influence on how Mister Crawford conducts his personal business regarding Jerome?" I asked curiously.

"In a manner as be expected by His Grace, ma'am—if I mayn't be out my place to remind."

"No—I mean, yes—I mean, I know there are expectations and formalities to be recognized. I would just like to know precisely how His Grace would be involved," I clarified after blundering. She glanced away from the flower caught between her fingers, preparing to shear it, and her sheepish eyes rested on mine, the second I seized another flower between my own fingers to clip.

"Jerome be wishin' to wed me, ma'am," she quietly disclosed, turning more reservedly shy than she already was.

"Really?" I sensed my brow rise abruptly with pleasant surprise.

"His Grace ain't familiar with Massah Crawford, as you

already certain to know, ma'am," she said, and I nodded a little, trying to keep up appearances that I was aware of this. "Jerome says Massah Crawford ain't got no place to fix the matter betwixt us even if Massah Crawford could spend his charity upon Jerome and me on account he ain't never merely had the fortune to polity greet His Grace at King's Chapel after Sunday service. Much less Massah Crawford bein' able to request an audience wif His Grace fo buyin' me from His Grace to add to his household fo pleasin' Jerome's wish."

"Taking you from us?" I suddenly gave her a worried look as I realized the situation potentially affecting the pleasant convenience of my friendship with her, which I strongly admired since she was my closest companion here, outside of Leif and Amity.

"Knowin' His Grace and his great fondness fo you, ma'am, he ain't never goin' to permit sellin' and removing me from here to satisfy nobody's wish," she expressed genuinely. "Besides, 'tis also well known by most everybody that he mercifully placed me into yo service, ma'am, fo which I is most pleased. Most pleased and grateful indeed, that he saved me and brung me to *Taigh Gràs* from a slavedriver who was certain to whore me to every man who would pay his price on the wharf." I nodded gently in response, acknowledging that what she was saying about what Leif had done for her was true. "So, I's won't be takin' no kinda leave from you, ma'am, any time soon."

As she continued looking at me, the sincerity of her deep appreciation for serving me was evident in her eyes. But while I knew the equal friendship bond we shared and the sentimental value it brought that was unique to us, I couldn't help the sharp guilt and sorrow I felt that she was being prevented from pursuing her own happiness because she was enslaved and waiting on me.

"Do you love Jerome?" I gently asked her directly, wanting to know. She paused momentarily. It seemed she was about to avoid answering when she glanced at the flower still held between her fingers for a second. Then, she returned to looking at me and focused, appearing not only reticent but hiding the possibility by the scarce hint in her hesitancy.

"He be a good God-fearing man, ma'am," Mercy responded quietly.

"It's very good that he is," I agreed. "As for loving him, though? Do you have feelings for him like that?"

"I is fond of him a bit," she disclosed cautiously.

"A bit?"

"Yes'm."

"I see... So, then, would that amount of bit be enough for your liking to marry him if you could?"

"I's afraid I ain't understanding yo meaning, ma'am," she replied respectfully in the most innocent tone. But a little smile came over my lips, because I knew better.

"Mercy?" I prompted. Then, a small smile faintly crept over her own lips, giving her away. "I see," I said, deducing the fact. "Well, maybe His Grace and I will have to arrive at a solution for both of you to be married." I gave her an encouraging little look.

"No, ma'am!" She gasped abruptly. Her eyes widened, blatantly conveying alarm on her face.

"Why not?" I was suddenly confused and very worried by her contradictory reaction.

"You mustn't, ma'am," she pleaded, extremely unsettled.

"Tell me why?" I wondered, honestly, and was also quickly concerned.

"*Taigh Gràs* graciously be my home I's most blessed and thankful fo. Although Jerome says Massah Crawford is a good massah, no manner can he be benevolent as His Grace be. I also ain't knowin' noffin' about Missus Crawford 'sep Jerome says she strict yet kind. 'Spite so, no missus compare to you, ma'am, that I knowin' to be true. You is known entirely fo yo charity and kind-ness in all of Boston. What's more, I is fondest of you, ma'am, so I don't cares to take leave fo none other massah's dwellin' and serve his missus that I knows I ain't certain of, since I knows better from bein' here with you. Excuse me fo bein' too bold, ma'am, as I's permitted by you to speak freely by expressin' myself fo you to know my mind. But whilst I do care fo Jerome, I ain't wishin' by no means to depart *Taigh Gràs* by weddn' him so I's can be taken to the Crawfords to dwell, and forsake what pleases me most by existing here and serving you," she explained anxiously. "No, ma'am. I ain't never wishin' for no such thing to become of me, since you don't mind my tellin' you so. That be the God honest truth. Indeed so, ma'am. Indeed so."

I quickly understood her fears as I also realized that by marrying Jerome, she'd be sacrificing her own security for the happiness she'd found by living with us. It would be a significant risk for her to give it all up to marry Jerome, who couldn't even legally give her his name, much less protect her if anything wrong ever happened to her. If this were ever to happen, he would be compelled to right the wrong not out of the legal right he lacked, but for the mere sake of it, from emotions alone—jeopardizing his very life to an immediate end. And most surely, as a result, she would be left widowed with the fruit of their offspring, who could potentially be separated and sold to different households.

That responsibility to guard her wellbeing would lawfully fall on Mr. Crawford, and who's to say how protective he'd be for the ones enslaved already working for him and his family? Any situation arising regarding the people he owned was left to his complete discretion, determined by the legal right he had and how much he sincerely cared for them. So, how could Mercy be asked to trust Mr. Crawford, or anyone else, to safeguard her wellbeing when she already knew and was guaranteed this security she'd certainly found here? It was a lot to ask of Jerome to ask her to place her trust in Mr. Crawford by marrying Jerome and moving into another household with him, no doubt—even if Leif would ever consider releasing her to this man. In a sense, because Leif and I were so lenient with our servants anyway, Mercy was freer to be more comfortable with us and do as she pleased outside of working. That, in itself, also enhanced her awareness of the value of living at *Taigh Gràs* rather than gambling on living anywhere else.

"I'm very sorry, Mercy. I didn't mean to scare you. Not at all. It would never be my intention to do that to you," I apologized sympathetically, feeling awful that I'd ever frighten her. "I understand your reasons for not wanting to marry Jerome, or anyone else. I hadn't realized your feelings until now. I wouldn't ever threaten your happiness here, because I love you as a friend. I'd miss you too much also if you ever left. So, please never worry—*Taigh Gràs* is certainly your home, and it's always here for you since it's where you belong."

She nodded slightly, appearing typically demure but calmer now.

"I's most grateful to you, ma'am. Indeed, I is. I thank you immensely fo regardin' me as you do," she responded meekly. But the sheer relief displayed on her face was reflected in her eyes, despite her deference. I also understood quite distinctly that I was precisely responsible for the stability of her personhood by having the highest influence over Leif's ultimate decisions.

"You're very welcome, Mercy. But you don't have to thank me. I just hope you know how important you are to me—that I care for you and want you to receive everything that's good, like I do hope for everyone else who is close to me," I said.

"Yo charity cannot be matched, ma'am," she responded gratefully.

"I'm not being charitable, Mercy. I fundamentally respect you."

"You be carryin' respect fo me?" Her eyes abruptly widened as her brow knitted in surprise and confusion.

"I certainly do. Of course."

"I beggin' yo pardon, ma'am, fo bein' contrary, but how can it be? I ain't nobody in the merest sense and you quite above me."

"I'm above no one, Mercy. And, to God, you are certainly somebody. That goes without question. He had the will and love to create you, not like anything else He made, and created you in His image, like all other human beings. So, because I'm in awe of all that He's ever created out of His love, I can't help but value the life He's given to everything that exists which includes you, and at least respect you for being—and of course love you just because I do—which essentially makes Him happy, as it does for me too. There's nothing complicated to understand. It's very simple, actually," I conveyed sincerely. She didn't immediately respond, seeming speechless, except the unexpected expression remaining on her face exposed her blatant shock over what I had just said.

"I's most grateful, surpassin' my ability to properly express myself. I's certain to be mo than pleased to sees that my missus is verily well waited upon by me. It be a true blessin' bestowed unto me," she resumed after a lapse. A nice smile eased over her lips, making her appear generously happy and pacified. The look on her face was genuine, and I smiled also, sensing that our connection had grown even deeper.

"Well, all I can say to you is thank you dearly for your attention to me. You should know that I truly appreciate you very much. For everything. Especially, for being my friend." Her smile widened while she remained humble, and I couldn't help but smile more.

We fell quiet with each other, then, and subsequently returned to peacefully clipping flowers around the garden, placing them into our baskets until they overflowed and filled the air with their rich, pleasant perfume. Satisfied with our collections, the four of us were ready to leave the garden for the house, intending to display the plentiful, colorful blooms in decorative vases throughout the mansion.

Twenty-Five

W e returned indoors with our thick bouquets. Amity, Winnet, Mercy, and I prepared the stems for placement and arrangement into several large, beautifully painted porcelain vases, which would be displayed throughout the house. When the colorful floral assortments were assembled, Amity and Winnet positioned the bouquets on stands and tables throughout the first floor, while Mercy and I did the same throughout the upper levels.

After Mercy and I had finished decorating the second story with vases full of flowers on various decorative pedestals, we proceeded upstairs to the third floor, carrying more large, weighty vases ready to decorate the halls further. Arriving at the top landing and beginning our way through the first corridor, as we headed for the end of the hall to reach the first pedestal, Captain Berkley was unexpectedly noticed approaching directly toward us from the opposite direction. Taken off guard as we recognized each other and came closer, I felt my brows drawing together as my eyes suddenly widened at the sight of him. I immediately wondered about the reason why he was here at this particular location within the house, when I expected he'd be out in the field like the other soldiers were for the day.

The clock at the end of the hallway, now behind him, had just begun chiming, telling the time to be twelve o'clock, noontime. There was no typical lunch period designated for this time, as there had been in my era, so no meal would be served here until dinner, which would have been the time he would have appeared. When soldiers grew hungry during the day, they broke from working and took refuge in the taverns or outdoors in the Common to eat and drink at irregular hours.

So, I was astonished to see Captain Berkley advancing toward us in the hallway now, clearly wandering where he didn't belong.

"Captain Berkley?" I started, giving him a strange look, my face filled with bewilderment and confusion.

"Your Grace!" he sputtered with a gasp, surely appearing equally surprised to see me also and caught off guard as he now arrived standing before us, looking directly at me.

"I thought you'd be around town. Is there something wrong for why you're here?" I inquired genuinely, sensing something awry.

"A matter?" he abruptly responded. The uneven expression on his face was nervous, and he seemed more than hasty in his desire to bypass us. But constrained to polite etiquette, he stood to acknowledge me.

"Yes, is there something wrong?" I reiterated, concerned about the possibility.

"Pray, no. All is quite well," he replied uneasily, making an effort to remain nonchalant as we gazed at each other.

"But you're here," I mentioned.

"Yes, indeed I am—apparently," he recognized uncomfortably.

"This wing of the mansion is private. If you'll remember?" I mindfully highlighted, keeping my voice polite, nevertheless, catching his further breach of confidence that I was aware of.

"I beg Your Grace's forgiveness, indeed—certainly—er, I am

merely in search of His Grace at the hour," he stammered, answering, beating me to the direct question for his presence. My eyes bounced beyond his shoulder, landing on the door directly behind him at the end of the hallway, leading into Leif's library. The door was closed, but suspicion suddenly edged into my mind.

"His Grace is at Fort Hill where he normally is. Where he can be found, of course," I said.

"Yes—presumably—I—er, however, rather believed his whereabouts might have been located here as he remarked interest in returning for tea whilst seizing his respite before journeying to the castle," he stumbled again.

"Castle William?" I was instantly surprised to hear this revelation, since Leif had mentioned nothing of this idea to me.

"Yes, Your Grace," Captain Berkley replied, sounding sure of it. "'Twas my understanding."

"I see." Leif certainly would have told me about his intentions if any of his regular plans for the day were different. If I hadn't already known well in advance, I would have known about it either the night before, the morning of, before he left *Taigh Gràs*, or through a dispatcher carrying his written note for me today. I realized then that Captain Berkley was lying as he was staring at my face. "Well, as you can see, His Grace is actually not anywhere to be found here."

"Thus, I have discovered," he said, looking at me with a wavering grin. The anxiousness he was trying to stymie and hide crept with insinuation in his unnatural expression, giving me the weird feeling that he was concealing something he didn't want revealed.

"It must be extremely important for you to want to see His Grace if you thought you'd find him here instead of at the fort," I continued, acknowledging his urgency.

"As a matter—I must say. The fort was first where I had landed in my search of His Grace, only to learn he was not there to be acquired."

"Well, is there anything terribly wrong, in that case? I'm now worried, of course, that there might be a newly dangerous situation that's arisen in the city."

"I mean none of Your Grace's concern due to my presence, for the city remains well at peace. 'Tis of a different nature for seeking His Grace on command of my superior officer."

"Oh. I see."

"Yes. Pray, rest assured that all is well," he insisted. I nodded slightly in response. "I must presently beg Your Grace to excuse me as I pursue my orders and take my leave."

"Of course," I replied, still somewhat confused. He shortly clicked his heels and bowed, then abruptly straightened as he whisked past me without a further word. I turned around a little, glancing over my shoulder, and observed him hurrying himself through the hallway, immediately for the staircase. Swiftly reaching the top landing, he rushed down the stairs and vanished, the sound of his footsteps receding.

Shifting my gaze from around my shoulder again, when he'd shortly disappeared, I glanced at Mercy, and her eyes met mine with a nearly impassive look, save for the slight raise of her brow indicating her odd curiosity for our encountering him also.

"Have you ever found Captain Berkley to be where he doesn't belong?" I asked, looking peculiarly at her.

"I have never, ma'am," she replied in her typically soft-spoken voice.

"Hmm. Strange..." I remarked, thinking to myself—in spite of the plausible excuse the captain had given.

"Yes'm." She gave a slight, slow nod, agreeing. Something in my gut told me there was something fundamentally off-kilter about Captain Berkley. Besides the aversion of his apathy and egotism, I couldn't exactly put my finger on it. The nebulous sense of his corrupted character swelled from his newly displayed dishonesty, and it began to permeate my consciousness, nicking the back of my mind.

Suddenly remembering the weighty vase I was holding in my arms as it was starting to grow heavier, I shifted my gaze from Mercy toward the pedestal against the back wall at the end of the hallway, near Leif's library door, and strode toward it. Arriving at the stand and gladly relieving my arms, I carefully placed the hefty vase on the tabletop as Mercy proceeded to do the same, setting the vase on another table situated against a different wall. After the vase had been positioned with the bouquet perfectly arranged to my liking, I turned from it, noticing she'd just finished fixing the other beautiful floral display accordingly. So, we rejoined each other in the corridor, ready to return to collecting the remaining bouquets resting in vases at the bottom of the second-story staircase, which had been brought to us with the helpful assistance from other maids.

After gathering the last few arrangements between us, we entered Leif's library, finally embellishing the room with these bursting, brilliant flower arrays. When I began positioning the first vase on the stand by one of the windows farthest in the room, away from his desk at the opposite side, I also glanced around, paying particular attention to the details, about to note whether anything seemed out of place from the ordinary. By superficial accounts, the library appeared typical while I primarily continued settling the last vase I'd gathered to place near the corner over Leif's massive mahogany desk by the window.

It wasn't until this was done and as Mercy was situating her last vase over the center of the mantelpiece, did I pause before leaving the library to take conscientious stock of any irregularities that I might have noticed supporting concerns of Captain Berkley's possible entry, because the door to the room had no lock. But as my eyes rolled over Leif's ordered desk, and the chair positioned behind it, I was compelled to slip my fingers over the handles of each desk drawer, pulling them forth to open to see if anything within them, like parchments and ledgers, seemed to have been disturbed. Leif was a precisely organized man in all of his customs, so if anything he kept within these drawers, laid upon his desk, or placed around the room had been seen the slightest disheveled, not only would it indicated someone's unwelcome presence but that the culprit for this disturbance could easily be associated to the delightful captain.

After making cursory assessments of the contents contained in every drawer and skimming the only items on the desk's surface: an ornate German cuckoo clock, quill, inkstand, and several open maps depicting the cape and Boston's harbor, with one other illustrating New England's northern coast, nothing was noticed amiss and everything appeared as it should, eliminating my wariness and setting me at ease.

At which point, aware that Mercy had finished arranging the last portion of flowers over the mantlepiece, I indicated that I had also finished. So, we proceeded out of the room together, and I reached for the door's handle, closing it behind us as we returned into the hallway, sealing the library closed.

Now that all the rooms and halls had been adorned with aromatic, brilliant bouquets, our work for the morning had been done. Suggesting that we rest for a nice break of tea, Mercy agreed with gladness. Amity and Winnet were found in the kitchen stealing bits to eat when I offered for the four of us to have tea and tiny cod sandwiches, our cook, Remember, made for us. Remember added cranberry bannocks, butter, and preserves for dessert to our meal, to our delight. We four sat secluded in the sunroom, enjoying our meal with a glimpse of the gardens beyond through the surrounding windows, as bright sunlight bathed the room and warmed us.

BEFORE DINNER WAS SERVED, I was in the bedroom using the privy closet, refreshing from the day. Leif hadn't yet returned from Fort Hill when I believed he would have done so by now, and thought instead he was going to be kept working for later hours this evening. It would be unusual if this were going to happen, and the anticipation of dining with soldiers without him wasn't anything I was actually looking forward to, since he distinctly controlled the conversation around the table when it might tend to deviate toward me. So, the thought of having to manage their topics of discussion without him was intimidating, as it was sure to place me out of my element and make the experience uncomfortable for me. In this case, I considered not participating in dining at the table this evening.

When I came from the privy closet, Leif unexpectedly appeared in the room. Arrested by the unanticipated sight of him, my steps automatically stopped, and I abruptly gasped.

"Oh! You're back," I expressed, shortly finding my tongue when I realized his presence.

"Och! I have given ye a start. Forgive me, *ceisdein*," he responded.

"It's okay, I'm so glad to see you," I replied, immediately relaxing.

"As I am verily pleased tae lay eyes upon ye as weel." He pleasantly gazed at me as his lips turned upward warmly.

"I was beginning to fear that you might have become stuck at the fort working late this evening."

"Aye, I regret that ye had the belief. The day had its fill, indeed. Yet I wisnae meaning tae delay my return any further by pressing my last duties. I wish tae relish dining with ye. The notion of ye dining in my absence whilst in the presence of wolves, disnae bode weel with me."

"Thank you," I appreciated.

"Aye." He nodded. He lightly seized my chin with his forefinger and thumb and raised my lips to meet his leaning kiss. After gently pecking my lips, he released me, letting his fingers slip away. "Shall we presently dine?"

"Well, if you wouldn't mind waiting for a minute, I was

hoping to simply change out of my boots into some slippers to ease my feet, finally," I said.

"Yoo're in boots?" His brow furrowed a little. He gave me a confused look when his eyes skimmed down the length of my skirts until landing on the tips of my muddied toes, which had now dried and caked. "Pray, dinnae inform me that ye had ridden yer horse astride in petticoats." His gaze rebounded to mine, apparently expressing disapproval mixed with concern.

"No!" I giggled, giving him an absurd look. "That's dangerous. Why would I ever do that?"

"Yoo're determined and capricious," he said definitively.

"But I'm not senseless. I know how to exercise caution. You have to give me some credit, of course." I shook my head at him, curving my lips into a little smirk. A brow cocked over his crystal ultramarine eye as the corner of his mouth deliberately tilted upward, indicating he discerned the guilt lurking on my face. "You should already know me very well by now."

"Quite weel."

"Then, you should know that I'm not reckless or silly like that."

"Yoo're determined and capricious," he reiterated in an even voice with articulated diction.

"For your information, I didn't ride Oakley today. So, you don't have to become chapped and wag your finger at me."

"Mustn't I, however?"

"Nope." I shook my head again, for sure, giving him a playful look inspired by his easy banter.

"Proceed. Explain yerself tae me, in this instance. Fur, I am most certain yoo'll attempt wriggling yerself out of receiving any reprimand if yoo're able tae assist it," he insisted as I recognized the twinkle in his eyes.

"Fine. I only have my boots on because I spent the whole morning in the garden, since the ground was wet and soft due to the rain last night. So, I didn't want to ruin any of my slippers, knowing it would be better not to wear them because of that," I explained. The slight, entertained smirk tilting his lips broke into a full grin as he stifled a chuckle.

"Yet, I shall mind ye weel and guid fur not considering the soil ye brought into the hoose," he said, scolding me further. I bit my lip, knowing he had a point, and the fact that my guilt ran through me.

"I'll make sure to apologize to the maids for cleaning up after me," I replied humbly.

"I ken that ye will, *àille dhubh*." He grinned at me, and his eyes twinkled as he lightly tapped the tip of my nose.

"Do I humor you?"

"Many occasions."

"But you just scolded me," I teased.

"Mustn't I reprove ye?"

"It's not fair."

"Fair?"

"No," I teased again.

"Yet, yoo're fond of it when I do," he quipped as I blatantly discerned the tempted look in his gaze.

"I suppose you need to be scolded too now, obviously."

"Fur whit reason?" His brow shot upward as the lingering grin remained, exposing the charm he was feeling.

"You and your hanky-panky."

"Hanky-panky?"

"Yes. Your shenanigans are nothing but trouble."

"Yoo're speaking of my mischief?"

"What else would I be alluding to?"

"But ye adore it from me."

"Do I?"

"Indubitably."

"Are you that sure of yourself?"

"Indubitably, once more."

"You're lucky I like you."

"Ye loove me."

"You're lucky about that, too."

"I cannae be contrary."

"I don't think so."

"Och. Thus, I have come tae see."

"Good."

"Regularly cheeky." He briefly raised a forefinger and lightly tapped the tip of my nose, making me giggle. Winking at me, I giggled again, noting the warm grin gracing his face and further attracting me as my eyes adhered to his.

"Hey," I started as a new thought entered my mind, shifting the subject.

"Aye?"

"Did Captain Berkley ever find you in order to meet with you?"

"He did not." Leif's brows drew together as he looked at me, suddenly appearing seriously piqued with puzzling curiosity. "Why do ye inquire?"

"Well, I discovered him in the east wing on the third floor in the hallway," I disclosed freely, now discerning that the expression on Leif's face had sharply changed. The unexpectedness perceived in his eyes as they immediately widened with alerted alarm, swiftly cooled as they hardened by the realization, and narrowed somewhat.

"Was he indeed discovered within the east wing, now?" The sound of his even response wasn't a question as much as it was a rhetorical statement from comprehending the idea, the instant he immediately became consumed by it. The look on his face turned deadpan and frigid.

"Yes, he was," I answered, nevertheless, mindfully aware while clearly reading the gravity seriously conveyed in his new demeanor.

"Elaborate further," he requested in a moderate tone, which I also knew was a directive.

"Well, it happened earlier today—at noontime, actually—

when Mercy and I were arranging the last of our bouquets throughout the house. That was the time we met him on the third floor in the hallway leading to your library," I proceeded, explaining.

"Continue," he urged without the faintest connotation that he'd ever been humored a second ago.

"It was definitely a surprise seeing him there when we arrived, and it seemed he was just as shocked to have seen us also. I don't think he was expecting to be found when we encountered him," I resumed.

"Aye, of coorse, as he would be stunned fur understanding his dereliction, clearly. Being quite weel awaur whaur strictly members of the household are permitted and soldiers are not, he is certain tae ken better," Leif stipulated. "Whit had he said tae ye upon this unexpected meeting?"

"He said he was looking for you, giving me the impression that he might have tried finding you in your library, since he was coming from that direction when we met. But I suggested that you'd be at the fort, where he could find you. Except, he told me that he'd already searched for you there and didn't find you because you weren't there. Instead, he said that he wanted to see you before you left for Castle William, and that's why he was in this wing by your library, believing he could find you in it."

"Had he believed it so?"

"Yes."

"Never was I tae take leave fur the island," Leif responded with a concentrated stare. From it, I perceived him seriously thinking along with his feeling of vexation.

"I know." I nodded, accordingly.

"I remained at the Hill the entirety of my day as regular," he said further.

"That's when I became skeptical of him," I put forth.

"Aye..." He drifted in thought, briefly pausing and appearing remote, comprehending Captain Berkley's deceit. "Had he been so brash tae intrude upon my library?"

"Not that I'm aware of. I mean, that's what had initially entered my mind when I saw him in the hallway by it. But soon after he left, Mercy and I went into your library to finish placing the rest of the flower vases, and I was sure to scrutinize the room," I explained. "And as I was carefully looking around, including looking inside your desk drawers, nothing seemed out of place at all. Even the maps on your desk looked perfectly laid out, the way you had them arranged before, without appearing slightly moved." He remained silent as I told him this. "So, I doubt that he was in there."

"He will suffer fur it," Leif resumed, his voice tight. My eyes widened as I quickly feared his intent. Given the discernible provocation he was restraining to a certain extent, it enhanced the aversion he held for the captain detailed in his eyes.

"Are you going to do something?" I asked carefully, concerned for his brewing temper and not knowing what to expect regarding the outcome of the situation.

"Tae have him flogged micht considerably settle matters, befitting him raither weel as he must be disciplined fur this infraction, accordingly," he replied bluntly.

"Flogged? But you can't do that," I responded, obviously alarmed.

"Indeed, I can." His brow sharply furrowed as he looked preposterously at me, utterly disagreeing and put off also.

"Except it's not equal to the crime," I rebutted, clearly knowing the savagery of the intended punishment.

"Contrary," he said curtly, maintaining the sharpness in his eyes. "'Tis most suitable fur the offense." The impenetrable look in his cold eyes told me he wasn't going to budge on his immediate decision.

"Okay," I said, realizing his position but continued saying, "I certainly understand your severe dislike for Captain Berkley, but you're not brutal like him according to how you've mentioned him being. And, I can very much understand how being annoyed or completely angry at someone can cloud the logic in our minds, since it makes it easier to act on emotions instead of responding with equal justification based on what's reasonable."

"His flogging is indeed reasonably warranted given the numerous offenses he has previously committed already. He has been spared from receiving such an apt consequence upon every occasion."

"Really?" I was suddenly surprised to learn of this while maintaining my gaze to his steely eyes.

"Aye."

"Oh."

"Captain Berkley is a capable man of which ye arenae awaur."

"I see. Well, you're right—I don't know him like you do," I admitted.

"Certainly. I shall have it ordered."

"Wait. So, you're telling me that he's never been reprimanded for anything he's done wrong? No matter how severe?"

"Aye."

"How's that possible, though? I don't understand."

"I huvnea quite understood his ability tae elude his due punishments at all turns. I fathom he is certain tae be within someone's superior protection in order tae have whit he must rightfully reap nullified. Who is screening him, I huvnae a notion. Yet, I presently have greater authority due tae my rank now that I am a colonel, unless 'tis Gage himself safeguarding him. Indeed, doubting it being the general's case, I mean tae have the order carried forth whilst discovering the patron protecting him."

"I see," I replied, understanding, pensively nodding a little also. "Well, I'm certainly not excusing him from not receiving any repercussions for what he did. All I'm saying is that if there's a better way to have him berated without jeopardizing his life, couldn't that measure be taken instead?"

"He ought tae be too grateful tae yer magnanimous compassion fur his sparing. Why must ye?"

"It has nothing to do with him, but rather to do with you instead."

"How? I perceive nothing of yer favor by yer compelling me tae release him from the execution of my judgment."

"Because, it's like I said about being emotional over logic. Obviously, you're extremely angry at him. I can see that. You also don't like him—at all—and that bias is likely enhancing your anger and clouding what's reasonable. I think that if you sentence him the way you want him to be because of how you feel about him, then it will be done out of pure resentment, not from objectivity, that will be just. You're a fair man, Leif. After all we've been through, don't let something so minuscule chip away at your humanity. You're cut from a different cloth altogether. You're not the type that comes from Captain Berkley's culture. So, don't become like those who are."

He paused for an extended moment, lulling the conversation, as he kept his eyes bound to mine. The hardness in his eyes was evident as he looked at me penetratingly. But as I sincerely held his gaze, I discerned the adhesion of my words churning his mulling mind. He was conflicted. I didn't know what to expect when he eventually spoke. I simply saw the severity of his annoyance, knowing he preferred to have the captain beaten.

"He will suffer punishment fur this offense," Leif resumed, finally.

"So, you're going to have him whipped anyway?" I asked, shocked that he'd decided this course.

"The punishment will be just," he said sternly. I suddenly couldn't help the wave of disappointment coming over me as I continued staring back into his gem-like eyes that were remote of leniency. It seemed exceptional of him. "Yoo're corrected, however. I am my own man. Concern yerself nae longer of Berkley."

"But, Leif—you have to re—,"

"He will survive anither day," he interrupted in a firm voice, promising me. I nodded in response, understanding his guarantee to spare the threat of cruelly jeopardizing the man's life. Slightly relieved by the conclusion of his reconsideration, I still didn't know exactly what he had in mind to punish Captain Berkley. But I was well aware that he was going to make him suffer his responsibility for the infraction—and it was the remaining severity of it short of death that lingered in my mind, concerning me now. And before I meant to say anything else regarding it, Leif reasserted, saying, "Proceed readying yerself tae dine. 'Tis time we join the chamber fur the hour."

"I won't be long," I responded, suppressing my thoughts and agreeing as I suddenly remembered how hungry I'd become.

Twenty-Six

After our conversation and while now sitting at the dining table eating dinner with Amity and the other officers, Leif's typical demeanor appeared to have resumed. In fact, I was impressed as I was witnessing his usual conversation and reactions to those with whom he was engaging at the table. It appeared that nothing had ever occurred to disrupt his mood, only a few moments ago when I informed him about Captain Berkley. Particularly now, when he acknowledged and observed the culprit contentedly eating his food as the captain himself incautiously partook in topics of discussion with members surrounding him, which included several exchanges with Leif.

However, Captain Berkley was without the scantest awareness of Leif's added anger toward him while sitting next to Lord Brimfield on his opposite side, who was carrying on a normal, robust conversation with Leif in general. Seeming composed as he was demonstrating himself to be, by all accounts, Leif was enjoying His Lordship's company. At the same time, they ate, reminding me again of the fine poker player that Leif was, unassuming and stealthy.

Occasionally, when he and Lord Brimfield encountered slight

lulls in their conversation, I caught His Lordship's gaze had steadied on me when looking up from my plate of food or after Amity and I had communicated. Without realizing it until these moments, it grew apparent to me that he'd been furtively watching me eat as Amity and I enjoyed each other's company while subtly conversing between ourselves, sitting at the opposite end of the table. But when my glance inadvertently discovered his attention adhered to me on every instant, an understated grin passed over his face, supporting the hint of interest lurking in his gray eyes.

The occurrences shifted to unsettle my unease, which heightened my awareness of an uncertain thought about whether my interpretation of him was correct. The trim level of discomfort was enough to unsettle a portion of my serenity about him. And the unanticipated realization that I was questioning Leif's friend only made me feel worse because of the guilt created for even daring to consider a potential issue being raised; *I could be very wrong about my misassumption that might not exist*, I thought.

Aware of the loyal friendship shared between them, to regard this question of Leif's friend was a nonstarter. And, I wouldn't dream of the possibility of ever breaching the trust binding them over a baseless thought inspired by a false interpretation of mine that I'd verbalized to Leif, simply because I found His Lordship looking at me seemingly in a distinctive way. It would be a mistake that I surely knew; their friendship appeared indeed grounded, solidified by strength in the time of my absence.

Recognizing their history of friendship, I returned my attention to Amity and the remaining food on my plate, smothering my inward awkwardness. When glancing away from him, I also factored in the idea that His Lordship was, in fact, harmless because of Leif.

So, my discomfort quickly abated as I reached for my cup of tea instead of my wineglass. As I drew the ridge of my cup to my lips and sipped, Leif captured my eyes as I glanced away from my teacup after returning it to its saucer positioned before me. Realizing then that he had undoubtedly been staring at me this whole time, watching, the recognizable warmth in his steady gaze was discernible. But the corner of his upturned mouth displaying a lazy smirk also made him appear artificial and predominantly smug. A characteristic I wasn't used to seeing in him. Then, his complacent grin buttressed his clear wink at me.

Suddenly, the temperature in my cheeks began to rise, heating my face. I knew they were noticed not only by him but also by Lord Brimfield, who was aware as he observed Leif's attention on me, and my response to him while witnessing. A large, captivating grin spread evenly across Leif's face, balancing the allure expressed in his steadfast eyes and dispelling all superficiality when fixing my gaze on his. Inhibited by the strength of his stare, my natural inclination to drop my gaze from him and look at the last bit of food remaining on my plate, in an attempt to curb my diffidence and expose myself, was prevented as I was compelled to look at him in return.

A little smile came over me as I felt my lips curl while striving to push shyness aside. Except, he winked at me again. Stifling the giggle that nearly eluded me, my lips naturally widened into a full smile instead.

"Indeed, you divert your wife, Monteith," I thought I heard His Lordship comment subtly to Leif from the opposite end of the table where they were sitting.

"I imagine," Leif replied in the same muted manner.

"One might say 'tis apparent." Leif slid His Lordship a conscious glance in response, and His Lordship caught it when he shifted a glance back toward Leif. "The tales prove true also."

"Tae whit tales do ye allude, Brimfield?" Leif inquired, returning his eyes to mine as I continued observing him, too.

"The fairest lady in all Boston lies captive within your palm," His Lordship replied before slipping a glance my way again, then returning to looking at Leif as his gaze remained melded to mine.

This time, I reached for my wineglass and began to sip, interrupting our interlocking stares. "A sight to behold, indeed."

When I returned my glass to the table, placing it before myself, Leif instantly turned his eyes from me to his friend.

"Micht it?" Leif questioned.

"In more ways than one," Lord Brimfield answered.

"Pray tell."

"A remarkable feat that you had ever wed, primarily. Yet, the beauty which you have procured would sway any man who might be so libertine to settle well. You have won yourself a magnificent prize, Your Grace."

"Lothario be warned. Admiration from afar is his limit, Your Lordship." Leif cocked an arching brow, giving his friend a cautionary glare coupled with a sarcastic smirk that enlivened his insinuation.

"Would he truly be so named?" Lord Brimfield's brow shot upward as his eyes abruptly widened accompanied by a snorting chuckle, conveying surprise.

"Irrefutably thus named as you are," Leif replied resolutely.

"As for his friend?"

"A changed man long ago. As he weel knows."

"He is abandoned," Lord Brimfield said, feigning sadness.

"Pity upon him isnae warranted. Lothario has proven weel secured in pursuit of his dalliances upon his own volition without any aid from a shadow to relish in such conduct from years past till present."

"Yet, his shadow has known of such conduct."

"Whilst in youth, which remains irrelevant tae this day. His shadow tae which he may refer, is naught more than a near monk, henceforth commencing many years ago. Let it be validated that his shadow is much gratified in monkhood these plenty days."

"*Near* monk?"

"He cannae be retrieved from the certain monastery in which he contentedly dwells, that is his wife."

"A true regret, there will be no game." Lord Brimfield seemed to lament in his light banter.

"*None*. Indeed." The tone in Leif's voice was absolute, equal to the look he was giving his friend despite the slanted grin on his face.

"Alas." His Lordship appeared half disappointed, save the ironic smirk mirroring Leif's expression. "Mayhap, to consider the attainment of an American wife into possession might presently be in order likewise, naturally."

"'Twould not be possible," Leif chuckled abruptly, obviously amused as the look on his face turned unexpectedly surprised.

"Of course, 'twould be so," Lord Brimfield responded, giving Leif an equal grin without laughing.

"Not so."

"A slight. Why must you contradict? The lack of faith cuts the heart," Lord Brimfield replied, sounding almost genuine.

"A pity. Yet, whit is merely said is true. A miracle it would be should it ever come tae pass, fur a leopard cannae change its spots."

"Wait to see. An American lass it very well might be."

"Meeting one's grave will prove prior above all."

"Care for a wager?"

"Benevolence prevents any such wager. I shall be thanked."

"If you and Gage have landed American beauties, then shall I?"

"Do ye reckon such a venture will bring joyful settlement? The pleasures ye seek are not presented in that confine given yer nature, unless 'tis a common mirage of devotion fur whit ye wish whaur ye will proceed as ye micht beyond the constraint. Let us be clear, Brimfield, yoo're not disciplined. Yer cheerful bride will suffer ye."

"You suggest to place the lesser sex above myself?" He gave Leif an appalling look.

"It must be. Fur the sake of happiness," Leif responded matter-of-factly.

"You are utterly daft, Monteith." Lord Brimfield laughed outright. "I shan't ever entertain such a ridiculous notion. 'Tis sheerly fatuous. I'm aghast that you have invented the belief. 'Tis quite the common tradition for women to fall happily in suit of their husbands' directions, whatever they are, thereby enabling their happiness entirely. If we are not content, then neither will be the women we wed. Adding to my position alone, any American lass at least with any mere connections to England would claw to have me wed her, should any one of them discover that I am in the emporium to suit."

"Thus, you have stated the apparent snag of yer perception, Brimfield. The gist being that ye wulnea suit happily, plainly, at all —despite yer nobility. 'Tis inherent. Yer lack of allowance or favor toward our counterparts is whaur ye tend tae falter. Ye regard them as lesser, when they may prove above and greater tae ourselves. Because of this, the essential premise ought to be to suit them, not merely to have them incline toward our wishes, but to uphold the effort throughout by way of our true respect of their existence, and fur the love we have claimed fur them. Fur a man tae serve his lass's happiness, is whaur true harmony within may be found betwixt the pair. And, there lies the true power of the bond between man and woman."

"Rubbish! Such a mentality will certainly lead to obfuscation, if not blatant confusion, to the whole order of society, should we argue for the sake of argument. What has brought you to this inane consideration? For you are most well aware of what a woman's place is to a man's. If we are not content, then certainly no woman would ever be. 'Tis quite a simple recognition, in truth."

"I am not discounting our own happiness. Yet, instead I precisely advocate fur it as I state whit is not merely within reason but sorely true. However, 'tis plain that ye dinnae comprehend this novel notion by my attempt tae bringing forth yer enlightenment."

"Proceed with your enlightenment of me. I confess that I am quite amused."

"Then, I shall enhance yer diversion by confiding that ye micht raither abandon blindness in yer regard fur lasses, and sincerely inquire of yerself whether tae settle within matrimony would be of any betterment tae yer morality."

"My morality? You are not genuine," Lord Brimfield scoffed with a sudden lifting of his brow before his expression returned to smirking.

"I am most genuine," Leif said, appearing more even in tone and manner.

"Since what occurrence? Come now. You, as well, cannot be this sanctimonious." Brimfield's brow now furrowed in confusion. Combining the slight gaping while looking at Leif, he also appeared shocked. "I have known you since our youthful days in London. You were no stranger to the theatre nor to any houses of certain repute. Finding it unfathomably impressive that you have not strayed from celibacy since our renewed friendship, I wonder why I do not admire it, as I have come to realize that I do not believe it is commendable. You say that you are a near monk, yet you are not one. And yet, whilst they are forbidden to wed, Vickers are not. Therefore, step down from your pious pulpit and relish the fact that you are, in fact, a man. Or, has my dear friend been reduced to the rank of a eunuch?"

"Far from it. My wife may attest tae the fact. I weel ken that ye would never doubt her raither certainly if ye waur tae ask, although her decency would prevent her replying. I say this, due to yer admiration of her already. Her word is worth more than gold, and her virtue is mine," Leif said, and the slanted grin on his friend's face increased as he didn't immediately respond, seeming to study Leif.

"You worship your wife?" Lord Brimfield resumed inquiring after a lapse, sounding struck by the novelty as the idea suddenly registered.

"Do you perceive it presently?"

"I fear that I might."

"Fear it. I do it without hesitation." He and his friend stared at each other for a second, as Lord Brimfield didn't seem sure how to reply.

"Mayhap, far be it for any man to come between him and his religion," Lord Brimfield said.

"One reason fur why a multitude of wars have begun throughout the ages."

"Touché." Lord Brimfield raised his wineglass, toasting Leif's words, and drank its contents, finishing the remnants to the last. After setting down the empty crystal before himself, he continued saying, "Nonetheless, if not to wed for the ideal of love, I shall pursue matrimony to bear an heir."

"Why not merely ward one already?" Leif asked sincerely.

"They are all bastards, as you know. I speak for none of them."

"Och, my dearest mistake. I have forgotten quite simply. 'Twould ail you tae bear such an undertaking. Being sensible of yer repute, forgive my proposal. 'Tis a rightful heir born within wedlock of which ye have presently professed. In other words, it is the way quite honorably to redeem yer bloodline. Yet, why not forego it altogether by pressing yer brother tae wed, releasing yourself in this event as it is certain that ye care not fur the institution of matrimony itself?

"Permit yer brother tae wed in yer stead. It may ease yer considerations to pass title tae his offspring, raither. Sparing yerself a prospectively disastrous matrimony with a wife ye wulnae loove, which ye weel ken would prove an empty union at its base. Relinquishing yourself will also grant yer retention tae continue experiencing yer existence as ye freely please without any further complexities, tae the detriment of an innocent wife. If it is yer happiness which yoo're in favor of seeking, do ye not already have it?"

"Do you truly propose such a notion? To sacrifice my inevitable responsibility? And what is it worth? For I'm certain to be surprised by your slight, if sincere," Lord Brimfield replied, now appearing serious as the crooked grin on his face acutely disappeared.

"Must ye continue retaining such vehemence fur Edward?" Leif asked as his expression turned just as earnest, if not a little more.

"You know my loathing of him," Lord Brimfield said grimly.

"It disnae serve ye weel by the hating of yer brother."

"Contrary. The forfeiture of Edward's wealth and any association to his peerage lies solely upon his own choosing once he abandoned our family for a more than a less desirable woman to whom he considers himself already wed. He has done so against our father's expectations and my command, and I shall never condone his doing so. Any diabolical offspring produced by his unsanctioned union is regarded at best as an illegitimate beast.

"Edward has wounded our father greatly in his actions, and is well aware that our father lies near death, whilst he beseeches Edward's return to our fold in London. Our father has written and dispatched many letters to him, to which Edward has never replied. He displays an utter disregard for him, and still, our father extends an olive branch to him. I haven't the merest understanding as to why. Yet, he has continually exhibited more compassion for Edward since his birth than for me—the one who bears the brunt of expectation. Edward is spoilt and undisciplined.

"Soon, however, I shall reach my inheritance and grant Edward's full wish by hammering the final nail to his own coffin, where he will be entirely severed from the family. Therefore, you will understand that I shall never be alleviated from the burden of producing my own legitimate heir, whereby I shall be forced to wed—ultimately."

Both men paused the conversation between themselves as they studied each other's expressions. I wondered what Leif was thinking, as I felt my objectivity toward His Lordship changing toward an unlikable bias. I didn't understand how Leif could have had a long, sustaining friendship with this man when their outlooks appeared to be diametrically opposing.

"'Tis perceived, Monteith, that your true fortune lies within the woman you have taken for a wife. A brilliant treasure of yours for any other man cannot help but to admire," Lord Brimfield resumed, staring honestly at Leif as the same candor carried in his voice.

"Ye may discover one who will suit ye best, Brimfield, should ye be fair," Leif said sincerely to him.

"In hopes," Lord Brimfield considered.

"Aye." Leif nodded a little, agreeing. Reaching for his wineglass, Leif drew it to his lips and drank what was left of it. Then, returning it onto the table, the conversation between them turned toward the events of the day about work that they'd each encountered.

Twenty-Seven

Captain Berkley's presence on our property and at meals was now missing. I later learned about the repercussions he had received for his violation when I inquired about the captain to Leif, and Leif told me that Captain Berkley had been imprisoned.

"He has?" I asked as my eyes suddenly widened, realizing the gravity of this consequence as we'd just entered the corridor from our bedroom, ready to head downstairs for this evening's dinner.

"Aye," Leif answered unaffectedly when sensing his fingers slipping around my elbow while he started escorting me through the hallways to the staircase.

"For how long?" I responded curiously.

"One month," he replied briefly.

"That's a long while, isn't it?"

"I reckon not."

"But is the length really justified?"

"Fairer than flogging, reasonably."

"But he could get sick and die, still."

"Pray fur his welfare, of coorse. I have already spared him."
Leif's tone was stout and resolute. I glanced away from him and

stared ahead as we continued pacing toward the staircase, falling quiet, knowing this topic had been closed for further discussion by him. But certain feelings remained about the harsh repercussion Leif had given him. So, I did say a little prayer for the captain; aside from believing that the punishment didn't fit the crime, I particularly didn't wish for this man to die as a result of Leif's sentence.

When we entered the dining room, the usual company attending, including Lord Brimfield and minus Captain Berkley, had met us and proceeded to take their places around the table as we joined them.

Much of the conversation circulating throughout dinner this evening focused on local affairs and the current situation occurring in Boston regarding troops and inhabitants. A couple of soldiers around the table wondered about solutions to the percolating problem of people's resentment toward them in town. Rumors were also rife that a growing number of soldiers were abandoning their commitments due to desertion, as they found living life here more appealing, and that they could improve themselves. This idea was better than what they'd already experienced living in England, and they'd abandoned the military after being pressed. It seemed, what I'd gathered from the conversation, that the stationed military was encountering instability on both fronts: from the exterior and from within.

"New orders have recently come concerning the particular of desertion," I heard one of the officers saying as I glanced up from my plate of food.

"Certainly, deserters will immediately meet death by hanging instead of being granted the chance of survival by flogging. This will curb a significant portion of the trouble," Lieutenant Jones said.

"Here," Lieutenant Davis agreed.

"These new orders, I do also believe, will give men pause to commit the crime. 'Tis much belated," responded the first officer I originally heard, named Captain Webber.

"Some, nonetheless, will risk to defy," Captain Miller commented pragmatically. "The matter will not be entirely resolved."

"You refer to pervading sentiments amongst rebels blighting them?" Captain Hanson assumed.

"Such sentiments attract those of ours like moths to a flame, given the understanding of squalor from the depths they have come and the visible temptation presented here for the perceived prospect of one's betterment," Captain Miller pointed out. "Therefore, what have they to forfeit but their lives for this prospect when their awareness of this risk to their existence may bring forth such achievement? These soldiers who were pressed know quite well that they are of little value, if none at all. The notion of escaping to the frontier to carve a life for themselves serves as an enticing risk to them than having been pressed from the dungeons of London to be finally spent. Consequently, men will continue to flee. Thus, the difficulty to retain them remains."

"Dastardly rebels and their foolhardy, insufferable cries for liberty, damning Tories alike without the merest compunction. They are too stupid to understand the discord they are engendering is the very reason for our presence," Captain Webber scorned. "Their resentment is utterly risible as it is hollow, and deservedly falls upon the Crown's deaf ears."

I glanced away from the conversing officers and observed Leif at the opposite end of the table, eating his food, with his silent attention focused on the surrounding topic of interest. Keen to the discussion, the expression on his face was impassive, however. Lord Brimfield was also listening, though he appeared somewhat bored while refilling his wineglass with Madeira.

When I returned to looking at my plate and proceeded to slice a small portion of my roasted potato to eat, distant sounds of gathered voices had unexpectedly become faintly audible from outside the surrounding windows. It was difficult to discern whether I was hearing cheering or disgruntled yelling. I wondered about the proximity of the origin. I replaced my fork over my plate to hone in on the voices emitting outside of the encircling conversation, and I caught a glimpse of Leif, who had noticed my attention had been drawn elsewhere as I turned my head toward the closest window near me.

It seemed a rowdy mob was gathering nearby on our property, yet at a distance, and those vocal individuals couldn't be distinguished through the dark, uneven glass pane windows, barely revealing the dimly illuminated moonlit front clearing. A mixture of curiosity and alarm crossed me, causing the stinging rise of adrenaline to shock my nerves. That's when one of our footmen, Elijah, entered the room and strode directly toward Lord Brimfield with a sealed note in hand, distracting my attention from the window.

Leif, like I, watched Elijah delivering the letter to Lord Brimfield. When the letter arrived, Lord Brimfield unceremoniously snatched it from Elijah as he had offered it to him. Lord Brimfield broke the seal and promptly began reading the letter as Elijah started withdrawing from him to leave the room. The message must have been brief because Lord Brimfield shortly slammed the parchment down onto the table, and he crumpled it, incensed. I was startled by his unexpected reaction. I sat there looking at him, more than slightly concerned, like the other officers who'd suddenly fallen silent and turned their attention toward him.

"Bloody rabble-rousers must all be hanged," he cursed as he turned his riled eyes toward Leif, who was intently watching him. Leif promptly seized the note between his friend's fisted fingers, turning it over to read it himself. Swiftly skimming it, he shifted his eyes back toward Lord Brimfield. "I am particularly reviled by the vermin as their persistence to blacken me is unrelenting, making me entirely aware of their hatred of me. The sentiment is mutual, and I shall make them suffer for it." Before Leif responded, Lord Brimfield sprang from his chair, immediately stepping away from the table. "Arm yourselves and arrest every damned louse," he continued, ordering the officers from the table to proceed with him as he hastily began his way out of the room.

Leif suddenly came to his feet, too, moving away from his position at the table. He followed the last man after Lord Brimfield as they were all hurriedly leaving the room. Before passing me, Leif caught my alert gaze, staring at him with questions, and shortly arrested his steps before abandoning me and Amity while we were still sitting alone in our chairs.

"Huvnae fear. I shall return," he assured quickly, pausing before continuing on his way from the room.

"But where are you going?" I asked anyway, aware that he perceived my unease.

"Outdoors."

"With them?"

"I must."

"What's happening?"

"I shall discover it." Without allowing me to reply, he shot out of the room instead and vanished, leaving us alone and me with an uneasy feeling coalescing deeply in my stomach.

The room quickly fell silent. Compulsively, I moved from my chair toward the window to peer out, attempting to catch a glimpse of the unexpected confusion unfolding across the clearing. As I scanned the distance, I suddenly discerned many burning torches in the background, and the officers were seen charging from the house out onto the field fully armed. I saw Leif and Lord Brimfield's shadowy figures hurrying and joining the other men; I anxiously anticipated some clash occurring at the location where they were all urgently heading and wondered why this brewing crowd had assembled on our property.

Having fixed myself to the window, I hadn't realized that Amity had stepped beside me until she placed a light hand on my forearm, drawing my attention away from the panes now toward her own concerned expression. The question on her face was obvious, and I promptly signed to her, informing her of what I knew of the situation that wasn't clearly known to me. After telling her this, she only turned her gaze toward the window and worriedly stared out into the moonlit darkness as I returned to looking through the panes, equally apprehensive.

We stood there together in silence, anticipating their return, when I jumped at the unexpected sound of gunfire resonating like fireworks in the room from the invisible distance beyond. My heart abruptly skipped a beat. My blood turned like ice water surging through my veins, chilling me. At a gasp, a shudder shook my limbs, and I jerked sharply away from the window. Stepping backward, fearful, and on impulse, I swiftly started out of the dining room. Amity, quickly noticing me, hurried after my steps. Rushing into the hallway for the foyer without forethought, I swept through the halls, forgetting that Amity was following me.

I arrived in the entrance hall with the intention of leaving the house, when I saw Quinn and Elijah, along with a number of other household men and women servants, were already gathered, blatantly alarmed.

"Return to your orders, the lot of you," Quinn was saying to the gathered servants who were his subordinates, responsible for directing them. "His Grace is certain to return so long as you pray for his welfare. Presently, move about."

The servants compliantly began dispersing, though the fright and worry on their faces remained evident. As they followed Quinn's directions and dispersed, they noticed me and Amity moving toward them in the foyer. While looks of concern lingered on me when they were disappearing for their duties, Elijah remained with Quinn, standing by the front door, with their attention now turned onto me.

"Do you know what's happened?" I anxiously asked.

"We fear not, Your Grace," Quinn answered in a calming voice. I quickly reached for the front door's handle to open the door, and an abrupt look of added stark concern flashed over his face. The same alarm was also expressed on Elijah's face as he stared at me. I suddenly recognized their hesitation but was compelled to continue grabbing the door handle, nevertheless.

"I'm only going to step outside. I won't go far, just down the steps. That's all," I responded unevenly, assuring them both of my safety, realizing their extra concern as I looked at them. The distance from the turmoil was far enough away, and I believed the buffer was safe to simply get a clearer glimpse of what was happening, as I primarily worried for Leif.

"We shall remain with Your Grace," Quinn replied, undeterred, committed to my wellbeing in spite of my assurance. I nodded appreciatively and proceeded to pull the front door open. Moving out into the balmy night air, I passed beneath the large portico and came down the limestone steps with Elijah at my side, alert to any nearby threat. Quinn, perched on the landing overlooking me, stood with Amity before the open doorway as she looked outward also.

Driven by nervous alarm, I was urgently uneasy over Leif's safety as I was desperate to know what was happening. However, due to the fluidity of the confrontation and its proximity, I was forced to remain motionless in my stance, having locked onto the vision of many burning torches in the background, before bands of trees bordering the field, leading up to the front of the property. From what I could discern in the moonlight, our stable master, Clive, along with our stable hands and groundskeepers, stood armed in the middle ground as I pinpointed the focal point of the disruption at the gate, manned by our gatekeeper, Levi.

Looking past Clive and our groundskeepers, realizing they were also armed with muskets, the tall iron gate could be heard clinking. This indicated that the rattling was due to the mob shaking the locked gate and their inability to burst through and cause any harm. As my feral heart pounded in my chest, I was steeped in uncertainty about how this situation would unfold, feeling the unbridled threat of disaster looming imminently. The realization that the gate could be breached escalated my fear, and the temperature of my blood dropped as I looked ahead across the property.

Unruly hollering continued to reverberate from the vociferous, angry crowd as flickering torches among them waved around in the air, streaking the darkness. Suddenly, more gunshots popped off into the atmosphere, freezing my blood and choking the wind in my lungs.

Then, it seemed voices from the hostile group began diminishing, until finally no one was heard anymore. At that moment, all but the native night sounds soon descended into silence as the air muted. Still, my feet remained planted and I unanimated, unable to withdraw indoors as I stood in the light breeze moments more, gripped to the earth, waiting...

Suddenly, air reentered my lungs when I saw Leif's striding silhouette, which was at last detected approaching from afar. While he was returning toward the mansion, Lord Brimfield was also noticed walking beside him, their figures becoming distinct in the middle ground as they arrived at the spot where Clive, the stablehands, and groundskeepers were standing protectively against the potential intruders. As the men encountered each other, Leif briefly acknowledged them in passing, then they all dispersed: Clive and the others returned to their quarters, while Leif and Lord Brimfield continued making their way back toward the house, more composed, and returned at ease.

Although appearing more composed and at ease when they arrived, neither seemed entirely settled like they had been before this incident. Lord Brimfield, in particular, scowling and cursing irately under his breath, was more intensely provoked as he surpassed Leif when he ceased before me. Lord Brimfield continued walking past us with blinders and climbed the front steps, disappearing into the house.

Shifting my gaze back toward Leif from his friend, all I felt was a surging wave of relief as our eyes met.

"What was that all about?" I asked with a combination of alleviation and apprehension as curiosity overwhelmed me.

"All is weel," Leif told me in a collected tone instead when I noticed a mixture of alarm and disapproval caught in the moonlight on his face, immediately sparking more of my concern. As I was about to inquire more about the situation, his hand slipped around my elbow, and he urged me away with him up the steps, returning me and Amity indoors.

Elijah and Quinn followed from behind into the foyer, and Quinn closed the front door. As Elijah promptly began withdrawing from the entrance hall, Mercy and Winnet appeared in our presence, ready to wait. Lord Brimfield's boot-heels continued to resonate over the planked floors and receded through the corridor until no longer heard as he returned to the dining room. Leif soberly instructed Winnet to attend to Amity for the final evening hours in her room. She bobbed a quick curtsy after his instructions and began guiding Amity away from us.

Then, turning his earnest attention to Mercy, he instructed her to postpone waiting on me until his further notice. Surely strange of him to do, I wondered about his unusual command. When I glanced at him as he directed her, I noted the severity in his expression. After his order, she respectfully curtsied before him and turned out of the front hall.

Remembering Leif's hand still possessing my elbow, he immediately proceeded, steering me through the foyer toward the large staircase and up the steps without a further word, giving me pause. Nervously biting my lower lip, I was aware then that something else was amiss, before realizing it, and knew his mood had been struck with additional displeasure. Heavier worry sank to the pit of my stomach like a lead weight as I tried understanding what more could be wrong.

Twenty-Eight

⟨flourish⟩

Arriving in the privacy of our bedroom, Leif promptly closed the door behind us, sealing us inside. Facing him as the door was mindfully shut, and when his eyes immediately shifted from it, locking onto mine, the intensity in them as he stared at me easily revealed the raw dissatisfaction and unnerved emotion he was feeling, bridled by discipline. He was angry, and it was clear.

Discerning him as the tension in his jaw was visible, squaring his chin more prominently, I opened my mouth to speak the second he broke my chance by superseding me and started saying, "Ye mustn't *ever* come from this hoose outdoors at the merest sign of peril."

The tone in his voice was not only measured but also forcefully blunt, carrying the sharpness from the weight of his disapproval and the demand of his directive that was full of worry.

"Please don't be upset," I blurted automatically, anxiously looking at him as I instantly initiated attempting to ameliorate his angry frame of mind, so that we could talk and that I could understand him. Certainly, I wasn't meaning for an argument between us also.

"Then, dinnae imperil yerself!" he replied gruffly, obviously concerned and malcontented.

"I'm sorry—I was—" I started unevenly, trying to explain, but was interrupted again as he continued saying, "I dinnae care fur the excuse ye mean tae present. Ye *wulnae* fall from my protection! Need I remind ye of whit occurred when the French took Fort William Henry?" he castigated with a deeply furrowed brow.

"No—you don't. I remember very well," I quickly responded as my voice unexpectedly shook.

"Ye must *ken* better, if this is true."

"I'm very sorry." My voice abruptly muted with meekness as the memory never left me, and the terror of losing him was real and brutally raw. A knot quickly lodged in my throat, and my eyes began stinging as saltwater emerged, glazing them. Not that I was at a loss for words, but to speak further would only hasten the dam to break. So, I just stared at him, silently.

The look in his ignited eyes sharply tempered, however, and a long sigh escaped his nose as his lips remained sealed. Forcing my gaze to stay with his as he continued staring at me, affixed, silence descended, and we only gazed at each other for a moment. Staring at him, I didn't know when he would speak and wondered what he was going to say the moment he did. Then, I felt the soft touch of his palm gently slipping over my cheek and embracing the side of my face when the pad of his thumb tenderly stroked a single, trailing tear away from the corner of my eye.

"I ken yer fear. 'Tis mine as weel. I shall exist forever a broken man if ever ye ceased tae remain whaur ye could never be retrieved," he finally expressed in a low voice that was now mild and lamenting. "The pulse of my heart, the reason it lives. Without yer presence, the universe is null."

"I'm sorry," I choked hoarsely. It was all I could bring myself to say as the floodgates would open, spilling waves of tears. His very words mirrored the essence of my soul.

"Aye," he replied, knowing how deeply my regret stemmed as I understood it in his eyes. He then pulled me into his arms, enveloping me when I sensed his lips pressing against my crown. "Ye and the bairns cause my greatest fear," I caught him barely whispering as his breath warmed my head.

As my arms wrapped around him, I tightened my grip and fastened him. His embrace strengthened, securing me against his broad chest.

"You're mine also," I scarcely uttered over his heart, beating soundly in my ear.

"We must take care."

"I will," I promised.

"Our fear fur one anither must be our guard. We mustn't let it fail us. We must heed its protection. Am I weel understood henceforth?"

"Very much so."

"Very weel," he responded calmly. "Yer period away from haur, from me, all these years is understood. I dinnae fault ye."

"Thank you."

"All is weel now." He pressed his lips over my crown in a kiss, then his arms slowly released me, and my hands slipped from around his back. We looked at each other again, and our eyes were complacent. He reached for my hand and drew my knuckles to his lips, planting a soft kiss over them.

When he affectionately lowered my hand from his mouth, his hand remained holding mine as a lapsing moment of silence passed between us. The look in his eyes had settled from the ignition of aggravation and heavy concern, and I knew he was relaxed and composed again.

"So..." I started pensively.

"Aye?" Leif urged, giving me an encouraging look.

"Will everything be all right?" I asked tepidly, carefully considering.

"I reckon. Why would it not? We have agreed tae mind ourselves. Have we not?" he responded genuinely.

"Yes. But I mean the crowd that came here tonight," I clarified.

"Och. I see."

"Yeah. So, will you tell me what happened? Why did they come? Do you know?"

Leif released my hand and raised his fingers to his brow, rubbing it, before they shifted lower toward the bridge of his nose and pinched the tear-duct corners of his eyes. A sigh escaped him. The question seemed to trouble him as he paused to answer. I watched his expression for a second.

When his fingers briefly fell from his face, he said, "They are men who are disaffected."

"Why are they? Are they angry at you?" I asked, unable to hide my concern as my eyes suddenly widened and my brow knitted.

"Imprecisely."

"What does that mean?" I continued, confused now, too.

"I am not directly their aim."

"What or who is their aim, then?"

He paused, seeming hesitant as we gazed at each other. He faintly released a breath, and his hands drew to his hips to rest, broadening his posture.

"Those men are among many who disagree with the Crown and are impartial tae soldiers who have come by its orders. As ye are quite awaur," he said after a second.

"Yes, but they targeted *Taigh Gràs,* and you told me that whatever few riots that happened were restricted to the North End—not here. So, I'm confused and a little concerned, of course, that they showed up here—unexpectedly. Are angry people going to start threatening us because of your uniform?"

"Nae," he replied assuredly, convinced as his stalwart ultramarine eyes held mine with certitude.

"How are you so certain? Maybe they won't care about your social prestige or military rank and will hurt you anyway, because you're working as a part of the system they hate. You can easily wind up being their collateral damage, since those people who came here tonight are obviously angry enough to throw any of that kind of consideration to the side. The number of soldiers living here with us didn't scare them at all. Doesn't their disregard make us vulnerable?"

"Ease yerself," he urged.

"I don't think I can," I said honestly.

"Those men hold my regard."

"They do?"

"Aye."

"They've got a funny way of showing it, then."

"Ye may be guaranteed that they do continue tae act upon my due regard," he reiterated calmly.

"How? Because if they respect you as you say, then they wouldn't have come here threateningly in the first place."

"'Tis not me they seek." Leif's large palms came over my shoulders, soundly possessing them with reassurance buttressed by the confident and comforting expression in his eyes.

"It's not?"

"Nae." He lightly shook his head. The truth in his admission was clearly perceived, and a faint wedge of relief edged into my unsettled thoughts as a breath slightly eluded my lips.

"Who are they after, if this is true?"

"His Lordship carries their interest," he disclosed seriously. His eyes became grave, and his face impassive.

"Your friend?" I felt my lips gape somewhat, coupled with widened eyes, when compounded shock and confusion abruptly hit me.

"Aye."

"I don't understand. Why?" Leif's hand slid from my shoulders as I perceived him arranging his thoughts, immediately anticipating his response.

"Lord Brimfield is a complex and difficult man. He has little compassion for any who micht contradict him, nae matter the case, that applies tae regional subjects," he started explaining.

"Well, I'm aware that he's apparently arrogant and wears the uniform," I admitted, genuinely. "But, isn't his arrogance typical of the elite in particular anyway? I mean, that's not unusual for someone like him. So why target him especially and not go after everyone who shares the same echelon as he does?"

"His repute is weel knoon, and he has made guid upon it."

"What has he done?"

"He is battle-hardened. Whit little humanity he once had, is nil."

"Little humanity?" I echoed, adhering to the operative expression, astonishing me by his confession about his friend.

"Aye."

"So, tell me, what's he done?"

"Yoo're presently acquainted with Captain Berkley?"

"Yes. What does he have to do with anything about Lord Brimfield?"

"Grant me yer perception of the captain?"

"Well, I suppose from what I've encountered of him, I can't exactly say that he's the most pleasant of people," I acknowledged.

"Nor is he the most moral of men," Leif added.

"I remember you implying that when you and he were conversing one time while we were all eating at the dining table— that he lacked mercy."

"Aye."

"But how does that relate to Lord Brimfield in any way?"

"Brimfield is his mentor. His esteemed mentor."

"You're saying Captain Berkley models himself after Lord Brimfield?" I fathomed.

"Correct."

"Oh."

"Thus, this would grant ye a wee bit of insight into Brimfield's own quality," Leif disclosed. My brow knitted further. Not only was I beginning to gain a clearer understanding of His Lordship, but I had also grown truly confused and was now struck with deeper worry, mixed with astonishment.

"Still, you're friends with Lord Brimfield?" I questioned.

"Aye." His tone was unapologetic.

"But why? You're so discriminating. Why are you choosing to have him remain your friend?"

"We have been shadows fur nearly a score. We soldiered together whilst in Guinea. If he hudnae risked defying our captain's orders by sneaking morsels of bread and canteens of water tae me, whilst I was imprisoned the month fur well-nigh killing one of our own soldiers fur having his way with that negro lass, I indeed wouldnae be in the midst of discussion with ye presently," Leif said.

"Oh. I see." I nodded slightly, gaining a better understanding of the unique ties that bound their friendship, distinct from the common bond. Lord Brimfield risked himself to save Leif's life.

"Once I had been granted leave from my post in Guinea for my return tae England, Brimfield had also been ordered his return tae England. We sailed together and landed in London. Shortly thereafter, war erupted with France. He was sent tae battle in Europe against France, and I was banished along with my commission tae fight fur England in America. Henceforth, I believed we would never meet again.

"Until he arrived tae serve in the same regiment as I within this colony after I lost ye. We warred with France and her Indians in the battle fur Fort Carillon. 'Twas a fierce battle. We didnae prevail and suffered abundant casualties. He is amongst them. Brimfield took pellets in his arm and was thrown from his horse, which landed upon him. His leg was trapped beneath the animal, and I hastened through the field and was able tae extract him. 'Tis the reason fur his limp.

"Efter the battle and upon our retreat, we became separated from our regiment in the wood whilst I had him carried upon my horse as we fled anither pursuit from an Ottawa war party. Once we had evaded the war party, 'twas Providence that we rejoined our regiment at its camp-site. It was then I decided tae perform the surgery upon Brimfield that I had witnessed ye perform many occasions upon soldiers at Fort William Henry tae retrieve pellets from the flesh," Leif expounded.

"So, you saved his life as well," I concluded, finally under-standing it all. "You guys are like brothers."

"In arms," he said. "He isnae Finley."

"I know. No one can be."

"I remain Brimfield's shadow, fur I must." I nodded a little in response, knowing now the loyalty shared between them. "He has nae other shadow but me."

"Likely because he relates to you the most due to your war experiences, that only the two of you can understand," I realized sympathetically.

"Reasonably so." Leif nodded slightly, agreeing.

"Hmm..." I muttered thoughtfully to myself, pondering still.

"Aye?" he prompted.

"I'm only thinking about how I now understand the impor-tance of the friendship you two have with each other. The fact that he risked saving your life sheds new light on my impression of him, and I'm so grateful that he did that. We wouldn't be together, belonging to each other otherwise," I realized.

"Truly," he said, already knowing as he nodded gently.

"Still, I confess that I'd like to also know what makes people so angry at him in particular for them to want to hunt him down to find him all the way over here at *Taigh Gràs*?" I curiously posed the gnawing question.

"Brimfield inflicts individual pain upon any subject who has crossed him, nae matter how minute, and who he deems fit tae receive his punishment."

"What sort of punishment does he give, exactly?"

"He is torturous. Deft at manipulation and a destroyer of men, leaving lasses in his wake—tae take or not—without a morsel of feeling," Leif disclosed candidly.

"Are you serious?" I responded, stunned by a little fright when digesting this extra disturbing information.

"Quite."

I became speechless while staring at him, as considerable thoughts signaled in my head.

"So, you feel that you can trust him? In spite of everything?" I resumed.

"I am the only man who bears tolerance fur him. He is weel awaur of it."

"So, you have the ability to sway his mentality?"

"According tae the support of his interests."

"How often is that?"

"As often as it suits his vanity. He will proceed in any manner suiting his preservation above all others. His ambition is his nemesis."

"Then, why would he ever listen to you if you deviated from his opinion?"

"My contradicting him, when I must, lures his vanity and appeals tae his weakness. That fault lies within himself, ultimately."

"Well, then, I suppose it's very fortunate that you saved his life," I commented contemplatively. A fortune that abruptly appeared was significantly obvious to me all of a sudden; examining his friend's volatile temperament, and the fact that Leif had also preserved his life, guaranteed loyalty between them. The thought settled my mind a little away from Brimfield's fatal personality flaw.

"Fur this reason, in the many years of knowing one anither, he has not yet crossed me. Therefore, I am skeptical that he ever will," Leif said, aware of the cautious thoughts swarming my mind. I nodded, acknowledging his assurance.

"I'm glad you told me. It's extremely good to know," I said soberly.

"Now, micht yer spirit be eased? The rabble nae longer exists," he assuaged.

"But won't more return some other time when he's here?"

"Unlikely. Men of this rabble are certain tae meet Brimfield's repute firsthand at the full pleasure of our governor, Sir Bernard, followed by Lieutenant Governor Master Hutchinson, and the commanding general himself, Gage. Tales of it will swirl the city and strike fear into more men, who micht be inclined toward participating in future in such events as in tonecht. Those particular men will consider twice before attempting such folly." I nodded again in response. Leif gathered my hands into his while his gaze remained fixed on mine. "Pray, be nae longer fretful. Thaur is naught at issue. All has been minded, and will continuously be."

"I'm not as convinced as you are, though. You've been to my home and you know what it's like. Remember the Fourth of July?"

"Aye."

"Well, it's not going to be a peaceful separation. Tensions are rising and we're on the cusp," I said. He didn't say anything, and we stared at each other for a second in silence. "So, it's something to consider." Again, he didn't respond. "Do you know what His Lordship's note said?"

"'Twas a foul threat. I care not tae repeat it."

"Oh." I nodded pensively, and he brought my hand to his soft lips and pressed a final kiss on my knuckles, resolving our conversation.

"I shall presently instruct Mercy's return fur yer waiting as I rejoin Brimfield in the dining chamber till his leave."

"All right," I agreed.

His palms slid over my shoulders again when he leaned his lips over my crown, sealing a finishing kiss. Then, releasing me, he turned for the door and opened it, proceeding past the doorway into the hallway. Watching him as he left our bedroom with the door closing behind him until it shut, I started for the dressing table where I sat and began removing jewelry from around my neck and ears to store in my jewelry box on the table.

Mercy soon entered the room and proceeded to assist me in undressing, and as she was quietly withdrawing my clothes, I started to say, "Mercy?"

"Yes'm?" she replied as she began organizing my clothes.

"Do you know about a note left on the dining room table tonight? It was left by Lord Brimfield's place setting."

"Yes'm, I knows of it."

"Do you know what happened to it after the table was cleared?"

"I seen His Lordship toss the missive into the fire."

"I see," I said, silently disappointed that I couldn't have gotten the note from her or any of the other servants before it was destroyed.

Twenty-Nine

The public recognition of Thanksgiving Day came this morning with snowfall. The recognition came on the third day of December under Governor Bernard's proclamation for the colony to observe, which was announced the first week of this past November. As snowflakes were heavily accumulating on the surrounding windowpanes around the room, I gazed drowsily out the window at the snow piling up on the windows near my bedside while lying in bed. I relished the fact that today would finally be spent at our leisure, as the city would be inactive due to the holiday, while staring out at the thickness of the new snow through the windows. Today, everyone, including soldiers and government officials alike, was on hiatus. Boston was peacefully at rest.

Leif's palm stroked over my bare breast and gently caressed it. Sensing him awakening now, I turned over in his embracing arm and met his dozy eyes, focusing on mine. An indolent grin upturned his lips, heartening his affectionate expression. I naturally smiled at him also, and we momentarily gazed at each other in companionable silence as I felt the tender touch of his fingers stroking obscuring ringlets away from my eyes, tucking them behind my ear when his palm cupped my cheek with a gentle sweep of his thumb and followed the arch of my eyebrow.

Simply staring at me the way that he was, without a word, the penetration of his striking deep blue eyes breached my inexplicable shyness that I only held for him. His grin widened, and I knew that I was sheer to him. My gaze suddenly fell from his as the heat in my cheeks began rising, and the urge to turn my face into the pillows was interrupted when his finger lightly tapped the tip of my nose, making me giggle.

"My wee *sìthche*, I ken yer secrets," he teased.

"What secrets?" I replied bashfully, smiling.

"The ones of which ye reckon that I am unawaur," he answered, continuing to tease.

"I don't know what you're talking about." My smile grew more, betraying me.

"Ye must."

"I haven't the slightest idea of what you're talking about."

"Have ye not?" He cocked an eyebrow over his sparkling eye.

"Nope."

"Hmm..." He drifted for a second, with a taunting smirk and mischievous gaze.

"What?" I prodded curiously, playfully looking at him.

"I micht punish ye."

"That's not a novelty."

"Och! Yer cheek!" He snorted as his brow shot up, and his eyes widened.

"Don't be so appalled," I giggled, knowing that I was entertaining him.

"Scarcely that, am I," he contradicted while smiling broadly also.

"Aren't you?"

"Not merely. Ye have proven yerself tae be once more untamed."

"How?"

"Although ye refuse tae express aloud what ye believe is weel hidden from me, I shall inform ye that I ken yer darkest secret."

"I don't have any dark secrets."

"Contrary. Ye quite do."

"All right, Sherlock. Name one." I gave him a goading smile, taunting him as well.

"A pleasure," he replied smugly, smirking still. The knowing look in his eyes was perceivable and suddenly I felt distinctly embarrassed, though I tried repressing it. His slanted grin only deepened as his thumb and forefinger carefully ensnared my chin, ensuring my maintaining gaze. "Namely, the darkest secret that ye possess is yer care fur my complete and utter debauchment of ye."

"Not true!" I gasped, shocked, and abruptly withdrew from his clasping fingers as I whipped my back toward him, throwing my face into the pillows on the opposite side from where he lay, suffocating myself. Scandalized and distinctly embarrassed, I wanted nothing more but for my surrounding blankets to fold inward and fully envelope me forever, and dissolve because I knew he was being truthful.

Just as quickly, he sharply flung me around onto my back as he pounced himself over me, locking me down. Feeling the solid weight of his body settling on me and caging me immovably beneath him, he forced my return to looking at his enlivened face.

"But whit I have said is indubitably true, Your Grace," he chuckled, obviously amused.

"It's not even close to being true," I claimed, shaking my head while giggling, as I playfully attempted worming myself out from beneath him. I knew he wanted to push the limit to our love-making boundaries and I couldn't help shying away from him. But he imperceptibly seized my wrists also, shackling them beside my head, preventing my escape, as we both were laughing: me, entertained out of guilt and he from the pure delight of it.

"Yer abashment strikes my heart with levity. Yet why argue the truth? 'Tis most apparent yer wanton desire of me exists," he said,

313

chuckling. Lowering his lips over mine, he began with soft, sweeping kisses.

"Wanton?" I questioned, feigning offense as I received his tender mouth, aware that I couldn't escape him even if I wanted to and tried.

"In all manners of the word," he declared warmly against my lips, calming us both from laughing.

"I'm not wanton," I muttered, returning his kisses.

"In my bed, I greatly differ. Nae siren can compare."

"But you did say that I was from Olympus. Didn't you?"

"Aye."

"Then, are you sure you can tame this goddess?"

"Are we not a fair match?"

"I suppose so."

"Whit should be had?"

"Okay, I must agree."

"Ye must."

"Fine. I do."

"In which case, ye may nae longer inquire whether I may be from the same region of the Mount as weel. I shall not harness ye entirely, although I can, fur I take deep pleasure in yer boundless spirit. It gratifies me immensely. I shan't ever spoil whit brings my true pleasure, that is ye. Yoo're free by my permission," he uttered between his kissing lips. "Presently, how grateful are ye fur this liberty?"

"Extraordinarily grateful, Your Grace," I muttered, smiling and kissing him back as his affection started warming my blood, turning me molten between my thighs, and aching my depths.

"Thus, present yer splendor and gratify us both," he half-whispered as his voice rasped. He proceeded indulging more kisses over my lips, growing in heat and trailed them past my jaw into the curve of my neck where they lingered and sucked, drawing the skin into his mouth causing a little pain. A whine eluded me from his inducing sharp, small pain on my flesh. My fingers dove into his loose, silky hair and buried themselves. I pulled his desirous mouth anxiously against my tenderizing skin in offering, as he compelled my thirst for him, and began to burn from the root of my core.

Raking my fingers through his hair, I arched my neck, pleading for him to take whatever he wanted, however he wanted. Forgetting myself and submitting to his touch, yearning was swiftly growing into a strength of uncompromising craving to envelop him in my full depths. Succumbing utterly to the will of his desire to steer himself in any way, known or unknown, as he would take me, I was susceptible to him and receptive to anything he'd do to me—knowing he would securely bring me to reach the apex of ecstasy with him—only intensifying our culmination, and binding us toward further perfection.

Releasing his consuming lips from my skin, he shifted from the curve of my neck, returning to my mouth, fervently fastening them over mine like a gasket, stifling my breath when the thrust of his tongue filled my mouth. Closely incapable of breathing while his plunging kiss took my mouth, and feeling searing blood coursing my veins, the sensation of him growing ardent was quickening. His domineering devouring pending to overrun me in a direction unexplored drew me further toward him.

Excited to heed the pull of his coercion to discover something new, I welcomed his powerful kiss claiming my mouth as my nails mildly scoured the flesh on his back. Sudden moans eluded him as our dancing tongues met. His tongue vehemently rolled over mine, shortening our breathing when irregular it grew, stifling us both.

While powerfully kissing me, he shifted slightly, pressing a knee between my thighs and I naturally widened them, aching to receive him. He easily adjusted himself as I proceeded, greeting him when I sensed the alluring, full strength of the tip of his bold shaft seeking to bury inside of me with boundless pleasure. Shifting my hips and spreading my thighs further apart, craving to envelope and ready to welcome him, I longed for losing myself to him, anticipating the dying sensation of his plummet into me and meeting the limit of my depths, burnishing our union.

But I abruptly froze beneath him and stiffened in his arms as a cold, intrusive thought unexpectedly sheared my mind with anxiety, halting me as I was rising. Suddenly crashing onto the hard stone of reality, I stopped kissing him and he ceased his kisses too, keenly sensing my unanticipated rigidity in his embrace. Instantly rearing himself upward from my lips just enough to glue his eyes to mine from my interruption, I met the unforeseen puzzlement in his worried eyes.

"Whit has occurred?" Leif asked immediately, looking unexpectedly with considerable concern as his brow furrowed somewhat. His steady eyes acutely bore the desire to know the reason for my interruption.

"I—I suddenly remembered something," I mentioned uneasily, regretting the interference.

"Aye?" he prompted.

"The day got away from me yesterday before remembering that it's time for me to give myself another contraceptive dose," I disclosed unexpectedly.

"Ye speak of yer nostrum?"

"Yes."

"Och..." he realized quickly, becoming silent for a second while we simply looked at each other. "Micht it bode weel should I retrieve yer storage in order tae mind caution as we proceed?"

"It would be really wise," I agreed.

"Neither shall we fret," he pacified and withdrew from embracing me, rolling himself off toward my side. Watching him easily shift out of bed, he strode across the room toward his armoire, pulling the doors open and positioning a portion of his clothes aside. When the back panel became visible and unobstructed, he pressed the corners in a certain way, then proceeded raising it as it slid over an invisible track until the panel was completely removed, revealing a hidden compartment. Reaching inside this hollow, Leif rummaged, seeking what had been hidden among everything else holding valuable secrets and was a priority for swift and easy access for retrieval. The other direst of secrets he'd kept securely undisclosed for safest keeping, and to our life's benefit were found in more undetectable locations within walls and floors in this restricted wing of the house. Inside these hidden areas, held items like the bulk of his massive wealth in Boston valued in coins and jewels, including the storage of personal articles belonging to me that had been manufactured in the future.

Discovering for what he was searching, I observed him now clutching a small, ornately carved ebony box in his hand containing the prescription I needed when he shifted his stance from the armoire. Turning away from his wardrobe, he approached and I raised myself from lying to sitting as I leaned against the pillows. The second I adjusted myself comfortably against the pillows, blankets concealing me slid from my torso, exposing my breasts, when he came to sit close beside me on the edge of my bedside. Passing the box to me, he simply watched as I received it from him and proceeded to open it.

"Oh my God," I gasped unexpectedly in horror, instantly peering into the cavity. My breath hitched in my throat as I stared inside the opened box. Nearly toppling the box over to the floor from the slip of my fingers, it landed stably in my lap. The sudden confrontation of icy reality thrust upon me, forcing my colossal fear now barreling down tracks in my immediate direction. The frigid reality doused me in freezing trepidation as my eyes locked onto the three decimated, shattered vial remains of Depo-Provera in my midst. Shuddering began in my fingers, and the temperature in my blood dropped, chilling my flesh as the tiny hairs on my skin raised with goosebumps.

Speechless, all I could do was stare at countless glass granules, appearing pulverized among the misshapen syringes. I was challenged to comprehend the reason for what I was seeing.

317

"Whit has happened?" I heard Leif asking in a quiet tone, sounding as confused as I was.

"I haven't a clue," I muttered, subdued as I struggled to reason past what was seen.

"They waur perfection upon placement before our departure from yer year. This box hasnae been since seen, or opened," he commented, almost rhetorically.

"I know," I replied, acknowledging.

"'Tis quite puzzling," he responded truly.

"I'm extremely confused also. I wasn't expecting this."

"Aye."

"Not at all."

"Aye."

"This is more than troubling..." I thoughtlessly expressed, falling deeper into abstraction.

Leif simply became quiet also, letting silence come between us as I kept staring at the destruction resting inside the box on my lap. As lapsing silence secured the air for a moment, I sensed him turning his eyes from gazing at the remains toward me again after a moment. As he was quietly looking at me, I knew he was waiting for an explanation for me to give him. Certain that he didn't understand the greatest significance of this facing circumstance—at least not yet, I began saying to him, "It seems as if the glass vials have imploded."

"Imploded?" The sheer look of perplexity was conveyed on his face when I raised my eyes from the box and met his. His brow was furrowed, clearly expressing that he didn't quite understand what had happened.

"Yes, they have imploded."

"How micht ye mean?"

"You're familiar with the concept of explosion, right?"

"Indeed."

"Well, just as objects can explode when forces from within it become greater than the outer forces applied to it, which enables the object to fail outwards, so is the opposite case when forces from outside of an object become greater than the forces within it that will enable the object to fail inward, causing it to collapse in on itself, known as implosion," I explained.

"Truly?" His brow lifted remarkably.

"Yes."

"Indeed, a novel conception that is quite brilliant," he said, understanding. He was mesmerized. I gave him a weak nod, acknowledging.

"Is this yer postulation of whit has become of the vials?"

"It's where my mind is leaning."

"Whit micht ye reckon the impetus tae have been fur this result?"

I shrugged slightly, shaking my head a little, wondering the same thing and returned to looking at the decimation in the box. Scrutinizing the granulated glass crystals, noting that they appeared like tiny, transparent, grains of sand, perfectly eroded into spheres not only presented to me the idea of the occurrence of implosion but that the glass had also experienced temperature changes combined with another agent like liquid to form their shapes the same way another natural element as in water behaved against rocks when grinding them away through the course of geological time.

The thought of time traveling rushed to mind and the effects of it, known and unknown, came into consideration. The extrapolation occurring to me was that the liquid-filled glasses couldn't withstand the pressure from traveling through the temporal vortex as time sped and reduced, possibly. Instead of exploding compared to known occurrences related to objects reaching outer-space altitude due to the reduction of external forces overtaken by internal forces, transportation through this wormhole through which we had traveled compresses matter that doesn't reach a finite. Otherwise, the glass, along with all objects, including ourselves, would have ceased to exist. *But how could Leif and I survive the temporal leap, and the vials had not? Plus, all of our other belongings had remained intact from the leap. How can that be explained, also?* I couldn't begin to fathom the physics of it. It seemed random.

The pressure was only enough to alter the glass and evaporate the liquid in it, as I noticed also no trace of the liquid in the box was ever indicated. Furthermore, as I studied the remaining contents in the box, the syringes were now malformed since their tubes curved. This left me with many more questions, not only about the range of quantum leaping, but the physical effects caused by it.

Given this different case, how in the world do our other belongings, like the phones we still have that are made with similar materials, remain perfectly assembled along with Leif and my intact biological forms when traveling through time?

This was the greatest conundrum of our lives—that we not only quantum leapt but survived with the ability to determine our temporal destinations. It was fundamentally apparent that I couldn't possibly be on the brink of figuring out the beginning of this equation, and I wondered if I ever could receive an inkling.

So, I just sat there in utter confusion, trying to comprehend the quantum physics enhanced by the absolute terror from what this potentially meant, with the evidence laying in my lap between my hands.

"Whit do ye fathom?" Leif inquired at last, quietly breaking the lull.

"We could be stranded here for a very long time," I replied subduedly, turning my gaze toward him again, locking our eyes.

"How micht ye mean?"

"The chances of us returning to see the kids again along with my family so soon, like we've planned, might be postponed."

"I remain puzzled."

"Without this medication, that I can't take any longer, the ability to safeguard against pregnancy has been jeopardized, disabling insurance for its prevention. The levels of this medicine currently in my body will certainly begin lowering as my own hormone levels begin adjusting to dominate my natural menstrual cycle," I started explaining to him. The look on his face was intently focused on me. He was paying close attention to what I was saying with gravity, even though he appeared to struggle to understand. "It generally takes about fifteen weeks for that to happen—for the medication to diminish—but I could become pregnant before it fully does—while it's happening. As early as twelve weeks after ceasing the last dosage."

"I see," he remarked, faintly understanding the mechanism for this new risk.

"Yeah—and, I've never experienced tapering from this kind of medication before since this is my first time having using it," I explained further, fully worried.

"I see." He became silent again along with me as we kept staring at each other.

"So... if that happens, then you know... leaping again, prematurely—before completing pregnancy full term could extinguish the baby from existence." Leif's eyes abruptly bulged, expressing horror by the thought.

"The similar quandary presented prior tae our return tae this period," he understood completely now, drawing parallels to my inability to travel on a plane ride for our honeymoon to Hawaii if I'd become pregnant too soon before the trip.

"Yes." I nodded slightly. "And in that event, we'd have to delay until I give birth."

"Aye," he responded remotely, as I perceived thoughts swarming his mind combined with steep concern in his eyes. The depth of his concern reflected mine as he was understanding me. But the added concerns brought by high risks to experiencing maternity, delivery, postpartum, and infant mortality being so prevalent in this era, thoroughly terrified me. I didn't want to die. I certainly didn't want our baby to die either.

Either way, the potential for experiencing a mortal risk to our next baby was very high odds—whether we traveled through time while pregnant or stayed here because of it.

Then, the memory of my family helplessly inserted into my thoughts: *how could we logically explain the incongruent new existence of an infant within our midst when returning to my family, without an explanation? And, without the explanation having the likelihood of revealing the lies I'd told them in the first place? The truth and lies are sure to devastate them, as it all being finally exposed?*

How can Leif and I ever explain this to them without the consequential harm inevitably happening...? And the aftermath of it all? I've no idea what the fallout would be in general—aside from effects on my family if the news of what's happened ever escaped secrets.

Plus, the next problem is: if my family ever became aware that I lived in an alternate dimension along the space-time continuum, existing in their absence, which prevented them or me from the simplest opportunity to see each other unless determined by time? They would liken this to my death, and try everything within their power to stop me from ever returning here again with Leif. A stark given. They'd unequivocally recognize the risk in doing so is much too high for guaranteeing my safety, returning to them by any whim to physically exist with them in the same dimension once again. Factoring in errors running parallel to the order of time, if any unforeseen factors emerged causing chaos to disrupt order, then timelines that were known to us on the continuum would not only be altered, but could rightly result with the extinction of Leif's and my existence—and quite possibly the annihilation of us all.

This possibility was terrifying as I considered it, and was enough for me to want to hide in denial. I pushed the idea outside of my mind. It was all I could do to keep my composure as I stared at the remnants inside the box while we were chained to our own thoughts in the added lull that had come between us.

"I cannae fathom," Leif admitted after a moment, gazing obviously stumped at me, if not more so as I understood when turning my gaze toward him again. "Yet, our bairns survived yer journey through time whilst ye waur bairned and didnae perish."

"Yeah, but I started my contractions after that."

"I see."

"But, it could have been happenstance—now that I'm thinking about it—since carrying twins to term is uncommon. Still..."

"Aye?"

"I don't think it's wise to risk it," I said, shaking my head. A distinct trepidation settled into my awareness, destabilizing me to the point of breaking down into silent tears as I strove to hold them back. "This is so bad..." My voice shook as I fought the knot that swiftly formed in my throat and struggled to push it down.

"Time wulnae foul us again, *ceisdein*," he vowed, gently bringing an arm around me and pulling me snugly against him.

"If we become pregnant while being here, away from the kids, it can do just that," I replied, pointing out the brutal reality. His body stiffened at the sudden realization. It was his ultimate fear.

"Merely string more beads and this situation will be remedied," he suggested sincerely, offering a solution with hopefulness in his voice, despite the tension in his chest while holding me.

"It isn't quite as simple."

"Fur whit reason?"

"It's going to take my body to find its equilibrium again for me to monitor my fertility cycle with the beads dependably," I explained. "So, it's going to be a while."

"Och." He nodded, seeming to understand. "Micht how many days must ye rely upon before ye may dependably use beads once more?"

"I'm not sure—only because I've never relied on this particular method of contraception before until we agreed upon me taking it when you first arrived in L.A.. So, I'm not certain how long it's going to take for my cycle to return to normal, since every woman's physiology is different."

"Yet, ye have sworn tae me that ye wulnae be left barren upon administering this nostrum," he responded, duly struck with further concern involving my health.

"I'm not barren. My body will just go through a period of hormonal adjustment as the medicine diminishes from it. When that happens, I'll receive my period cycle again, and then I can monitor myself using the beads."

"I see," he responded, appearing less skeptical.

"Yeah, so, as clinical studies have shown, women who've used this medication can take about fifteen weeks to menstruate again. That would include me. So, in the interim, the potential for pregnancy exists, since the regulation from the medicine will no longer be guaranteed—which also means I won't be able to depend on the cycle beads until I begin menstruating again," I said. Leif nodded, maintaining a pensive stare. "Until that point, it won't be safe for us to depend on them like before."

"Should this be so... I shall refrain my touch," he said, realizing.

"Do you think you can wait so long?"

"I had vowed abstinence one day whilst in London, which carried throughout my experience within the colony, till the day my meeting ye."

"I remember when you told me that."

"Half a score before my laying hands upon ye until we met," he said. I nodded a little, continuing to remember. "Anither has been added since my losing ye."

"I believe that I even heard Lord Brimfield teasing you about it when at the dinner table not too long ago."

"Aye. Pardon his lack of delicacy."

"I'm sure he can be a lot worse without my presence," I replied, excusing the male conversation I'd heard between them.

"Nonetheless. My apology fur it. Yer ears are too fine." I smiled at him a bit, charmed by his sensitivity.

"Well..."

"Aye?"

"Thank you. For not only the consideration to abstain, but for being completely loyal for so long."

"Never will there be aught tae bring us asunder. Unless, it be by our Heavenly Father's will." Leif's arm pulled tauter around me and he leaned his lips gently but soundly upon my temple, reinforcing the promise of our union. My anxiety began settling as his lips lingered before drawing away. He then tenderly leaned his head against mine, pressing them together with his arm still wrapped around my shoulder, sitting quietly with me for moments longer, until he knew I was at ease again.

Thirty

T he streets were crowded with many pedestrians, horses, carriages, and marching soldiers on patrols as I rounded the corner into the marketplace with Mercy, along with Amity and Winnet. The morning sun this late fall was bright, shining brilliantly in a cerulean sky embellished by patches of fluffy white cumulus clouds. The sunlight beaming down on us felt warm, still, among the snowpack surrounding us as we moved over the masonry and brick-laid walkways. The breeze from the ocean was cutting, numbing the skin, and would have frozen the bones if not for the protection of heavy woolen clothing and furs, which warmed us.

We'd just left the spice shop with my purchase of special ingredients, including cocoa and vanilla beans, nutmeg, cloves, cinnamon, and a refill of ginger for use in recipes for the upcoming Christmas dinner celebration. As we stepped off the shop's last step, returning us to the square, Amity had asked me if it would be all right for us to go to the adjacent knick-knack shop to acquire new silver buckles she'd suddenly seen and liked, displayed in this shop's window. Sure to indulge by making this purchase for her, we moved in the new shop's direction when an unfamiliar middle-aged, strawberry blonde woman made eye contact with me while approaching from the opposite direction.

Our paths were sure to cross as she continued uninterrupted along the path I stepped. She was being escorted by a tall, young black male of an ebony complexion, appearing to be in his late twenties, possibly early thirties. Intending to courteously move aside for them to pass our company before reaching the next shop, the woman and her escort shortly arrived directly in front of us, interrupting me as I was beginning to take a turn up the shop's steps leading my company's way, and ceased before me, stopping us all.

"Your Grace," the woman very politely said as she deeply curtsied in front of me. Surprised, I oddly wondered who this sudden stranger was as she rose and now kindly but demurely stared at me while facing each other. "Pray, forgive me. 'Tis merely my great wish to make Your Grace's acquaintance. Many admire the Duke of Monteith, as my husband, Master Crawford, and I must also have equal fondness for His Grace's wife. The reason for my boldness upon sighting Your Grace through the flock to seek a kind introduction."

"Hello, Missus Crawford. It's very nice to meet you also," I responded with a smile, acknowledging how gentle and polite she had presented herself. I was finally glad to meet her.

"The pleasure lies entirely with me, Your Grace," she replied, reciprocating a modest smile with a special look of surprise that I would've known who she might be. My gaze shifted toward her escort, acknowledging him with a pleasant expression. Her glance slipped sidelong toward her escort, and he politely bowed without a word. When he straightened, the look on his face not only seemed dutiful but also kind and pleasant, meeting my eyes with deferential regard.

Not holding my gaze, his eyes immediately shifted onto Mercy and I discerned the nearly impassive expression on his face soften somewhat further when he scarcely grinned. Inadvertently glancing at Mercy standing beside me, I caught the reciprocal look expressed as her own lips barely acknowledged him with a diffident smile of her own. Aware of me, the meager smile swiftly vanished as her eyes modestly dropped to the packages she was holding in her arms. But this man was far from distracted as he kept his silent eyes steady on her.

He must be Jerome, I instantly realized.

"Pray, permit me to express that I shall not intend to deter Your Grace for much longer. Yet, only shall I wish Your Grace good day," she resumed after the little pause between us.

"Thank you very kindly, Missus Crawford. I wish you a very nice day also," I said genuinely.

"Very generous of Your Grace. I thank you most humbly." She curtsied once more as her escort bowed alike, politely waiting for me to make my way up the shop's steps with my company following, then proceeding with him walking again past the building.

I glanced over my shoulder as they disappeared into the crowd when entering the new shop. The shopkeeper had been holding the door open for us, anticipating our entry since he noticed us through the windows and didn't close the door to the building until we were fully inside.

"A great pleasure, Your Grace. How might I serve you this fine morn?" the shopkeeper, Mr. Bains, promptly asked me with a pleasant demeanor.

"Good morning, Mister Bains. It's nice to see you also. My niece is very interested in having the buckles that are displayed in the window," I responded politely.

"Aye. Certainly, a must," he amiably agreed. "Permit me to acquire them."

"Thank you, Mister Bains," I appreciated.

"Indeed, Your Grace," he replied.

Mr. Bains subsequently turned away from me to retrieve the buckles from the window. After gathering them, he went to the counter to wrap them. While he was wrapping them, I turned to

Winnet, who was indentured, and offered to let her seek out anything she wished to have for herself, for me to purchase as well, as I suddenly considered her.

"Verily obliged to you for your kindness, ma'am," she expressed thankfully. She curtsied and parted from us like Amity had already done to peruse more interesting items that were in the shop.

Left alone with Mercy now, I, too, started strolling past the shelves filled with intriguing merchandise imported from England. Spotting a collection of fine silk ribbons on spools in hues of ochres, umbers, carmines, crimsons, violet, Prussian blue, and white, my mind remained pasted on my encounter with Mrs. Crawford—with particular attention to Mercy's reaction to the man admiring her. Reaching my fingers to examine a spool of violet ribbon, I couldn't help the curious thoughts running rampant in my head.

"Was that Jerome we had met outside a moment ago?" I quietly asked her, turning an inquiring eye toward her as she merely stood beside me, admiring the ribbons also with her eyes. Her gaze immediately shifted from the spools and met mine with a sudden look of bashfulness and surprise.

"Yes'm. 'Tis him," Mercy admitted softly. I also perceived some embarrassment in her eyes.

"I see," I commented with passivity in my voice, not wishing to make her uncomfortable. "I'm glad we encountered Missus Crawford this morning," I added. Her lips subtly turned upward. The faint smile reflected the guarded delight exposed by the glimmer in her eyes, inciting me to smile further. Returning my attention to the ribbon, I then proceeded to say to her, "Do you like these ribbons?"

"I reckon I ain't knowin', ma'am, for them alls be splendid," she considered honestly.

"Hmm... All right, then, I suppose that I'll have to get a sampling of them all," I decided, since I agreed with her that they were all so beautiful, making the choice a bit difficult.

"As you wish, ma'am," she said.

After Mr. Bains had finished wrapping the buckles, Winnet had also presented to me a new needlework hoop of her choosing for me to acquire for her. Receiving the hoop from her, I gave it to Mr. Bains to add to our collection of goods and expressed further interest in obtaining three yards of each of the ribbon samples. He promptly did me the favor of measuring and gathering them, then completed nicely wrapping everything for purchase, bundling them together.

Once I had paid for the goods, we left the final shop and found my carriage for our ride back home.

UPON OUR RETURN inside the halls of *Taigh Gràs*, Amity pursued her own devices with Winnet in her company, leaving Mercy alone with me. Mercy started withdrawing my mink cape from my shoulders when I caught her attention before she moved to place it inside my armoire as I presented the lovely wrapped package, complete with silk ribbons, to her. Simply taking the package from me, believing that I'd preferred for her to set them aside before tending to my outer garments, I interrupted her while she was turning away from me to do this and said, "Would you like to choose a ribbon, Mercy?"

"I's beggin' yo pardon, ma'am?" she replied suddenly. Her eyes suddenly widened, expressing significant surprise.

"I thought you would like to choose a ribbon for yourself," I repeated.

"A ribbon fo me?" Her brow knitted now. The bafflement on her face was clearly perceived.

"Yes." I nodded. She hesitated a second as her eyes bounced from me down to the package in her hand, then returned to me with the appearance of not knowing what to say. "You said you'd liked the colors, didn't you?"

"I do, ma'am. Yes'm." She nodded, obviously trying to under-stand my gesture.

"Well, I thought you'd simply like to have one," I said sincerely.

"Beggin' yo pardon again, ma'am, yet what wills I ever do wif such fineness?"

"You're extremely skilled at sewing, along with your embroi-dery, I only thought you might like to use something like one of these ribbons to include in any one of your projects."

"Yous always be terribly kind to me, ma'am, as I's continually be frightfully grateful fo you bein' so. Yet, I caint be seein' how I shall be graced by receivin' this fine gift if I caint find fit use for 'em."

"What do you mean? You're creating beautiful things all the time."

"Fo you, ma'am, only."

"Oh."

"I don't be carin' to be bringin' no business to myself neither —if I might be permitted to recall by sayin'."

"I remember. I'm sorry, I wasn't meaning to imply anything close to the idea of having you dismissed, Mercy. I've already told you that's never going to happen unless you desire it. My only intention was to make you happy with the ribbon as a show of my gratitude toward you."

She paused a second, then said, "A mighty fine deed is you showin' me, ma'am. I caint say my full words by tellin' you the great fondness I hold fo you also, indeed."

"That's so nice of you to say, Mercy. Your words mean a lot to me, as do you, personally."

"Thank you, verily."

"Then, I hope you'll have a ribbon and will use it. Perhaps you can incorporate it into clothing for a special occasion," I suggested.

"My mind fails me in reckonin' what occasion that be, ma'am? Beggin' yo pardon."

"What about for your Sunday best?"

Her eyes widened as she suddenly paused again. The abrupt lack of response from her as she hesitated quickly made me reconsider my offered idea. I realized just then, while forgetting to acknowledge that not only was she deferential because of her position, but she was naturally modest and free from vanity. Combining these aspects of her disposition, her genuine demeanor was never revealed in the time that I've ever known her. She was never presumptuous over others despite her lofty position as a duchess's maid. So, I unexpectedly understood that if she used the ribbon for herself, not only would it display privilege but also brandish it against everyone who'd question whether she's deserving. She would shy away from making herself so bold, I realized.

"It's all right, Mercy. I'll understand if you don't wish to have the ribbon," I proposed understandingly.

"No, ma'am. Yo gift be verily kind," she contradicted suddenly, decisive about it.

"So, you'll keep it?" I wondered, a little confused.

"I will, ma'am."

"But if you do, I won't exactly appreciate you making anything for me, or for Amity, out of your gift that's meant specifically for you," I told her, fully aware that's exactly what she'd end up doing.

"Yes'm."

"I want you to enjoy whatever it is that I give you for yourself. You're worth more than a simple present given to you, and it'll make me happy knowing you'll be happy with anything you receive from me. Use it however you want—just not for me, or Amity."

"Yes'm." She nodded a tad. Then, a small smile crept over her lips. "I got me a good bonnet only meant fo my head to worship on Sundays in. Mayhap, it can use a ribbon upon it."

"Maybe so." I smiled. The timid smile curling her lips spread gladly, brightening her eyes, though still holding her modesty.

We looked at each other for a smiling moment, perceiving the recognition of gratitude coming from us both. The moment was brief, but deeply felt and understood. With my cape still draped over her arm and holding the packaged ribbons in the other, she resumed turning from me for my armoire. Before returning my cape inside the wardrobe, she first arrived at my dresser and placed her gift on top of it, setting it in a position visible to her so that she wouldn't forget to take it with her when it was time for her to leave the room.

A RAPID KNOCKING CAME through my medicine room door while I was carefully pouring freshly concocted saline solution into amber glass vials. The rapping sounded urgent. I topped off the current vial and corked it. Setting it aside with the others that had already been filled, I moved from the work counter due to the unexpected interruption and opened the door.

"Mercifully beggin' your pardon, ma'am," Faith started excitedly, blatantly panicked, with Mercy at her side.

"What's wrong?" I asked, staring at them both, immediately piqued by the alarm of their expressions.

"'Tis wee Oliver," Faith answered anxiously.

"What about him?" I replied, suddenly struck by concern for our youngest household member, who Remember was primarily nurturing. She had assumed a maternal role in Oliver's upbringing as a result of his mother's death days after bearing him. Leif had acquired Oliver's mother, Hildegard, who'd been left destitute and enslaved as an unmarried young woman soon after the war with France had ended during my absence. I'd learned that she hadn't been more than nineteen years old when she appeared on the streets of Boston begging for food and shelter, when Leif had encountered her by the wharf. He'd learned the circumstances under which the man she was to marry had been killed in the battle for Fort Carillon, and her family had been killed on the frontier.

Leif considered her dire position that had left her vulnerable to further harm.

Whether it was true that she was to marry the deceased soldier as she'd claimed or was a camp follower branding her with ill repute, it had no bearing on his decision to bring her to *Taigh Gràs,* knowing she was doomed to the cold streets to die or to prostitute for means of survival by the hands of deviant pimps mastering the sex trade in town.

Given the alternative to receiving guaranteed safety, clothing, food, and shelter with the option to come into Leif's possession to serve him as the rest of his servants properly, Hildegard easily accepted his offer without qualms, regarding it as a blessing. It had also been revealed to me that Hildegard's health had already been deteriorating and further declined as her pregnancy continued, despite being rescued from the abusive streets and assuming responsibility as a scullery maid. And from what I understood, it was a miracle that Oliver was born at all, and survived infancy. Now well into his childhood, he was a spunky little boy in apparently very good health and proving to be an adventurous handful —rattling the nerves of his surrogate mother along with the rest of the house servants who loved him as aunts and uncles.

"Beggin' for your mercy, ma'am," Faith pleaded urgently again.

"What's happened to him?" I asked suddenly, my concern heightened.

"Oliver stole away with the other lads to sled down the street. Whence sledding down the hill toward the end of the run, a sleigh was seen at the foot, and the horses reared upward as he and the other lads tossed themselves off of their sled to avoid trampling. The lads flew from their sled, off the street, into a drift and landed upon it, crushing wee Oliver beneath them. 'Tis merely the lads have carried the babe all this way, returning him to us at present," Faith explained excitedly.

"Oh no! Is he conscious?" I demanded quickly.

"Aye, ma'am. His eyes be open whilst he wails something fierce," she said.

"All right," I replied, grateful for the fortune of his state of alertness. "Where is Oliver now?"

"Remember looks after him as we seek you. I fear he is crippled!" She suddenly burst into tears, and Mercy was close to doing the same as she wiped breaking droplets from her eyes.

"Crippled?" My heart plunged further than it already had by this dreadful speculation.

"Fearing it true," Faith cried.

"He hasn't moved since being brought home?"

"I cannot say, ma'am."

"I'm coming quickly." I abruptly spun from them and swiftly grabbed some extra supplies, adding them inside my medical bag.

Hurrying in their direction, I arrived out of the room, shutting the door behind myself, and followed them through the hallway leading toward the farthest end of the house where the maids' quarters were. Before arriving, Oliver's wailing was heard emanating throughout the hallway from Remember's room, since the door to it was open and had drawn the attention of some of the other maids who'd worriedly congregated by her doorway while standing in the corridor. Noticing my approaching, onlooking maids hastily dispersed to return their attention on their responsibilities before I'd arrived at Remember's door and entered her room.

Her eyes shifted from six-year-old Oliver, distraught in her arms while sitting on a chair, immediately aware of me the second I'd arrived.

"Have mercy, Your Grace. Wee Oliver has suffered," Remember sputtered, striving to stem tears in spite of the anguish clearly expressed on her face.

"Of course, I'm here. I've been made aware of what's happened," I assured while stepping deeper into the room and arriving before her holding the sweet little boy. I instructed her to

335

carefully shift him out of her lap and slowly lie him aside, stretching on his nearside little bed against the wall. As she attempted to move him, Oliver's weeping pitch heightened as he was clearly fearing to be removed from the comfort and safety of his mother's hold.

"Come now, my wee Oliver. 'Tis Her Grace to visit you," Remember tenderly informed him in a mollifying manner, trying to urge his settling.

"Hello, Oliver," I started gently, leaning a little as I stretched light fingers over his brow, brushing platinum tendrils to the side of his ruddy, damp face, clearing them away. His howling suddenly fell to whimpering, but his reluctance to abandon Remember's arms persisted. I suddenly wished that I had a simple piece of candy or small toy to kindly offer to him in order to coerce his cooperation.

"Are you not fond of Her Grace as you have said, Oliver? You tell us all quite regularly your wish to visit with Her Grace. Yet, presently your wish is granted, therefore won't you have a mere look to greet her presence and graciously thank her for her kindness to appear?" Remember compassionately told him. He then turned one of his buried eyes from her breast and latched onto my gaze with the shockingly unexpected realization that I'd actually come to see him. I gave him a compassionate look with encouragement, and his crying waned. Still, the anxiety that I knew he was feeling hadn't quelled by his remaining resistance to letting Remember remove him from her arms to have him more comfortably placed on his bed.

"It's all right, Oliver. I understand that you've had a frightening accident, and it worried me. So, I've come to see you to know how you are," I began saying, and he seemed to be receptive. "If I ask you a question, will you answer it for me?"

"Aye, Your Grace," he said timidly, muffling his response into Remember's chest.

"Good. Now what I'd like to know is, do you know what candy is?"

"Nay, Your Grace," he replied, again muted. His answer was what I'd anticipated, so now I was rather encouraged.

"Well, then, I'll let you know that it's a special sweet made from sugar. I know of a kind called rock candy and I like to put a bit of vanilla in mine to have it extra special. I was thinking of making a bit of it to share with someone after visiting with you, and I wonder if you'd like to be the one to try a bit of it to enjoy to eat? It tastes very good, I'll warn you. You might even want to have more than one sample," I said.

"Will I truly be granted a wee bit of your special sweet?" he dared asked, looking uncertain of his permission to inquire and if I was meaning my offer.

"Of course," I promised. "Except, in order to receive the treat from me, you must agree to let yourself be placed on your bed in order for me to examine how you are doing. Is this something you're willing to do?"

"Aye, Your Grace," he replied more clearly as he slightly turned his face from fully hiding.

"Very good. I'm happy we agree." I smiled at him. The fact that he'd calmed down now, including the fact that he'd coherently conversed with me, indicated that he may not have been as seriously injured as initially believed, relieving my paramount horror.

Now relaxed in Remember's arms, she was able to move him to his bed, where she mindfully placed him lying on his back. I drew the stool from the corner of the room and positioned myself sitting beside him at his bedside. Retrieving my timepiece kept in my pocket, buried within the folds of my skirts, I proceeded to gauge his vitals by first determining his pulse.

Remaining still as he lay on his back, frozen, complying with my proceeding examination of him, I scrutinized his head, neck, and glands along with his stomach and ribs, looking for any bruising on his head and in the abdominal regions. Noticing several abrasions and some bruises on the side of his ribs, I instructed him to take deep breaths to witness any potential respiratory constriction caused by pain, which might imply injury to his ribs. However, fortunately, he demonstrated sound lung capacity without showing any pain, relieving me further.

After having him successfully wiggle his limbs, fingers, and toes as I checked his joints, his bones appeared unbroken with no hint of nerve damage, and eliminated my fear of paralysis. Except for the noticeable skin abrasions covering his knees, exposed by ripped breeches and shredded stockings, they would need proper cleansing and bandaging. After thoroughly examining his spine, I instructed him to straighten up from touching his toes.

Once all of this was done, I assured Remember, along with Faith and Mercy, who'd remained to support her while observing and showing their concern for the little boy, that Oliver was not only seriously unharmed by the trauma of the sledding mishap but that he was evidently as strong as a little ox. The maids brandished full smiles of relief and released gladdened sighs between them as Oliver's wounds were finally bandaged.

"Now," I said, turning my attention toward Oliver when he followed my direction to return to his bed and sit facing me. "It's a real blessing that you haven't become so badly hurt, for which I, like everyone else, am extremely grateful. You've given everyone a terrible scare. I know you, yourself, are also very happy that you can run and play some more, but you're not allowed to run off with your friends without first asking permission to do so from now on. It has to be known where you are and where you wish to go with your friends, if it's believed that you'll be safe from the risk of getting hurt. None of us wants you to become seriously injured. Do you understand that you must follow this rule?"

"Aye, Your Grace," he said meekly.

"Good. I expect you to follow it," I said. "In that case, I promise to give you the candy I offered as soon as it's made." I smiled at him, giving him a gentle pat on his crown, and a shy little grin curled his lips.

Standing from my seat on the stool, Remember promptly removed it out of my way and returned it to the room's corner when I began assembling my medical belongings together, returning them inside my bag. After collecting my things, ready to leave the room, Remember and Faith bobbed curtsies.

"Bless Your Grace, for your mercy and kindness," Remember said after straightening from curtsying.

"Thank you, Remember," I responded.

When I returned to the medical lab, replaced my materials, and tidied up before entering the kitchen to prepare a batch of rock candy, I relieved Mercy so she could enjoy a break. Once the cooking ingredients for making the candy had been arranged, I began preparing the treat. When the solution was prepared, I set aside the supersaturated mixture to cool on sticks, knowing it would take three to five days before the candy was ready to be enjoyed and consumed with joy.

Thirty-One

$\sim\sim\sim$

Days later, I took the newly hardened candies, which had crystallized on petite wooden sticks, and placed them inside a small cheesecloth pouch, drawn closed by a string. Ready to gladly give Oliver his candy, I was informed that he was assisting young Desmond, who was working in the stable. So, I suggested that Amity join me for our daily walk in the snow, since we hadn't taken one yet to enjoy today. Joined by Mercy and Winnet, we were all happy for the fresh air, clear skies, and bright sunlight shining down on us. Even the wind chill from the shore wasn't too numbing to bear. It was a nice break from overcast days with little snowfall.

As we strolled through the orchards, arriving near the edge of the clearing where the barn and stable became visible in the middle ground, I was surprised by the unexpected presence of two men who had joined us in our walk from behind.

"Good day, Your Grace," Lord Brimfield said, pacing alongside me while he slightly limped with the company of Captain Berkley at his side.

"Lord Brimfield—hello," I stammered, caught off guard as I realized their unanticipated accompaniment. I glanced at Captain

Berkley, and he caught my eye, holding it for a second with an expressionless face. But the look in his disdainful eyes revealed the caustic resentment within them. I inferred that it was a result of the punishment he'd received from Leif, which included me in the fallout. It was the first time they reencountered each other after his imprisonment. He turned his eyes from me and started pacing forward, leaving His Lordship alone to continue pacing with me and Mercy, until arriving at Amity's side while Winnet was on her opposite. I became certain then that Captain Berkley did not like me. The feeling was mutual. "Has His Grace arrived also?" I asked Lord Brimfield, wondering as my gaze locked onto Captain Berkley now strolling ahead of us as he made himself comfortable in Amity's presence while he paced with her.

"Upon our departure from Fort Hill, he expressed his intention to detour upon King's Street before his arrival to join us here," Lord Brimfield said, informing me.

"Oh," I replied only as I realized my disappointment that Leif wasn't already here.

"Might I seek your company to enjoy this stroll?" he asked presumably. It was obviously his intention, deemed by the look in his self-satisfying eyes when I returned to looking at him.

"If you wish," I replied, remaining polite. "Did His Grace give you an estimated time for his return?"

"He did not," he answered.

"I see."

"Yet, he instructed that I shall assure you his promise to have arrived sooner before 'tis time to dine."

"Thank you for letting me know."

"Indeed." I shifted my gaze from him and adhered my eyes to the captain again as he continued walking closely beside Amity. He intermittently stared at her without any reservation, certainly striking me with the idea that he was interested in her. A thick lull came between me and Lord Brimfield while I continued observing Captain Berkley. But I also grew aware by my peripheral vision that

His Lordship followed my line of sight and was aware of my attention. Then, he turned his eyes back to me and said, "'Tis a fine afternoon, is it not?"

"Yes, I believe so," I replied simply, keeping my gaze ahead.

"The pleasure of your company during this amble brightens it further," he complimented.

"That's nice of you to say, Lord Brimfield," I responded reservedly and smiled a little, feeling the instinct to place some social distance between us.

"The charm of your dialect enhances all of it—let alone your beauty, which uplifts my spirit," he further complimented.

I suddenly looked at him again, automatically, noting the extra compliments. This was the first time that he and I were relatively alone in each other's company, where the opportunity for conversation between us was ever had. Before now, discussions always took place between him and Leif, along with other male company, particularly during times of dining, which never included me—least of all during one-on-one occurrences involving me like now.

"Where have you acquired it?" he proceeded to ask.

"Acquired what, Your Lordship?" I replied, sounding rather innocent and polite.

"It all. Your beauty and dialect?"

"That would be from my parents, of course," I answered, unfazed. He smirked. Quite obviously, really, it was seen. But he didn't seem offended and appeared entertained—or attracted, instead, by my frank reply—at least, from what I sensed.

"Thus, where have your parents originated?"

"America."

"Which colony?"

"Would you happen to be familiar with the distinct regions within the colonies?"

"I must say that I precisely am not."

"I see."

"Which is the reason for my begging to inquire. I care to be enlightened regarding such subjects beneath the Crown."

"Well, at the risk of truly boring you with details of my background, anyone else whose roots remain in England is surely found more interesting. Our simple lives here are known not to compare," I said with a delicate smile. He caught his tongue for a second, looking at me as if he wasn't quite sure how to digest my reply.

"Nonetheless. This territory fascinates," he resumed anyway.

"Does it?"

"Quite certainly."

"Interesting. Why would that be?"

"It whets the appetite for any adventurer to seed wealth. Land is plenty and attainable," he answered pragmatically.

"Have you also invested in the colonies?" I asked curiously, adhering to the double meaning of *adventurer*.

"I have land surveyed near Schenectady aside from having my abode in Boston."

"You do?"

"'Twas acquired after the war. Although, I must confess that I have made little use of Schenectady and fail to regard myself as a proper venturer, unlike your husband. Removing the merest slight, his savvy rivals the notorious Master John Hancock as he also has his venture by sea," he said. "If I were not ready to retire my commission, the notion of obtaining a schooner to go the same route entertains me quite well. However, England continually beckons for many more reasons."

"Well, it is difficult to sacrifice ever returning home when opportunity presents itself for experiencing it again," I said, feeling a modicum of fear when he compared Leif to John Hancock.

"Quite," he agreed. "Might you ever dream of experiencing England given the opportunity?"

"I can't say that I ever do," I replied honestly.

"Never?"

"I'm afraid not."

"Yet, there is an abundance to enjoy that one cannot discover here, which you may find strikes your fancy."

"Thank you for the suggestion, but I'm certain that I'm very happy right where I am. Traveling is something that doesn't quite interest me. My susceptibility to illness is always concerning to me —when traveling. I'm sure you might understand," I said, lying for any excuse to snuff out this trending subject.

"Mmm," he considered thinkingly. It seemed he was accounting for the visible state of my overall health, that was apparently far away from frailty given the way he stared at me. "Your husband speaks fondly of London. My suspicion is he might cater to the occasion for returning should it present."

I felt my brow knit a bit in confusion as I wondered if Leif's friend was blind to the fact that he'd been banished here by the government. But I didn't respond, considering the possibility that Leif hadn't revealed this information to him and respected the case if he purposefully withheld disclosing it. Still, I was curious to think that his friend had not already known Leif's fate.

"However, the prospect mayn't ever arise," Lord Brimfield rejoined after considering a second.

"Why do you say that?" I inquired, probing to see if he knew.

"'Tis apparent where his interests lie."

"And where do you suppose that would be?"

"Why, with you, of course," he said directly. "Your unwillingness to explore London further grounds him here. Given his mind is inseparable from the mere thought of you, he is far from daring to remove himself from the sight of you by his own volition, unless 'tis by your will. One can easily understand his adoration, shown by your return. Especially because of it, your husband is much admired. Candidly, he is also envied. His guarded devotion to you is well and apparent. It is simple to perceive why. The belle of Boston is unmatched."

I suddenly shifted my gaze from him without responding,

uncomfortably struck by his allusion to aspects of my appearance and realizing the unexpected feeling of his attraction toward me. I didn't like this feeling. It was troubling.

"Good day, Your Grace! Good day!" Oliver was suddenly recognized, shouting among the apple trees on his running approach toward us. He was surprisingly spotted by me and I smiled at him. Fourteen-year-old Desmond was also seen jogging right behind him, accompanying him. Both were happy to see me. Particularly Oliver, as I was also happy to receive them both as they arrived, and I was relieved for the distraction.

"Hello, to the both of you," I greeted pleasantly, smiling at them when they shortly arrived before me. Catching Winnet's attention also, she gently notified Amity and they came to stop as did the captain, observing my interaction with our newest arrivals.

"Good day, Your Grace," Desmond politely responded with an instant bow as a sunbeam glowed over his wooly crown. Oliver immediately followed Desmond's suit.

"How are you two today?" I asked.

"Faring well, Your Grace," Desmond answered respectfully for both of them.

"I'm so glad to hear it," I replied. I turned my gaze toward Oliver and regarded his expectant face. "How are you mending, Oliver?"

"Grand, Your Grace," he said.

"I like hearing that also."

"Me and Desmond comin' from mindin' the stable."

"Yes, I know. I was actually making my way to see you."

"Nay say, Your Grace?"

"Absolutely."

"Your Grace got a treat for me presently?" he eagerly guessed.

"I sure do. The reason for coming to see you." I withdrew a hand from my muff and held out the pouch full of the treats inside for him to take. "Here you are."

"Verily thanking Your Grace in all the world!" He excitedly

took the pouch from me and pulled the closure apart to open it. Peering inside, his eyes abruptly widened as his jaw dropped. His shocked expression quickly shifted toward Desmond's interested eyes, and he shoved the opened pouch up toward Desmond's vision for him to also have a clear look inside. "Her Grace promised me, she did!" Desmond's eyes became large as well, making him appear equally impressed. Then, Oliver returned to looking at me, utterly amazed. "May I be sharin' with Desmond, Your Grace?"

"It would be very nice of you, Oliver, if you shared with Desmond, of course," I encouraged. He immediately reached his hand into the pouch, drawing forth a stick of candy, and gave it to Desmond. When Desmond received the treat, he silently stared at the unfamiliar edible he was now holding between his fingers in wonder, surely curious about what to do with it.

"By your leave, Your Grace," Oliver requested.

"Don't eat them all in one sitting. Save portions for later to enjoy. Now, go right ahead," I said before agreeing for him to continue on his merry way.

"Aye, Your Grace." He quickly bowed again, following Desmond's manners, then took off running, dashing again between the trees with Desmond on his heels, and the pair vanished from us.

Now that the candy had been happily delivered to Oliver, I was ready for our return to the house. I intimated to Amity and Winnet for them to begin accordingly by preceding me as I would follow them again on our way back through the orchard. Meaning to maintain an eye on Captain Berkley as he continued to move ahead with Amity when they started toward the house, I began with Mercy at my side to follow. But Lord Brimfield called my sudden attention away from proceeding with the others.

"A moment," he said unexpectedly as I observed him leaning to grasp for something and retrieving it from the snow by our feet. "Missing your handkerchief, Your Grace," he said, the minute he straightened. "It has fallen from your muff." He offered it to me between his fingers.

"Thank you. I didn't realize it was gone," I replied, taking it from him and tucking it back into my muff along with my hands. When I took my handkerchief from him, the tips of my fingers accidentally grazed his, and I noticed him grinning in response. His grin was bold and comfortably placed on his face, supporting the temptation in his eyes, leading me to believe he was certainly attracted. Averting my eyes and proceeding to pace with no regard, I intentionally behaved as if I hadn't witnessed the meaning expressed on his face, and I stilled my vision ahead while resuming to walk. I was silently uneasy by the impression I was receiving from him. Not any more inspired to converse with him, I was eager to return indoors for my haven within the house until Leif's return before remaining in His Lordship's company any longer.

"Is it common to proffer delectables to your slaves?" he inquired oddly, questioning the unorthodoxy of my kindness and continuing to pursue more conversation with me.

"We're very fond of our staff, Lord Brimfield," I responded simply, intending to stifle this topic.

"Staff?"

"Yes."

"I fear 'tis a novel term for my understanding," he commented curiously. I didn't respond as I only kept my gaze on Amity and her company. "Yet, why have you displayed favor for the boy, as well as spur his appreciation for the Negro?"

"What?" My eyes shot toward him, glaring at him in sheer appall that I couldn't hide. Suddenly, I felt my temperature rise and my cheeks grow hot, as I immediately caught the initial forthcoming scalding words at the gate of my teeth from my reaction, when simultaneously realizing the significance of tempering the composure of my response. "The premise of our morality, Lord Brimfield, determines our behavior to treat all life with respect since we hold it sacred. Being kind especially to people who are vulnerable for being forced to live among social strata that may lend to their harm by those who live in hierarchical positions, bears upon us the essential responsibility for their protection from members living in higher societal echelons like we, as it is mandated," I replied uniformly, striving to ensure that I sounded exceedingly polite also to hide my ire, and not to chafe him for Leif's sake.

"Intriguing philosophy," he patronized.

"It's morality. Not philosophy. They are primarily different," I replied.

"Are they not similar, however?" he differed absolutely.

"They're not. I assure you."

"Yet one may influence the other."

"In one direction only. Philosophy derives its existential thought from moral constructs formed by religious belief in God. Noting the Ancient Greeks had also formed their philosophy according to the belief in their gods, as did the Romans, to establish my example exactly."

He paused for a moment, seemingly taken aback as he continued holding my gaze, studying me.

"Yet, would not morality be innate?"

"I don't believe so."

"According to Master Francis Hutchison, one of Scotland's popular philosophers, aligns his reason with Cicero's. That morality is based upon the nature of our sense of feeling rather than reason at all."

"But I might respectfully deviate slightly from that logic and counter it by saying that the sense of what is right or wrong is not inherent, except is built on the foundation through the experience of being instilled codes of conduct derived from social canons found in elements of Biblical texts to unify society, in order to strengthen it toward perfection as a whole. Also, if you would consider it, the truth is that human nature is confined to fundamental conditions exposed by external states, rendering its flaws and separating it from its ideal.

"One condition being the preservation of one's self at the expense of others. An ugly truth, that if we're being honest, should be regarded. For example, if two individuals enclosed with each other were suffering from famine and a single piece of bread had been given to them to eat, do you think they'd inherently share the food between them rather than for the one's single consumption, negating the other?"

"I propose that one would succumb to the feeling for the need to share with the other in order to sustain them both, determined by the sense of guilt," Lord Brimfield said. I couldn't help the ridiculous giggle faintly escaping me.

"Guilt?" I replied, giving him a slightly quizzical look.

"Yes."

"That's a learned value."

"Is it?"

"Of course. Why would anyone sacrifice himself for the sake of another person before preserving himself first, if his life depended on it? Consideration for others is also an instilled value, sharing the consequence of guilt. If none of it were true, then we'd all be living in an idyllic world where the natural condition of selfishness wouldn't exist, permitting everyone to happily live by freely sharing their own interests with their fellow person, understanding there'd be no threat to themselves by anyone if it were done. And no one would question the indulgence of a given treat, or whether it was shared with another who is considered a friend. But that's not the world we're living in. Is it?"

He silenced himself for a moment, perceivably thinking. I understood that he was aware that I'd suddenly questioned his integrity in spite of my pleasant demeanor.

"Morality is a system of rules, that are not innate, to regulate society's virtue, and it is instilled in individuals to achieve it," I concluded as he remained quiet for a minute longer.

"How have you come by your reason?" he resumed. He appeared genuinely curious, I discerned by the light furrow in his brow and the curiosity in his eyes. It seemed that he couldn't fathom it.

"I've been surrounded by intellectuals my whole life. Discussions apropos to civilization were common to me while coming of age among family and friends," I disclosed.

"I see." He paused again, seeming to account for what I'd just said and mulling me over some more. Then, he decided to ask, "Yet, how are you certain that morality is not inherent?"

I turned away from looking at him, considering how I was going to answer him. Darwinism aside, knowing that I couldn't even prematurely introduce his revolutionary nineteenth century theories of evolution, further bound me from revealing to His Lordship any origin of my most contemporary knowledge to preserve my risk: that I'd stemmed this information based on extractions of scientific observations of sociological and psychological case studies of infants and toddlers interactions among each other, and their transformations from their beginning behavioral patterns and emotional stages following throughout to adulthood.

The results from these abundant studies not only demonstrated and proved the inherence of human behavioral tendencies but advanced the continued cementing of my own spiritual belief that human beings are imperfect beings removed from God by natural sin.

"Just like botany, Lord Brimfield, people can be studied too—physically and emotionally—as in any other science, if honestly considered," I chose to say, making a basic analogy.

"Novel. Indeed. Your Grace's assertion to claim the nature of man may be studied within the realm of science is pioneering. Your contemplation is bold," he replied. "I shall also confess to say that I have not been left disappointed."

"Disappointed?"

"Indeed."

"What do you mean?"

"I am stirred by your reasoning."

"Really?"

"Truly."

"That's interesting."

"Agreed. 'Tis rumored that you are uncommonly learned for a woman. Presently, my experience being in discussion with you marks this hearsay as truth. My skepticism stands corrected and now I am further intrigued by you. A woman possessing beauty and mind is unconventional. Discovering one with such presence of mind rivaling a man's is particularly unique, separating from beauty. I find my interest has been certainly piqued along with my admiration for His Grace. He is fortunate to have claimed you before I," Lord Brimfield complimented frankly.

My instinct told me rather clearly that he was never one to tolerate differences of opinion from anyone, least of all from a woman, despite his own claim to objectivity. I was sure he would use a woman's intelligence against her as a basis for his resentment and punishment of her, only to keep himself in obvious control by keeping her submissive and accountable to him. So, I realized just how lucky I was to meet Leif before meeting any other man like Lord Brimfield.

I gave him a little smile in response, which I knew was fake but couldn't be detected, only to appease his compliment and satiate his arrogance.

"Your husband must permit you to have many novel discussions with him as your unique considerations stimulate him, for he does gravitate toward those exhibiting distinctive intellect uncommon to others," he said.

"Well, I will say that I'm very grateful that he appreciates that I'm a critical thinker and have a mind far from groupthink."

"Another irregular term—groupthink. How is it referred, precisely?"

"Its meaning is based on the general understanding of collective thought that influences people's behavior as a unit and discourages creativity and responsibility, being a byproduct of it."

"An original notion," he said with a slight furrow, attempting to understand my precise meaning. "Is it a colloquial term?"

"Unique to a specific location where I'm initially from."

"I see." He silenced himself again, and I turned my gaze from him to look ahead at the company pacing before us. "Explaining the reason for the existence of your Negro maid, I presume it rests upon the agreement you hold for your husband's own original attitude. Although I do not admire it altogether," he acknowledged candidly, continuing to speak again. "Nonetheless, I do commend your husband's unyielding ability to inspire controversy and his lack of care in doing it. Whether 'tis justified, I will not say. However, he is daring. People take note of him. Suiting his repute reaching the Crown."

"What has the Crown noticed about my husband?" I inquired, returning my eyes to him. I was curious to know how much he was aware of Leif's specific problems with the government, while silently fuming at his irreverent hubris by the further insults I believed he just made about Mercy. And now, I was acutely repulsed that he was friends with Leif.

"Merely 'tis said that due to Lord Loudoun's accusal of your husband being a Jacobite 'tis well known at Court, that Lord Loudoun blames your husband for his own nullification because of your husband's accusal of His Lordship to the Crown. Your husband had assisted in proving His Lordship's incompetency during the war in the colonies, and he spearheaded Lord Loudoun's removal as commanding general. As a result, Lord Loudoun was recalled to London, and the Crown recognized your husband's expertise in politicking."

He laid a slight emphasis on the word, *politicking*. I wondered why for a second. I didn't know the reason for it. So, I let the attention on the word fade. I was generally more angered by the type of person he was so proudly portraying himself to be. Having now drawn a final opinion of him, I determined that it wasn't at all good.

"I see. Well, I don't know anything about my husband's political activities. But I will say, as it relates to the war and the Crown's decision to remove Lord Loudoun from his position to direct the offensive here, does appear to have worked for England's best interest. Doesn't it?" I responded realistically.

"Reasonably well, it has, evidently," he agreed, then grinned at me again, appearing distinctly comfortable in my presence.

"My husband is a fair man. An attribute of his I'm sure you're already well aware of, since you've been friends with him for so long. It's one of many characteristics he has that I love so much about him. The other is loyalty. He never betrays." The grin on Lord Brimfield's face diminished faintly as we kept looking at each other, but his eyes were still gripped with seeking to further probe. "As for my maid, there is no issue. I'm sorry, but you may have wasted your opinion considering it. I'm afraid."

What was left of his smile vanished completely. I thought I discerned a breach of sudden surprise in his eyes that he met the realization he'd been challenged. I couldn't tell if he'd been insulted, though. It was only a glimmer that I'd noticed. But I think that he understood me now.

Our attention suddenly shifted from each other, caused by the sound of footsteps crunching in the snow heading closer toward us, perpendicular to the trees. My heart abruptly leaped in my chest, and I automatically broke into an enormous smile the second my eyes met Leif's as he advanced. I couldn't have been happier and relieved to see him now, and that he was joining me, finally.

I instantly moved away from Lord Brimfield to greet Leif as he shortly arrived. Grinning at me with obvious pleasure also, I removed my hand from my muff and slipped it around Leif's firm bicep when he promptly revealed it from beneath his coats for me to take. He received my encircling palm and seized it with his free hand, securing it snugly in his possession.

"Fancy tae see ye, *ceisdein*," he welcomed warmly in a low voice meant for me.

"You too," I greeted softly, smiling at him.

"I am returning my wife to myself, Brimfield. Ye have had enough indulgence in her lone company," he said, redirecting his attention toward his friend. Lord Brimfield subtly bowed his head, acknowledging Leif without a word and stepped aside, making room for Leif to assume his place between his friend and me as he proceeded to escort me and Amity back toward the house. Friendly, general conversation began between Leif and Lord Brimfield as we walked along the way. I was happy to be relieved from the responsibility of supporting his friend's attention alone any longer, and now let my attention fall to the enjoyment of the pleasant wintery scenery surrounding us, refusing my disgruntled feelings toward his friend to irritate me further.

I glanced at Leif as he engaged Lord Brimfield in conversation and noticed his gaze had locked onto Captain Berkley as he remained pacing ahead of us at Amity's side. I knew by the stony expression on Leif's face that he was not pleased.

Thirty-Two

Christmas Eve.

Extensive preparations were made for our holiday dinner ball, which Leif had charged me to orchestrate like the previous time during my first experience living here when we were newlyweds. And as before, Christmas decorations containing holly and evergreen garlands highlighted with green pears and red apples decorated the banisters throughout the house, and embellished outside windowsills, featuring it with cheer. The spruce wreath enhanced by interlacing green and red silk ribbons, pears, red apples, holly berries and a large carmine silk bow at the center top, finished the front door from the outside, and the rest of the mansion's exterior. Finally, Leif indulged me with a trimmed Christmas tree attraction set in the drawing room, adorned with lace chains, gingerbread men, and a crocheted angel on its pinnacle, in the drawing room once more, delighting me.

The celebration was planned for Boston's most prestigious residents, including officers already boarding with us and visitors consisting of Sir Francis Bernard, the governor, and his wife, Amelia, along with Lieutenant Governor Thomas Hutchinson and his wife, Margaret, including General Thomas Gage and his wife, Margaret. And to my pleasant surprise, Mr. and Mrs. Craw-ford, Edward and Sarah, relatives of the Hutchisons through Thomas's wife's side, Margaret.

Lastly, sharing in this afternoon's festivities was Miss Annabel Cox: a young woman among Boston's Tory elite in her late twenties. She was regarded as a determined spinster for her refusal to marry after her father and fiancé were lost at sea on their return from England. It was well rumored that she never favored marrying anyone from the start, which caused friction with her father, as he was determined to see her paired for the rest of her life.

When she had learned from her mother the actual reason for her father's voyage to England to acquire his nephew, her cousin, Richard, to bind her in marriage to him, she was ready to escape Boston for New York City without notifying her mother the very day a visitor came to report to her mother the news, that the ship sailing her father and cousin back to Boston had wrecked in a storm with remnants near the cape.

Now that her mother had been widowed and was fragile, Annabel assumed charge of the family's wealth as a result of being the only living child. With her mother's blessing, she vowed to never marry for reasons of her own, like the Virgin Queen. Instead, she would stubbornly model her autonomy, like Queen Elizabeth the First, for the remainder of her life. Curiously, though, as I contemplated her seemingly sound intelligence while observing portions of her conversations with others at the dining table, I wondered the reason for her affiliation with Lord Brimfield, who'd brought her here as his guest. They seemed to flirt quite a bit with each other as they spoke while sitting close. But their rapport wasn't genuinely struck as they engaged, since they found pleasure in tormenting each other by belittling each other in the form of their little joke exchanges unique to them. Certainly, they were familiar with each other. Still, I tended to believe that they didn't like each other and only found the other tolerable in spite of their familiarity.

Perhaps both essentially found the other mutually beneficial to themselves for whatever reason. It seemed she was still the sort of person who respected and stayed within civil norms and held an air of tactfulness, according to her demeanor. Being mindful of herself in this way, she was granted some leeway to mingle with someone like His Lordship, who was known for subscribing to loose mores specific to his social associations with women without tarnishing her reputation.

After forming my reserved opinion of Miss Cox, I turned my attention away from the couple seated at the opposite end of the table near Leif at the head, and caught his eye while he was speaking with the governor before my focus fully redirected toward Mrs. Crawford. Leif grinned with a subtle wink at me, causing my own reaction to him as I gave him a reciprocal smile. Turning my eyes completely now to Mrs. Crawford, I gladly responded to the compliment she'd paid me over the flavor of the stuffing she and her husband were currently enjoying. She admired its unique taste and inquired about seasonings that had been used in its recipe, leading us into a pleasant conversation about the flavors found in food in general—despite the more robust political discussions surrounding the table in the background.

When the last courses were served and consumed, along with countless refills of Madeira, moods had grown comparatively relaxed, as more trivial conversations emerged and veered from the gravity inherent in earlier parliamentary topics that had dominated the table. And with the introduction of chocolate crème pies appearing and being served as a conclusion to the meal, everyone delighted in the novelty of the dessert, further elevating the atmosphere in Christmas blithe.

By the time everyone had their fill of food, the evening had comfortably settled in. Madeira and rum continued to flow as some guests remained leisurely sitting in conversation in the dining room, and others relaxed in the drawing room where Miss Cox entertained on the harpsichord. After a while spent in the drawing room playing chess with Amity, she indicated to me that she had grown weary and wished to withdraw to her room. So, I left the room with Amity to have Winnet contacted for Amity's assistance.

After meeting Winnet's prompt arrival in front of the grand staircase, I wished Amity goodnight with a hug and kiss on the cheek. She turned with Winnet to climb up the stairs to settle for the night. As I was returning to the drawing room to continue my conversation with the ladies, I felt a noticeable draft sweeping coolly through the hallway leading toward the ballroom. Finding this unusual, I entered the room and discovered an unexpected breeze entering through one of the French doors that had been left open.

Assuming someone had stepped outdoors onto the marble patio to gain fresh air and escape the abundant heat emitted from roaring fireplaces and candlelit chandeliers throughout the house, I moved in that direction to see whoever it was and inquire after their enjoyment. Except when I arrived on the patio, there wasn't any indication of anyone having come to breathe fresh air. So, I was a bit stumped for why the door had been left open, until something strange caught my eye, and I stepped forward toward the marble balustrades against the railing. A cloaked figure, wearing a hat and appearing to be a man, moved swiftly like a shadow beneath the glowing moonlight. He vanished in the middle-ground, before abruptly making a sharp disappearance into the bordering band of trees.

Struck by the oddity, an ominous feeling came to me; the man's urgency in hurrying away from the house was apparent that he was either escaping from or going to something. And, I was convinced that it wasn't any of the servants he was leaving, since this man wasn't fleeing in the direction of any one of their quarters built apart from the house. I briefly considered, then, maybe it had been one of our guests having an emergency, forcing his early departure. But I just as quickly acknowledged that, being a guest, he would have properly informed us of leaving before departing through the front door.

So now I was immediately concerned someone unwelcome had interloped. By this swift realization, I was going to bring what I'd just witnessed to Leif's attention. But the second I turned from the rail, I was startled at the unexpected sight of Lord Brimfield standing directly behind me, only several paces away.

"Your Grace. Pray, forgive my alarming you," he said calmly, before I could simply acknowledge him through my surprise.

"Lord Brimfield," I gasped, staring in shock at him as I was entirely taken off guard. His footsteps weren't even heard crunching on the icy snow while advancing. "Are you always so stealthy?"

"'Twas not my intention to use deftness to cause you any fright. You appeared too entranced for any interruption. Therefore, I believed it better to quietly make my presence to you known without my abrupt interference, which might lend to your fright. Yet, I have failed in my attempt, nonetheless. I beg your forgiveness," he explained while coming to stand beside me at the rail. He stood close, in fact, I noticed—ignoring the idea of one's personal space. I shifted a couple of paces away from him, creating more appropriate separation between us and he remained standing where he had arrived.

"Well, I'm actually returning inside, now. I only please ask that you close the door after yourself once you're through catching some fresh air, if you wouldn't mind," I said politely, assuming getting some air was his purpose.

"But might I inquire before you take your leave? 'Tis quite brief that you indulge me, that I beg," he posed, sounding somewhat curious and considerate simultaneously.

"What is it?" I asked cordially, hiding my disdain for him as I stopped myself from leaving.

"Merely that I inquire whether you are faring the evening well? The hour grows late and 'tis been a most eventful day, to your compliments. 'Twould be expected if you have found yourself weary, as a result. It appeared that you might be near a fit of the vapors upon discovering you here. Thus, my concern for my dearest friend's wife—of course—and the reason for my appearance," he explained easily.

"It's very kind of you, certainly. Thank you. No—I'm all right," I assured.

"I am pleased to understand that you are indeed well. Then, 'tis not past assuming that the frigid outdoor air warrants fleeing toward the prevalent heat within indoors."

"Yes, the warmth inside is actually preferred," I agreed. "But were you trying to find me for some reason that brought you here aside from my wellness?" I was a little skeptical of him because of his stealth.

"Simply my service in locating you for your husband's favor."

"I didn't realize that he was looking for me."

"Soon. I imagine."

"Well, I shouldn't have him start wondering where I am, in that case. Please, excuse me while I return inside," I said, beginning to move now from the rail to abandon him.

"He is far into discussions, however, with the governors and the general, presently. The discussion won't have yet concluded, readily. The interruption is not expected, providing you a moment's spare," he replied, causing my pause again.

"I see," I realized. "Well, I'll take the moment inside to wait."

"The frost is quite uninviting," he acknowledged.

"Yes," I responded simply. I resumed turning from him, nevertheless, and moved toward the open door for the warmth of the ballroom inside.

"The winter season is harshest of all. Fairer weather brought upon spring is what I favor most. Would you not agree?" he asked, when I realized he was following closely behind me to enter indoors also.

"Spring is rather nice," I agreed simply again, hoping to break away from him and the growing conversation he was pursuing.

"What do you favor most about the season?"

"All the flowers that bloom in the garden that my husband has planted for me. They're stunning when they bloom during the season."

"I have seen them in your quaint garden. And so, they are appealing. Yet, I must say that if you were to see the garden my aunt keeps in York, you are certain to be thoroughly amazed by the comparison."

"But I'm perfectly happy with my little garden, because it's mine and given to me by my husband, who designed it especially for me. He filled it with obscure perennials that are very hard to obtain and struggle to flourish in England, as I'm sure you might have already noticed," I replied, understanding the pedigree and wealth he was posturing against Leif's, which silently ruffled my feathers. Leif was the wealthiest man in the colony, with the Hancocks being second. Leif's estate was far from minute, exhibited and buttressed by the examples of the gardens he kept for me, and had expanded. They were the envy of Boston, while rumors of their admiration had spread widely across New England and as far south as Maryland and Virginia.

Lord Brimfield didn't respond after my reply while he continued pacing behind me and followed as I came through the door, entering the ballroom. He stepped past me and shifted aside, watching as I moved to close the door, freezing the cold air out. I felt that he realized that I wasn't impressed by him after I punctured his comparison, which I believed was snide.

Turning from the closed door, I went toward the roaring fireplace to retrieve my nearly emptied wineglass of Madeira resting on the mantle when I noticed that a second full tumbler of rum had been set beside it, touching mine. Suddenly repelled to finish consuming my wine, I was uncomfortably aware of him striding with me toward the mantle. Regardless, when I arrived by the fireplace, I reached for my glass intending to deliver it to the maids in the kitchen for washing, along with the other used dishes. As I was carefully wrapping my fingers around the stem, he also moved a hand to gather his full tumbler when the tips of his fingers not only brushed mine, but enfolded them with a little grip.

Feigning that I had overlooked the encounter, I indifferently removed my fingers from his along with my glass, completely. He said nothing of it either, and the look on his face was undisturbed. Maintaining his nearly deadpan, gray eyes on me, however, as he brought the rim of his glass to his mouth and sipped, it was discerned in his stare that he hadn't committed an accident. The purpose was there. Abruptly, Jasmine entered my mind, and I unexpectedly knew the feelings Leif had felt regarding her. Except, I wasn't in a free position like Leif was, where I could influence his friendship with this man; Lord Brimfield had literally saved Leif's life, in addition to having known him for a decade or more.

"I suspect that I might be partial to settling in a climate presenting more temperate weather to neglect the harsher winter, given the opportunity. As in Virginia Colony where I'm informed snow does not accumulate for long," he resumed after swallowing the rum he just sipped and pulled the tumbler from his mouth that he was now holding.

"Is that so?" I replied pleasantly, trying to devise a courteous exit strategy from him as it was becoming increasingly clear that he was being insistent.

"There are those preferring the irregular difference of more clement weather, which may be offered to elude what trials snow does bring."

"Yes, I suppose that would be a likely reason for interest in living in those regions."

"My younger brother, whom I hate, attests by his experience of benefiting from such weather once he fled us from England to reside permanently in Jamaica. He stated this in the only missive I have ever received and read from him, after his flight."

"I see."

"He amassed his allowance, surveyed land there, and purchased it. He has made it a plantation for sugarcane and indigo."

"He has?" I asked simply, faking interest, though I was beginning to learn even more about him.

"'Tis a fact," Lord Brimfield said plainly. "Edward has also claimed a woman to be his wife whom he has no right to wed."

"You mean aside from your disapproval?" I surmised easily from a previous conversation I'd remembered he had with Leif. And now, I'd grown somewhat curious in spite of my aversion to him.

"The reason for my perfect disapproval," he said bluntly.

"Which is what?"

"My brother has made himself a criminal," he said bluntly.

"A criminal?" I automatically responded with surprise. Hearing this was unexpected, and I was confused as to why, when I suddenly clued into the potential reason for his brother's derogatory labeling and disparagement.

"I see that your husband has honored my shameful secret by not disclosing it to you," he deduced by the look on my face. "Your husband proves his trust once more."

"You detest your brother for having a black woman for his wife," I posed the explanation carefully, realizing him.

"He will suffer imprisonment if ever he should appear in England again," Lord Brimfield said.

"Interfaith marriage, I'm aware, is mandated illegal by the Crown. However, I'm unaware that it has applied a similar prohibition related to people of various races. Has a new law been introduced?" I replied sincerely, remembering the famous painting by David Martin of Dido, who was the daughter of an English nobleman and his black wife, and her beloved white cousin, Lady Beth Murray, who came to live with her aunt and uncle in England.

"Prohibition of it does exist within several of the colonies, whether the law exists or not, I shall see to my brother's public humiliation," he guaranteed. "He would make a beneficial example to counter any leniency to support such diabolical marital relationships in the face of new stirs from members within London's society for convincing Parliament of the business of slavery, of which I am aware. Anyone swayed toward that line ought to be publicly castigated. Those experimenting with that mentality would soon rather see the empire in ruins."

I didn't respond while holding my tongue. I didn't know what to say when I realized I couldn't say anything without exposing myself.

"But interracial marriage isn't illegal, is it?" I put forth anyway, unable to stop myself from questioning him.

"As of yet? No," he said. "However, I hope that it is done."

"Then, your brother isn't a criminal. Isn't it harsh to label him as one?"

"Naming him a criminal is quite apt. With or without the judgment of his wedding, his enterprise is familiar with smuggling and for that he is deserving of what the law will bring."

"Do you know for a fact that he does this?" I asked curiously, feeling a beat of dread hit me.

"My mere speculation," he admitted.

"I see." The fact that Lord Brimfield would accuse his brother of crimes he didn't commit or had no proof of him committing, left me with a distinctly bitter feeling about him and made me question his loyalty to anyone he considered a friend—namely Leif, who was his only friend and brother in arms. "Politics is a weary subject for me, Lord Brimfield. It is not my forte," I demurred instead, meaning to curb the conversation.

"Forgive my tedium," he regretted.

"Apologies aren't necessary," I said, sounding polite.

"I entreat you not to bear my brother's scandal against me."

"I judge everyone's actions independently."

"You are noble, indeed. I thank you most generously."

"Of course," I accepted, then proceeded to ask while maintaining my innocent tone, "Perhaps, I should rejoin the ladies. I'm sure they're wondering where I've gone. Maybe, Miss Annabel is wondering where you might be also?"

"Ah, yes, Miss Annabel Cox," he remembered. "Quite doubtful that she is."

"Oh. It seems you are nicely acquainted with each other."

"For the matter," he commented flippantly.

"Oh."

"We are not well suited."

"I wouldn't have guessed otherwise."

"We are merely fitting for the present. I fear she tires quickly of me. Furthermore, she is lacking."

"Lacking in what?"

"I find she no longer stimulates me. Her wealth does not remove the commoner that she is, and she refuses to wed. If I cannot seem to manipulate her hand into wedlock, then who? She is stubborn and not worth the patience. Thus, we have settled upon a familiar acquaintanceship," he explained.

"I see," I said.

"Apart from it, I am certain there will be another who will intrigue me more. Miss Annabel is certain to lament my abandonment. Yet, what care have I? Greener pastures lie ahead. I shall assure my own suit. All within time, of course."

He drew the tumbler to his mouth again and sipped some rum without yielding a glance from me. Interpreting the direction of his comment while he stared at me, an unsettling feeling came over me. I didn't know quite how to respond. So, I didn't. Instead, I turned my eyes down toward the Madeira in the wineglass I was holding, more inclined to withdraw from him. But the sound of new male footsteps advancing within the ballroom caught my attention as well as his when I gladly recognized Leif entering the room. Relieved, I instantly moved away from Lord Brimfield, deserting him by the fireplace, and approached Leif as he continued advancing into the room.

Grinning kindly at me as we met in the room's center, his smile widened, inciting me to smile back at him. Grasping my fingers among his, he tucked my hand beneath his arm while saying, "Our guests begin to depart. We must bid them farewell."

"All right," I agreed pleasantly. Steps echoed as they proceeded, moving toward us from behind me. Leif's eyes shifted from mine, sighting his friend past where I stood. The look on Leif's face was impassive while he kept his eyes steadily on his friend as he continued toward us.

"Your wife is commendable, Monteith," he said to Leif as he was arriving at Leif's opposite side. "A tribute to your betterment. One can easily perceive the reason for your choosing her. She is a rare sophisticate. A pedestal of feminine reason and intuitiveness. Quite remarkable indeed that one philistine as yourself would have the ability to capture a maiden so fine."

"A noble view in the looking glass would reveal the undoubted philistine betwixt us, Brimfield. However, I am in full agreement that my wife doth lure my greater quality, of which I am all beholden tae her and rejoice my debt," Leif quipped with underlying cautionary doused in irony by the smirk on his face.

"My envy."

"A deadly sin," Leif countered, still holding his smirk. A lesser grin slanted Lord Brimfield's lips as the men looked at each other. Lord Brimfield didn't reply. Then, Leif turned his attention ahead and proceeded comfortably, escorting me out of the room to bid our guests farewell for the evening. Lord Brimfield accompanied us to meet our guests without a further word, until he left with all of those departing for their own homes this late evening hour, and wished us an amicable good evening also.

ॐ

WHEN LEIF and I had settled ourselves into bed, ready to rest from today's festive Christmas dinner, finally, I remembered to inform him of the strange encounter with the open ballroom door and the unidentifiable man I'd witnessed leaving the grounds. He took note of it and agreed that it was an unusual circumstance; all our guests were present except for Captain Berkley, which Leif considered odd. So, he promised he'd examine the captain's situation following the early morning, before we attended King's Chapel in observance of Christmas Day.

After doing so the next day, according to Leif, when he finished questioning Captain Berkley, it seemed the captain had a reasonable excuse for his disappearance during the ball last night, which was a result of his having vanished into the privy closet. Still, as a precaution, the itemizations of valuables on display throughout the house took place after church, which included the private east wing. An accounting of livestock had also been made, and discreet questioning of servants regarding any unusual activity they may have witnessed taking place last night. But nothing was reported to be amiss. So, the concern regarding the man I'd seen running in our field last night was dispelled without further regard.

Thirty-Three

N ew Year's Eve quickly arrived. Leif and I were invited to the governor's ball and were greeted by Sir Bernard and Lady Amelia when entering their governor's mansion, Province House. Among their guests were familiar faces, including Lieutenant Governor Hutchison, General Gage, Master Crawford, and their wives. Many other high-ranking officers were also in attendance. Including, for sure, Lord Brimfield, who wasn't accompanied by Miss Annabel Cox this time, but by another woman, appearing a few years younger than she, accoutered in a carmine silk gown. This was Miss Lauret Rancier. The color of her gown alone was not only daring but highly risqué for the era, as it was synonymous with inferences of scandal and entirely carried the stigma of shame, if not branding her *une dame lâche*—which was all too flagrant.

Despite it, though, she wore it with obvious confidence, vainly doused in pride. Dismissing negative, silent, and whispering opinions cast by critical female eyes thrown in her direction, she didn't seem at all influenced by their questioning or disapproval. The bold statement her appearance expressed in her high-fashion gown, despite its color, male attendees were well aware of her laissez-faire attitude and reputation, and were lured by it. Her demeanor was arrogant, enhanced by the bourgeois air she held as the elevation of her nose literally touched the stratosphere. Given her attitude, I knew she and I would mix like oil and water when forced to socialize on this evening's polite pretenses.

Adding the fashionable white, lead powder all over her coiffed hair for embellishment, and used as oil facial foundation heightened by rose matter painted cheeks and lips, along with a perfectly positioned charcoal black painted mole just below the left corner of her blue eye, gold filigree ruby dangling earrings and matching necklace, fit the perfect mold for an elite, well kempt European socialite that was no doubt a courtier. A Huguenot, she was a fresh transplant from France visiting Lord Brimfield. He was accommodating her at his local manor and had arranged for her to stay with him indefinitely. By all observations, it seemed his philandering hadn't failed him in the slightest.

A quartet was playing minuets in the ballroom as guests danced. Port wine flowed from silver fountains molded into large fish, situated in the corners of the room, which was the novelty of the discussions as indulgent guests stood drinking animatedly around them. Leif had escorted me past crowding, cheerful partygoers congregating around the ballroom's perimeter toward a center clearance along the perimeter. There, he led us into the middle of the ballroom with dancers arranging themselves to begin anew as the following minuet was about to play.

We partook in several minuet dances nonstop until members of the quartet broke for a respite. During this time, we drifted toward the flowing fountains where Leif drew us some wine pouring from one. Enjoyably sipping a bit of it from our crystal glasses while facing each other, General Gage and Lord Brimfield, with Miss Rancier attached haughtily to his arm, made an appearance, joining us. Genial conversation began between the men while I interestedly listened to them speaking and continued sipping wine. Miss Rancier appeared to be doing the same. But when I coincidentally glanced away from sipping my wine, I caught her stare when I realized her gaze had been fixed on me for a notable moment.

She gave a smug little smile, drew the rim of her wineglass to her lips, sipped, then withdrew it, all while her eyes remained on me as she delicately swallowed her wine. Evidently, she had been studying me, and it was then I knew she'd certainly rubbed me the wrong way without a doubt, not only due to her pomposity, but it seemed she was trying to compete with me for whatever reason— and none of which I was interested in taking her bait for sporting any challenge.

Insolence was discernible in her eyes. Struck by it, I, too, steadied my gaze on her, meeting her expression with my own deadpan eyes, as I took another tiny drink of my wine, scrutinizing her as well. Then, her gaze turned from mine and latched onto Leif's tall, lean, robust figure as he was speaking with the general and his friend. It appeared she was interested in him now. I was observing her closely, watching as he engaged. Never wavering her gaze from him, it was clear Leif had replaced Lord Brimfield.

Sampling the last droplet of my wine, Miss Lauret Rancier's gaze had turned unabashed toward Leif with a flirtatious, closed-lipped smile upon her face that lacked any consideration for me or His Lordship's companionship. Mutually, His Lordship didn't seem to care at all either, whether she discounted his presence or not, obviously ignoring her while in conversation with his mutuals without even tossing a glance her way. It was clear that neither he nor she held any genuine, heartfelt affection for each other; instead, they were simply superficially connected.

Bringing her nearly finished wineglass to her lips again, taking a single sip, Miss Rancier smiled once more after pulling the rim away. Still staring at Leif, it was evident that she had placed her full attention on him; Jasmine entered my mind. Suddenly, Miss Rancier's eyes shifted, returning to mine, and we discerned in each other's quiet gazes that both of us were carefully cognizant of the other. But a full smile dimpled her cheeks, highlighting the coquettish sparkle in her eyes, which had delivered a slight slap. Automatically reciprocating a genuine smile in kind, my delivery was perhaps precisely targeted, with a harsh sting, when the grin on her face abruptly faded, as my expression was benign, with no hint of insecurity in my smiling eyes.

Nature suddenly called, forcing me to turn my attention away from her, and I delicately garnered Leif's attention from the discussion he was having with his surrounding male company to excuse myself from the group politely. He nicely received my glass from me and excused my withdrawal. Leaving the room now, I wandered the halls full of jovial guests as I sought the privy closet. Fortunately, I found a maid to guide me to the proper location and followed her through a lone, window-lined corridor until we reached its end, where she presented a footman to me who was holding a chamber pot while standing, guarding the door beside himself.

Arriving before the footman, the maid promptly curtsied toward me, then retreated, making her return through the hallway. The footman then respectfully offered the pot to me and opened the door for me to enter into the privy closet. After the door had been closed, I carefully positioned the pot on the stool, mindfully drew my skirts, and happily relieved myself.

Once finished urinating, I completed caring for myself by rinsing my hands in the freshwater basin, then looked myself over in the standing looking glass by candlelight bouncing off walls from sconces. Pleased with my appearance, I emerged from the closet when a chambermaid came to collect the pot, as a fresh one had been given to the footman to hold for another guest.

While I was pacing through the vacant, isolated corridor, making my return to rejoin Leif in the ballroom, I saw a tall male silhouette approaching from the opposite direction in the darkness, caught between moonlight entering through evenly spaced windows lining the hallway walls. As this man came closer, he was not a stranger; I realized when silver moonbeams poured over him through the window, where he now stood directly before me. My heart tightened in my chest as I stared at the caddish grin of Lord Brimfield, gazing at me as my steps were impeded by him, bringing me to a halt. There wasn't a way for me to bypass him without being rude. So, I was at his mercy for being congenial, which was also dictated by the circumstances of this party and his relationship with Leif.

"A splendor it is to meet Your Grace once more," he complimented, forcing my engagement as he stood closely facing me.

"Thank you, Lord Brimfield," I responded quietly, giving him a modest look.

"Seamus does not quite formally address me. Might I invite you to regard me as George as well?"

"But isn't it reserved?" I asked, oddly, about the unexpected invitation.

"Merely for ones deemed privileged," he said.

"Oh," I realized, noticing him grinning somewhat also. I hesitated, not inclined to give any informality between us, only to uphold my boundaries with him.

"I am willing to implore, if I must, simply to have you aware of me. Thus, I beseech your kindness found in friendship," he insisted in an even voice.

"But aren't you better off as my husband's friend? I'm sure you'd find me lacking otherwise."

"Pray, do not miscalculate yourself when I have discovered the glory of my dearest friend's wife strictly shares the throne upon which he sits, but who is equated to his wit and intrigue that draws my interest quite precisely. Therefore, do address me personally to let pretenses be done."

"If it is what you prefer," I responded reticently, giving in to his wishes. He grinned, seeming satisfied. But something still felt ambiguous about him, and I only desired to put my finger on it just then, but I couldn't.

"I do so prefer it. And, I thank you," he replied chivalrously. I nodded a little in acknowledgment, but was disinclined to reciprocate the same invitation. However, the interpretation in his gaze told me that he was waiting for a similar response from me as a lull in our exchange emerged between us. It was discernible that he held the same expectation to regard me more intimately, with my permission for him to use my first name. The answer to this was not forthcoming, as my negative response was pending, with the hope of not disclosing my impoliteness and any hurt feelings he might feel, while I hesitated. "Sylvina is quite a lyrical name. Beautiful and rare. Fitting for your appearance as regal as a princess. 'Tis a Spaniard's name, is it not?"

"Derived from Spain, yes. My origin isn't Spain's, however," I said.

"Most intriguing."

His expression conveyed the combination of scrutiny and attraction. Seeing it prompted skepticism in the back of my mind and an uncomfortable feeling within me.

"George is a German name, isn't it?" I heard myself asking, despite my desire to move around him and pass by to continue walking through the corridor, distancing myself from him altogether.

"I do not share a Habsburg's name, I assure you. The Bourbons' adoration for their dynasty is no consequence to the Hanovers'. And, any Frenchman not a Huguenot deserves all of England's wrath. The Pope may keep them. Our liberation from the Vatican has risen us to be its envy as we master the world. Our dues are our own."

"The right to self-determination is the root cause of separation from the oppressor by the oppressed, isn't it?" I replied curiously to his opinion.

Given: the essential reason for King Henry the Eighth's renunciation from the Vatican was sexually driven above moral principles of matrimony as stated in the Catholic Canon. It ultimately fell to the argument of the power of Free Will granted by God to justify England's separation from Rome, as the king developed his own theological argument, found in Leviticus. Still, I was wise enough not to broach the argument with the man I was now facing as he cocked an eyebrow and gave me a considering look.

"The right to self-determination, you say? Stimulating. 'Tis quite novel to believe that any one man is subjugated, is it not? Your vocabulary is unique by expressing the word *oppressor* rather than *taskmaster*. One cannot dispute how astute you are, for your remark is untenably shrewd. Commendable for a mind belonging to the female persuasion, for it makes one who is not inclined to consider the contemplation of such a new argument," he said.

"Well, as you might already know, I do read abundantly as well as observe. So, there is some room for thought," I replied and unthinkingly placed my fingers to rest on the ledge of the windowsill close beside me.

"Indeed." He also shifted his stance a little closer toward the window while maintaining his stare focused on my eyes. "One may acquire prudent knowledge by observation."

"Yes, I believe so."

"Quite admirable to understand. This brings to my consideration that we may share a sort of commonality betwixt our minds that is unique—if you will. I do find the merit of our discussions strangely aspirational to the deepening understanding of the other. Pray, forgive my forward posture in my admission to you, yet I must confess how I am lured by your originality and seek that I shan't be punished for it."

"Except, it also seems Miss Cox is highly intelligent and matches your interest rather well. Doesn't she? Despite your differences, you and she apparently are still close friends. In that case, wouldn't she prove not only better acquainted with you and therefore be more suitable to your intelligence?"

"She is standard, however. Entirely dull. Dreary, in fact. To disregard her birthplace is quite generous of me to say."

"Oh. I wouldn't have known."

"I assure you 'tis the case. We are fair when necessary, regardless. She is convenient, I will say, suffering amusement."

"How does she bore you?" I asked curiously again, trying to understand the trajectory of his meaning, exactly.

"'Tis regular," he dismissed, closing the idea for further discussion.

I unexpectedly felt his fingertips brushing mine, and I recoiled my hand from his touch. But he caught my palm in his and enfolded it, holding it. Thrown off-kilter, suddenly, my voice stifled as my words caught in my throat when my next thought flew from my head. Stunned, as I watched him raise my hand to his lips where he planted an indicative kiss on the back of it for a prolonged second, I naturally attempted to withdraw my hand from his, except he clasped his hand firmer around mine, inhibiting my withdrawal.

My heart clenched, and my stomach contracted when he wouldn't readily release my palm. I was suddenly made aware of his intention, and he held me captive to his whim as he strongly impressed his attraction to me specifically. All I kept wishing was for my hand to be removed from his and for me to escape him. But I was frozen in place, remaining before him and hoping for any interruption from a partygoer, passersby, or a servant. It didn't seem that I was able to elude him soon enough.

"I shall forget Miss Cox. Nor shall I recall Miss Rancier, for her intellect fails miserably along with her amusement, which does not master intrigue at its closest. My compliments to you, of course, Your Grace," he said after his lips parted with my hand finally. Not too soon, I carefully removed my fingers from his, retracting them fully and safely as I clasped my hands together, securely entwining my fingers before myself.

A grin crept across his emboldened face, and though he seemed unintrusive or gentle, I imagined that he might not be so if persuaded otherwise, more suitable to his surrounding male comrades, disposing of women a dime a dozen at his discretion also. Observing his grin, there wasn't any doubt in my mind that he epitomized rakish behavior and was a complete cad. So, the leery feeling I had of him was only underscored in my mind.

The flame bouncing in the nearby sconce flickered in his gray eyes. His pupils were dilated, revealing tunnels of blackness I was certain matched his soul and combined the licentious temptation glaringly discernible in them. His overture hit me like falling bricks as I understood his willingness to risk betraying his best friend, whom I had married. My heart immediately sank as a chill swept over my skin, recognizing now the deceit in Leif's friend that I was experiencing. As a result, I knew that Lord Brimfield was not only a danger but also a malignant man.

"Lord Brimfield," I started mindfully, "please understand, with all courtesy, that I must insist that we continue addressing ourselves appropriately in a formal manner—since I still believe it appropriate to consider my husband's feelings. I hope you'll under-stand, of course?"

"I—I imagine, therefore, I must," he stammered as his eyes slightly hardened, indicating the sudden withdrawal of his spirit. He didn't like that I had changed my mind to address him less formally.

"Thank you. I'm certain you value the friendship you share with my husband, and you wouldn't want any misunderstandings to arise because of our familiarity."

"In truth, not."

"Then, you're probably already aware that because you and he are true friends, he doesn't choose friends lightly and regards them well while expecting the same reciprocal honor."

"But of course."

"I'm very glad that you understand. So, thank you for respecting the boundaries my husband and I share. My husband must be able to trust his friends as well as I."

"Forgive me," Lord Brimfield offered with embarrassment.

"If you'll excuse me, I'm sure His Grace is no doubt wondering where I am at the moment."

Without hesitation, I took the opportunity without giving a chance to gauge the reaction on his face as I stepped aside to move past him and swiftly resumed pacing through the corridor toward the ballroom to rejoin Leif. As the distance grew from His Lordship, I sensed his eyes lingering on me from behind. My heart returned to beating again, and warmth returned to my skin as I drew in a deep breath of relief and released it.

I wrestled with what had just happened, but I knew I had to disclose it to Leif. I struggled with this fact because of the potential damage it could do to their friendship. The urgency to tell Leif was pressing, but I had to choose the most opportune time to broach this topic, knowing how delicately the subject needed to be handled. The fallout was unknown, and I feared it because of the longevity of their friendship. Despite this, however, I only wished that I could take Leif aside right now and inform him of what his friend had done.

Flustered, I entered the reception hall from the hallway. Carefully meandering around the animated guests crowding the area, I veered into a separate hallway leading toward the ballroom. Passing more partygoers along the way, when nearing an entrance to a different room, Leif and I spotted each other a distance away through the crowd. We approached from opposite directions, with Miss Rancier glued to his side as a companion.

As the crowd slightly spread for them to move through, he separated from Miss Rancier and continued forward toward me alone. Miss Rancier, left standing alone by him while being suddenly interrupted in the middle of their conversation, appeared noticeably put off when she discovered the reason for his departure, as her eyes scanned and discovered me in the crowd waiting for Leif's arrival. Her brow knitted before a contemptuous little smile slanting her rosy lips, and pairing her sneer. My eyes shifted, dismissing her mockery, and I met Leif's advancing, easy expression. His glinting eyes and warm grin were obvious, and I was glad to see him, too. Placing a gentle hand over my shoulder as he soon approached, the pad of his thumb lightly rubbed my neck. Standing directly before me, he leaned in for a pleasant kiss on my cheek.

"Ye spare my dread of that insufferable lass," he muttered against my cheek before pulling his lips away. "I am ever more within yer debt."

"Is that so?" I smiled softly, aware that she was still watching us. Normally, I would have found his response amusing and giggled. But I was more unnerved by the unsettling feeling left by Lord Brimfield, and I was barely able to force the smile I gave in reaction to Leif.

"Indeed. Brimfield's selection of lasses sorely lacks till this day. Miss Cox does the man the favor tae indulge, yet he goes tae the likes of Miss Rancier. He argues that English standards are superior to Europe's, in general, being second, and America's wanting. That is his reason fur entertaining Miss Rancier beneath his roof. Truth being, they dinnae differ from one anither, and are weel matched," Leif divulged, unimpressed, sounding faintly annoyed also.

"But she's French," I commented.

"Precisely," he replied ironically.

"She's watching us," I informed him, slipping a glance around him and catching her jeering stare.

"I reckon that she is. Grant her naught. She is not worthy of the mind that she desperately seeks. Alas, wantonness does not cease and is played in no matter the era." He gathered my fingers in his and raised the back of my hand to his lips, pressing a natural little kiss on my knuckles. I instantly returned to looking at him and smiled softly in response. "Permit my abandonment solely tae use the pot," he said after lowering my hand. He winked at me, eliciting a full smile from me. But it involuntarily diminished, and he noticed. The lighthearted expression on his face suddenly turned odd, with a bout of concern noted in his attentive eyes. "I shan't be long, however," he apologized, reassuring me.

"No, it's okay. Go use it, of course," I insisted apologetically. His eyes held steady with mine, examining me momentarily without him readily responding. His pause, I knew, was a result of his questioning my confidence. I perceived him beginning to determine that something was awry. He sensed it.

Intercepting the opportunity for him to inquire, I smiled nicely at him, masking myself as well as I could. "Use the closet like you must. I'll be right here waiting for you when you return."

"Aye," he replied pensively, and hesitated still. Maintaining a studying eye on me despite his agreement to leave to relieve himself, I couldn't help the slight uneven curling of my lips.

"Go ahead. I'm not going anywhere," I reiterated, insisting again, curtailing his ability to unravel me.

"The midnight hour does grow near," he acknowledged instead, still appearing attentive.

"Then, you should hurry, for sure, before the chimes toll in the New Year. It'll be a shame if we miss it together."

"Indeed." He gave a subtle nod. "I vow that I shan't be long."

"All right." I gave him a little smile again, and he began stepping away, notwithstanding his reluctance. Following him with a gaze over my shoulder as he shifted from me, he moved in the direction behind me through the lone corridor leading toward the privy closet. While receding through the hallway, to my dread, he encountered Lord Brimfield, who was shortly seen approaching from Leif's opposite direction in the same location, and they slowed their steps as they encountered each other.

"Monteith," Lord Brimfield naturally greeted Leif as they were passing.

"A fine masterpiece, Brimfield. Certainly, ye have stolen Miss Rancier from Caravaggio, and thus he weeps," Leif bantered, teasing his friend.

"All the more reason to gloat, for I am positive that I am his envy," Lord Brimfield quipped back, and they chuckled.

"Paintbrush tae canvas as chisel tae stone is all an illusion," Leif joked again, having the last word with his back facing while continuing on his way through the hallway past Lord Brimfield. Leif chuckled, but Lord Brimfield didn't, as he continued to smirk instead.

Lord Brimfield fully turned his glance from Leif and unexpectedly met mine, realizing that I was observing their exchange. His expression was sedate when we looked at each other, and I sensed his mood had changed. Confident in knowing the cause of his altered vein, I was sure that I was the reason for it when he impressed this fact by staring at me without yielding. Breaking his mineralized stare, I turned my attention toward the minimal crowd congregated in the room beside me and stepped inside it. As I did so, my breath lightly escaped me in relief when saving myself from his close encounter once more, while passing me within the hallway as he was just about to do.

Alleviated to escape his impersonal stare as I entered the new room and vanished from sight, away from the doorway when he passed by, further unease struck; not only had I felt his opinion of me turned, but the sudden bitterness I'd just detected within him had materialized in him and had solidified as it might have taken root. A feeling that swept over me, deep regret, since it determined the likely negative impact it would have on Leif. And, if honesty had any bearing, it wasn't going to allow for this truth to be hidden from him. Making it all the more painstakingly raw once he was made aware of his friend by me.

Standing near a wall-covered painting just beyond the doorway, I now patiently waited for Leif to appear, glancing around the room as I observed the lightly congregated crowds, divided into happily conversing groups that included tipsy members. The air was surely merry, enhanced by the sound of violins and cellos emitting from the ballroom, mingling with resonating chatter and laughter. Glimpsing passively at one corner of the room, Mrs. Crawford and I recognized each other as she stood among friends, including Lady Bernard, Lady Dearfield, Mrs. Gage, and her cousin, Mrs. Hutchinson.

Mrs. Crawford smiled, and I reciprocated when she politely excused herself from her friends and approached me. Without particular regard for her withdrawal, they continued their delight in gossiping; no doubt, the gossip was more interesting than their friend's absence.

"Hallo, Your Grace," Mrs. Crawford nicely greeted in her New England accent as she arrived, standing before me, smiling genuinely.

"Hello, Mrs. Crawford." I also kept an affable smile on my face.

"Pray, might I beg for your company as I do hope that you will indulge?"

"Of course."

"I thank you most benevolently for your rescue."

"Rescue?"

"Indeed. Without any doubt, I am grateful to escape my cousin and lady friends."

"Oh?" I looked at her a little curiously.

"Not only do they find pleasure in hearsay, they often kindle it. I fear that I am not of that mind," she explained.

"I see." I nodded slightly, understanding her position.

"They are delighting in the scandalous new Miss Rancier for her ill repute and for His Lordship's flagrant presentation of her this fine evening. They condemned her a courtesan—no less. Certainly, she will answer to God for it, yet the ladies let His Lordship elude equal condemnation, though he aids her sin. I am quite in the minority of my opinion, as it may seem, and I have not the strength to contradict them. My cousin cannot bear me already as she found me troublesome the instant I wed my good husband, a Quaker from Philadelphia."

"I'm very sorry to learn of the irritation between you and your cousin," I sympathized sincerely.

"Master Crawford endeavors to make the best of our residing here. In truth, he is wearied by Anglicans' diminished practices. Forgive my admission most genuinely, I implore. Yet I must avow that he has us remain for my sake as my family are Bostonians—my mother and younger sister also being survivors of my father's passing. To remove us would be my mother's undoing. The burden would lead her toward an earlier grave.

"Further, my sister would certainly long for her doting cousins. Thus, for any anticipated future, we keep ourselves here. Whilst I am grateful to Cousin Margret, I am her nuisance. She and I are of contrary minds, and regretfully, we do not share the same humility as I continuously remind her to acquire it like a pricking needle in her gown. She often likens me to Boston's sour, accordingly. Alas. 'Tis the difference betwixt us. Why must relatives be rather disagreeable?"

"Well, I can't exactly say... Except, perhaps it could be the result of differences that are specific to internal familial workings that influence attitudes and behaviors, varying them among extended families," I considered honestly, supposing.

"Hmm... A novel notion to mind. Quite a wise one, indeed, I shall say, for I have never heard anyone suggest it." She coincidentally glanced over her shoulder, and her eyes rebounded to mine with a perfectly petrified look. "Good heavens! They all come this way."

I glimpsed past her and realized her panic as her cousin was approaching us, along with her encircling friends.

"Whilst my cousin does retain her shortcomings, Mrs. Gage leaves much more to question," she warned worriedly. Before another word was shared between us, the ladies arrived and joined our company. Cordial greetings flittered as the pair of us received our new companions, and the conversation they were having earlier continued with our invitation to participate.

"Lord Brimfield does strike the eye immensely well—I shall grant you the observation," Mrs. Hutchinson said with a bit of irony to Mrs. Gage.

"More than well, I declare," Mrs. Gage replied, smiling coyly before sipping a bit of her wine.

"Be that as it will, yet dare I say that Mrs. Gage places her attention elsewhere, for the man is worth more strife than what you have seen. Sir Bernard tells me well of him, and from what I am aware, you will hate him when all is said and done," Lady Bernard warned Mrs. Gage.

"You are too certain?" Mrs. Gage asked Lady Bernard after pulling the rim of her wineglass from her lips.

"Quite," Lady Bernard affirmed.

"Well, I am not," Mrs. Gage differed, equally sure.

"Have you no qualm for your general?" Mrs. Hutchinson asked Mrs. Gage.

"What qualm has he of me? He has forgotten me of late," Mrs. Gage sulked.

"Would it not be due to his duties pressing him to manage the whole of the British army?" Mrs. Hutchinson presented.

"Indeed. To be fair, Missus Gage. Might this not be?" Mrs. Crawford agreed carefully with her cousin.

"To be fair? Do you inquire?" Mrs. Gage laughed. "You humor me, Missus Crawford. Too many husbands are not fair at all to their wives in the slightest. You and our lovely duchess seem to be the most fortunate amongst us all. For ourselves, the tale is far different. Therefore, our husbands hold no innocence and are negligent of their wives—what is indeed fair?" No one answered. Or, seemed to want to reply as she sipped more wine from her dainty wineglass. "Permit me to divulge. A meandering glad-eye poses to remedy any injured spirit. In which case, I am owed a measure of pleasure whilst my husband heeds not. Isolation makes for poor company."

"I beseech you to speak to your husband to remedy qualms," Mrs. Crawford proposed sympathetically.

"A wasted effort, I assure you. He dismisses me," Mrs. Gage said.

"Regularly?" Lady Dearfield asked, unsurprised as she seemed to better understand Mrs. Gage's plight.

"Enough," Mrs. Gage answered. "I grow weary of it. The times are too plentiful."

"His Lordship is dastardly, yet. He will serve you ill no less. Seek elsewhere if need be," Lady Bernard cautioned again.

"Yet, your husband, the governor, and his lieutenant highly favor him," Mrs. Gage responded paradoxically to Lady Bernard.

"As well does the general," Mrs. Hutchinson pointed out.

"How perfect," Mrs. Gage said, carelessly smiling. Then, she attentively shifted her gaze toward me. "Might I inquire of Your Grace's opinion of Lord Brimfield?"

My throat felt a little dry, and I suddenly swallowed, feeling it had grown scratchy; I wished I had a glass of wine myself. "I don't regard any other men but my husband, Mrs. Gage. But if there is any warning that Mrs. Crawford has given you, I think it would be wise to consider it."

Mrs. Gage didn't reply so quickly as the other ladies fell silent. Pursing her lips, it was apparent that she was thinking for an instant. "If I may, 'tis my finding that he is all too jaunty for our majority to caution. Nonetheless, I thank Your Grace for your mind," she said after a second.

"By all means," I replied demurely, noting her flippancy.

She had her intentions set despite the advice surrounding her, minus Mrs. Crawford, it seemed—which made me consider the overall shock of their conventional marriages, which wasn't tradi-tional to me and mocked the institution of matrimony. It made it easy to believe that these kinds of members of society were incapable of holding simple trusts that were found and dictated within friendships. And I knew inside of this politely acquainted group, there were none to regard as friends, except perhaps Mrs. Crawford, who was easily seen as genuine and loyal to her husband, as she and her husband mutually upheld each other, respectively. She was a serious woman who adhered to Puritan values and conducted her life reverently, as evidenced by her devotion to God and humility, which was reflected in her genuine appreciation for others in her interactions.

I unexpectedly felt a masculine palm slip around my elbow, capturing my attention from the ladies' company. I was warmed to see Leif's pleasant presence greeting me when I turned my head and glanced at him.

"Pray," he said in a mild voice that was usual to me, seeking to urge my attendance away from the surrounding company amiably. The women promptly curtailed their chattering and curtsied, acknowledging Leif's joining appearance.

As he intended to draw me away from the women, I kindly said to them, "Have a nice New Year," wishing them well, and they amicably reciprocated in their delicately polite fashion. Afterward, Leif withdrew us from their company and escorted me out of the room. We returned to the ballroom a minute ahead of the chimes sounding off from all the clocks in the mansion as Boston's bell tower and church steeple's bells rang out in unison, resonating across the city along with gunfire, ushering in the New Year. More wine made an appearance among the guests as a concerto began to play. While the bells tolled amid gunfire at midnight, Leif affectionately pressed his lips softly over mine in a sweet kiss as we innocuously stood together separately in the shadow of one corner of the room.

"A bonnie New Year, *ceisdein*," he said warmly when his lips parted mine.

"Happy New Year, Leif." I smiled at him with equal tenderness. He winked and I couldn't help giggling, noticing the dazzle glinting in his eyes caught by reflecting flecks of bouncing candlelight.

Once the chimes had ceased and we'd finished our wine, we concluded the celebration with a final dance.

Thirty-Four

R iding home in the carriage from the party at Province House, the night had worn, and we eagerly anticipated our return to *Taigh Gràs*. I tiredly leaned my head on Leif's shoulder, relaxing, and he wrapped an arm around me, pulling me snugly against him. The conversation between us was almost lacking, save for the light exchange about our returning home and diving into bed before sunrise. I felt his lips gently pressing against my temple and rested a second before drawing away when he began saying, "Waur ye weel entertained at the governor's mansion this evening?"

"Yes... I suppose," I said faintly.

"Merely suppose?" he asked.

Glancing up at him, I discerned a questioning grin curving his lips, and if I hadn't known any better, he would have seemed more confused than not.

"Well—I did enjoy myself with you wholeheartedly, of course," I assured, primarily.

"Splendid." His grin grew into a full smile, indicating his great satisfaction.

I didn't have the heart to spoil his good mood and belief that

387

I'd equally enjoyed myself at the governor's ball as much as he, without the problem his best friend had posed to me. So, I let the issue slide for a more opportune time and returned a pleasant smile to Leif as he held his warm gaze to mine. His eyes further warmed as his smile deepened, and he leaned a second kiss softly on my brow before I returned my head to lean comfortably on his shoulder to enjoy our ride home.

EARLY THE NEXT MORNING, New Year's Day, I'd awakened at the crack of dawn before Leif had even opened a drowsy eye as usual to begin his day. Today was going to be a rather lazy day as far as commotion within the town was concerned, as it recovered from celebrating the year's end and ushering in the new one. So, it seemed, like the rest of the community, he was going to be able to take the opportunity to have an easy start to his day without reporting to Fort Hill immediately this morning to tend to service duties, and may very well have the day off in this case. And that he was still sleeping so soundly was evidence of how much wine and rum he must have consumed over the festive evening. It only served his best interest this morning to remain lightly snoring in bed.

I, however, couldn't fall back to sleep, though I was still dead tired from the night before and only wished to remain dreaming. Instead, my mind kept whirling with the memory of what occurred with His Lordship and how I was going to expose this to Leif and when. The sooner, the better, no doubt. But how soon?

I must have tossed several times beneath the blankets because I noticed Leif rising from them from the corner of my eye when I turned my gaze and saw him rise to urinate in the pot placed at his bedside for ease of use instead of his need to stumble toward the privy closet last night. I suppose my tossing beneath the blankets encouraged him to awaken sooner rather than later and take care of his urgency to relieve himself at the same time. When he'd finished and slid beneath the blankets again, he glanced at me and realized that I was awake, catching my gaze with a warm grin. Reaching an arm around me, he tugged me against his body and spooned his bare chest snugly against my back when I felt his lips press gently behind my crown.

"Yoo're widely awake. How can this be?" he muttered within my loose ringlets, feeling his palm cup my breast hidden beneath my shift.

"I just woke up early and can't seem to rest easy again," I murmured also.

"Whyever not?" he asked curiously, sounding relaxed and groggy with his voice deeper than usual.

"I just can't help thinking," I admitted.

"Whit presses yer mind, loove?" he inquired lazily as if returning to sleep.

"I had a strange encounter," I began cautiously.

"'Twas all but a dream. Naught tae trooble yer spirit as daylight has come, and yoo're presently awakened. Yoo're safe and soond." He gently kissed the back of my head again, comforting me simply.

"That might be the problem," I said under my breath.

"In whit manner?"

"It was at the party last night—at the governor's ball, where I had the encounter."

"Whit are ye meaning?" He turned me over in his arms to face him, and now we were closely staring at each other as he tucked long ringlets behind my ear. The look on his face was receptive and sincere as he intently looked at me. Now, I knew that I couldn't avoid him or the emerging subject between us as I gazed seriously at him, and the look in his eyes turned earnest and confused.

"I mean, unfortunately—I think—I might have had a negative experience with Lord Brimfield. I hope I'm misinterpreting it—I could be mistaken—but I don't know," I responded insecurely.

Leif's brow suddenly drew together, and the furrow was deep as he seriously looked at me, also, no longer drowsy with full attention locked onto my eyes now.

"I quite dinnae understand. Whit occurred?" He asked precisely as I felt the pad of his thumb lightly stroking my cheek.

"Do you remember when I left you to use the privy closet?"

"Aye."

"Well, it was on my return to you when we encountered each other in the hallway. He stopped me along the way to talk for a moment."

"Not quite curious, however."

"No. But we had a conversation."

"Och. Whit was entailed?"

So, answering his question, I told Leif the entirety of His Lordship's conversation with me, including the seemingly innocuous little brushing of fingertips and kiss on the back of my hand. Once I'd told him, his eyes deadened and became impenetrable, and the hue in his face rose as his lips pinched into a line, a look that I had not recognized. But it was the expression in his mineralized eyes holding the unknown that landed the worst feeling I'd ever received from him. I couldn't read what Leif was thinking or feeling. Essentially blocked from knowing what was running through his mind and from his burst of emotions, I'd recognized for the first time ever since knowing him cold, lividness seizing him—and it was frightening—as it was controlled. He shut down, and his gentle hand that had cupped my cheek and rested on my shoulder slipped from me.

"Are you angry at me?" I ventured carefully as he held my gaze to his.

"Why micht I ever be thus? Heavens nae," he answered, certainly in a ridiculous tone. I suddenly felt foolish for asking, but I wasn't certain. His palm tenderly came over my shoulder again, and his fingers softly stroked me, reassuring me and all that was between us. Then, he withdrew them and anxiously raked them through his long, loose hair before pinching his tear ducts and nose bridge, once letting them fall to the blankets he tore off himself. Without a moment's hesitation, he hauled himself out of bed and began returning the shirt he wore last night over his head, which was carelessly hung on the back of a wing chair, and shoved his legs through a less formal pair of breeches. Grabbing his boots, he sat on the foot bench and plunged his feet into them, each at a time, as I sat up among the covers and watched him swiftly dressing himself.

"Where are you going?" I asked worriedly, sounding strange as I was suddenly feeling nervous.

"I shan't be missed fur long," he said determinedly, standing from the bench. He had quickly put his boots on and stormed toward his wardrobe to yank his coats off the pegs after swiftly buttoning his waistcoat completely closed.

"Why are you leaving this early in the morning? Don't you have the day off from work?" I continued asking with concern, nevertheless, while watching him quickly shove his arms through the sleeves of his coats.

"Rest weel. Be not alarmed. 'Tis a simple matter of import tae which I must attend. I shall soon return." Before I could say anything else, grabbing his hat, he was already at the door, opened it, stepped out of the room into the passageway, drew the door closed, and vanished.

A clear hour had passed while lying in bed and remaining awake, unable to drift to sleep again now that I'd been stimulated by curiosity regarding Leif's sudden order of business and where he'd gone. My mind churned with ideas, and I only hoped that his urgent duty wouldn't delay his return for a more restful and pleasant New Year's morning. But after an hour, I'd fallen back to sleep for a couple of more hours and had awakened with no indication that he'd returned to our room.

So, I covered my shift with a dressing gown and followed a hunch leading me up the third flight of stairs to his library. Quietly pushing the door open, he was discovered smoking his pipe at his desk while contemplating and staring out the nearby window. A silver tea set had been positioned in front of him on his desk, accompanied by a piping hot cup of tea that steamed from it. He hadn't touched his tea yet and was waiting for it to chill a bit when I realized that it had just been delivered to him.

The second I entered the room, he immediately turned his gaze from the window toward me as I carefully closed the door behind me. Noticing his greatcoat and hat, still snow-dusted, hanging on the pegs beside the door, I gathered he must have just returned from outdoors.

"*Ceisdein*," he greeted mildly.

"Yes?" I replied, noticing the hue on his face had returned to normalcy along with the affectionate expression I was used to seeing. Any indication of his guarded, vitriolic temper from earlier had vanished—or so it seemed—superficially. I wouldn't have known by the tone in his voice either. Therefore, whatever his earlier issue had been, it now seemed settled, and he appeared to be in a much better temperament.

"Mind me fur a moment, will ye not?" he requested politely as he motioned for me to sit in the chair opposite him across his desk.

"Of course," I said equally. I moved through the room toward him and comfortably sat down in the chair.

"Micht ye care fur a spot of tea?" He offered, drawing the teapot for pouring into the cup.

"Tea would be nice, thank you."

"Very weel."

"Did you just return from where you had to go earlier?" I asked, watching him pour fresh tea into the cup as steam rose together from the spout of the teapot and the cup.

"Aye. I fear that I micht have been deterred longer than antici-pated, as anither matter promptly consumed my attention," he answered. He passed the filled cup to me and gave me a modest grin. I naturally smiled as well, and while noticing his grin, it told me that he was still thinking and was partially removed from the new conversation we were having.

"Oh," I responded simply. "Will you have the remainder of your day free from working?"

"I reckon," he said, leaning back in his chair and puffing more contentedly on his pipe.

"That'll be nice. I was wishing for you to be able to rest today."

"It seems that I may."

"Where did you have to go so early this morning in the first place?" I carefully took a sip of tea and swallowed.

"I called upon George Winton this fine morn," Leif disclosed in a casual manner matching his tone as he calmly puffed away on his pipe.

"George Winton?" I didn't recognize the name, and my brow knitted a little.

"Lord Brimfield," he clarified.

"Oh." My voice suddenly became a bit withdrawn. I didn't think Leif would have quickly visited his friend, and now I cautiously and curiously wondered what occurred between them.

"Aye. I called upon his manor and met with him quite plainly."

"I see. Well, is everything all right between you two—now that you've met? You seemed incensed before you left, and I was particularly worried about you. I wasn't sure what to expect."

"All is raither weel, *mo ghaol*," he assured.

"It is?"

"Quite. Merely ken that from present till future, George's appearance at *Taigh Gràs* shall nae longer exist. He and I are nae longer acquainted as shadows; rapport betwixt us is nulled."

"You mean you and he are no longer friends?"

"Precisely."

"I'm really sorry to learn that the friendship you both had with each other has ended," I started regretfully with sincerity. "I have to say that I was fearing that this might very well be the case when I told you what'd happened last night, but I was hoping for the best

—and wishing your friendship could be salvaged—some way—given how long you've both known each other, including the history also."

"Aye, weel..." Leif dismissively shrugged and smirked at the irony of how his friendship transpired.

"So, there was no way for you both to merely talk with each other to come to an understanding for him to respect your boundaries?"

"Micht I remind ye that this had already been done months prior, once ye had newly arrived home once more? We waur dining if ye recollect it," he replied. I suddenly remembered and nodded a little in response. "Furthermore, I had brought tae his mind also that I shall not have him vie fur my wife's affections as the opportunity disnea exist. I warned him that he could never win. Agreeing tae not duel, George accepts tae never again appear at *Taigh Gràs* or attempt communication with ye—ever."

"Duel?"

"Aye."

"It's illegal to do that, though."

"Regardless. Many a man does it still."

"Why would you ever consider doing anything as extreme as that?"

"'Tis nae difficulty tae the imagination tae consider such a resolution tae not amend the affront or any other such slight. Dueling is satisfactory."

"But not only could he be killed and then you be charged and executed for murder, but you could be killed also, and then where would either one of us be?"

"Ye mustn't concern yerself, fur this isnae the case. However, in the event of my passing, ken that yoo'll remain with much wealth as I have provided, and ye will persevere."

"You've got to understand, Leif, how much I hate talking about anything bad happening to you," I said specifically. "It's frightening when men say they'll fight each other with fists, but dueling brings extra consideration. It's altogether terrifying for me to even think about you doing anything like it."

"Ease yerself, *mo ghaol*. It remains as said. It wulnae occur as the terms have already been stated and on which they have been agreed tae this matter," Leif reassured in a calming voice. "Furthermore, Brimfield is unwilling to risk his person. He is more Latinate than he cares tae admit and would raither live tae see anither day than tae ficht, which is a quality that nae longer remains within him as once before. He fancies the loove of lasses than tae battle. He is a fop. Therefore, the matter betwixt him and me is sealed. Therefore, he and I benefit tae experience anither day with the hope of more tae come."

When Leif concluded with this last statement, I gratefully acknowledged that the benefit was ideal. I reflected that because there would be no dueling, it was a true blessing that neither man would be injured and that Leif would remain safe and alive, something that was immeasurable to me. As I took another sip of tea while watching him continue to smoke his pipe comfortably in his chair, I considered how he had ended his friendship with Lord Brimfield drastically, cutting off all contact except when they were in professional settings. It was a regrettable situation for their friendship of so many years to have suddenly disintegrated after the trust they'd placed in each other's lives, only to have been tested by a mistake. It somewhat reminded me of what had occurred between me and Jasmine, but to a lesser degree, since Jasmine and I hadn't had our lives dependent upon each other—literally.

So, it was futile to attempt to convince Leif to soften his decision to abandon his friendship with His Lordship because not only did I understand, but he knew more intimately the workings of his friendship with him and was capable of making the correct determination. Something inside me quietly agreed and was relieved.

PART FIVE

Bellwether

Thirty-Five

I t's been two months since Lord Brimfield was last seen at *Taigh Gràs*. As a result, a burden seemed to have been lifted from me from the anticipation of ever encountering him on our property in the future. To an equivalent degree, the same couldn't be said for Captain Berkley. These days, he had made himself more present around our grounds at the most unsuspecting hours when it was believed he'd be with other officers in the field away from *Taigh Gràs*. His newly heavy presence had garnered my attention; it became apparent to me in particular that he'd developed an interest in Amity that wasn't as obvious to her as he seized any moment he could to be in her company on the pretense of seeming innocuous as he ate meals with her, or joined her in the sitting room while she darned or embroidered.

Although Captain Miller also seemed attracted to Amity, he was modest, if not highly so, and regarded his obligations by seriously tending to them regularly during the day away from *Taigh Gràs*, meeting whatever professional expectations demanded of him. Comparing the two men, it entered my mind that Captain Berkley was being derelict in his duties and favored hooky instead to lure Amity's trust to slip into her good graces.

Being that my laboratory was small, I couldn't quite fit Amity and Winnet comfortably inside the room for Amity's sake, to safely remove her from Captain Berkley while I worked. So, I had strictly instructed Winnet to not only remain present with Amity at all times, but she must remove Amity from Captain Berkley's presence on every account, particularly in circumstances like today. Very well understanding my position, Winnet was keen to comply, and I was secure in the belief that Amity's wellbeing would remain safe from his schemes while I now worked inside my medical room.

I had just completed creating a calamine mixture and was pouring the fresh concoction into vials with Mercy's assistance. Once the amber bottles had been filled and corked, she and I began moving them into one of the cupboards to store them while we were engaging in light conversation.

"Once Church completed yesterday, somebody took notice of the ribbon upon my hat," Mercy mentioned demurely, giving me a subtle, shy smile as she placed one of the vials inside the cupboard.

"Oh?" I glanced at her, surely piqued with interest, while drawing another bottle between my fingers to position it beside the one she'd just placed.

"Yes'm."

"Did the person say anything nice?"

"Quite nice, indeed, ma'am."

"That's very nice. What was said?"

"The body comes ta me, and then I's told that the ribbon becomes me."

"That's very nice, again. Who told you that?"

"Jerome be the one tellin' me them kind words."

"Jerome?"

"Yes'm."

"Really?"

"It be true, ma'am."

"Well, how exceptionally nice is that?"

"I imagine so."

"I'd agree." I smiled gently at her with delight. "Did you say anything about his compliment to him?"

"Yes'm, I did thus quite propah."

"And what was it that you said to him?"

"I thanked him kindly fo payin' me the compliment, modestly —o' course."

"I see. That was equally polite of you to acknowledge his kindness."

"I'm supposin' so. He then be aksin' me where I come upon fineness such as that."

"Then, what did you tell him?"

"I told him he's foolish for aksin," she giggled faintly, still being bashful.

"Did you really tell him that?" I responded, suppressing my own little giggle.

"I's most certainly did do it," she replied, smiling more this time.

"Oh, my goodness! Why were you so harsh on him? It was a simple question, wasn't it?" I smiled back at her, entertained.

"He already be knowin' the truf about it. Therefore, why he gonna aks and be foolish."

"Maybe he was trying to start a pleasant conversation with you, that's all."

"He already be beginnin' a discussion wif me when he tells me how lovely the ribbon be on my best hat that is on my head. Beggin' yo pardon, ma'am, yet I's beginning ta question Jerome's mind," she said with a little smile, being somewhat playful.

"Well, don't let him hear you say that," I joked also a bit, smiling at her too.

We giggled softly, and she continued saying, "Aside from all that business, I told him the ribbon be granted ta me out of the benevolence of my mistress's heart—fo which I am most grateful ta you, ma'am, fo all of yo goodness ta me."

"You're more than welcome, Mercy. It's my pleasure."

"Thank you, ma'am. Indeed," she replied graciously with evident and sincere gratitude. "Once I told Jerome all, he smiled a large smile at me and be sayin' more foolishness."

"Like what?"

"Like he ain't certain he be wantin' me to be waitin' and bein' a fancy maid due to his foolish wishes—sayin' he didn't want ta look at me as the grandest maid in all of the town, and if he could have it his way, he'd run off wif me—you see, fo me bein' wife ta him. Yet, that ain't nofin' but nonsense—entirely. He merely fancies that be merely it. He nothin' but foolish. Pray, do not be misinformed by me, ma'am, fo 'tis all in jest—I hope you do not mind me tellin' you thus."

"It's quite all right, Mercy. There's no harm in letting me know. It sounds like you and Jerome had a delightful conversation after church." I smiled at her again, and she reciprocated bashfully.

"Yes'm, 'twas fine," she admitted.

I glanced away from her toward the next vial and reached for it, grasping it from the facing counter to position it in the cupboard with the others. She resumed doing the same. Silence came between us for a moment, and a new consideration entered my mind as I pondered her situation more in-depth.

"Mercy?" I began thoughtfully.

"Yes'm?"

"May I ask you a question, if you wouldn't mind?"

"Ma'am?" She gave me a puzzled look.

"Yes, I just wish to ask you a question, if it's all right with you."

"I can't be understandin' why 'twould be any bothah ta be pleased," she responded, still appearing confused that I'd ever ask her permission.

"But it's a little personal—the question I'd like to ask—if it might be all right with you for me to proceed."

"Certainly, ma'am."

"Well, I'd like to know... What I wish to ask you—is if you'd ever consider... What I mean is—I'd like to know from you—that if it were a perfect world without any fear for you to consider, and if you were presented with the opportunity to marry Jerome, would you be happy to agree to take the opportunity to do it? If it's what you would both like?" Her eyes suddenly widened, and she certainly appeared caught off guard that I was bold enough to ask her this question. She held her tongue for a second, and I could perceive that she was considering her response carefully. But the faint smile curling her lips, expressing her feelings, gave her away.

"'Sep I care not ta abandon you, ma'am. So, I fear my answer ta yo question is no, ma'am. There ain't no bettah place than bein' at Taigh Gràs," she replied for certain.

"But what if you didn't have to worry about leaving here? What if things remained suited to you and your wishes? Would you care to marry him if that were the case?" I pursued asking considerately.

"I never even thought of such an occurrence—truth be tellin'."

"But imagine it now and tell me what your answer is. I'm only curious and would like to know."

"I 'supposin' if I must politely regard your question, ma'am, I reckon I might tolerate Jerome enough—if the Lord Almighty sees fit."

"Tolerate?" I smiled gently at her, catching her subtle playfulness.

"Yes'm. 'Twould be all I could bear seein' how Jerome is too merry in my presence."

"I see."

"Not ta disregard the Lord Almighty no less."

"No less."

"Yes'm."

"Agreed." We smiled at each other again, then continued positioning the bottles inside the cupboard until the task was done.

LATER THE SAME DAY, after Leif and I had shared afternoon tea with each other from his break, visiting subordinates in the Commons, he and I took a sleigh ride to the marketplace and strolled the icy cobblestones. Along the way, after visiting several shops, our conversation was as it typically was: light and jovial. Until a different thought popped into my mind that was leaning a bit more on the serious end of things, and which I wished to address with him.

"Leif?" I started mindfully as I slid my palm around his arm while he carried some packages with his other arm.

"Aye, *mo ghaol?*" he replied receptively with a warm little grin.

"Well, hmm—first, let me preface this by saying that I learned something from Mercy not too long ago."

"Och? Have ye now?" He appeared interested suddenly, even though his sidelong glance toward me was casual.

"Yes."

"Whit news have ye from yer maid?"

"Well, I've come to understand that she has had a long-lived admirer," I divulged simply.

"Ye speak of a suitor?" Leif's eyes widened, making him appear piqued by the unexpected revelation and gossip. I couldn't help smiling at his sudden reaction, and it grew as we stared at each other for a moment as I witnessed the realization dawning on him.

"Yes, that's exactly what I mean. She's got suitor," I said, smiling widely at him.

"A suitor," he repeated contemplatively, looking raptly at me, which only kept me smiling at him.

"Yes." I nodded. "And he's extremely nice."

"Micht he be?"

"Yes, he is."

"How micht ye ken that he is pleasant?"

"I've met him."

"Have ye?"

"Yes."

"Upon which account?"

"It was a while ago when I met Missus Crawford here at the marketplace as he was escorting her."

"Why have I not been awaur of this?" he asked, ignoring my last statement.

"You've been too busy to hold any kind of conversation like this, and besides, I'm making you aware of it now."

"Whit is his name? Micht I ken of him?"

"Yes, in fact, you would know of him."

"Then, whit micht his name be?"

"Jerome. You know the man who works for the Crawfords?"

"The Hutchisons' relations?"

"Yes."

"Explain more."

"He's Mrs. Crawford's escort in place of her husband and their driver."

"Och," Leif realized. "Fur how long has Jerome fancied Mercy?"

"I believe since she was seventeen years old."

"A while yet."

"For some time, I'd agree."

"I reckon they have encounters during their times of worship?"

"Yes, that's the only time they're able to see each other and communicate."

"Hmph," he responded, considering this new information.

"And there's more you should know," I continued.

"Aye?"

"Mercy has the same feelings for him, also," I disclosed. Leif's eyes widened again, and now I felt him anticipating me further. But I discerned that the look in his eyes became skeptical.

"Does she now?" he asked.

"Yes."

"I see."

"Yes, well, but—" I broke off, wondering how I was going to venture forth.

"Proceed. I care fur yer thoughts."

"Well—they both love each other. Perhaps you should know that also."

"Is it so?"

"It is.

"I see."

"So, what I'm wondering is—you know, since they've loved each other for so long—and since they'd both like to become married—would there be any way for us to assist in helping them in doing so?" I suggested mindfully, and I noticed him furrowing his brow a little.

"'Twould be a matter of some consequence," he said.

"You mean legally? Because they're slaves?" I asked, wondering.

"Not of that high consequence."

"Oh. I don't understand."

"Our colony disnae forbid slaves tae wed as England disnae prevent different races tae doing the same beneath the law."

"Then, I'm still confused. What would the consideration be?"

"Yoo're quite fond of Mercy. Are ye not?"

"Yes, of course I am. Why do you ask?"

"Then, 'tis wisely presumed that ye dinnae care tae have her vacate *Taigh Gràs*, and therefore yer service?"

"Absolutely not?"

"Mayhap, Master Crawford isnae willing tae part with his servant either."

"Right. I hadn't thought of that," I replied, disappointedly. "But, just tell me—if there was a way for them to be married, would you be impartial to the idea of them being married?"

"Is it of much import tae ye, micht I inquire of ye instead?"

"Yes, it's very important to me. I'd love nothing more than for them to be together in that way."

"I see."

"How about you? What are your feelings about it?"

"The matter requires thought. Thaur are the other slaves I must consider. Mercy's precedent will inspire their desire tae wed as weel. Furthermore, I have not considered the notion of expanding the number of slaves already within my possession."

"Oh. But is it wrong for them to want to be married?"

"On the contrary. Too many other matters have taken the lead fur any focus upon the notion of any one of their proper unions."

"I see."

"The matter deserves consideration, in truth, and I shall ponder it in more depth. Then, I shall relay my answer tae ye anither moment later with regard tae Mercy," he said, sounding resolved, and I nodded in response, which brought the conversation to a close.

The last thought that entered my mind about this conversation was that if I could help facilitate Mercy's happiness, which would result from sharing it with the man she loved and with whom he loved in return, then that would bring us all an added blessing of joy. I was also satisfied that Leif was open to at least considering the idea of her possibly being married, while knowing it would open up the same possibilities to the other servants in our household.

"One last matter as we discuss Mercy," he continued.

"Yes?" I replied curiously.

"You do care fur Mercy?"

"Yes, of course. You know that I do."

"It has been brought tae my attention that ye have given her a gift. A ribbon tae be precise."

"Yes, I did."

"Are ye awaur that thaur are rumors abound because of the ribbon?"

"What rumors?"

"That the lass has stolen it from ye."

"Stolen it? That's absolutely not true. I gave it to her."

"Be that as it will. Ye have caused harm tae the lass by your gift, though yer intention was pure," he said.

"It was only a ribbon, though," I justified.

"'Twas not a simple gift as ye perceive it tae be, Sylvie. Gifts are reserved fur equals, and the sort of gift ye had given her was fine."

"But I also gave Winnet a gift. A hoop for crossstitching."

"Once more, this is out of place. Our servants may be blamed fur thievery. Furthermore, Mercy is a Negro, and I ken that ye would not care fur anyting ill tae befall her due to yer negligence that stems from yer kindness," he explained. I didn't respond so quickly as I started to think and realized that he was right. I felt horrible that Mercy had been accused of theft.

"I understand," I said after a second, as my guilt ate at me.

"Very weel," he replied.

"I have to do something about Mercy. I don't want her to be thought of as a thief and her reputation ruined."

"I have already quelled the situation as it is now known that the ribbon is a gift from ye and 'tis the only gift she will ever receive from ye. It is also known amongst our servants that the mere gifts that they receive from me are food, shelter, and clothing. I am certain ye will agree tae my wishes, will ye not?"

"Yes. I don't care for any misunderstandings from anyone."

"Guid," he said, concluding our conversation.

Thirty-Six

My hormones had adjusted to their natural balance sooner than had been anticipated, and I began charting my fertility with newly constructed cycle beads after my menstruation resumed and was completed. Having abstained from each other for three months, I was glad to indicate the risk for us had waned when I playfully swung myself over Leif's torso and rested on his chest as I delivered a sweet kiss over his lips.

"Whit is the meaning?" he chuckled out of surprise as his eyes abruptly widened before he smiled.

"Don't you miss me?" I giggled, raising my lips from his and staring back at his brilliant face.

"My missing ye is my constant." The look in his eyes suddenly changed, and his grin widened, exposing his pearly white incisors.

"I'm so sorry you've suffered for so long," I pouted and gave him a sympathetic peck over his soft lips. He chuckled again and gripped my waist with both hands, securing me over his chest.

"How micht ye pity me in truth?" he asked, smiling at me.

"Do you truly wish to know?"

"Aye. Yet, tell me whether we are not safeguarded primarily."

"We're more than safe."

"'Tis cast within yer beads?"

"Yes."

"Ye have become troublesome once more."

"It would seem so for you. Not me," I joked, giggling.

"Lord Almighty, have mercy upon my soul," he laughed. I laughed also and lightly kissed his lips again before returning to looking at him. "Have ye nae notion of the torture I have endured upon this entire lonesome time of mine?"

"But I missed you too," I replied, smiling.

"Rubbish tae my torture."

"Rubbish?"

"Precisely."

"How can you say anything close to that?"

"My mere lacking tae deeply lay my lips upon yers was an unbearable temptation that I couldnae risk."

"Well, I have to confess that I didn't like your simple kisses on the cheek or hand for three months. You've spoiled me otherwise. So now I'm here to collect my debt, which is a lot. Hope you can afford it."

"Cheeky lass!" He laughed outright and walloped a light-hearted palm on my buttock cheek, sending an echo throughout the room. I instantly yelped at the little sting and laughed, too.

"Hey!" I started chastising playfully, but was immediately interrupted when he lightly tapped a finger over my lips, silencing me.

"Mind yer tongue lest I punish ye further," he teased while gently holding his finger to my lips. "Presently, be a guid lass and explain yerself."

His finger slipped from my lips, and I said, "What does His Grace care to know?"

"He wishes tae ken the meaning of yer behavior," he quipped, arching a golden eyebrow.

"Well, I was trying to tell you that if you wanted to pay me for the debt you owed, then I'd be happy to take it," I said, smiling at him.

"That I owe?" He questioned, smirking.

"Yes."

"Och, certainly?"

"Certainly."

"Yet, are ye not the gatekeeper of this particular arrangement?"

"Well—I—uh... Gatekeeper?"

"Aye."

"But—you know, all for good reason—of course."

"Quite understood."

"So, it doesn't quite negate the fact that you owe me now."

"Weel, I am a man of extensive means. Therefore, the question becomes, are ye able tae store all whit I can give?" he teased again. I felt his palm firmly squeezing my other buttock cheek, almost pinching as he began desirously massaging it. I gasped a little between a giggle, caught between surprise at his keen reply and his seduction.

"Um." That was all I could say.

"Did ye not say tae me that it was a magnanimous debt ye are collecting from me?"

"Yes."

"How many chambers must be placed into commission?"

"Chambers?" My eyes abruptly widened by his innuendo, and my lips parted as I gaped at him.

"Aye," he replied definitively as his teeth gleamed now that his smile opened.

"Leif!" I gasped, shocked and giggled in spite of myself, looking into his mischievously twinkling eyes and the slanted grin on his face growing wider.

"Whit appears tae be the matter?" he joked.

"The matter is that I am not a harlot."

"Yoo're better. Indeed."

"I'm much better. Without a doubt."

"Then, I shan't argue the fact. Thus, I shall inquire once more. How many chambers must fill my debt?"

"Incorrigible!" I squealed, feeling a bit embarrassed despite everything.

"I am," he chuckled, confessing. "I care not tae disappoint my debtor in the least."

"One chamber will suffice," I replied, giving him a playfully shameful look.

"Fur the present," he goaded again.

"Yes, for now," I said, shaking my head.

"Be that as it will," he responded, feigning disappointment and causing me to giggle.

"Don't sound so sad."

"I merely care tae generously meet my debt. 'Tis all."

"Well, I can still help you with that. Don't forget so quickly."

"Then, grant me a stupendous kiss tae begin. I care tae recall whit I have missed the past countless weeks."

"Fine."

"Make it so."

I giggled again and pressed my lips over his. I could feel his other hand seep into my ringlets at the back of my crown and begin massaging as he pushed my lips more fervently upon his, deepening my kiss. My mouth slightly parted for me to catch my breath, but was immediately stolen when he thrust his hungry tongue inside and probed with vigor. Staggering my breath, I strove to inhale and stabilize my breathing. But it was difficult to do. My heart raced, and I felt his also pounding against my breast. It was all too real how much we'd missed being with each other as I felt the heat of his unsteady breathing breaking unevenly against my lips.

Moans eluded us while our tongues swept and drank. As his fingers slipped downward from my ringlets, roved down my back, meeting his other hand fondling my buttocks, the pressure of my lips over his became gentle again without diminishing my enthusiasm for him. His hands suddenly gripped my shift and raised it, compelling me to break from kissing him as I reared upward, allowing it to be pulled overhead and off my body.

Without hesitation, his arms enveloped me, returned me down over him, and I was tossed onto my back with him caging me as his lips came over mine again. Drawing my tongue into his mouth, he sucked, then forced it back into my mouth and joined mine with a deeply rousing continuous kiss, stealing my breath all over again. The intensity was strikingly reminiscent of the moment we'd reunited after being apart for years. I thought I was going to die, and the ache between my legs amplified.

Overwhelming me with his powerful kiss, I understood once more all that I'd meant to him and how I was compelled to reveal the same to him. Anchoring my arms around his neck, I secured my body to his as we continued kissing each other. Feeling light-headed, I naturally moved my thighs apart, anticipating him, yearningly. My blood coursed heatedly, making me hot, and the dizziness I was experiencing placed me in a cloudy state of mind where reality fell away.

Dragging my nails faintly down his back, a moan escaped his ravenous lips, and his kissing mouth became more heated over mine, dominating it. Delighting in his ruling lips, my fingers raked his back again, and a low growl eluded him when I sensed him reaching a hand down between us. Desperation was consuming me; my thighs widened, and my hips wriggled. I sensed him then seizing himself and stroking the head of his formidable shaft between my cleft, locating my entrance. In one vigorous thrust, the sensation of him entering and filling me cast me into delirium, scaling upward.

Joined, he kissed my cervix as he surged to the hilt, pushing the wind out of me. Withdrawing, I gasped as he began thrust-ing, determining a rhythm for us. He easily shaped time between us, and he ebbed and flowed with sublimity, commanding my blood to boil and me to flood between my legs. My body begged him to return on each withdrawal and welcomed him on each return.

Pulled closer toward the apex of disintegration, my flesh around him began tightening as he powerfully pumped, and I held onto him, meaning to savor the spellbinding moment of our journey. It seemed that while we climbed, it all was slipping by too soon, since I was so close to dissolving completely. But I knew he was close, too. Panting passed between us, bringing the quiet room to life, save for the crackling fire near the hearth and warming the atmosphere in addition to our own heat.

Incapable of helping himself, he surged deeper and with more fervor, driving himself into me with zeal as beads of preparation formed on his brow and dripped over my lips. My palms slipped from his shoulders as his skin had grown moist and warm. Breaking from kissing me, he turned my head and trailed heated kisses from my cheek toward the curve of my neck and sucked, hurting me a little. Then, his mouth returned to mine as new depths were explored within me.

He found my cervix again and landed a vigorous kiss on it, sending a sudden shockwave that electrified my nerves throughout my body. Abruptly, my flesh pulsed around him, and I shuddered in his arms. While wild spasms coursed and clamped down on him, trembling me, Leif seized, and a guttural groan eluded him. Scarcely aware of his enormous moan reverberating throughout the room, I launched into soaring euphoria as my breath caught in my throat.

As I sailed back down to reality, the sensation of him violently throbbing between my legs was distinct, and the heat filling me seared a path into my womb. In a moment, he was drained and slumped over me, burying his head into the curve of my neck as his essence poured from me. Feeling the warmth of his heavy breathing against my skin, I was aware of our hearts pounding synchronously, and the sensation was fierce.

Silence passed between us as we listened to each other, our

voices calming. After a minute, he raised his gaze to mine, smiling languorously. The indolent grin curling his lips was evidence of his complete satisfaction, and he tenderly pressed his lips over mine. My fingers gently stroked his moist back when he returned to looking at me. His cheeks creased as he grinned again, and I smiled, too, feeling dreamy. He softly kissed a last kiss over my brow, then rolled off to the side and drew an arm around me, tugging me close as he fitted me against him, spooning. Whipping the blankets that had been kicked aside, he covered our nakedness inside a cocoon, and we quietly drifted to sleep.

Thirty-Seven

February.

Recently, my attention was drawn back to my conversation with Leif about Mercy and Jerome, and the possibility of them being able to marry. We hadn't furthered this conversation since last month during our outing to the marketplace, and I was very curious to know what Leif thought about the issue. I hoped for his support because I not only believed that she should have the right to marry if she so chose, but I ultimately wanted her to be as happy as possible with the man she'd loved for so long. So, I thought I'd seek Leif in his library now to discuss it.

I had just finished climbing the third-level staircase and paced the hallway toward his study when I noticed the door ajar and male voices emanating from the room. General Gage was recognized as having a conversation with Leif, and I stopped short in my steps, half tempted to interrupt politely.

"Do you have a list of all the men involved?" the General asked Leif when I realized the middle of their conversation was serious. So, I decided to remain quietly still from retreating as I'd just stepped on a squeaking floor plank near the cracked door and didn't wish to draw any attention to myself unexpectedly.

"Aye, General. 'Tis haur," Leif replied to him.

"Permit me to see it, Colonel," General Gage said. The sound of weighty parchment rustling in the air was heard, and a moment of silence ensued.

"Are these all of the men who are members of the association?" the general asked.

"At present. Yet more may join as it grows," Leif answered.

"I see," General Gage responded, sounding pensive. "You are certain of their scheme?"

"'Tis understood the Mechanics mean tae see their convictions through," Leif said.

"We shall see about it," General Gage said with noticeable displeasure in his voice. "Have you knowledge of how they exchange missives?"

"They have them posted upon an elm tree in the Common," Leif disclosed, sounding as serious as the general.

"Do they?"

"Aye."

"'Tis brazen of them."

"'Tis named the Liberty Tree and believed the location to be simple fur discovery as any man may be seen posting, reading, or removing missives from it," Leif said.

"The impudence," General Gage scoffed. "Have you seen this infamous tree, precisely?"

"Aye, I have."

"Make certain to have yer men rip the missives down and deliver them to me. I must be privy to their plots."

"Aye, General," Leif said.

"Now, then, the matter regarding stamps. Might you have any awareness as to who is counterfeiting them?"

"I fear not as of yet."

"In this case, I have a missive—fit for the Mechanics. Have them aware that once I discover who the counterfeiter is, he and his cohort will be tried for the felony and hanged for treason. Let it be clear," General Gage threatened.

"Indeed, general," Leif assured.

"Good. Have you any other intelligence for me, Colonel?"

"Rumors are afloat amongst the Mechanics that they will riot and burn customs agents from their dwellings," Leif disclosed.

"Indeed?"

"Aye."

"When will this occur?"

"The subsequent week."

"Which day?"

"Unknown. Yet, likely whilst all are asleep."

"Then we shall have our guards posted at officials' residences all of next week, and arrest any man loitering there about," General Gage ordered.

"'Twill be done," Leif said. "Stamp officers' safety must be included as weel in this order, general. They too have been threatened this week tae be burnt."

"Very well, make it so. Have any more particulars come to light?"

"It may also be of interest tae ken that the Mechanics recruit our soldiers who wish tae abandon their loyalties instead fur becoming spies fur them," Leif continued.

"More gallows are warranted, then. See to it that it is done. All will see how we handle traitors, Colonel. 'Tis our provision." General Gage's tone was detached from any sympathy as he made his last statement.

"Aye," Leif responded, sounding the same as his superior officer.

"Any more particulars?"

"None at present, general."

"You are of good service to the Crown, Colonel. I shall let it be known to His Majesty."

"Thank ye, General."

"Indeed."

Chairs abruptly resonated over the oak floor, and footsteps began advancing toward the doorway from inside the library. Hearing this, I instantly began carefully making a turnaround over the squeaky wood-planked floor as the men continued their advancement toward the library door and moved toward the staircase, before I hoped to be discovered. Except for making it nearly halfway through the hallway, I spun on the ball of my foot when Leif was recognized from behind me, saying, "Och! Hullo, *ceisdein,*" as he and General Gage stepped past the doorway from the library.

"Oh! Hello," I replied as naturally as I could when facing them.

"The General and I have merely completed our meeting," Leif said, acknowledging General Gage without seeming curious about my appearance.

"How nice," I responded pleasantly. "It's always very nice to see you, General Gage."

"The pleasure belongs to me, of course, Your Grace," he said graciously.

"How is Missus Gage?" I asked with interest.

"She fares well," he replied.

"That's very nice to know. Please give her my best wishes."

"Indeed, Your Grace, I shall."

"I was only hoping to borrow a book from the library to read, but I realized that you were in a meeting, and I didn't wish to interrupt." I suddenly found myself lying as I now gazed at Leif.

"Yet, we have merely concluded our meeting *mo ghaol.* Pray, the library is empty. Peruse all ye wish as I see the General tae the front door," Leif said.

"Thank you." He gave me a subtle wink, which made me smile. I then stepped past them as they began moving toward the staircase again.

When I entered the room, they had already advanced down the

steps, so I went to one of the built-in bookcases lining the back wall to begin scanning titles for a book to read, despite my original intention.

After locating a book that had caught my interest, I pulled it forth and sat on the sofa, waiting for Leif's return. A good moment had passed before he entered the room again. I raised my eyes from the book in my lap and noticed him attired in coats over his uniform, which made me wonder whether he had just come in from outdoors or was leaving for a while.

"Are you leaving?" I asked, looking curiously at him.

"I must mind my remaining duties fur the day. Yet, I shall make my return this evening fur my dining with ye, of coorse," he said easily as he approached me.

"All right," I said, a bit disappointed. Gathering my hand in his, a comforting little grin curved his lips, and he raised my fingers to them, pressing a soft kiss on my knuckles.

"Be a guid lass," he responded afterward as he drew his lips away. Then, with a light forefinger, he gently tapped the end of my nose, making me smile once more. Turning from me, he proceeded to leave the room, and now I was left to wait for another favorable time to discuss the topic that was most interesting to me.

POPE DAY HAD COME and gone last November, when anti-Catholic sentiments were high and celebrated by hordes of people in the streets. Today, an immense crowd had assembled in the marketplace again as Leif and I were strolling in the area. As we looked to see what was taking place, it appeared that a crowded procession of another mock funeral was underway. This time, it was for the *Death of American Liberty*.

Not wanting to become separated among the crowd, Leif firmly wrapped a hand around my elbow and worked at steering us through people blocking our way. As we made our way past onlookers, I peered past them to meet my curiosity to get a glimpse of what had caught everyone's attention when I spotted an effigy of Mr. Hutchinson, the lieutenant governor. It was being placed in a pine coffin as demeaning and degrading statements and shouts about him bellowed from the gatherers at the effigy. Then, once the effigy was laid inside the coffin, the men closest to it raised it and began parading it around the center of the marketplace square, captivating everyone's attention.

Many in town who weren't close to the lieutenant governor hated him, and he was no one's friend. Hutchison had become the bull's-eye target of people's anger and disdain. Most of this was due to the fall of the economy here after the war with France. Straining the matter, the only acting banker in town, Mr. Nathaniel Wheelwright, who was a wealthy merchant, suddenly stopped his debt payments and fled to Guadeloupe, leaving smaller merchants, artisans, and shopkeepers in debt as a result. And because of his departure, he effectively crashed the whole economy here in town. Commercial creditors and depositors suddenly fell into debt and also began defaulting. So, they fled the city as well, exacerbating the situation all around.

However, Hutchinson saw an opportunity and seized it after the General Court passed the Bankruptcy Act. Aside from being the lieutenant governor, he was the chief justice of the Superior Court, where he began issuing warrants for fugitive debtors and collecting substantial fees for managing bankruptcies and seized properties. What's more, he was blatantly ambitious and profited from those payments as he monopolized government positions for himself, which also included being probate judge for Suffolk County and commander of Castle William. He claimed the reason for his profits was compensation for his excessive responsibilities to the Crown. Further deepening public resentment, his shameless practice of nepotism, as evidenced by his hiring and exclusive promotion of family members related to the Hutchinson family, was fully on display.

No wonder the customs officials who were related to him were the targets of the mobs—according to what I'd overheard Leif telling General Gage recently. The officials were rich and greedy from the fees collected, evidenced in their mansions and wealthy lifestyles. It was also a wonder that Leif and I weren't targeted too, in general, for appearing to be elite Tories associated with the likes of Lieutenant Governor Hutchinson—along with the Governor, who didn't escape disdain either.

Leif and I remained sandwiched in the square, far outnumbered by angry people holding Whig sentiments, as he determinedly guided us through packed onlookers gazing at the effigy of Hutchinson's corps being tarred and feathered before them. After tar and feathers had been doused, a man threw a lit torch over it and set it all ablaze. The crowd roared and cheered at the sight of it raging into flames.

With Leif's hand securely wrapped around my elbow, he guided us between people, as he eventually cleared us from the crowd and began making our way toward our waiting carriage. But as we walked, an unfamiliar man bumped into him, catching his attention.

"The tree speaks tae ye, Your Grace," the unfamiliar man said to Lief in a low voice that was almost inaudible as he brushed by his shoulder. I glanced at the man as he passed us, peering over my shoulder. He continued walking as if nothing had occurred, disappearing into the congestion of people behind us. Obscured in a black great-coat and a large matching tricorn hat covering his face, getting a good look at him was a failure.

I glanced back around, turning my attention toward Leif, and noticed a folded note had just been pressed into the palm of his hand by the strange man. Leif promptly tucked it inside his coat pocket and continued meandering us away from the ruckus at the market square toward the street where our carriage was waiting.

When we entered our carriage and were safely tucked inside away from the crowd, we began riding along the streets, heading back to *Taigh Gràs*. While on our way, he pulled forth the note from his coat pocket and proceeded to read it. Curiously glimpsing at the script myself as we sat next to each other, I wondered what it said. He read it swiftly, folded the note, and tucked it back into his pocket, concealing it.

"What's it about?" I asked him curiously, simply wondering.

"A matter of business which influences my duties," he said, turning his eyes toward mine.

"Oh?"

"Aye. 'Tis of nae concern. I shall also not bear yer ennui with the particulars." He then pressed a quieting kiss against my temple, laying any further questions I might have had about it to rest. I wanted to have a conversation about the note, but Leif diverted the discussion to what had happened in the mob. This made an interesting topic for conversation. But I also found it somewhat worrisome that we were so closely associated with the lieutenant governor and governor, who were so hated by half the population.

Thirty-Eight

As I was rounding the banister of the grand staircase near the foyer one morning, I met Mr. Crawford, who'd just come down the last step on his way out the front door.

"Your Grace," he greeted graciously as we met each other before he proceeded to leave.

"Mister Crawford," I replied politely.

"A certain pleasure to see you, naturally, Your Grace," he continued.

"Thank you."

"I have merely met with His Grace."

"Oh?"

"Aye. The Crawfords will miss our servant Jerome greatly. Yet, I am certain he will be of irreplaceable service to the Duke and Duchess of Monteith," he said courteously, and before I could respond, he continued to say, "Good day to you, of course, Your Grace. I best be on my way, if you'll please."

"Yes, of course. Have a nice day also," I replied nicely. Mr. Crawford then politely acknowledged with a slight bow and continued through the door as our doorman opened and closed it for him when he stepped outside and vanished.

Reminded again about Mercy and Jerome and the overdue conversation I wanted to have with Leif, I climbed the staircase and went up the levels toward his library. When I entered the room, he had just snuffed out his pipe and laid it on his desk in front of him before standing from his chair and moving aside. He appeared ready to leave the room when he suddenly noticed me entering.

"Àille dhubh," he greeted, smiling at me. Striding toward each other until we met, he slipped his palms around my shoulders and pressed a gentle kiss on my brow.

"Hi," I replied, glad to see him, smiling back at him when we looked at each other again. "I saw Mister Crawford leaving."

"Had ye?"

"Yes."

"He and I met tae resolve yer happiness fur Mercy's sake."

"You did?" I asked as I now gazed curiously at him.

"Aye." Leif's palms slipped from my shoulders as we continued gazing at each other. "My discussion with Master Crawford appears tae have brought about a resolution tae the matter."

"Really?"

"Apparently."

"Well, what? Please don't keep me waiting. I have to know instantly."

"Ease yerself, fur I shall promptly inform ye," he said.

"I'm waiting," I replied, nevertheless.

"As ye wish. I have purchased Jerome," he said, cutting to the chase.

"You have?"

"Aye."

"But, I thought that we might discuss solving the situation together," I said, feeling uneasy that Leif had purchased Jerome.

"Ye brought the matter tae my attention and therefore I have remedied it."

"Yes, but. You bought him. Did you have to do that?"

"Of coorse, I must."

"Why?"

"'Tis the only means by which I may acquire him fur Mercy."

"You know how I feel about people being bought and sold."

"Aye," he said. "Ye recall the period in which we live?"

"Yes, but it doesn't make it moral."

"Sylvie—"

"No, wait. Listen to me for a second. He's a human being, not an animal."

"Micht ye not understand 'tis the only manner in which I micht acquire him tae suit Mercy without ruining yer own happiness?"

"Does he have to be a slave, though? Why can't he be indentured like the other servants, then, at least?"

Leif didn't readily answer, except gazed at me, appearing to consider my words. "Tae indenture him may inspire envy amongst the other slaves," he resumed.

"I understand," I said. "But couldn't you simply indenture them as well?"

Leif paused again. His lips pinched into a line as he faintly nodded, appearing pensive with even deeper consideration.

"Whit of Mercy? Yer fondness fur her is evident. In whit manner shall she be regarded?"

"Well... Why not indenture her also?" I suggested persuasively.

"The other lasses?"

"You could do the same for them. At least this way, they won't be slaves and can earn their freedom just like the others."

"Aye. Yet, keep in mind that their freedom wulnae come fur years tae come as I huvnae the means tae free all our slaves."

"I see."

"However, I understand yer reason."

"Thank you." A faint smile came over my lips as I gazed at him and realized that not only was he inclined to please me, but he was beginning to understand the significance of my beliefs.

"As ye wish," he said, persuaded.

"Thank you," I said again, grateful.

"Aye. Ye must also understand that Jerome is the Crawfords' most beloved manservant?"

"No. I didn't realize that."

"Yet, he is."

"Oh no. What will they do in that case?"

"I presented a guid sum tae Master Crawford in order fur his family tae obtain two more servants the likes of Jerome in his stead. Only then was Master Crawford swayed tae part with him."

"I see," I realized. "Does this mean he'll be coming to live here now?"

"Not till Jerome is wed tae Mercy."

"So, not until their wedding day?"

"Correct."

"How soon will that be?"

"Mayhap the middle of April will be suitable."

"That's only about a month away," I realized. March was already here, and spring appeared on the twentieth day with light morning frosts, plenty of showers, and damp soil.

"Aye, it is merely so," he acknowledged. I also wanted to make the day a celebratory day for Mercy.

"Would you mind if we made it a nice celebration for her and our household in general?" I asked, considering his opinion.

"The notion hudnae entered my thoughts in truth," he confessed.

"Do you think it would cause a scandal?" I wondered.

"Scandal or not, 'tis my standard tae bear. Furthermore, my wife's pleasure is my own, which is my standard alone. Therefore, do as ye will, bring happiness tae yer maid and our remaining servants by bringing yer celebration tae them. I see nae qualm," he said.

I suddenly threw my arms around his neck and said, "Thank you so much. You have no idea how happy you've made us all."

"Thaur is more yet," he informed me as I sensed him embracing me also.

"Really?" I pulled back from him a little, only to catch a glimpse of his eyes.

"Aye."

"What could it be?"

"I reckon it most proper fur the newlyweds tae have their own quarter."

"What do you mean?"

"I mean that I shall have a modest abode built past the stable fur them tae keep."

"Seriously?"

"Quite," he responded definitively. "'Twill be my gift tae them as weel. Weel constructed yet modest."

"I never imagined. You're very kind, Leif," I acknowledged. I reached and kissed him gently on the lips, and he reciprocated with a soft one of his own. When I withdrew my lips from him, I said, "I'm so excited. I have to tell Mercy right away."

"Whilst ye please, I must take my leave fur the time being tae the fort. I shall return later," he said, informing me as he released his arms from me, letting me go from his embrace.

"All right," I replied, nodding, and my arms slipped from his neck, releasing him also.

Afterward, he went to the pegs holding his coats, and he covered himself with them. Then, he took his hat off the last peg, and we walked out of the room together; he was on his way to the fort, and I was on my way to look for Mercy. When I found her in the sunroom sitting with Winnet as they were darning stockings and while Amity was reading a book, I withdrew Mercy from the room and brought her into my medicine room to tell her the exciting news. After telling her everything that had been discussed between Leif and me regarding her ability to marry Jerome, she appeared nothing short of dumbfounded in a way that was cautiously happy, mixed with her demure disposition.

"Ma'am is you meanin' His Grace gone ahead and got Jerome from the Crawfords fa him ta be present here wif me?" she asked, shocked.

"Yes, he did," I responded gladly. Mercy didn't appear to know what to say or how to react exactly and just shook her head for a second.

"Thus, Your Grace tells me that Jerome and I can wed after all?"

"Yes."

"I'm beggin' yo pardon, ma'am, but this comes ta me as a dream of a sort."

"It's not a dream, Mercy."

"I'm a bit surprised, however. Truf be told."

"I imagine that you are," I agreed, and she lightly shook her head again. "Aren't you happy about it?"

"Well, I shall say that I's can't imagine not bein' so. I never dreamt it in the least bit truf be told some more. Jerome gonna be comin' here..." she drifted in her thoughts. "He and I gonna be wed? I's gonna be his wife?" The look on her face turned happy as a smile distinctly curled her lips, and for the first time, it seemed she was genuinely impressed by a happy idea that benefited her.

"Yes, to all of it," I said, smiling with her.

"His Grace given' us our own abode here too?"

"That also, yes," I said. "So, now we've got to think of what kind of wedding dress you'd like to wear for your ceremony and the kind of refreshments you'd like served for the occasion."

"I don't know about no fancy gown, ma'am. I ain't too good for any kind of—"

"Please don't worry about anything like that. I'd like very much to give you some beautiful fabric to suit your gown," I offered easily. Leif had given me bolts of beautiful French silks, muslins, linens, pieces of cotton, and lace he had taken off one of his smuggling shipments the time we were visiting Nahant. So, I was more than happy to spare some of this material for her use.

Understanding that a full silk gown would be overstated for her comfort and position, she still had plenty of silk ribbons to embellish a fine linen and muslin gown that would better accommodate her station. She could have this gown created by her own hand and with the assistance of one of the other maids if needed.

When I presented this solution to her, her demure smile heartened, and she said, "I thank you most deeply, ma'am. Yo kindness is much too good fo me."

"You're very welcome, Mercy. It is all my pleasure. I'm just happy for you," I replied. "Now we just need to consider the sort of refreshments you'd like served for the reception. Would you have any idea at the moment?"

"Well—I supposin' that I might reckon to fancy a fruitcake and that lemon water you named lemonade," she considered thoughtfully.

"Good. That'll be nice for everyone. Now that the time for the wedding has been arranged, perhaps we should look at some fabric kept in one of the closets for you to choose from in order to start designing your gown. Would you like to start on it?"

"I reckon I might so, ma'am. 'Tis mighty kind of you, indeed, ma'am. I thank you tremendously."

"You're welcome, Mercy."

We exchanged smiles, concluding our conversation. We left the room together, and I closed the door behind us as I led her upstairs through a series of corridors until we arrived at one of the lesser-known storage closets near my bedroom, which contained bolts of fabric. Perusing past the silks, she spotted some chintz fabric with pink roses accented by moss-green leaves. Complementing the gown, she also desired the matching green linen for the petticoat. Adding some of the silk ribbons that I'd purchased a while ago was sure to bring a wonderful finish to her modest gown.

Once I had cut the number of yards of fabric needed for her to construct the gown, I excused her so that she could begin the project.

Thirty-Nine

E arly one morning, after I'd gotten dressed for an anticipated outing with Leif before he was to report to the fort, I entered the library seeking him. As I entered, I was noticeably startled to witness him frantically rummaging through his desk, looking for something he obviously couldn't find, which was either misplaced or lost. Frazzled, I had never seen him discombobulated as I was seeing him now—ever—while he searched his desk, which had also had a portion of it dismantled. Panel pieces belonging to it had been placed aside, leaning against the nearest wall. Without even acknowledging that I'd entered the room, he was overwrought as papers and ledgers were strewn over the desktop and on the chair pushed away from him while he scoured.

"What's wrong?" I asked suddenly, closing the door behind me. His eyes shot up from searching his desk and locked onto mine as I turned from the closed door and faced him. The look on his face was alarm combined with devastation. His cheeks were ruddy, his brow was drawn together, and his lips were pinched, expressing anger also. He raked his fingers through his unbound hair and exhaled deeply, exasperated and distressed. Seeing him like this struck a deep, unnerved chord in me as I stared at him with growing concern and confusion.

"I have been thieved," he blurted, flustered, running his fingers through his hair again. "Damnation!" His fist suddenly pounded on his desktop, rattling the inkstand and causing me to jump a little.

"Thieved?" I asked spontaneously, looking at him in shock.

"Aye."

"What do you mean?"

"I have been robbed of one of my ledgers and several correspondences privy tae me."

"Private?"

"Aye."

"When did you notice them missing?"

"This morn when I meant to store anither correspondence newly received by me with the others inside a private compartment within my desk."

"Oh." I approached him at his desk, where he stood behind it, and noticed the hidden chambers that the removed panels had revealed beneath his desk. "How would anyone know that you could store anything in those compartments? It's all so well hidden, as it appears that this portion of the desk was made in one piece. I never knew your desk could come apart like this, so how could anyone else know?"

"Precisely. How micht one else ken this ability that my desk holds? This desk has been amongst my possessions since the craftsman who created it fur me whilst I was in London, and not a single soul would ever ken its secrets but I." He pinched his lips hard, and the jaw muscles pulsed.

"Then, your things were taken very recently if this was the most recent time you've noticed them missing, right?"

"I cannae say. 'Tis been months since I last opened my desk in this manner to store matters of import."

"Except, there's a lock now on the library door from the time

Captain Berkley was found looking for you in this wing of the house."

"In this case, I suffered thievery conceivably before the present."

"Yes, it is very possible," I replied, thinking. Then, the thought of the man running from the mansion during our Christmas ball entered my mind. "Do you remember when I mentioned to you about the man I'd seen running from the house during the night of our Christmas ball?"

"Aye."

"Maybe there is a correlation. I mean, maybe that was the time your things had gone missing, since we never found out who was running away from the house that night. That person could be the burglar," I conjectured by the odd occurrence.

"To note, indeed. The circumstance ye had witnessed, I had believed, was not necessarily consequential. Yet, fur your concern, had mine risen as a result. Therefore, I now question the occurrence also," he agreed.

He placed a hand on his hip and let the other sift papers around over his desk, idly searching when his gaze dropped from mine. He became silent for a second, as if thinking.

"It seems like a very strange thing to take. Why would anyone want to steal your ledger and letters?" I asked. Leif didn't answer. It appeared he was still contemplating. But I also knew he'd heard me. "What was written in the ledger and letters?" I continued delicately.

"Primarily, information pertaining tae my business dealings— shipments into the colony," he disclosed. My eyes widened, and I didn't say anything in response. The gravity immediately bombarded me, and suddenly, I realized his exposure to breaking the law and the harm it was going to bring him: treason and death. "Aye." That was all he said, confirming the horrified realization expressed on my face. "I mean tae discover the dastard thief. Make nae mistake about it. Once I do, may the Lord Almighty have mercy upon his soul, fur I shall not. I merely pray that 'tis done before the torment comes tae pass upon me."

The last statement was said under his breath, but I heard it—and I felt the exact anguish his subdued comment expressed—and I prayed.

Without another word, he proceeded to reassemble his desk by returning the paneling over the secret compartments, and I silently watched him do this with ease. Then, gathering the rest of his less critical papers and ledgers that had been strewn about, he compiled them over his desk into a relatively neat stack. When this was soon all done, he moved toward the door, grabbed his coat off the pegs, and briskly shoved his arms through the sleeves.

"Where are you going?" I asked curiously, observing him snatching the library key out of his waistcoat pocket before he buttoned his coat.

"I must take my leave before the morn grows any later," he said.

"Oh, of course," I replied, remembering his duties.

"Fear not, *mo ghaol*. All will be weel." He placed a reassuring palm over my shoulder, comforting me as he read the distraught look on my face. I only hoped he was right as I watched him turn for the door and pass through the doorway into the hallway, where I followed him.

After locking the door, he returned the key to his waistcoat pocket and hurriedly buttoned his coat before swiftly making his way through the corridor and down the staircase. As he hastily moved through the hallways with determination, I assumed it was to prevent himself from being tardy for work. When he reached the grand staircase to the first floor, he galloped down the steps, leaving me to watch on the top landing as he snatched his great coat off the pegs by the front door and shoved his arms through the sleeves, then yanked the front door open and vanished outdoors as he closed the door behind himself.

Left with an immense sense of devastation that his private

belongings had been stolen, the worry about it was extraordinarily pronounced between us. It was very difficult for me to focus on the better part of my day as I tried pretending everything was normal in front of others. Still, all I could do was closely deny that it had ever happened and that his life wasn't placed in jeopardy for the time being, to keep my own semblance of emotional balance as I wondered who had committed the offense and when, let alone for the reason why.

ONE LATE AFTERNOON, when Mercy and I were finishing a stroll after picking vegetables from the garden beyond the floral garden, a loud disturbance of male voices was heard resonating from the floral garden near the gazebo. The shouting was obstreperous and uncharacteristic, drawing our attention in its direction. Alarmed, I wondered what the commotion was about, as Leif's voice was recognizable and entwined with another man's, and bellows clashed.

When I arrived in the garden with Mercy, several of the soldiers boarding with us had gathered and surrounded the scene where Leif was shouting at the top of his lungs, berating a man who was painfully screaming. As I pushed through the surrounding onlooking soldiers, it was frightfully obvious why Captain Berkley, now recognized, was miserably yelping while being beaten by Leif's merciless swinging cane over the head and back.

Freezing in my steps and steeply confused over what was happening, shock held me in place when I realized Leif's temper had exploded beyond recognition.

"David Jones! May the Devil take yer soul, Berkley! I shall see 'tis done!" he bellowed with vitriolic detestation. "How dare ye come beneath *my* roof! Ye insufferable, damned bastard! Scoundrel! Be damned! Git yer swiving arse out of my secht lest I kill ye! I shall ship ye tae England in a pine box! Damnation! Hell-hound claim this minion!"

Captain Berkley suddenly collapsed to the ground, bloodied over the head and with it streaming over his temple. Abruptly pierced with more fear now that the captain was physically inca-pable of escaping Leif at all and that he was going to make good on his threat to kill him, I found myself rushing forward toward them as Leif kept whaling his cane over him now in a fetal position on the ground.

As I quickly approached, I called out to Leif to gain his atten-tion and cease his beating. But to no avail, he kept striking the vulnerable captain, continuing to thrash him to a pulp. When I arrived at arm's length and snagged his coat and arm, he suddenly stilled the last blow in mid-air before hitting the captain once more and turned his wild eyes toward me, and realized that it was I attaining his attention.

"Please, don't!" I gasped in appall, pleading with him as my hand clutched his coat-covered arm. His eyes had locked onto mine, and the unruly fury visibly in them scarcely retreated behind the gate of his control as he now stood motionless, staring at me. A semblance of self-dominion seemed to come over him shortly, and he swiftly turned from me and gathered Amity out of the gazebo, who I hadn't realized was there, witnessing the violent disturbance until now, and was weeping.

Taking her by the upper arm and leading her toward me, he passed her to me to guide as he proceeded out of the garden without a further word, with the expectation for us to follow him. As we did, and were joined by Mercy standing nearby, Captain Berkley was left beaten and bloodied on the ground while several of the surrounding soldiers looked on. Leif's ill temper remained visible as he plowed ahead of us in large, hurried strides toward the house in the direct direction where Winnet was standing on the outdoor steps before the sunroom, sobbing.

Flaring with anger as we approached her up the steps, Leif

brusquely asked her, "How are ye absent at Amity's side, Winnet?" He glared at her, demanding to know, and she could barely get a word out between hyperventilating sobs.

"Captain Berkley claimed to relay a missive from His Grace informing me that Your Grace wished to have a word with me," she forced between tears.

"I sent nae such missive," Leif refuted stoutly. "The scoundrel," he hissed. "Have a moment tae collect your wits, Winnet. Then, promptly return tae Amity."

"Aye, Your Grace," she replied gratefully and immediately turned from him, heading back indoors.

Leif drew in a deep breath, seeming to strive to calm himself further before entering the house again, stalling us as Amity's tears kept flowing and as we watched Winnet retreat through the doors.

"What on earth happened?" I asked, finally, drawing his attention toward me, deeply confused.

"That hellhound steals our niece's innocence," he seethed with clenched teeth.

"Steals her innocence? How?" I looked at him in shock since this was unheard of to my awareness.

"Deceiving her maid presented his opportunity tae manipulate our niece into stolen kisses. She was hardly inclined when I had discovered them upon my return from the Common with several soldiers fur dining," he explained.

"Oh, my goodness!"

"In a phrase, more than my sentiment, exactly, indeed."

"I recognized that he had an eye on her for a little while."

"Had ye?"

"Yes. I wouldn't have put this past him to do something like this."

"Aye, weel, he has certainly, and I shall have him tossed out of *Taigh Gràs* promptly and not a moment sooner." With this last statement, he stepped away from me, turning for the door, and stormed into the house, seeking Quinn to order the staff to throw all of Captain Berkley's belongings out past the property and into the street. As this began to take place, the captain was no longer welcome here, and with the assistance of another soldier who was a friend of his, he helped pick him up off the ground where he was lying and brought him carefully to his feet to escort him off the property.

When Amity and I arrived in her bedroom, we moved toward her bed, where we sat, and I finally embraced her, calming her tears. After she had calmed, my arms slipped from her, and we were able to discuss what had taken place between the captain and her when he'd placed himself in her company when she was alone with him inside the gazebo. Claiming that she was all right after I had first asked her before beginning our conversation, I was unsettled that she had become frightened over the whole experience with him. This led us into a much-needed discussion over sexual relationships between men and women—despite the assumption that she would have had a similar, though very delicate, conversation with her Aunt Beth earlier. Still, I found it beneficial to have this sort of discussion with me since I was a bit more frank and realistic about aspects of this topic, in addition to giving her the opportunity to inquire freely.

When our conversation came to a close, Winnet entered the room ready to assist and keep Amity company. She now appeared to be collected and prepared to focus on her task of aiding Amity. So, I kissed Amity on her temple and wished Winnet well before leaving them both to themselves. As I was walking through the corridor and rounding another corner, servants could be heard shuffling and moving heavy objects through the hallway toward the grand staircase. It was clear that these items, consisting of trunks and cases, belonged to Captain Berkley and were hastily being moved out of the house. When I was passing some of the male servants hauling trunks and several maids carrying bundles of dirty bed linens, Prudence, one of the maids, called my attention, stopping me in my tracks as I faced her.

"Beggin' your pardon, Your Grace," she said politely.

"Yes, Prudence?" I replied.

"This got the Stewart crest upon it. So, reckon it belongin' to His Grace." She presented a leather-bound ledger to me, and I received it. Curiously, I opened it and discovered Leif's writing with all of the shipping records and receipts he'd been keeping. I instantly believed this was the missing portfolio he claimed had been stolen from him, and couldn't believe that it was now in my possession.

"Where was this found, Prudence?" I asked her oddly.

"'Twas discovered between the mattress and platform of Captain Berkley's bed, Your Grace," she responded.

"Thank you," I said, shocked, and resumed through the busy hallway, hanging on to the ledger, realizing the captain had stolen it. Suddenly, I fully suspected that the man whom I'd seen running from our house during the night of our Christmas ball was Captain Berkley, escaping his theft of the ledger and possibly more. While I had the evidence of the ledger in hand, I wished that I had the advantage of a camera recording him committing the crime to prove his guilt. Either way, my resentment of this man rose equal to Leif's.

Not knowing whether to journey up to the third floor for Leif's office or head straight for our bedroom, it was a toss-up where he'd be located at the moment. But the thought of dinner soon beginning led me to believe that he'd be in our room, tidying himself to dine. So, I went to our room and entered. When I entered the room, I was relieved to see him and noticed that he'd changed into a pair of new breeches from the bloodstained ones he'd worn previously and had just finished gathering his hair into a queue. While not nearly as animated with ferocity as before, he did appear more subdued, even though the agitation was still visible on his hardened face.

"I believe what's been stolen from you has been found," I

began as I strode toward him, hoping this new information would subdue him further.

"I beg yer pardon?" He replied, noticing me coming to stand before him. I presented the ledger to him, and his eyes bulged as his brow lifted and then furrowed with a combination of surprise, relief, and confusion. His hand grasped it as it slipped from my fingers when he asked, "How in heaven have ye come by this?"

"Prudence gave it to me as we met in the hallway and said that it was found in Captain Berkley's room between the mattress and platform of his bed," I informed him.

"The man be damned," he uttered.

"I wonder why he would have stolen your ledger?" I asked.

"I am certain it was tae spy upon my business dealings."

"I don't quite understand why he'd be interested in doing that."

"Because I have one vessel that comes tae port in Boston filled with guids which may amount tae more than the tariffs, as I have heard him question the possibility of it with another man at the tavern. Captain Berkley claimed at the time when I spied upon his discussion with this particular man that he was puzzled by my opulence and trade. Therefore, he stole my ledger to examine my records of the guids and tariffs I have paid. I am certain 'tis the reason why fur his theft," Leif explained.

"But why would he even care about what you do?" I replied, confused and worried.

"I do not stand fur his arrogance and I have too often commanded him tae his place. He detests me because I am Scottish and wishes tae see me hanged," Leif answered.

He opened his ledger and also discovered his receipts and remaining pertinent papers as he thumbed through the pages. "Bastard," he muttered, uttering it barely under his breath that I almost didn't hear him say it. "Whilst I am quite alleviated to have my ledger returned tae me, my scalp may not yet be fully saved."

"Why? What do you mean?" I asked, looking at him with grave concern.

"Five correspondences of mine remain mislaid from my desk. If merely I kent, who possesses them, I micht have a notion as tae how tae proceed."

"Maybe they might still be in the captain's bedroom and have been overlooked," I fathomed.

"Aye, likely so," he agreed.

"I shall promptly explore his quarters prior tae dining and make an inquiry of Prudence regarding the possibility."

"Good idea," I agreed.

"The captain hid my possession fur quite a time," Leif remarked, making an observation.

"If he took it during the time he was discovered near your library several months ago, or if he was the one escaping the Christmas ball with it, then yes, he had it for quite a while."

"Aye."

"But I wonder what he was going to do with the information he'd stolen, eventually?"

"I fear tae speculate. I merely believe that he found naught amiss within my records tae report to General Gage or Sir Bernard, our governor, and had nae opportunity of returning my ledger without appearing suspicious."

"Yes, I think you're right. But what's his reasoning?"

"Tae imperil me one way or anither."

"How could he have known about where you kept your belongings in your desk's secret compartments? I'm really raking my mind over it to understand."

"Likely when the door must have been slightly ajar whilst I was working in my library and had hid them in it without my awareness of his presence prior tae his discovery in the vicinity by you."

"Likely so," I agreed.

"He is a spy. I shall have ye awaur. Although his spying is not beneath my command, despite the fact that he is a subordinate of mine."

"Oh, I see. Then, are you saying that he's a rogue?"

"I am awaur that he has spied fur other commanders. However, I have never given him such orders. It is as I have told ye, he is undisciplined and would rejoice tae see me hanged," Leif said, and I swallowed hard, understanding that no one around us could be trusted. "Fortunately, he had not realized the accounting in my ledger had been modified to suit the tariffs on the guids imported into the colony. He cannae accuse me of being a smuggler."

"We call that cooking the books where I'm from," I remarked, relieved about the potential accusation.

"Aye, weel, 'twas done to hide what has been smuggled. Berkley is certainly displeased tae discover nae evidence against me."

"His unhappiness is my joy," I replied, and he nodded pensively, still.

"Yet, my correspondences remain lost," he said, appearing seriously concerned about it. "Permit me. I must go to his chamber tae discover whit I micht without the servants prior tae my acquiring Prudence's attention before dining," he said. I nodded in response, and he proceeded out of our bedroom.

Later, Leif told me, to our misfortune, that nothing else related to his belongings had been found in Captain Berkley's room, according to Prudence and himself, after scouring the furniture and the rest of the room. While Leif was relieved that his register had been returned, snuffing out the threat of evidence that he had smuggled, he remained concerned about the letters that were still missing. Only revealing the importance of the letters to me in that they were political in nature, without disclosing details, I understood more about the reason why he wished to have them in his possession again. But without knowing where they'd gone, he was at a loss and expressed his unease as he continued to fixate on where they could have vanished.

Forty

fter Leif banished Captain Berkley from *Taigh Gràs*, he was rescued by Leif's ex-friend, George, Lord Brimfield, when he promptly received him to dwell in his manor. The house had grown noticeably subdued with the leftover soldiers still boarding with us, as both flippant influences with strong personality traits were no longer here. I was happy that the atmosphere had returned to somewhat calm and normal, despite the company we still kept. I was enjoying our spring day in the floral garden today, clipping flowers with Amity, Mercy, and Winnet and placing them into our baskets.

When our baskets were full of hyacinths, daffodils, and early rose blooms, we gathered them and went indoors to have them arranged in vases and placed around the house. As Amity and Winnet were decorating the first floor with floral vases, Mercy and I were talking about the flowers she would like to have for her wedding bouquet, realizing her wedding was quickly approaching the following week. Afterward, we began arranging the remaining floral vases throughout the second floor.

As we delightedly spoke and arranged flowers on the console table by the room Captain Berkley once occupied, I staggered in my conversation as I detected His Lordship making an unexpected appearance through the hallway as he was advancing toward us. Ceasing what I was doing, Mercy noticed me and had the same stunned reaction as he arrived, standing directly in front of me. Shocked, I wondered why he was here and how he could have appeared on the second floor of the house, without the direction of Quinn or Elijiah, and all in Leif's absence.

"Lord Brimfield," I gasped, turning my surprised attention to him.

"Forgive me," he said, not so sincerely. The look in his eyes was shallow, and any feeling he had appeared remote.

"You never come here," I mentioned.

"'Tis been a while, I declare," he replied coolly.

"Yes, it has. You'll be disappointed to know that my husband remains on duty and hasn't come home yet if you wish to see him," I informed him, knowing that he likely should already know this.

"A pity. Yet, as His Grace and I remain estranged from the exchange of mere words, I presumed that I might have a word with Her Grace instead, as she may deliver what I have to say to him promptly," he explained without a smile, appearing earnest in tone and manner.

"What you have to say must be urgent. Otherwise, I could have met you in the drawing room, not upstairs unexpectedly," I replied, suddenly concerned and giving him a strange look.

"'Tis grave, indeed."

"Please tell me what's wrong, then?"

"What I must say is extensive. A word in private. Leave your maid." He gestured toward the open doorway into Captain Berkley's empty room. Placed on the spot, I exchanged a cautious look with Mercy and moved away from her as I proceeded to lead His Lordship into the vacant room. When we entered the room, he took the liberty to close the door, and now I was staring uncertainly at him, along with concern for what he had to say. Standing alone in the room together, he gazed at me for a lagging second, making me uncomfortable because not only was his attraction to me still vivid, but the expression on his face was stern, and the hard bitterness was crystallized in his eyes. I almost moved to open the door ajar, except he was standing directly in front of it. So, I moved toward the low-burning fireplace that had been helping keep the cool house warm this late afternoon and faced him.

"What seems to be the trouble, Lord Brimfield?" I asked him directly.

"I am under the distinct impression that you and your husband are quite unique in that you share a high level of confidence," he started.

"Yes, I believe we do," I agreed.

"Then, presumably, it would not be of any surprise to you to know that your husband delves into dubious affairs."

"Dubious affairs?" My brow knitted as I gave him a perplexed look.

"Yes," he responded curtly.

"I believe you're mistaken."

"Believe me that I am not."

"What sort of affairs are you meaning, specifically?"

"The deceptive sort."

"I'm quite stumped since I don't know what you mean. Would you mind being clearer?"

"The work of a spy is a cunning and perilous business. It requires much prudence and discreetness, and if one is discovered, it will certainly mean death," he said pointedly instead.

"A spy?" I responded, still confused. But my heart started to race.

"Yes," he said frankly.

"I imagine that if he does spy, it's for the Crown, and so I would agree that it is a dangerous line of work."

"Yet, the rebels are fond of him."

"Wait a minute. You're accusing my husband of being a spy for the rabble rousers?" I questioned, astonished.

"I have not charged him of anything where the Crown will be pleased should it be known," he replied.

"But he hasn't done anything of the sort. So how on earth can it be possible that he'd ever be charged with such a crime?"

"Forgive me for imparting this revelation to you. Apparently, I have been mistaken about your confidence." Lord Brimfield smirked, and now my heart was beginning to pound.

"How can you make this accusation when it's false?"

"I have been made privy to information pertinent to your husband's secret affairs."

"My husband is not a spy," I insisted.

"Yet, he is quite that."

"Did it ever occur to you that he may be under General Gage's orders to spy on the rebels for the Crown, and to do so, he may have had to infiltrate their network?" I questioned, remembering quickly the conversation I'd overheard between Leif and the general several months ago during the winter.

"The possibility is curious," he considered skeptically with a disdainful smirk again.

"The possibility is a fact when a conversation was held between the general and my husband about doing this against the rebels. He is spying on them for the Crown on General Gage's orders," I countered seriously, gazing unbelievably at him.

"I might verify your claim myself with the general if it were not for what I have been given into my possession, which draws question."

"What are you talking about?"

Instead of answering, he reached inside his coat pocket and pulled forth a series of five folded parchments in the form of letters and presented them to me. Indicating for me to view them, I reached toward his hand and gathered them from him. Opening the first letter, I proceeded to read:

October 1, 1768:

It is with much gratitude from the Sons of Liberty that you have chosen to sponsor our Circular and have provided this support in the cause to rid ourselves of the Crown's Tyranny.

Yours respectfully,
Master John Hancock

Uncertain of what this specifically was all about, my heart began pounding harder, and my breathing grew somewhat shallow. Folding the letter and curious about the next one, I unfolded it and began reading:

November 20, 1768

Upon receiving your missive and after our meeting of like minds, Master Hancock, I shall consider your request for further means to aid others against the Crown's machinations.

Its Tyranny must be rid. Yet, be forewarned, there are many enemies as well as friends amongst us. I have discriminated against many of them betwixt our friends and acquaintances. Be wary of those who freely claim to be friends, for they may very well be Tory plotters.

Cordially,
Duke of Monteith

Now that questions were beginning to enter my mind, I folded this letter and opened the third and last one I was intending to read:

December 19, 1768,

I humbly request Your Grace's attendance at the Green Dragon Tavern tonight.

Much needs to be discussed. We must acquire information from the Governor's ball. Men will protest at the marketplace and at Fort Hill tomorrow. We continue to recruit soldiers to spy by your charge.

With due respect,
Master Samuel Adams

After reading this final correspondence, I was not only deeply confused because I had never been made aware of these letters from Leif before, but the idea of Leif being a turncoat to support Whig sentiments was also frightening. My blood ran cold in my veins, and my pulse shot up with terror, knowing what could happen to him. But I found it extremely difficult to believe that he'd threaten our security in this way. Then, as I realized how terribly worried he'd been since his secret correspondences had gone missing, I understood that His Lordship had now delivered them to me as I finished reading the final one.

Despite what I'd just read, I hung onto the better inclination to believe that these letters resulted from Leif's spying involvement for the Crown by General Gage's orders. Believing this gave me some semblance of having the ability to gaze calmly at Lord Brimfield while continuing to hold onto the correspondences in my hand that had begun to tremble.

"Quite a startling revelation, is it not? Your husband plotting with the likes of Hancock and his scoundrels is disappointing, at minimum. I am certain Sir Bernard, our governor, will be pleased to understand this revelation, as you do know he detests Hancock to all extremes. The governor will certainly hate your husband too once I reveal my discovery after my word with you is finished, madam," Lord Brimfield rejoined, watching the expression on my face.

"It's as I said. General Gage has my husband spying on rebels for the Crown," I replied. "And these letters are conceivably a product of that."

"Or not. I shall inform you that I have eyes as well," he countered, narrowing his eyes slightly at me.

"Speaking of which, how did you come by my husband's personal possessions?" I asked, figuring him.

"That is entitled information."

"Entitled?"

"Quite."

"I differ. No one is entitled to my husband's belongings, Your Lordship. So, if you'll be so kind as to tell me, it would be appreciated if you'd let me know how you've obtained these private belongings?"

"As valued as the inhospitable disposing of Captain Berkley."

"Captain Berkley? What does he have to do with this conversation?" I asked when I immediately realized his culpability in all of this as Lord Brimfield's mentored spy. "So, Captain Berkley is your agent?"

"He is subordinate to me, of course, yet he had no reason to spy upon His Grace."

"Until when?"

"Captain Berkley has informed me of his suspicions of your husband when he witnessed him frequenting the Green Dragon Tavern, which is a den of Whig charlatans, last autumn. The captain also questions why it would appear that your husband would associate with Master John Hancock, as he has visited his dwelling on occasion."

I couldn't answer the latter part of his statement, as it also made me wonder. Instead, I spontaneously asked, "When did the captain give you these letters?"

"When he was tossed out. Why might you inquire?"

"I'm only wondering if he was a lone thief or if he was hired." Lord Brimfield didn't respond. "Because you see, my husband's belongings have been missing for quite some time, and it seems it might have been premeditated for ulterior motives."

"Blackmail. Mayhap?"

Blackmail. All of this was beginning to look less in Leif's favor if General Gage hadn't had him operating under covert orders not known to anyone else. This was the only thing that I could think of that was reasonable.

"I'm afraid there's been a mistake, and this issue needs to be addressed with General Gage since he's ordered my husband to operate under secret conditions," I said.

"The mistake is yours, I fear," he replied tersely.

"How?"

"If I visit the general with this information regarding your husband, and he is exposed as a traitor to the Crown due to your lack of knowledge of the situation, the Crown will execute him. Do you care to risk widowhood, Your Grace? I don't mind obliging," he said. His words suddenly sent an electric current through my bones, shocking me as I realized that he hated my husband. I found myself incapable of answering him as I stared unbelievably at him. "Your silence speaks for itself. In this case, permit me to expound further. Quite naturally, you may not be aware of this situation, either of which I am about to reveal to you. You see, prior to our estrangement, I asked your husband for a loan, to which he simply let sail without further acknowledgment. His Grace surpasses Master Hancock as the wealthiest man in the colony, and since Master Hancock has been revealed to be a smuggler and charged for it, there is no question as to how he has obtained such opulence.

"Therefore, considering your husband's indebtedness to the

Crown and supposed lack of wealth, it begs the question, of course, of how he has acquired his opulence beyond that of Master Hancock's. Certainly, His Grace would not be smuggling, would he?" Again, I didn't answer, as I didn't know how to respond, since I was taken off guard and somewhat frightened. "Regardless. I propose, due to your fair standing with your husband, that you grant a word upon my behalf. Impress upon him to grant me the loan for which I had asked him. If granted, then I shall not deliver the missives into General Gage's hands, and I shall not encourage an investigation as to whether he pays proper tariffs upon his shipments into the colony, where he will be accused and charged with smuggling."

My fingers tightly gripped the letters, and I slipped them inside my skirt's pocket, hiding them from him. He stepped forward toward me, and I moved backward away from the hearth, bumping into the bed behind me. He stopped short directly in front of me and glowered. My heart pumped ferociously as I wondered what his next reaction was going to bring. If I could have maneuvered myself around him, I would have done so, but as it was, I was blocked by his broad and taller frame.

"Excuse me, Lord Brimfield," I started, attempting to move around him anyway.

"I know your husband is a Jacobite. Give the letters to me," he demanded, inhibiting my ability to step away.

"I won't," I affirmed fearfully.

"Give the letters to me, presently."

"No."

"Give them to me, or else," he threatened, raising his voice, clearly losing his temper. He scowled, and his eyes widened, causing me to panic. I wedged myself around him, and he grabbed me tightly around the upper arm.

"Let me go!" I responded suddenly, raising my voice also from sheer alarm.

"Not till I receive the letters!"

"Let me go!"

"Give them to me!"

"No!"

Suddenly, I saw stars when a forceful sting slammed over my cheek, knocking me backward onto the mattress on the bed. Dazed, I realized that I'd been impacted by his heavy hand, and my vision was quickly restored. I immediately moved to sit up when a second series of stars crossed my vision, and the collision forced my head back onto the quilt. Moaning, I didn't know what was happening until I felt my skirts being summarily raised above my knees, and I thrashed, trying to escape him.

"If I shan't receive the letters, permit me to send my best regards to His Grace. A traitor's wife makes the best whore," he growled as I felt him falling on top of me and pinning me down beneath him before I could elude him on the opposite side of the bed. "Jacobites and Negro lovers be damned alike," he hissed as I now wildly flailed my fists, punching him in the head and shoulders. "Fight as you might. 'Twill be done quickly."

"Get off me!" I screamed, feeling him quickly adjusting himself between my thighs when abruptly I sensed him plunging into me and began violently thrusting, burning me, and causing me to scream again. Whipping my fists against him as much as I could, I caught a glimpse of the door swinging open, and Mercy peered inside the room. Horrified, she backed away from the doorway and ran through the hallway, vanishing.

What the fuck is going on? I can't believe this is happening! Is this real? No, this is not real. What he's doing isn't real... it can't be... It's not happening... It's not happening...

The moment distended as he surged while I strove to remove him from me with punches and scouring scratches over his face that made him howl. When he soon groaned and gritted his teeth, along with the hue in his face flushing, he reached his climax as my eyes landed on the nearby candlestick over the nightstand, and my palm grabbed it. Swinging it off the stand, the weighty silver stick crashed against the back of Lord Brimfield's skull, and abruptly, he became lifeless.

Slumping over me now, I dropped the candlestick and struggled to push his body off mine when I noticed blood staining my hands. Further terrified, not knowing if I'd killed him, I was able to shove him beside me, and I raced out of the room. I continued whirling through the corridors and fled down the staircase toward the back of the house, where I escaped outdoors and ran.

I had no idea where I was running. I simply kept running. I ran until I dropped to my knees in a band of spruce trees where Leif and I had ridden our horses. Curled in a fetal position, I wept aloud, wanting the earth to open and swallow me whole and never give me the opportunity to face Leif or see *Taigh Gràs* again. I wanted to vanish from all that existed.

Forty-One

❧⟡❧

Soon, the sound of Leif's gentle voice came to me, along with his touch over my shoulder, as I continued lying in the foliage beneath the trees. As I kept weeping, I didn't have the strength or will to acknowledge him—least of all, turn a glimpse toward him. Except when he found me and his soft hand came over my shoulder, I inadvertently moved backward, hitting the tree trunk at my back. Incapable of seeing him through my watery gaze, I sensed his touch coming over both shoulders this time as he moved to embrace me, and I reacted, pounding his chest with my fists for him to abandon me.

"All is weel, lass. I'm haur, presently, Sylive. Yoo're safe with me," he comforted, taking me into his arms and binding me in his secure embrace. But I kept screaming and crying, wanting to dissolve from him, believing nothing could be fixed. Still, he unrelentingly held me close, consoling me, begging for me to calm down and to listen to his gentle words. "Sylvie, *mo ghaol*, yoo're safe. 'Tis Leif. Recall? I am haur. Nae more harm will come tae ye. 'Tis Leif. Yoo're safe. I am haur. All is weel. I am haur. All is weel. I promise ye. Ease yerself if ye micht, *mo ghaol*. I have come fur ye."

"Is he dead?" I cried.

"He remains alive," he answered.

"Is he still here?"

"He has fled."

"How?"

"Berkley has rescued him. Mercy tells me."

He embraced me for as long as I struggled to free myself from his arms and sobbed. I didn't want to be held. I just wanted to disappear. But he held me soundly until I no longer had the strength and buckled. Then, he gathered me altogether into his arms, lifted me off my feet, and began carrying me out of the woods back toward the house.

"No! Don't take me back! I don't want to go back there!" I whimpered anxiously.

"'Tis alrecht, loove. I am haur. Yoo're safe. Yoo're safe," he repeated in calming whispering tones.

When he finally arrived indoors, he carried me through the hallways to our bedroom and carefully placed me on the bed. When my head touched the pillows, I sat up and moved to stand from the bed, telling him that I wanted to have a bath.

"I shall have the maids draw yer water fur it," he said. "Yet, lie till 'tis done. Ye must rest." His tone was soft and soothing, and I was encouraged to take his advice. So, I returned to bed and lay against the pillows, waiting to cleanse myself. As he was about to leave the room to fetch the maids, I noticed that his coat had not been removed from his shoulders as usual. I knew he wasn't going to stay with me longer to return outdoors.

"Where are you going?" I asked weakly, meeting his gaze. His eyes flared with roaring rage, mirroring the hue in his face as his jaw muscles throbbed.

"I shall visit Lord Hathnell," he answered gently but with determination. The visible outrage within him was guarded like the sound of his voice as he controlled himself.

"Lord Hathnell?" I responded.

"Aye."

"Who is he?"

"An anchorite. We fought together in the war. He is an honorable man and a loyal friend."

"Oh. Why must you go see him?"

"I seek a favor."

"What sort of favor?"

"I seek his favor to be my second."

"What?" I suddenly raised myself from the pillows, started to my feet, and approached him with terror. "Leif, please don't."

"I must."

"Please. I'm begging you not to duel." My mind began racing with all the things that could go wrong. Dueling was not only illegal; it could kill him instead—and if he killed Lord Brimfield, then he'd be charged with murder, jailed, and executed. Either way, the risk was too high for him to avenge a wrong. "Please, don't do it."

"Return tae bed, *mo ghaol*. Rest. I shall have the maids promptly draw yer bath as ye wish. I shan't be absent fur too long. I swear it." With those last words, he turned from me, left the room, and closed the door, vanishing.

THE NEXT MORNING, as dawn broke, I was awakened by his movements in the room as he dressed. Exhausted, my eyes slowly focused on him when I remembered what had happened yesterday and his intentions to settle the offense with His Lordship, dispelling anything that seemed like a dream. While watching him buttoning his waistcoat, I wondered if he was going to follow through with a duel after his meeting with Lord Hathnell.

"You've met with Lord Hathnell?" I asked while lying beneath the blankets.

"Yoo're nae longer sleeping?" Leif replied, turning his gaze to mine while finishing the top buttons.

"No."

"I beg yer pardon fur awakening ye. Ye must continue tae gather yer rest, however."

"I can no longer sleep. What did Lord Hathnell say to your request?"

"He is tae be my second."

"Leif, please," I said, suddenly removing myself from bed and arriving to stand before him. "Please don't do this. It's too dangerous all around. It's illegal. You know it is. Worst of all, you could get killed."

"Whether or not, 'tis agreed," he responded unyieldingly, appearing fearless also. He grabbed his coat from his armoire, and I watched him stride to his dresser and pull forth the pistol box resting on top of it. He tucked it under his arm and clutched it. Suddenly, my blood curdled with fear when I realized what was going to happen this morning. I rushed toward the door and stood, blocking his exit, and he approached me, stilling himself before me as he drew in a small breath and gave me a determined look. "Remove yerself, Sylvie. I must pass."

"No, I won't let you die," I replied nervously.

"Be a guid lass. Do as I say."

"It doesn't have to be rectified this way."

"How else micht it be?"

"We—well, you—can charge him with the crime and have him arrested."

"Nae."

"Why not?"

"'Twill not suffice."

"Why not?"

"Such trials are salacious, and the criminal is typically inadequately punished. Furthermore, our exposure is unwarranted. 'Tis a private matter. Thus, the resolution is privately dealt."

"Would it help if I told you that I have your stolen letters?" I asked, trying to distract him from leaving. His brow furrowed, and he paused.

"Whit do ye mean?"

"I have them."

"How?"

"Lord Brimfield had them and showed them to me yesterday. It was his reason for coming here. To blackmail you," I disclosed.

"Indeed?" Leif's eyes widened and his brow lifted high, making him suddenly look shocked.

"Yes. Apparently, Captain Berkley is the one who stole them and gave them to Lord Brimfield," I said. I proceeded to tell him everything that had happened with Lord Brimfield and the letters yesterday. "So now that everything's returned, perhaps consider what is actually at stake because they both can corroborate each other's accusations against you—especially if you participate in this duel and you survive—even if they no longer have the evidence against you. They each could divulge their information about you to General Gage or the governor, surely. Particularly if they feel threatened by you in any way, think about the consequences of that. Won't you?"

"Whaur micht the letters be?" he asked instead. I moved from the door and went to my writing desk. Opening one of the top drawers, the letters were revealed, and I took them into my hand. I closed the drawer and returned to where Leif was standing at the front of the door, now, and gave him the letters. He quickly opened them and perused each one.

"Pray, return them to your desk. I shall acquire them upon my return," he said, returning them to me.

"Leif," I started begging again.

"All the more reason tae settle this affront," Leif defied, minding his temper. "Dinnae fret. I shall return."

Then, he opened the door and left the bedroom, closing the door behind himself. A tidal wave of dread swept over me, and the letters in my hand began shaking. There was nothing I could do about him or this situation, and the thought of him being shot and dying, or at best, jailed and executed, raced through my mind like a freezing ice storm, which paralyzed my stance. I didn't know what to do. There was nothing I could do; I was left with no choice but to accept.

Without thinking, I mechanically went to my writing desk, replaced the letters in the drawer, and sat in the chair, gazing out the window beside it at the new morning green scenery. Tearfully consumed with anxiety, I watched sparrows chirp in the surrounding trees.

IT WASN'T until hours later, after remaining in my room, that I noticed, when looking out the window toward the direction of the stable, Leif galloping over the field on his horse. Rushing out of the bedroom and extremely relieved to see him, I hurriedly made my way out of the house and went to the stable to meet him. When I arrived, our stablehand was nowhere to be found tending to Leif's horse as expected. Instead, his horse remained saddled and standing by the stable's entrance while shouting was heard emitting from the side of the building.

I swiftly went around the stable and, to my great alarm, discovered Leif wildly swinging and stabbing his sword into stacks of hay. He was roaring at the top of his lungs, outraged and having entirely lost his temper. Flabbergasted to witness him in such an uncontrollable state, I stood there watching him violently expressing his tirade. Approaching him, I suddenly stopped and stayed there, watching in shock. So, I remained behind him, out of sight, only staring as he writhed through his kinetic emotions.

He drove his sword into the haystack with force a final time, then abandoned it and proceeded to walk out into the field, now bouncing in the breeze with tall grass and wildflowers. Not knowing that I was there behind him, I followed him at a distance into the field until he arrived in the middle of it and ceased walking. Drawing deep breaths, his breathing was settling while he perspired and raked a hand through his disheveled hair. When I approached at arm's length, I reached a gentle palm over his shoulder and felt his perspiration soaking through his shirt. He turned his eyes toward mine, and they met. His eyes scarcely widened, though I knew he was surprised to see me, and I noticed they were glazing over.

"Why do ye come outdoors?" he asked as his voice croaked.

"I saw you returning through the window. I wanted to meet you," I replied. The sunlight caught perspiration dripping over his brow and cheeks like crystals as the light splintered through the droplets.

"Yet, yoo're weary, and ye must rest," he replied in a softer voice which cracked again.

"I'm all right right now to see you," I said softly, too. "I'm just so happy to see you again." He didn't respond, except he kept his eyes frozen on me. "Did you kill him?" The worry I felt was so severe, I was afraid to ask. As I anticipated his answer, I also didn't want to know it.

"I shall kill him," he vowed, straight-faced and with passion in his eyes.

"What do you mean? I thought that was the reason for your leaving early this morning."

"It was precisely for that reason. Yet, when Lord Hathnell and I arrived in the Common tae meet Lord Brimfield and his second, we waur delayed by their tardiness. 'Twas not till somewhat later did Sir Banford, Lord Brimfield's second, arrive in the field at our location tae disclose that His Lordship broke the agreement and has fled Boston."

"He has?"

"I have raked the city high and low for his whereabouts only tae be met with futility when I learnt from General Gage that he agreed tae Lord Brimfield's wishes tae immediately transfer him tae New York City tae impress the Quartering Act. 'Twas done after General Gage discovered that Brimfield's manor had been ransacked last night and burnt tae the ground like whit had occurred tae Master Hustchison's dwelling years earlier. Brimfield is hated within Boston, and many subjects threaten him. His life is at stake, regardless. They want him scalped as do I.

"I have nae inclination of his lead as I do not know how many hours ago he took leave from Boston. General Gage does not ken whit has occurred betwixt Brimfield and me. Yet, I mean to track Brimfield down and kill him," he said, still visibly outraged.

"How will you manage to leave here? Won't General Gage say something if you suddenly left town?" I asked, obviously worried and frightened for him.

"I shall manage," he replied resolutely.

"But what about what I said earlier? If you survive, you'll surely get caught for the crime, and they'll try you for murder and then execute you. You're already on weak ground with the Crown as it is. Please don't risk it, Leif. It's not worth it."

"Not worth it? Not worth it?" he questioned unbelievably, raising his voice also. "Yoo're worth it all! Dinnae tell me such nonsense! Yoo're worth my existence! Dinnae demean whit ye mean tae me! Yoo're my life, my happiness, my joy! Dinnea stand in my way, Sylvie, fur I shall kill him!"

He suddenly turned from me and started determinedly pacing through the field again, back toward the stable.

"Leif!" I called out to him, quickly chasing after him, but he kept moving ahead of me, ignoring me. "Leif! Please! I'm begging you! Leif! Why are you the one who is so angry?"

"Ye waur violated!" he shouted back at me.

"I was and it wasn't you! So tell me why you are really so angry?"

"Ye waur violated!" he hollered again.

"That's not it! You don't want to avenge me! You want to avenge yourself!"

"Ye are my woman!"

"You only want to avenge yourself because of what others will say about you!"

"I wulnae have that bastard slip from my vengeance! He will receive whit is owed tae him! 'Tis final!"

"Don't pity yourself! I'm the one who got hurt!"

"I am yer guard! I shall bring whit he did tae a conclusion!"

"It won't end by you killing him!"

"He will be extinguished!"

"But what he did won't and if you truly love me like you say, then you won't leave me! You swore it—that you'd never leave me!" I shouted at him as he kept walking ahead of me. He didn't answer but kept moving swiftly. "Liar!"

He abruptly stopped walking and collapsed in the field, concealed by the tall grass and flowers. When I arrived at him, he was seen buckled to his knees, wheezing with visible tears streaming down his face. Kneeling to my knees before him, my own eyes quickly welled with tears and streamed down my cheeks as we stared in anguish at each other.

"How do ye beseech me?" he asked with a cracking voice, looking defeated.

"Because I love you," I wept.

"I loove ye more, do ye not understand? I vowed yer safety. I vowed tae keep ye safe—that nae harm would ever touch ye. I have failed. I have failed ye," he wheezed emotionally. I didn't respond. There was nothing I could say. "Aye, ye have been harmed. Validated. Not I. I beg yer forgiveness, though I dinnae expect ye will ever grant me yer forgiveness. Yoo're my most precious possession. I cannae bear that ye waur hurt. I ail fur ye. I am most enraged at myself. Most enraged at myself, indeed."

"But if you were to die... my heart would break, and I would die too."

"He mustn't live."

"But you must."

"Sylvie..." He drifted in tears, and so did I. "I have failed ye," he grieved when he was able to catch his breath. "Ye will return tae *Serendipity* and remain. I shall return tae this land and I shall kill him."

"No!" The thought of our separation anguished me more than I could fathom. I couldn't go through that again. And if he died...? The thought was too much to bear.

"Yoo're harmed and I have failed."

"No—you haven't. How can you ever say that?" I wept.

"How am I worthy of yer loove? Therefore, we part and I shall seek tae annihilate him. If it will be so, merely when 'tis done, mayhap ye will understand my reason. Aye, I am prideful and I am enraged, yet he is an evil man and I care tae bring us justice for yer violation and his betrayal of me."

"But if you die, then you will have failed me—and I would never forgive you." His eyes locked onto mine in a sudden way that quickly registered my meaning and struck him profoundly in an unusual manner. His arms abruptly whipped around me, and he drew me into a tight embrace, and my arms came around him also.

"Whit ye implore of me is tormenting. Yet yer hate of me will be my death beyond the grave," he said against my cheek, anguished. "If ye should never forgive my failure tae guard ye whilst we live, I shall remain alive for yer sake than to be cursed with your loathing of me beyond my living days. I cannae bear that ye have been harmed, fur yer death is mine."

"Yours is mine, too," I reiterated.

"Yet, I remain in fear that I may never rest so long as Brimfield breathes. I shall pray for the Lord Almighty's grace tae grant me solace fur our sake," he whispered as he quivered. "I loove ye, Sylvie. Ye may not loove me in return. Yet ken that I shall never forsake ye." He kept holding me in his vice-like embrace as if never to let me go, and I remained. "I shall never forsake ye," he repeated, sealing the vow a final time as he held me.

❧

IT WAS A BEAUTIFUL MID-APRIL MORNING. The sky was a rich cobalt hue, and the titanium-white cumulus clouds floating by appeared like cotton puffs. Seagulls flew inland from the Atlantic, and the geese returned to the ponds and walked through our floral garden. A light breeze stirred from the shore, and the air was mild and fragrant from all the surrounding lilacs in bloom.

I found myself in a surreal state of mind, like denial. I tried to push what had occurred to me with Lord Brimfield far into the back of my mind. But every time I closed my eyes, the image of his face came to my mind like a photograph. I experienced him all over again: his yellow smile and rank breath, putridly panting over me, the sound of him groaning and heavily choking, his rancid, stale body odor, the sweat on his face, and the feel of him dirtied.

When I opened my eyes, the beauty of the day was pronounced. It impressed the senses, incapable of pulling forth the dark emotions lurking in the back of my consciousness. I looked on from a slight distance at Reverend Haskell, who'd come here upon Leif's request, to say nuptial blessings while presiding over the wedding for Mercy and Jerome.

Mercy looked extraordinarily lovely in the gown she'd fashioned with the assistance of a couple of the other maids, Mable and Prudence. The material she'd selected perfectly complemented her appearance as she stood with a pleasant expression on her face beside her handsome Jerome, who was also gently grinning. I had given her a little bouquet to hold for the ceremony, and she modestly received it from me with a gentle smile. She was a beautiful bride, radiating a glow. I felt joy for her and smiled to see her on this lovely spring day.

When Reverend Haskell finished the ceremony, he left to complete his work at the almshouse for the day. Light refreshments, consisting of Mercy's favored fruitcake and my lemonade, were placed on a table inside the gazebo, and all the servants gathered to eat and celebrate. Leif and I remained at a distance beneath the boughs of a maple tree, observing the merriment, and when I glanced at him, his eyes met mine. Torn between experiencing complete happiness, the pain in his eyes remained half-cloaked, mirroring the way I felt. He was concealing the actual anguish he felt to spare my grieving and replace it with this supposed joyful day. Knowing him, though he had promised never to leave me, I knew within the deepest recesses of my soul that he would not rest the remainder of his life until he knew Lord Brimfield never walked the earth again.

My sense of security had been shattered, and the idyllic space I had once known had disintegrated, revealing the reality that evil had been lurking and betraying me. I desperately wanted to return to my era and escape what had happened, denying that any of it had occurred as I lived my familiar life again. *Seeing our children, my family, and friends again would bring me joy and restore a sense of safety,* I believed. My eagerness to leave Colonial Boston for Los Angeles was compelling, and it seemed the days couldn't move fast enough until the time came.

Since Mr. Putnam had returned from London and notified Leif of the king's decree, Leif was successful at convincing the king to release him of his debt and keep his duchy intact so long as he continued to serve the king in his army. Making our lives work in my era, Leif and I had already discussed this earlier in depth, and he and I both knew that he wouldn't last in my century in time. His happiness was as important to me as mine was to him.

But if Leif couldn't trust his friend, then who could either one of us trust here?

I had no idea. But for now, I wanted to focus on Mercy's wedding day because she was a beautiful, happy bride. It was a lovely day, and I wanted Lord Brimfield far from my thoughts.

I smiled gently at Leif as a sign of thanks, gratitude, and love for this day that I was able to spend with him once more. He didn't reciprocate, but the expression in his soft eyes exhibited his appreciation and mutual love ahead of his melancholy demeanor.

Then, he said, "Yer smile lifts my spirit. Always. I cherish it and shall permit it tae guide me evermore."

I slipped my palm into his hand, and he clasped it. He started away from the festive venue, leading us out of the garden. He guided us on a stroll through rustling trees in the breeze, and we knew our time here was coming to an end as May was nearing our return to the sanctuary of my era, where we'd reunite with our beloved children and my family again.

Thank You For Reading

Are you curious to know more about Leif and Sylvie? A forthcoming installment will continue their story.

Join the author's email list to receive newsletters whenever E. C. Roderick publishes a new book and for exclusive sneak peeks and author news.

Thank you; I appreciate your interest in my books!

Enjoyed The Book?

You can make a difference!

If you enjoyed this book, it would be greatly appreciated if you would spend a few minutes to leave a review on the book's retailer page found on the website where you purchased the book. A simple written line or two for your review would be extremely helpful in spreading the word. Thank you so very much!

Acknowledgments

First and foremost, thank you to my husband, Alan, who believes in everything I do. Without your support, this story would have never been written. I'm immensely grateful to you for encouraging me in all of my creative endeavors and for inspiring me to create them. I love you. Also, thank you to my family, who have given me the same wonderful support. I love all of you.

Thank you immensely to the beta readers who read the manuscript. Your input was highly regarded and strengthened this story, for which I'm entirely grateful.

A huge thank you to my editor, Candy Leondard, for your attention to detail so that the manuscript read smoothly and for all of your encouragement. You're incredibly appreciated.

Also, a wonderful thank you to Mary Ann Smith for creating the perfect cover for this story. I can't tell you enough how grateful I am for our collaboration.

Finally, but certainly not least, thank you incredibly to readers like you. I treasure that you took a chance on a new emerging author like me and have followed this story from the beginning. Without you, I would not be able to bring more stories for you to enjoy and continue my love for writing while being with my family.

Thank you!

About the Author

E. C. Roderick is an emerging author of romance fiction. Her award-winning historical time-travel romance debut novel, TAKEN, which is also a number one Amazon bestseller, begins the saga of Leif and Slyvie. Once a classically trained fine artist, E. C. Roderick taught fine art to both adults and children for many years and found it rewarding. While she enjoyed the creativity inherent in the art process, she discovered her love for writing.

As she raises her family with her husband, finding the necessary space and time to paint has become challenging. Consequently, she focuses on creative writing whenever she has the opportunity. This particular medium for creativity has proven equally rewarding for her, as she delights in developing strong characters and their environments for readers to enjoy.

When E. C. Roderick takes a break from writing, she enjoys spending time with her family and going for long walks with her husband on the beach in southern California.

Connect with the author

www.ingramcontent.com/pod-product-compliance
Lightning Source LLC
Chambersburg PA
CBHW052342110726
47901CB00005B/1329